The Drowning River

The Drowning River

Christobel Kent

FELONY & MAYHEM PRESS • NEW YORK

All the characters and events portrayed in this work are fictitious.

THE DROWNING RIVER

A Felony & Mayhem mystery

PRINTING HISTORY
First UK edition (as *A Time of Mourning*) (Atlantic Books): 2009
First U.S. edition (St. Martin's Press): 2010
Felony & Mayhem edition: 2011

Copyright © 2009 by Christobel Kent
Reprinted by arrangement with Thomas Dunne Books,
an imprint of St. Martin's Press, LLC

ISBN: 978-1-934609-90-3

Manufactured in the United States of America

Printed on 100% recycled paper

Library of Congress Cataloging-in-Publication Data

Kent, Christobel.
The drowning river / Christobel Kent.
    p. cm.
ISBN 978-1-934609-90-3
1. Private investigators--Fiction--Italy--Fiction. 2. Florence (Italy)--Fiction.
I. Title.
PR6111.E58D76 2011
823'.92--dc23
                        2011025302

For Donald

ACKNOWLEDGEMENTS

I would like to thank Angus MacKinnon, without whose stead-fast intelligence and belief in Sandro Cellini this book would not have been written, and my agent, Victoria Hobbs, for her clear-eyed and constant support.

The icon above says you're holding a copy of a book in the Felony & Mayhem "Foreign" category. These books may be offered in translation or may originally have been written in English, but always they will feature an intricately observed, richly atmospheric setting in a part of the world that is neither England nor the U.S.A. If you enjoy this book, you may well like other "Foreign" titles from Felony & Mayhem Press.

For more about these books, and other Felony & Mayhem titles, or to place an order, please visit our website at:

www.FelonyAndMayhem.com

or contact us at:

Felony and Mayhem Press
156 Waverly Place
New York, NY 10014

Other "Foreign" titles from

FELONY&MAYHEM

AUTHOR'S NOTE

I have tried in *The Drowning River* to be true to the geography of Florence. However, although when I first visited the Kaffeehaus in the Boboli gardens, it was open for customers and entirely possible to sit on its terrace overlooking the city, it has been in restoration for six years and is at present not operating as a café.

The Drowning River

Chapter One

IT TOOK FOUR days for the knock at the door. Four long, quiet days in the fading light of an unseasonably mild November, and plenty of time for Sandro to decide whether he liked the two rooms Luisa had found for him to use as an office, if not to make up his mind about what he was doing there in the first place.

It had not occurred to Sandro that he'd be in at the deep end with the first job. He thought he might get eased in gently but, then again, the world doesn't work like that. It was a lesson he should have learned long ago, that life doesn't owe you a warning.

The rooms Luisa had found were on the second floor, square and light and plain in a peaceful street off the Piazza Tasso in San Frediano. The street was the Via del Leone, with a small glassed-in shrine to the Madonna on the corner and at least four candles burning, the sign of a God-fearing neighbourhood, or a superstitious one, depending on how you looked at it. Sandro Cellini stood somewhere between the two, born Catholic, naturally enough, but a rationalist by thirty years of police training. He was too ambivalent as a result to go to Mass more than a couple of times a year, Easter and baptisms, but he liked the shrine, anyhow. And where there was God, there were old ladies. When he had been in the police force—a phrase that still knocked him back—Sandro had found pious elderly women always ready to provide detailed testimony as well as to light candles for divine intervention.

The buildings of the Via del Leone were humble, no more than three storeys, and as a consequence the street itself was sunnier, quieter than his home turf, the acoustics less grating on the ear when the first of the morning *motorini* whined down it on their way to the centre. Born and bred north of the river in Santa Croce among noisy, narrow streets the sun never found, as he stood at the window that looked into the street on his first day, Sandro didn't know if he'd ever get used to it.

It was Florence, undeniably it was, but it wasn't the city he'd woken up in every morning for fifty-eight years, where only a shard of blue sky was visible and the street outside vibrated with din from seven in the morning. A cacophonous opera made up of the crash of bins being emptied, the squeak of the buses' air brakes, the rumble of taxis, the first tourist group of the morning stopping on the corner to be informed loudly in Spanish or German or Japanese of where Dante had been born and Galileo buried.

Looking down, Sandro saw that it might be quiet, but it wasn't deserted after all. He watched as an old woman led her small, overcoated dog to the kerb so it could crap on someone's front tyre; soon enough, he thought, he'd know whose car that was and whether he cared or not. She was carrying a bedraggled bunch of chrysanthemums, heading for the cemetery, no doubt. Coming the other way, he saw a pretty girl; a student maybe, with long hair, long legs in dark jeans, stupidly huge studded and tasselled handbag. She was running, in a hurry; almost opposite the house she sidestepped the old lady and her flowers and her dog, and, as if she knew he was up there, the girl tilted her head and was looking back at Sandro. Her eyes slid over him and, ashamed, he ducked away. He wasn't in this to eyeball passers-by, was he?

Sandro retreated to his desk. It had been found for him, like the flat, like every other piece of furniture from the grey filing cabinet to the elderly but respectable computer, by Luisa. In the silence he reflected that the lack of tourist groups, at least, was a mercy. A fondness for the sound of a Vespa or buses' brakes might be his own private perversion, but he'd never learned to love the guided tours. Luisa had pointed out that he'd better start learning to love the tourists, because they might turn out to be his bread and butter, just like they were hers.

❀ ❀ ❀

'I'm going to start tomorrow,' he'd announced when she got home from the shop the previous night. It hadn't gone down well.

'Ognissanti?' Luisa said with flat dismay. 'Really?' She stood in the kitchen with her coat still on, smelling of woodsmoke from the street.

Ognissanti was All Saints' Day, the first of November, followed by All Souls' the day after. Two days when all the leaves fall at once, and flowers are laid on the graves of loved ones. Tradition was, Ognissanti should be a day for quiet reflection, and the consideration of mortality.

'Why not?' Sandro said, defensively. 'They called this afternoon to say the phone line's been installed. I've had enough of hanging around.'

But he knew why not. Religion, habit, duty to the dead, not to mention that it might be obscurely inauspicious to start halfway through a week. And although Luisa was no more religious than he was, the tug of familial duty was stronger; her mother more recently dead. She had to get up early to take flowers to her mother's grave out in Scandicci, before heading in to the city

'You'll be at work yourself, after all,' Sandro said.

Like many other religious days, the feast's status as a public holiday was being eroded, particularly in the big cities with their wealthy, godless visitors, and Luisa's employer, Frollini, had given in years back. They did good business in November, with the stock room crammed to overflowing and the windows full of sheepskins and velvet and party dresses. Luisa didn't like it, but it was the new Italy.

'It seems like bad luck,' she said uneasily.

'I don't want to put it off any longer,' said Sandro with finality, and she could see that that, at least, was true.

Grumbling, she had got up even earlier than usual to cook for him.

'Your first day, you'll take something hot to eat,' she said, when he wandered into the kitchen, bleary-eyed, to remonstrate with her. The pristine lilies she had bought the night before for her mother stood in the sink.

She'd given him *baccalà*—salt cod stewed with tomatoes— and when Sandro prised open the foil dish six hours later at his new desk it was still just warm; but then again, it was barely midday. He had been on the job three hours, and had done nothing but ogle a girl through the window and open a file on the computer for his accounts, before closing it again. Expenses to date, five thousand euro, give or take. Income, zero.

Sandro devoured the rich salty stew in five mouthfuls, suddenly starving. He spilled a little of the sauce on his desktop and although he rubbed at it immediately, cursing, it left a tiny orange stain. A good start, he thought to himself. What will the clients think, supposing any ever materialize? He felt ready to hurl something at the wall; what a slob. That night he told Luisa he'd maybe experiment with the local bar for lunch; she eyed him warily.

'Gone off my cooking?' He shook his head. 'As if,' he said. 'Just—well. I need to get to know the neighbourhood.' She nodded, deciding not to be offended. He didn't tell her the *baccalà* incident had made him feel like a small boy on the first day at school, on a knife edge of misery.

'How was the visit?' he said. 'The cemetery?'

She was pale; he remembered she had been up since six, and he cursed himself for letting her work so hard. He could have just said, *I'll start tomorrow*, couldn't he?

'Fine,' she said. 'It was good.' She smiled and he could see that for all her pallor and weariness, it had made her happy. For Luisa a visit to the cemetery always kindled something; she still spoke to her mother, standing at the grave, once she had spent twenty minutes arranging the lilies. It was another example of her mysterious superiority, that Luisa was not afraid of grief.

Sandro had been nineteen when his mother died—she had had cancer, though Sandro never knew where—and just coming to the end of his military service. He came back for the funeral in his uniform, unable to cry. His father went to his own grave a year later; they had been hard-working country people with no time for the expression of emotion, and although he'd been no more than sixty the loss had simply been too much for him to bear. Sandro had found himself stunned into silence by their abrupt absence.

It was suddenly too late to ask them anything; within six months he had met Luisa, and asked her to marry him. At the time it had seemed like the only way to survive; within five years he realized that he couldn't remember his father's face without taking up the framed photograph he kept in a drawer, and staring hard at it. They were in his head somewhere, the pair of them hand in hand in old-fashioned clothes, but he did not want to think about them; he didn't have Luisa's trick of taking sadness by the hand and making it a friend.

'I'm a very lucky man,' he said to her back as she stirred something on the stove. 'Very lucky.'

❋ ❋ ❋

One of the things Sandro turned over in his mind as he sat there on day two—All Souls', a little cloudier than day one, the November light a little thinner and paler—was this alteration in his relationship with Luisa. Thirty years married—or was it thirty-one?—and suddenly Luisa was in charge. While he'd been in the force they'd run along separate tracks, two blind-sided locomotives, each oblivious to the other's direction. With pain he thought of the big police station out at Porta al Prato on the busy *viale*. Standing guard at the north-eastern approach to the city, the warm, busy corridors, the long, shuttered windows, the camaraderie. Misguided nostalgia, he reminded himself; where was the camaraderie now?

That was unfair, clearly it was. He still saw his old comrades now and again in the city; they'd nod and exchange a word in the street; he thought they'd stand him a coffee if he ever found himself back in the bar on the *viale* they used to frequent. But what conversation would they have? 'Sorry, mate'? The murky old Caffè Tramvai—there'd been trams running past the Porta al Prato once, before Sandro was born—with its Formica tables and sixties decor, and the best *trippa alla fiorentina* in the city. He thought of those lunch-breaks now and again, when his guard was down; they would all crowd in there at twelve-thirty and stand eating the ragout out of little bowls, steaming, sweet, garlic and tomatoes and tender fragments of meat. But that friendly shared coffee was never going to happen, was it? Sandro had avoided the place like the plague since the day of his departure on a cold, dark January day nearly two years ago.

Sandro was no longer a police officer. At least, he considered gloomily, he had not been discharged, dishonourably or otherwise; at least he had been allowed early retirement. It had been more than a face-saver; it had meant he could work, because the opportunities for a disgraced policeman were limited. If there'd been any sympathy for his offence among his colleagues, Sandro didn't seek it out; he didn't want to be forgiven. The offence of relaying confidential information to the father of an abducted child.

The child's disappearance had come at a bad time; if you believed in astrology, at some disastrous conjunction of planets, it had always been inevitable that further tragedy could only follow from it. It had been a long time ago, with Luisa the wrong side of forty, and the possibility that they would never have children of their own was turning to stone-dead certainty for both of them. The girl—nine years old—had disappeared from a crowded pool, her body found at a bend in a river in the Apennines a week later, caught in reeds.

No arrest had been made, though they'd had their suspect all right, and Sandro had kept in touch with the child's father. Why? It was obvious why, people sometimes said to him, it was the human impulse, it was out of sympathy, but Sandro had offered no excuses at the disciplinary hearing; he had remained silent when they were asked of him. He had merely admitted that he had, yes, kept the bereaved, the now childless father, informed; had supplied him eventually with the name and whereabouts of the chief suspect in his daughter's murder, with every scrap of information. And when, fifteen years later, the suspect—against whom no charges had ever been brought—was found murdered, the whole thing unravelled. Sandro had known immediately that he was responsible for the paedophile's death, whoever had in fact held the knife against his throat.

The dead man had been guilty, they knew that now, but it had still been wrong. One little breach in the rule of law and the whole thing comes apart at frightening speed; the murderer is murdered, and one of his victims ends up with blood on her own hands. And once you have lied to a man who trusts you, to your partner of more than a decade, you cannot be sure he will ever trust you again.

And that was how Sandro came to find himself adrift. But thirty years in the police leave their mark; it was too late for him to become anything else.

Pietro was still a friend, of course, his partner of thirteen years and as close to a marriage as you can get. Pietro still called at the apartment every other Thursday, religiously, to haul Sandro out for a drink, to talk about football and Fiorentina's death plunge down through the divisions, a grumble about the new *commissario* seconded from Turin, nothing too close to the bone. They didn't talk about Sandro's disgrace, and though Sandro felt the warmth of Pietro's sympathy he shied away from voicing his gratitude; it wasn't the relationship he wanted.

Thirteen years in the same grubby fug of their allotted police vehicle, you get to know the smell of another man's socks, his aftershave, what he eats for breakfast. How he takes his coffee. *Caffè alto*, for Pietro, down in one then another on its tail, to kickstart the day; there are some questions that don't need asking, after thirteen years. Sometimes now, taking his coffee alone, Sandro had to close his eyes so as not to wish it all back again.

Perhaps Luisa had always been in charge. Sitting in the thin sunlight, eyes closed, Sandro felt curiously comforted as he mused on that possibility. Those long years of quiet unhappiness together during which each had shouldered his own burden—the lack of children, the ugliness of daily police work, the shrinking of expectations—Luisa had been in charge all along. Biding her time for the moment when her superior skills would be called for.

Over those four days in the Via del Leone he did come to the conclusion that Luisa knew what she was doing, all right. He'd come with her to see the place, and he hadn't seen its potential; if truth be told, he'd been downcast by it. Luisa had found out, through the usual mysterious means, that it was about to come on the market, a second-floor walk-up, two rooms and a tiny kitchen inhabited by an exhausted-looking elderly couple and their disabled daughter, who were about to be rehoused in 'more suitable' accommodation. That should have given him the hint; public housing was hard to come by, and the *comune* didn't step in lightly. The disabled daughter turned out to be middle-aged, brain-damaged and quadriplegic since birth, parked in a tiny kitchen in a wheelchair. The apartment had no bathroom, a fact that did not dawn on Sandro until they left.

'My God,' he'd said in the street below, thinking of all those years carrying their helpless child up and down the stairs, while she turned into a middle-aged woman. Luisa had squeezed his hand. 'It's a sad place,' she said. 'I think that's why they haven't been able to find a tenant.'

That and the builder's yard below the window, currently full of orange plastic tubing, maybe. But there was a sliver of a view of the back of Santa Maria dell'Carmine, if you were disposed to concentrate on that instead, on the frescoes inside that Sandro hadn't seen since he was a boy, the Adam and Eve, Eve with her hand up to her mouth. These things all settled in his mind in those idle hours. He wondered where they were now, that couple and their ageing daughter, and whether they missed their view. Nonsense, Luisa would say briskly. Modern bathroom, ground-floor access, lifts and bars and all sorts after forty years hauling the grown child up two flights of stairs? Nonsense. It'll make a good office, and they're better off where they are.

Day two, just before lunch, Sandro found himself looking down into the street again; he saw the woman with her dog, and realized he was watching for the girl. Out of police habit, getting the lie of the land, or because she'd been pretty? He turned tail, unable to give himself the benefit of the doubt. She *had* been pretty.

Safely at the back of the building Sandro had spread his copy of *La Nazione* out on his desk and went through it as though that was his job, reading every story in the paper. He stared at the big stories first, national news. Garbage collection in Naples, dioxins leaching into the food chain from toxic waste. A new book out on the Camorra, and a piece about Calabrian gangsters buying up property in Tuscany. His stomach felt sour and leaden; my country, he thought, staring at the page; there'd been a time when it had been his business. Out at Porta al Prato, buckling on his holster, slapping the peaked cap on his head, jostling out through the door with Pietro, they'd laughed bitterly at their dismal clean-up rate, at all the shit still out there waiting for them, but it hadn't felt like this.

He worked his way down to local stuff: illegals employed on building the extension to the Uffizi; a hit and run on the *viale*, involving a child. A doctor found to be a member of a satanic cult drowned in Lake Trasimeno. Sandro worked his way right through to the end before he closed the paper, impotent.

In the afternoon Sandro went out into the street, so as to have something to tell Luisa when he got home. The food in the nearest bar was lousy; a stale roll and some dried-up ham, and the floor was dirty. It had turned chilly, too; after a brisk turn down to the Piazza Tasso and back—on the corner seven candles had been lit for the Virgin this afternoon; Sandro resolved to keep a proper eye out one day for the devout, his future informers—he hurried back to the flat, where the ancient radiators were clanking loudly to keep pace with the cold.

Climbing the draughty stairs Sandro had tried to imagine the place in July, when San Frediano, built for the street sweepers and humbler artisans, the carpenters and stonemasons, had the reputation for being a sun-bleached desert, without high stone façades and deep eaves to protect its inhabitants from the heat of the sun. Did people need private detectives in July?

And, as Sandro found himself reminded once again that that was what he was now, a private detective, he had to fight the urge to put his face in his hands, and groan.

Chapter Two

THERE WERE HOARDINGS along the motorway out by the airport, advertising the agencies. A picture of a young man in a peaked cap, toting a holster, or a Pinkerton's-style badge. A Discreet and Thorough Service, Any Investigation Undertaken. Financial, Personal, Professional. Experts in Surveillance. They had laughed at them, when Sandro was in the force, though the laughter had been uneasy. Some private detectives were borderline criminals themselves, and smart with it; some of them were close to conmen, some were lazy, some were stupid. But it was others—the *laureati* with their degrees in IT and control engineering: modern, computer-literate, hardworking—that inspired the unease, a kind of envy, in those embedded in the creaking old machinery of the state police.

Where was the room for someone like Sandro, a village idiot where computers were concerned, old school, a one-man band, among this lot? It was a shark tank, a snakepit. It had, of course, been Luisa's idea.

'You're brilliant at your job,' she said, to his silence. 'You've got the basics on computers.' True enough; he might be old school, but even the Polizia Statale had been computerized. 'You speak a bit of English.' Sandro grunted at this. His English had hardly been honed to perfection during twenty years of taking down notes from tourists on their stolen purses, struggling to interpret a dozen different accents, Louisiana, Liverpool, London. 'I could help you with that, anyway,' Luisa said, thoughtfully.

Sandro had made an effort, asking mildly, 'Do you really think there's a—what d'you call it, a market? For a one-man operation?'

Head on one side, Luisa said firmly, 'Yes, I do.' He waited. 'Look,' she said earnestly. 'The old ladies.' Them again. 'The—I don't know, the grannies, the individuals, I'm not talking about big corporations, *caro*, though I suppose there's money in that and I don't see why...' But seeing his face at the thought of selling his services in some boardroom somewhere, she changed tack, frowning. 'Real people, little people, who can't get anywhere in the system.' Despite himself, Sandro had nodded at that. There were such people.

She leaned forward, encouraged. 'And the foreigners. Not maybe tourists, they're only here a couple of days, a week at most. But the ones who live here, the ones who would like to live here? The expats?'

Sandro's shoulders dipped again. 'What would they need a private detective for?' he said. 'Don't be daft.' And almost immediately regretted it. Luisa was on her feet then, striding round the kitchen table, her little heels clicking on the *pavimento*. She had just come in from work, still wearing what he thought of as her uniform. Had she been thinking about this all day on the shop floor? She'd barely taken her coat off, she was so fired up.

'You have no idea, Sandro,' she said. 'No idea at all. She had raised her voice without thinking; Sandro glanced at the window, open in the September heat, and that seemed to annoy her even more. 'For example,' she said, holding up a finger to get his attention, 'a client came into the shop, a very nice old lady, English, has lived here for years. Fifteen years at least. Her landlord is saying things about her because he wants her out of the flat. He accuses her of subletting her rooms, he is tampering with her heating to freeze her out. He refuses to carry out renovations. She is helpless.' Shamed, Sandro chewed his lip. Of course, these things happened. But a private detective?

'Any number of divorce cases, infidelities,' Luisa went on hurriedly, knowing this would not appeal to Sandro. 'A couple who were sold a house in the Chianti with six hectares only to discover none of the land belonged to the seller, and it was too late to recover their deposit? Two hundred thousand euro?' That was the deposit? Sandro's eyes popped at the figure.

'Don't you see?' she said, taking his hands in hers. 'They get married, they buy property, they start a business, just like us. They need help more than us, they don't know the system. You could advertise, in the free papers, the little magazines for foreigners. And for locals, in *La Pulce*, that kind of thing. You don't even have to call yourself a private detective, if you don't want.'

Sandro studied their hands together on the table, Luisa's pale and puckered with washing, clean, short nails, her plain gold wedding ring. He should have bought her an engagement ring, shouldn't he? But they had never had the money. He thought about what she had said. A niche, that was what she was talking about, and he had to admit, he didn't object to the word. And, as Luisa was too kind to say out loud, what else was he going to do?

Taking a deep breath and without knowing if it was true, Sandro said, 'I don't mind that. It says what it means, doesn't it? I don't mind being a private detective.'

First thing on day three, Giulietta Sarto turned up, like a bad penny, he thought with something like affection. 'Oi,' she shouted into the intercom. 'Only me.'

She was looking better these days, though Giulietta could hardly have looked worse than she had two years ago when, emaciated from living on the streets, she'd stabbed her abuser and so played her part in the story that had ended with Sandro losing his job. She'd been placed in custody, of course, and put through the mill, but they'd got her off on mental health grounds, then Luisa had taken an interest. Giulietta had put on some weight and was living in public housing, Sandro dimly remembered, not far from here. San Frediano, he thought gloomily as he heard her quick footsteps on the stairs, public housing and old ladies. It's not going to pay for Luisa's engagement ring.

'Hi, Giulietta,' he said warily. 'What are you up to?' Standing in the lobby, she didn't look bad at all, as it happened. She was wearing a dark suit, cheap but it fitted her. Hair thin from malnutrition but brown instead of the rainbow of red and rust and greenish blonde. Wrists still as thin as chicken bones, but fuller in the face.

'How did I track you down, you mean?' she said with rough good cheer. She took out a pack of cigarettes, turned it over in her hands, put it away. 'Have a guess.'

He nodded. Luisa. 'She thinks I need keeping an eye on, does she?'

He saw Giulietta survey the room from the doorway without answering, lips pursed. 'Bit quiet,' she commented, and he shrugged, helpless.

She eyed him. 'Don't need a receptionist yet, then?' She must have seen the alarm in his eyes because she burst out laughing then, her rusty, smoker's laugh. 'Don't worry, Commissario—' And when he flinched, she looked apologetic, started again. 'Don't worry, Signore Cellini, I'm not offering. I don't need a job, as it happens.' She eyed him for signs of surprise and, seeing none, went on proudly, 'I'm working at the Women's Centre. On the Piazza Tasso.'

Bit close to home, Sandro thought, guiltily. He wasn't sure he needed to be worrying about Giulietta Sarto on top of everything else. 'Sit down,' he said, pulling out one of the plastic chairs.

'Two mornings a week and all day Saturday to begin with,' she said quickly, as if she knew what he was thinking. 'Only, when I bumped into Luisa at the baker's she told me you'd got yourself a little office here. Said I could pop my head around the door.'

Sandro relaxed. What else was he doing, anyway?

'Thanks,' he said, smiling for the first time. 'Maybe you could drum up some business for me, down at the Women's Centre.'

They both laughed reluctantly at that. The Centre provided emergency contraception, advice for battered wives, rape crisis telephone lines. Halfway house for women like Giulietta, not a *centesimo* to rub between the clientele.

'You'll be all right,' she said, cautiously. Then, becoming more thoughtful, 'Seriously, though. I will say. If anyone—not, like, liabilities, I can see you can do without that, but anyone serious, decent—wants a bit of help, I'll recommend you.' Sandro had been her arresting officer, two years ago. She looked puzzled at the turnabout in their relationship the offer entailed.

Sandro sighed, the irony weighing a little heavier on him than on her. 'Thanks,' he said again. There was a silence during which she fiddled with her mobile phone and he wondered if he should offer to buy her a coffee. But before he could say anything she stuffed the phone into her bag and leapt up.

'Oh, God,' she said, panicky and apologetic all at once. 'It's ten o'clock. I can't be late, it's only my third day!' And she was off, as abruptly as she'd arrived.

Six hours and four coffees later, the desk drawers now stocked with stationery, *La Pulce* folded and unfolded a dozen times so he could stare uncomfortably at the ad he'd placed last week ('Ex-officer from the Polizia dello Stato offers thirty years' investigative experience and discreet and conscientious service. No job too small.'), Sandro wished he'd asked her to come back for a spot of lunch. Found himself feeling envious of her two mornings a week of being needed.

That night, Luisa chattered on about the day at the shop. A *marchesa* had been caught shoplifting. Seventy if she was a day, she rattled around in a vast, freezing nineteenth-century pile on the hill up towards Fiesole and had given an Uccello to the Uffizi, but the Americans who used to rent her *piano nobile* for cash in hand must have got cold feet, what with all the terrorism, because she was clearly broke. Broke, but refusing to admit it. She'd swanned through the shop being gracious to all of them then put a handbag under her ancestral fur coat. The alarms had gone off when she'd tried to leave.

'Are you listening?' said Luisa. 'I thought you'd be interested.'

'Sorry,' said Sandro. He'd been wondering how long he should sit there in the Via del Leone, before calling it quits. 'Shoplifting?' He wondered if she was about to suggest he should look for some work as a store detective, or private security standing by the cashpoints or the jewellers' shops on the Ponte

Vecchio in a toytown uniform. He'd have to hide whenever a real uniform turned up.

She looked at him. 'You're not going to give up, are you.' It wasn't a question.

❀ ❀ ❀

As it turned out, Sandro nearly missed his first client. He had advertised his hours of business on the plate he'd had made at the door as well as in the small ads, as eight-thirty until twelve, two until seven. On the doorstep at eight twenty-five on day four, Friday, his key in the lock, he thought, to hell with it. Who turns up at eight-thirty? Not in the crime stories, they didn't, in the *gialle* of Rex Stout and Raymond Chandler, they turned up around whisky time, beautiful hard-boiled women with long legs. He should have known, after thirty years, that trouble gets people up early in the morning. People lie awake in the early hours, waiting for it to get light. And private detectives often found themselves drinking whisky by ten, even in the *gialle*.

But, getting slack already, Sandro had put the key back in his pocket and turned away from the door, from the thought of all those hours to kill. He took a step towards the square, where on the way home yesterday he'd noticed a nicer-looking bar than the grubby one on the corner of the Via Santa Monaca. It was a big, bright place with a marble counter frequented by the market stallholders; he could almost see it from where he stood, full of real life. You could stand there and watch the little kids playing on the slides, the mothers with their bags full of vegetables. He'd had enough of his view of half an inch of Santa Maria dell'Carmine and eighty square metres of orange plastic tubing. He'd had enough of silence and solitude; he was going to the bar.

But something made him turn around. An apologetic cough, a small sigh, ten metres behind him, at his own front door. He turned without thinking, and there she was, a copy of yesterday's *La Pulce* in her hand.

Chapter Three

IRIS MARCH BURROWED under the duvet and listened. She could hear the drone of morning traffic in the street the other side of the three-foot-thick walls, but the big, dark apartment was as quiet as a tomb, and as cold.

Iris wanted a cup of tea. Her nose was cold; her feet were cold; the apartment was colder than anywhere she'd ever been in her life, and it was a long way across uncarpeted stone to the kitchen. It was colder than school in England, where the windows rattled and the radiators were never more than tepid, and you sat pressed hopelessly against them turning mottled under your uniform without ever getting warm. The apartment was also colder than home, the terrible mildewed glass house built in the only cold, damp, north-facing site in the whole of the Ventoux by an experimental architect Ma had been having an affair with when she'd dropped out to paint—well, mess about—in the South of France, at nineteen, which happened to be exactly Iris's age.

A pov, they called her at school, in her discreetly hand-me-down uniform. If you hadn't sent me there, she used to say to Ma, we could have rebuilt the house. Or put in proper central heating. Iris remembered falls of snow that killed olive trees, and hunters going out on New Year's Day in hard frosts, blasting away with guns on the hillside below them. Then, feeling herself getting all homesick, she forced herself to remember the days and days of rain, too, the water seeping under the cracked concrete floor of the terrible house. He was fairly famous, now, the architect, though Ma's house was one of his projects that never got photographed for magazines. He had a shock of white hair and a wrecked red face, and he'd made a pass at Iris, once. She turned over in disgust at the memory, pulling the inadequate duvet over her head.

Made a pass, that was one of Ma's phrases, always delivered gaily, fondly. 'Oh, lovey, David Bailey? Twenty years older than me and made a pass before he even knew my name.' There would have been very little point in blowing the whistle on the architect, even if he had been something like forty-five years older than Iris.

Ronnie's mother had found the flat. Ronnie was short for Veronica. Being called Iris was bad enough, but she couldn't imagine how anyone could come up with a name like Veronica for a girl born in 1988; Iris supposed that under the circumstances Ronnie was all right. Ronnie's mother had racing stables outside Newmarket and a new boyfriend, and wanted Ronnie, mooching around at home between school and whatever was going to be next, out of the way.

'Bitch,' Ronnie had said as they unpacked their bags. 'Why does it have to be stinking, boring Florence?'

Ronnie throwing silk underwear around, chucking expensive boots on the floor. *And why*, Iris had thought as she looked at her own favourite dress, dark red rayon with a ruffle that was suddenly looking cheap, *do I have to come with you, Ronnie?*

They'd been default friends at school, and had exchanged emails since, Iris dutiful, nostalgic even, after coming home to France to do the International Baccalaureate because Ma had run out of money for school fees. Ronnie's emails had been easy, boastful, condescending; Iris had the idea Ronnie's mother, Serena, was telling her to write them. Serena had a thing about creative people and, Iris being from a creative family, she wanted Ronnie there for some screwy, snobbish reason to do with that. If you only knew, Iris wanted to say. The life of the artist. Ma illustrating children's books for a pittance. Selling watercolours of Mont Ventoux in a crappy gallery in Aix, at the rate of one a month.

But of course when it came to it, Ronnie *didn't* want Iris to come with her to Florence, not much; it had not been her idea at all. It had been Serena's, of course, and Ronnie didn't try very hard to disguise the fact. Iris was going to be the sensible one who'd keep Ronnie out of trouble, and the creative one who encouraged her to keep up the classes. And most of all Iris was the one whose mother was so broke the offer of a course in life-drawing and free accommodation in Florence for three months would be snatched off the table.

'Do I have to, Ma?' Iris had said sulkily, then, hearing how graceless she sounded, pleading, 'I hardly know her, these days.'

'But it's in Florence, sweetheart,' Ma had said, a dreamy, faraway look in her eyes. Iris assumed from the look that passes had been made in Florence, too, and sighed.

Ma's focus had returned to Iris then. 'And you've got talent,' she'd said, with a determination that unnerved Iris. Ma didn't have a determined bone in her body, or so Iris had always thought.

'Ma,' Iris had muttered, looking down at her feet. 'Don't.' Because Ma would say that, wouldn't she? Her only child had to have talent, at something. It was no joking matter. She sighed.

'Darling,' Ma had said, and Iris heard the worry in her voice. 'You've got to decide on something. You can't stay here all your life, working in the bar.' Why not? Iris had thought stubbornly, still looking at the floor. You did. She heard Ma clear her throat. 'There's always London.'

Shocked, Iris had looked up then. By London, she knew, Ma meant Iris's father; she meant that she'd move heaven and earth to get Iris into Camberwell or Chelsea or Goldsmith's or any other London art school, and she would live with her father and his new family, in Dulwich. With the baby and the four-year-old and the ten-year-old twins and the second wife she'd never met, and her father. Her father whom she barely knew, who had taken absolutely zero interest in his first, grown child. Not now, not ever.

'Ma,' she'd said, alarmed, and it was Ma's turn to look away. This was serious. Grow up, Iris told herself urgently. What does it matter if we don't get on? Florence might be stuffy and gloomy, but Italy was Italy, right? Michelangelo and Leonardo da Vinci and coffee and sunshine. Even in November. And three months' proper grown-up life-drawing. It'd be all right.

What it was, was lonely. Resignedly Iris sat up in bed in the dark, sniffing in the cold air. High-ceilinged, north-facing, the room was full of the outlines of things in the gloom; every morning, it seemed, she still woke up wondering where on earth she was. There was a colossal wardrobe on one wall with something like an eagle carved on top of it, and big dusty curtains hung in heavy swags over the shuttered window. She pulled back the duvet. It was warmer outside than in this place, even in November. She crossed the smooth, icy tiles in bare feet, stubbed her toe on some great huge bit of furniture, an oak chest or uncomfortable armchair. 'Ow. Bugger, bugger, bugger.' She sat down on the scratchy stuffed seat, rubbing her toe.

Around her the apartment was still quiet; only the ticking of the ancient heating cranking up—or it could be cranking down, for all Iris knew. It never actually seemed to get warm. Iris stood up, opened the shutters and looked out.

Now that she'd got to know the city a little better, Iris sometimes thought she would have lived anywhere but Piazza d'Azeglio. A vast, gloomy nineteenth-century square just to the north of the centre, it was too grown-up, too big, too ugly, too much of a hike from the drawing school on the other side of the river. The massive buildings flanking the dull square of grass and trees were either owned by banks or, like this one, by ancient families who couldn't afford to keep them up and let little apartments stuffed with hideous old family furniture to foreigners like Ronnie and Iris. They saw her coming, Iris reflected on Ronnie's mum; had she even seen the place before she handed over the deposit?

The view out of the back was odd; it wasn't the Florence she'd imagined. The smallish garden, with bits of statues in it and lots of black ivy, and the synagogue, although she hadn't known that when they moved in. It looked like something from South Kensington, a green copper dome and mottled beige stonework, Victorian. Iris softened; on a morning like this, with muffled sunlight trying to get through the mist, the view was nice. The roofs, some far-off hills just about visible to the south. Iris pushed open the window on impulse, leaned out on the cold stone of the window ledge. It was warmer outside. There was a smell of smoke and the air was mild.

In the summer, Iris supposed, pulling down the sleeves of her T-shirt, you might be glad of the chill inside, and the dark, and the bath that really was made of stone and therefore instantly cooled the water down to barely lukewarm, but they wouldn't be here in the summer, would they? For the first time, Iris felt a stab of regret. Or maybe she was just dreading what she'd have to do once this reprieve was over. Somewhere a church bell began to clang and she pulled the window shut. Time to get going.

Before she left Iris looked in at Ronnie's room, out of duty if nothing else. It was bigger than hers, though that wasn't strictly Ronnie's fault. Iris had claimed the smaller one, grumpily assuming the role of paid companion; she had been reading Edith Wharton preparatory to coming—Ma's idea—and saw a number of quite satisfying similarities between herself and the impoverished heroines in the novels. She was supposed to make herself agreeable, or useful. Iris wasn't sure if she was good at either.

Ronnie hadn't seemed even to notice. 'All right,' she'd said carelessly. 'Whatever.' And actually, Iris reflected now, it was likely that she really didn't care. Ronnie probably knew how things were going to pan out, that she'd only be spending one night in three here anyway, and the rest coming in at two in the morning, singing to herself, high as a kite on dancing and drinking and flirting. And maybe it was because she'd never been short of money, but one thing Ronnie wasn't, was mean.

The room was dark and fusty and empty; clothes everywhere. The shutters were almost closed, but not quite; Ronnie never did anything thoroughly. The bed was unmade, the laptop left on, a box of Tampax spilling its contents on the bedside table and two pairs of knickers on the floor. Iris went over to the small table—inlaid, rickety, like everything in the flat it was more decorative than useful—and stared at the screen; Ronnie's MySpace page. A picture of her upside down, her dark brown hair with the blonde streak across her face, and a dozen friends' pictures up; her MySpace name was Da-doo-ron-ron.

Guiltily, Iris scrolled down to check out the messages people had posted. There was a lot of cheerfully insulting stuff from people back home, *saw ya last night, what are you like, love and kisses, loserrr.* Florence is Grrr8, Ronnie'd posted on Monday night, and she'd pasted in a Leonardo drawing; she's changed her tune, thought Iris. A couple of weeks ago she'd have mimed a big fat yawn at the mention of Leonardo's name.

Knowing she shouldn't be doing this, Iris minimised the page, flicked to the mailbox, surfed up and down Ronnie's messages; there was a man, she bet there was, Ronnie'd never head off just to hang out with friends of the awful Serena, even if they did have a castle.

But if there was a man, he wasn't emailing her. Iris read a couple, cool, non-committal messages to her mum, stuff to Antonella Scarpa at the school about the course, paying her bill for supplies, thank you for the extra lesson to the course director. So formal, so unlike Ronnie: *It was very kind of you, I am most grateful.* Maybe she was growing up. Nothing about any man, nothing about this trip to Chianti; you'd have thought she'd be boasting all over MySpace.

Iris didn't do MySpace; it made her nervous, like being back at school, all that bitching and bullying and those snide remarks, but Ronnie loved it. Ronnie'd never been got at in her life, she didn't have anything to be afraid of.

In fact, Iris didn't have a computer of her own; wasn't that weird, everyone said, like she was an Amish or something. Which was stupid; she knew how to use one. But Ma didn't like them; there'd been computers at school and when Iris came back to do the IB she'd bought her a big old desktop, second-hand from Emmaus the other side of Marseille, but that was her limit. She didn't have the cash and, anyway, computers were a distraction. 'Not every day you get to go to Florence,' Ma had said wistfully when Iris asked about a laptop to keep in touch. 'Do you want to spend it all in front of a computer?'

Iris bent down and picked up the little carnival mask off the rug, a cheeky little black satin eyemask, no warty old rubber witch job for Ronnie. Halloween seemed a long time ago; Iris remembered the flat full of people as if it was something she'd seen in a film. She'd worn a red feather mask, and her dress with the ruffle. She remembered a couple collapsed on top of each other on the hard sofa, and the old lady—the landlady—bashing with a broom handle on her ceiling below, telling them to be quiet. A drunk American boy asking Ronnie loudly who the fat girl was. 'Who's the fat chick?' Meaning Iris.

The huge studded front door clanged shut behind Iris and she struggled through the iron gate to the street. Sometimes it felt like a great big 200-year-old prison, the keys she needed just to get out of the place practically filled her bag, never mind her sketchbooks and pencils and apron. Outside the square was cold and grey and quiet, the tall, bare trees motionless in the mist.

After a week or so of trying—and failing—to work out bus routes, they'd settled on walking. Iris liked walking, Ronnie didn't; she grumbled all the way, when she was there at all, not refusing to come out from under the duvet, not rolling in at dawn and climbing into bed just when Iris was climbing out. Still, Iris preferred it when Ronnie was there, because they talked a bit about stuff, because Ronnie was nicer for being a bit subdued, and because when Iris got in to school on her own, she always had to spend the first half an hour making Ronnie's excuses for her.

She might have said, thought Iris. Given me an idea when she was going to come back.

The mist was thicker over the river, more like fog. Iris's route to the Scuola Massi, which was in the Oltrarno on the south side of the river, took her across the plainest and most modern bridge over the river. The Ponte alle Grazie may have been ugly but it had the best views on a clear day, the Ponte Vecchio on one side and the mountains of what Iris calculated from her examination of the guidebook must be the Casentino rising up on the other. Ronnie would jeer at the crowds thick on the Ponte Vecchio; *tourists*, poring over the blue guide just like Iris. As if the two of them were anything else.

Today the Ponte Vecchio was barely visible, and in the other direction thick low cloud rolled all the way down to the city. At the foot of the bridge there was one of a series of hoardings the *comune* had put up, with blown-up photographs of the flood, forty years earlier, that had filled up all the cellars and washed the cars into gardens. Iris read the caption to a photograph of a cavernous warehouse with documents spread to dry on trestle tables and an earnest, bespectacled white-gloved figure picking through them: *From all over the world lovers of art came to help us restore our city.*

All Iris could see clearly was the river below her, turned yellow with all the rain that had fallen last night, and the buttresses of the bridge cluttered with branches and detritus washed down from the hills. Sad stuff, rags and shopping trolleys that made Florence just like any other city; a whole tree torn up from some country riverbank. The muddy water swirled and churned, and Iris watched, not moving.

Before leaving the apartment, Iris had stood a long time— for her—staring into the mirror in the bathroom. Like all the other rooms it was badly lit, the ceilings too high, electric light all wrong under the vaulting, but when looking at herself in the mirror Iris didn't mind that. She'd wished for Ma at that moment, to rest her hand approvingly on the small of her back and say, you're well made. You're lovely.

Not lovely, she'd decided, looking at herself as if for the first time. But not fat. She had swallowed, blinking at the insult. She hated him, whoever he was; for an instant as she'd tugged on the light pull to extinguish the sight of herself, she'd thought that if she had an instrument, an etching tool or a kitchen knife or a hammer, she could kill him.

On the Ponte alle Grazie Iris felt the cold of the rail under her gloves. She hauled the bag higher up on her shoulder and set off towards the far bank and another day at the drawing board. She'd be first to arrive.

Chapter Four

Had HE PASSED her in the street, Sandro might have thought she was a nun, if he'd noticed her at all. She didn't have a nun's veil, but a band over her hair that made him think of one. The hair itself was quite white and cut severely, a fringe just above pale blue eyes, then straight across behind, just below the ears. Like a schoolgirl, or at least, Sandro reminded himself, not the kind of schoolgirl you get these days, chewing gum with long hair and jeans, but a schoolgirl from his own childhood and one, furthermore, in whom vanity was being firmly discouraged.

Standing on his doorstep, waiting for him, she demanded closer inspection. There was something nun-like about her clothing, too, the colours all grey and black and white, the skirt just below the knee, the flat, laced black shoes, but like the severe haircut the whole ensemble suited her somehow, it had not been imposed on her, as a nun's habit would have been. He thought she was perhaps seventy years old.

They stood, a dozen paces apart on the pavement, and he could see her grip tighten on the newspaper. Their eyes met, then both turned to look at the new brass plate, *Cellini Sandro, Investigazioni*, and the sight of his own name propelled Sandro towards her at last, late for an appointment he hadn't known he had.

'Signore Cellini,' said the white-haired woman, quite formally. She looked at him with a directness he was not prepared for, or perhaps it was the blue eyes that took him by surprise, clear and pale and luminous.

'Yes,' said Sandro, although it had not been a question. 'Please.' He gestured towards the door and showed her up the stairs ahead of him out of a chivalrous instinct, then found he had to struggle back past her to get the door open. A fine start, he thought grimly.

To his relief he had left the office clean the night before; he had even emptied the wastepaper bin of his sandwich wrapper. Almost as a distraction he found himself wondering if he would need to employ a cleaner, whether that was something he might ask Giulietta to do or whether she would be offended. Concentrate, he told himself.

Taking off his coat, offering to take hers—she refused, sat down with it still buttoned to the chin—Sandro realized that his first client, or so he assumed, reminded him of school; he felt as though he was in the presence of a teacher. Sandro had been educated by nuns, and several, if not all, had had precisely the quality he felt from this woman, whose name he did not yet even know. A quality combining quiet authority, composure and economical gestures. He realized that he was very nervous, and might be about to start babbling. Don't be ridiculous, he told himself; this is your first client. This is not about you; this is about her. With the woman already having seated herself, Sandro went back behind his own desk.

She stayed quite still in front of him, ankles together and her handbag and newspaper on her lap, waiting.

'Well,' said Sandro, 'Mrs...?' And with that innocuous and inevitable first question he saw her composure falter. He could not have defined it, but he knew it when he saw it. And he had seen it before, in years of interviewing witnesses and suspects, the innocent and the guilty, the moment at which a crack appears in the subject's certainty, and negotiation can begin.

Her mouth opened a little, then closed. She looked at him very hard, without blinking, and he knew she was trying to master some very strong emotion.

He saw her pale throat move as she swallowed. 'My name is Gentileschi,' she said. 'Lucia Gentileschi. My married name.

But I am not—My husband is not...' She stopped, and Sandro waited. 'My husband is dead.'

'I'm sorry,' said Sandro gruffly, and she looked at him as if she had no idea what he meant. 'I'm very sorry for your loss.' He could see that her hands were folded in her lap very tightly. 'Is it—was it...'

Lucia Gentileschi sat up very straight in the cheap chair, and took a small breath, then another. Despite her name, and her unmistakeably Florentine accent, there was something foreign about her. 'I am sorry,' she said. 'It is difficult. To say what I want to say.'

'Take your time,' said Sandro, and seeing a jug and two glasses on his desk that he did not at all remember putting there, he poured a glass of water and held it out to Signora Gentileschi. He smiled wryly. 'I don't have a queue.' Signora Gentileschi nodded gravely, and her shoulders relaxed a fraction. She unfolded her hands and took the glass.

'Claudio died nearly three days ago,' she said so quietly that he had to strain to hear her, looking down into the glass of water, not drinking. 'My husband of forty-nine years. I am a widow now.' She said it with dull wonder.

'I'm so sorry,' said Sandro again.

Nearly fifty years, he thought. She must have married young. And as he narrowed his eyes to examine her Sandro felt professional detachment returning to him like an old friend, tapping him on the shoulder after two years away. He realized that he could not yet be absolutely sure of the emotion she was trying to control. Death produces many more reactions than grief; some wives of forty-nine years would not grieve the passing of their husbands. He had to remind himself that Signora Gentileschi was coming to him as a client, not a suspect; he did not have to question her motives. All the same, he did not feel quite ready to ask her outright why she was here.

'Was your husband ill?' He asked, cautiously. 'Was he... very much older than yourself?'

Lucia Gentileschi frowned a little, alert, and he saw that she was a woman of intelligence; he saw her grasping for an accurate response. She set the glass down on the desk and returned her hands to her lap.

'Yes,' she said simply, and when he waited, she continued. 'I suppose, yes to both. He was beginning to be ill, in the early stages. He was eight years older than I am. He was eighty-one,'

'The early stages?' Sandro felt uneasy; he didn't feel yet as though he was asking the questions he really wanted to ask. But he could tell this was a woman who hated telling her business to others, and he needed to take it slowly.

'Well.' Her fine, clever face seemed to collapse a little, and in her lap her hands fell apart. 'He was becoming forgetful.' She looked away from Sandro a little, towards the window. 'He forgot ridiculous things. I bought him a book, for his last birthday, in June. A study of Viennese modernist architects. He forgot it was his, almost immediately. He picked it up as if he had never seen it before, three times. *Where on earth did this come from? he said. Is this mine?'*

Still she wouldn't look at Sandro; as she gazed past him through the window he saw her eyelids tremble, and he felt very sorry indeed. It was to be dreaded, wasn't it? This Alzheimer's thing. They all dreaded it.

'He was an architect?' he asked, to ward off the subject, somehow. Then she looked at him, and she smiled, and he saw how beautiful she must have been. A young woman with her child's haircut and the beautiful arches of her eyebrows.

'He was,' she said with gentle joy. 'A wonderful architect. Not famous,' she added hastily. 'Modest. But very clever.'

And then her face clouded so suddenly and devastatingly that he felt she must be about to cry. Sandro felt absolutely helpless.

'Signora Gentileschi,' he said quickly, wishing he had something to forestall the tears, wishing he had Luisa with him, a box of tissues, anything, but in their absence he extended a hand uselessly across the table. 'I am so sorry.' But again she controlled herself; he knew now, though, what that emotion had been, at least; he recognized grief when he saw it.

'Signora Gentileschi,' said Sandro, 'tell me how can I help you.' And then, knowing that they would have to come to it first, 'How did your husband die?'

Her head tilted and her blue eyes looked at him, pale and luminous as the moon.

'They told me he killed himself,' she said.

✾ ✾ ✾

The fog cleared around noon, just as they were breaking for lunch at the Studio Massi, but as Iris pulled off her apron and stashed her pencils and erasers away, she still felt as if something heavy was in the air, something hanging over her.

It wasn't fair. Ronnie went off to live it up with some friends of her mother's in a castle in the countryside, and Iris had to come up with her excuses.

'Tell them yourself,' she'd said, outraged. Ronnie had been sitting up in bed, hungover but still pretty. And Ronnie'd pulled out all the stops, pleading, it was the chance of a lifetime, blah, blah. 'Anyway,' she'd finished slyly, 'it'll only be Antonella. You can handle Antonella.'

And so far this week, it had only been Antonella Scarpa, the short-tempered studio manager: Iris had a strategy for dealing with her, just get it over with, her bark was worse than her bite. Head down, nodding to agree or to accept criticism on her own behalf or on Ronnie's. But to her dismay, there was another coat hanging by the door, a heavy black wool overcoat next to Antonella's fur-trimmed jacket, and when Iris came around the corner into the big room there he was, the course director. Paolo Massi, off wheeler-dealing somewhere, to whom she had not yet had to explain Ronnie's absence. She had assumed he'd be away all week; her heart sank.

Massi was just the kind of Florentine Iris had been led to expect from paintings—long straight nose, tall and lean, permanently frowning; she bet Ronnie's mum had liked him when she'd signed them up for the course. Serena (Ronnie often called her mother by her first name, with a sneer) had been here on a mini-break with the new boyfriend, and it must have looked like a golden opportunity, something to keep Ronnie busy for a bit longer while they worked out a plan of action.

Ronnie's A-levels had been disappointing. And they'd been impressed with the school, a long pedigree, an old family business with testimonials all over, a printing press that had been kept running during the war to help the partisans. Though as Ma said, if it was anything like France and everyone who said they'd worked for the Resistance really had, the war'd have been over a lot sooner.

At first Iris wondered, when Massi and Antonella both looked up at her from whatever it was they'd been examining on the big trestle table, if this was a deliberate strategy. *We need to talk about Ronnie.*

But they said nothing, Antonella smiling faintly and superciliously, fine-boned, long-nosed and androgynous. She had sharp black eyes and very short black hair, a crew cut with a bit of grey in it. I wonder if they're having a thing, thought Iris, just for a second. Or—no. He's married.

'Our best student,' said Massi. 'Good morning, Iris.' He pronounced it in the Italian way, made it sound more like a flower. *Ee-ris.* She didn't know if he was being sarcastic or not, and mumbled something, like sorry.

He smiled, a little stiffly. 'It's all right, Iris. I was being sincere.' And he gestured around. 'Always first. Always ready for work.'

'I'm sorry about Ronnie, I mean,' said Iris, feeling foolish, then regretting saying anything at all. He passed a hand over his high forehead, hair springing back, wiry, with threads of grey. He sighed.

'Veronica?' He spoke lightly, but she could tell he was taking it personally. 'I'm disappointed in Veronica.'

Iris bit her lip, ashamed.

Only last week Ronnie'd been asking him about supplementary reading, making a good impression, her speciality of course, until she spoiled it. She always spoiled it, though in this instance she'd excelled herself; he'd fallen for it, hadn't he? Offered her some of his own books to read, given her a pass for that tour of the Vasari corridor, the famous passageway from the Pitti Palace to the Uffizi that only the cognoscenti ever got to see. And now Iris had to carry the can.

She looked at her feet while he spoke.

'Do I bother to ask where she is today?' he said, stiffly.

'I don't know where she is,' she said, and Paolo Massi nodded, studying her. 'These students,' he said. 'But not you, Iris, eh?' He nodded towards the row of hooks, where her apron hung. 'To work, OK? I think the one I should speak to is Veronica's mother, perhaps.'

Bloody hell, thought Iris as she turned to begin work, then, when he didn't look up again from the table, *He's bluffing*. But Ronnie's mother probably wouldn't care, anyway; it was probably all the same to her if Ronnie was learning to draw or rubbing shoulders with English aristocrats in some castle in Chianti.

It had turned so mild by lunchtime that Antonella Scarpa opened the glass doors into the courtyard and Iris slipped out there to eat her sandwich. Only half a dozen had turned up today, anyway; forget it, she thought, why are you feeling guilty? She wondered again what would happen if Massi did call Ronnie's mother. Maybe she'd be out on her ear, for failing to keep Ronnie on the straight and narrow.

The centre of the large, high-ceilinged studio was now occupied by a long table, where they could sit and eat or draw. Six or seven people; the workers. Even today, even preoccupied with Ronnie's bad behaviour, Iris liked Fridays. Right from the start—and this was, what, her fourth Friday? Or maybe fifth— certain students on the course didn't turn up, because the partying started on Thursday night. It meant the noise levels were down and, more importantly, the social pressure was off. There was none of the, *Where did you go last night? Did you see so and so? I was, like, so wasted.* Ronnie could handle it, of course, Miss Congeniality; Ronnie was interested.

But Iris wanted a quiet life, and on Fridays that was what you got. She surveyed the heads at the table. She liked everyone who was in today, liked Hiroko, liked Gaby, even liked weird Traude from Nuremberg. The absentees were Sophia, from Gloucestershire, and Jackson, from some college in Vermont. Iris didn't know where Vermont was, exactly, but it didn't look poor; even Iris found herself looking sneakily at Jackson's iPhone, mesmerised by the tiny glowing screen and Jackson moving the pictures along with a fingertip, like a magician. Jackson had laughed at her, not unkindly.

Sophia was prone to oversleeping, and so hopeless at drawing Iris felt for her; it was to her credit that she kept going at all. To date Iris didn't think Jackson had come in once on a Friday, and on the days he was in he was almost detached, sleepy and careless and gangly. Out of place, just killing time in the studio while waiting for the evening when he'd head off out with some other Americans to the Zoe, a bar around the corner from the school where their evenings always started. A place full of posh, wealthy Florentines, young men in blazers and crisply ironed shirts and women in heels, with long blonde hair. They'd move on to the happening places, the other bars and clubs, and as often as not Ronnie would go with them. Sometimes they asked Iris, but she didn't have the money, and she didn't want to freeload. Would she have gone if she had? Maybe.

Jackson had asked after Ronnie yesterday, or maybe it had been the day before. The day the rain started; they'd been eating their sandwiches at the table, listening to it fall on the glass roof. He'd shown no sign of surprise when Iris had told him, under her breath, that she'd taken a little holiday. 'Somewhere hot, I hope,' he'd said, nodding at the rain. Iris had grimaced, thinking of how mad Ronnie would be, no chance of swimming pool action at the Chianti castle.

Antonella hadn't really gone over the top about it, either. Iris pondered if this always happened, the parents coughed up for the course, and the students just quietly drifted off to do their own thing after a week or two. Nice enough for the teachers; maybe that was why there seemed to be an etching school or a life class around every corner in Florence; she passed at least five brass plaques on her way in every morning. You ended up with a handful of committed students, and a nice quiet studio.

Iris yawned; she'd slept like a log last night, in the huge cold flat with its blackout curtains and shutters and cavernous spaces, but it had left her feeling even more tired than usual. She squeezed her eyes shut and when she opened them again she found herself looking at a drawing that with a sick feeling she recognized as one of hers. It had been pinned up on the wall, by Antonella, Iris assumed. It was a sketch she'd done of Ronnie lying on her back, hands behind her head, one knee up and the other leg slung over it carelessly, a book resting on her thighs. She'd handed it in at the end of last week to be marked.

Flushing, Iris found herself glad Ronnie herself wasn't here to remark on it, to say something languid and sarcastic, her voice floating through the studio. The space had deceptive acoustics, transmitting sound around corners and into alcoves; the higher registers carried a long way under the lofty, vaulted ceilings. Iris turned away from the picture; she wished Antonella hadn't put it up.

The model this morning had been a man for once—she thought Sophia and Ronnie might even be pissed off to have missed him. He'd been young too, in his twenties perhaps, but it had been hard to tell because he was very thin. Iris had wondered if he had something the matter with him, he'd seemed unnaturally knobbly, all bones and joints, and although he had black Italian hair, his skin was whiter than any she'd ever seen, his chin blue with stubble. He hadn't said anything but, then, the models often didn't. He'd been very good at keeping still, on a wooden chair, knees apart and elbows resting on them.

They didn't have a live model every day. They spent a lot of time drawing from jointed figures and photographs, which Iris thought at first was a bit of a cheat but when she kept at it she could see it helped. She liked drawing from life, though; after the first week she had started looking at clothed people, people in the dark streets or in bars, and imagining drawing them in the studio, undressed, how their flesh would sit on their bones. Fat was hard to draw. It was a weird feeling, interesting, not for any pervy reason but because it made them all equal, somehow, and in addition it seemed to qualify her to examine people shamelessly.

Going into the studio's small kitchen to wash up her plate, Iris found herself wondering what Paolo Massi would be like to draw, and just at that moment he walked in. She felt herself blush, turned slightly so he wouldn't notice her and her hot cheeks, and made a lot of drying her plate then putting it away. He didn't say anything—perhaps he hadn't registered she was even there—but began to assemble the pieces of the aluminium coffee pot, and she quickly went out.

Iris seated herself at the table as the blush subsided, scrabbling in her bag for her sketchbook. Perhaps it was because he'd been away that she was noticing Paolo Massi suddenly, wondering about him. He'd been there all the time their first three weeks after all, and she'd hardly registered him. He gave the introductory talk in the big studio, Ronnie and Jackson tittering at the back over something, rudely. He had taken them round the Uffizi and to look at drawings in a private room. Michelangelo, mostly; Iris thought she might go back and look at them again. Massi had been distant, and she remembered thinking it must be boring for him, having to say the same thing, every three months or so, to another lot of them.

'Hey,' said Hiroko's soft voice at her elbow suddenly, making Iris start. 'Are you OK?'

Iris turned, surprised; she must have been staring off into the distance. Hiroko was a quiet, self-contained person; modest was the word Iris would have used, or perhaps it was a Japanese thing. She didn't ever talk loudly, or put herself forward, like the rest of them.

'Fine,' said Iris, with a sigh. She smiled, half curious, half grateful for this display of interest. 'I'm fine.'

Hiroko nodded. 'You're distracted this morning.'

'Just a bit,' said Iris. She had an idea Hiroko was living across town beyond the railway station, a bleak, noisy part of the city with concrete, Stalinist hotels, although Hiroko never complained or even spoke about it at all. All she knew about Hiroko came from one conversation overheard. Iris had been sitting next to Traude when she asked Hiroko where she came from, and had marvelled silently at the information that her father was a Buddhist monk in Southern Japan, outside a city Iris had never heard of. She imagined Hiroko as a small, serious girl sitting alone under cherry trees, with her straight black fringe. And she wondered how it would work, having a monk for a father.

Hiroko was looking at her. 'She hasn't been here since Monday. Has she gone back home?' she said in her soft, apologetic tones, and for a moment Iris wondered what she was talking about.

'Back home?' And then she realized she meant Ronnie. 'Oh, no,' she said quickly, because if Ronnie'd gone back, she'd be going back too. 'She hasn't gone back. To England, you mean?' She shook her head at the very idea, no, no, no. 'No. She's... around. Somewhere.' And she laughed.

Hiroko looked at her in puzzlement. 'You don't know where she is?' Maybe it sounded worse to a Japanese person; perhaps like Italians they left home in their late twenties, weren't used to teenagers being allowed to roam the world on their own. And as she spoke Iris became aware of the school's director at her shoulder with a small metal tray of coffee things. He set it down. There was a silence.

'Oh,' said Iris, 'it's some guy. Well, you know Ronnie.' She hesitated. 'Well, I suppose you don't...' She gave Hiroko an agonized look, incorporating a meaningful glance at the course director, who had sat down at the end of the table and was frowning. Hiroko still looked baffled, but she shrugged.

'OK,' she said, eyeing Iris curiously. 'But you're not lonely? Living on your own?'

'I'm not living on my own,' said Iris quickly, feeling the director's eyes on her as he waited for an explanation.

Antonella came out of the kitchen and began to collect the small coffee cups. Iris sprang to her feet to help.

'Back to work,' said Massi.

They were to do charcoal studies of a small Etruscan statue Antonella had set up against the glass doors, but they had hardly sat at their easels when a bell rang. It was only the doorbell but today to Iris it sounded ridiculously loud, a raucous, grating sound like the alarms that called farmers in from the fields in France. In the peaceful space it reverberated, stopping them all in their tracks: Hiroko, Traude, Sophia, who'd turned up breathless just as they packed up their easels from the morning's sitting, looking around for someone before sitting down, Antonella in her work apron behind the delicate, beautiful statue. Massi came out of the office that sat on a *soppalco*, a kind of loft platform in the space above them, and looked down.

Antonella shrugged in response; she made as if to take off her apron and go to answer it but Massi made an impatient gesture and came down the stairs.

'Come along,' said Antonella, turning back briskly to her small audience as Massi passed behind them on the way to answer the door, a tiny frown puckering her forehead. 'It's nothing to do with you. *A lavoro.*'

But none of them even picked up the charcoal; they were listening. There were men's voices, lowered but serious, at the end of the wide corridor that led to the street door. Massi's voice was raised. Then there were footsteps and the voices came closer, and seeing the expression on Antonella's face as she looked down the corridor, they all turned, and Iris stared along with all the rest. Two carabinieri in dark blue uniforms with guns startlingly real, matt black and substantial on their hips, were following the course director back into the studio and up the stairs to the office. One of them was carrying a large plastic envelope by the corners; it was opaque, and seemed to contain something bulky.

All three men's faces were averted from their curious audience as in unison the heads below followed their progress; there was a tiny gasp, from Sophia, when the nearest policeman's holster came into her line of sight. She began to say something in a whisper but stopped when Antonella raised a hand.

Iris saw Antonella make an effort. 'Really,' she said to the small, open-mouthed group with an attempt at her usual authority, though Iris could see she was shaken. 'Please.'

There was a stirring and settling but the door on the *soppalco* remained firmly closed and eventually, reluctantly, they took up their charcoal. By the time the policemen re-emerged from the office close to an hour had gone by and Iris had almost finished her study of the statue, though it wasn't any good, she could see that. The sound of the door, though, jerked all their heads back up from the easels immediately, as if none of them had had their minds on higher things, not even Hiroko.

Slowly the director came out on to the gallery. Iris saw Antonella shoot him a frowning glance from below, then, bunching her apron in one fist she said nothing to any of them this time, only mounted the stairs and disappeared into the office.

It was only when Antonella came back out and Iris saw her face looking down at them from the gallery that she felt it, a jolt of panic. *Ma,* was her first thought, because home had always been the first thing she worried about. What would she do without Ma? She darted a look at the others; Sophia was open-mouthed but Traude's face was only politely interested, and Hiroko's patiently expectant. Calm down, she told herself.

Antonella was alone on the gallery; behind her in the office Iris could see the three men, standing, two in their dark blue uniforms, the course director half a head taller. Antonella's eyes swept the room, and she cleared her throat. She blinked; her gaze settled on the drawing on the wall, the girl lying on her back with her book. And just as Iris was wondering what the connection could be between the arrival of policemen in the school and her drawing of Ronnie, Antonella turned and looked directly at her.

Iris got to her feet in a daze; she felt them all watching.

'Iris,' said Antonella. 'If you would come into the office.'

Chapter Five

For A LONG TIME after Lucia Gentileschi had gone, Sandro sat at his desk and thought about memory and what it must be like to lose it. Unwillingly, he conceded to himself that he knew the pattern of the disease all too well, whether they called it Alzheimer's or something else—and apparently, Lucia Gentileschi had told him, in her dead husband's case, it was something else. It had always been around—on the bus there was inevitably an old lady who would say every two minutes, *Are you getting off here? Is this the station?* But these days everyone knew someone who had it. Luisa's mother had certainly had it, although there had been so many other things gone wrong with the poor creature that she hadn't had it long.

'It's because people are getting older,' Lucia Gentileschi had told him with sorrowful precision. 'We are an ageing population.'

The most recent memories crumbled first; you forgot setting a pan on to boil, or what you had gone to the refrigerator for, the names of recent acquaintances. Then you would confuse your children with your siblings, then with your own parents, then you would fail to recognize them at all. Sandro realized he had not asked Lucia about children. What stage had Claudio been at? The earliest, his widow had said, barely noticeable, unless you knew him inside out as she did, unless you knew the quality of his mind and his meticulous attention to detail.

'He stopped reading,' she said, then halted again and folded those pale hands back up in her lap. And although Sandro had never been interested in reading more than the newspaper in that moment he could see the two of them reading together, scholarly, silent, companionable. And then one of them stopped reading and—did what, instead? Stared, vacantly? Panicked, silently?

'I started to find little sticky notes he put around the place,' she said with a tiny gasp. 'Two or three times, saying *Teeth*. Things like that. Reminding himself to clean his teeth.' And he saw her press her lips together.

They did say that the earliest stages could be the worst, when there was still considerable lucidity and the implications of the memory loss could be understood by the sufferer. He had seen that terrified look in Luisa's mother's eyes for a brief few weeks, before other parts of her brain had shut down and shielded her, mercifully, from her loss.

He called Pietro, with a heavy heart; he hadn't anticipated how much he would hate this. The calling in of favours. He was out on a call; carefully Sandro left the message, that he wanted to talk to him about the death of Claudio Gentileschi, gave details of the date, age, address, everything he knew would speed things up. The desk officer—whose name he had avoided asking—took down all the information, his voice remote and uninterested as if Gentileschi had died a hundred years ago. Sandro hung up, his mind ticking through the whole hopeless business; what does a man do who sees the end of his life rushing towards him?

By the time he stood, stiff in the failing light, and reached for his coat, although he had liked her perhaps more than anyone he had met in years, Sandro was dreading his next encounter with Lucia Gentileschi.

❀ ❀ ❀

Nothing had happened to Ma, though the moment Iris understood that fact she had to fight the urge to phone her mother, tell her she loved her, despite being a stroppy, censorious and ungrateful only child who'd never said it before.

She couldn't; she mustn't. 'Don't worry about phoning,' Ma had said, squeezing Iris's hands in hers, roughened with turps. 'Too expensive. Too distracting.'

The look Antonella had given her as she'd come past on the gallery had only confused Iris further. Then Antonella had stepped out of her way and gone down the metal staircase to the dwindling group of her students.

Once inside the office, Iris had seen it on the desk, laid out on the plastic ziplock bag the policeman had brought it up in, and Ma was out of the picture.

'Iris,' said Paolo Massi abruptly, 'I'm sorry, please sit down.' She looked from one face to another, and hesitated, her eyes fixed on the table. Massi pulled out a chair for her, then another for himself, and then, reluctantly, she sat. Awkwardly the policemen took off their shiny peaked caps and followed suit, as if only belatedly realizing that Iris might need putting at her ease.

'Where did you get that?' she asked, her throat dry as a bone. 'That's Ronnie's.'

It certainly looked like Ronnie's bag. Iris had been with her when she bought it from one of the Nigerian street traders three weeks ago, and for a second, remembering the conversation they'd had about the fines they'd started making tourists pay for buying fake stuff on the street, the circumspection with which they'd checked out the Via Por Santa Maria for policemen before handing over the twenty euros, she thought they might have come after her to pay.

Only a second, though, before she asked herself, well, if they wanted to fine someone, why wouldn't they fine Ronnie herself? Because where the bag went, Ronnie went, arm clamped over it to ward off Vespa thieves. She loved that bag.

Iris pulled her chair a foot closer to the table, staring. The bag was big, dark brown with buckles and cleats and a big brass padlock with the designer's name on it; she remembered peering at the seams with Ronnie, deciding that it wasn't real leather. Ronnie'd had her bag nicked, was that it? She put out a hand to touch it but the closest policeman, a short, solid man with shiny black hair, cleared his throat; it was a warning sound, and she stopped. Iris could smell his aftershave, and she felt a kind of tension in her cheeks, as if she was about to be sick.

'Is this Veronica's bag?' asked Paolo Massi.

'I think so,' she said, warily. The bag was empty; how could they have known whose it was or where to bring it? But as if she'd asked the question out loud the other policeman produced a smaller, transparent plastic bag from a nylon suitcase at his feet, and she knew. Ronnie's grubby make-up bag; and her purse—still stuffed with old receipts, thought Iris, puzzled, wouldn't a pickpocket just chuck all that stuff?—her keys on the designer keyfob some ex-boyfriend had given her. No phone.

'I don't understand,' said Iris. 'When—? Ronnie hasn't...' She stopped then, feeling Massi's eyes on her. She couldn't tell them, could she, that Ronnie hadn't been in the city for days. That she'd had no intention of doing any work this week, and that for four days Iris had lied for her.

But how had Ronnie managed to get out to the country— and at that moment Iris wished she could remember the name of the town or the people she was staying with or anything but her mind was a complete blank—how had Ronnie got there, bought her train ticket, without her bag? It didn't make sense. 'Where did you find it?'

And then as she stared at the plastic bag Iris became aware of a dusty scent, somewhere below the policeman's aftershave, a smell at once familiar and incongruous. Out of place here inside, in the brightly lit office. The smell of what? Of the dry earth under trees, of hummus and pine needles and leaf mould. Against her better judgement Iris leaned to look closer and she saw the bag was scuffed and grubby, sifted with fine grey dirt inside. As though it had been rescued from a rabbit hole, like a terrier she'd seen hauled out of the ground with powdery grey eyelashes. As though it had been buried.

Iris felt something rise inside her, huge and nameless. 'I don't understand,' she said. 'If she'd lost her bag, she'd have come back, she'd have—What's happened to her? What's happened to Ronnie?' She struggled to hold it back. 'Where is she?'

Both policemen, perhaps at the panic in her voice, began talking at once, in Italian, and although her Italian had been improving, Iris couldn't understand. She looked from one of them to the other, and then Paolo Massi stood up, holding up a hand to the policemen. Taking control. He turned to Iris, and gratefully she found herself able to take a breath.

'Iris,' he said, and she could tell he was trying to keep his tone easy, 'I'm sure Veronica is fine. They just need to know when, when did you last see her? See, ah, Ronnie?'

And at the words Iris felt a strange humming in her ears, her line of vision narrowed until she could only see the bag, the brass padlock and the designer's name, off centre, the hallmark of a fake, they'd agreed. Narrowed until all she could see was the grey dirt inside Ronnie's bag.

'I—ah—I—sorry—' she stumbled, but Paolo had turned away to say something to the carabinieri; she focussed on the sound of his voice, and slowly the world reasserted itself. Stupid, she thought, what was that all about? She understood that he was asking if they'd like him to translate for the moment, and they talked together about how long it might take to arrange an official translator and then they agreed. If they spoke slowly, she wanted to say, she'd be able to follow, she wasn't useless. But then she gave in. She needed to be sure of what was happening, didn't she? This was important. There was some nodding and shrugging, then Massi turned back to Iris.

'Sorry,' she said. 'What did you say?'

'I asked when you last saw Ronnie,' he said. 'Or when you last spoke to her.'

Iris felt cold and sweaty at the same time.

'I last saw her the morning after Halloween,' she said slowly. 'We had a Halloween thing at our flat. A party.'

An absolutely rubbish, dismal party, she wanted to say, thinking of the American boy, and no one nice came.

'On Monday, then,' said Massi. 'And you last saw her on Tuesday morning.'

Iris nodded, staring at him, trying to think. 'She was in bed,' she said. 'I came here. To the school. The morning we went to the pottery class.'

'And you told Antonella she wasn't well,' said Massi flatly.

Embarrassed at the lie, Iris shrugged uncomfortably. 'She had a hangover,' she said. 'She really didn't look that great.' Actually, she'd been fine. Sitting up in bed, looking excited.

Massi turned and relayed the information succinctly to the tall carabiniere, who nodded. 'You were here on Tuesday?' she heard the policeman ask him. 'In the school?'

Massi looked at him curiously. 'I was hanging an exhibition, he said. 'In our gallery. All week, in fact.'

Plenty of people weren't in that day, thought Iris defensively; it was only a visit to a potter in Fiesole. Practically optional; Antonella had even left them to it and come back to the school.

The policeman nodded. 'So you didn't know Miss Hutton was not attending her classes?'

'Antonella might have mentioned it,' said Massi, frowning. 'Veronica would not have been the first student to play truant; obviously we do our best. We have excellent results.' He sounded defensive.

'But you yourself were not here. You were not teaching.'

'No,' said Massi, sounding angry.

Uncomfortably Iris watched them. Sooner or later she'd just have to say. She took a deep breath.

'I knew she wouldn't be in this week,' she said, looking down into her lap with shame. 'Well, no, actually I thought it would be a couple of days, but you know…' She'd been going to say, *you know Ronnie*, but for some reason the phrase raised panic in her. 'She said she was going off to stay with some friends of her mother's.' The name of the place came to her, and then the name of the friends. 'The Hertfords,' she said, almost triumphant until she checked herself. 'In Greve.'

Massi gave her a look, half-dubious, it seemed to Iris. 'Ah, well,' he said with false joviality, 'there's the answer.' Did he still not believe her?

'It seems she's in Chianti,' he said, turning to the policemen, explaining. They seemed to relax, almost grow impatient as they talked back to him. Massi turned again to Iris.

'You've spoken to her since she got there? She didn't mention her bag?'

'I, um, I—well, no,' said Iris slowly, feeling the panic rise in her again at the question.

'That is, I called her a couple of times, but there wasn't—it said the number wasn't active. Or something. Sometimes—well, if there's no signal?'

They asked for Ronnie's number, and the network she used, and then it dawned on Iris that the phone hadn't been in her bag, had it? Which was odd because that was where she usually kept it, but perhaps she'd had it in a pocket, or perhaps the person who took her bag only wanted the phone. Iris felt her head hurt with the possibilities. Why take the phone and not the money? It occurred to Iris that the keys to the apartment weren't in the bag, either.

So Ronnie had her phone, and her keys. That was better.

'We could try her again,' she said, pulling out her phone and dialling before they could stop her. That would be the way to deal with this. Please, she repeated in her head as she waited, Just speak, Ronnie, just answer. Just let me hear your voice, one more time. And only later did she think that it was then, listening to the dead air before she heard the wooden Italian recorded message once again, that she knew something was wrong.

❋ ❋ ❋

'Would any wife believe it?' asked Luisa, arms folded. 'That her husband would commit suicide?'

'Sit down,' said Sandro impatiently, pulling her chair out. Between them on the kitchen table was a dish of *pappardelle* with hare sauce, his favourite, the pasta ribbons glossy with meat juices. The kitchen was warm, the overhead light low over the table, which was laid as always, cloth, clean glasses, water jug, napkins. It had lifted him just to see it, but Luisa's reaction could capsize the whole mood. 'It'll get cold,' he said, mildly.

Sandro had been looking forward to this, all the way back. As though by prior arrangement the rain had stopped briefly and he walked home by moonlight. Through the great emptiness of the Piazza del Carmine, its cobbles gleaming; when he reached the great dark palaces of the Via Santo Spirito and saw silvery light shining down its majestic length, the Florence he recognized, then he began to return to himself. Halfway down a photographic hoarding was suspended from a façade; peering at it, Sandro saw that it showed an image of the great flood of 1966. November 1966: the photograph was of a pile of rubble up against a shopfront, and a car overturned in a tide of sludge. Sandro had been eighteen, and on military service; he had not yet met Luisa.

Walking on, he could see them now, the waters that had risen, stealthily, unstoppably, four decades before, up to the *piano nobile*, washing through ancient cellars. Remembered the mud and filth it had left behind and the months of back-breaking work of hauling and sluicing and rebuilding, the trucks full of ruined worldly goods parked everywhere, and men crying in the streets. And briefly Sandro marvelled at how the city had survived. How he had survived, the eighteen-year-old Sandro full of frustration and temper and irresolution; he'd found himself a job, a life; he'd found Luisa, and held on to her. Like the cleanup of the city, it had turned out to be a matter of hard work all along.

In the kitchen Luisa sighed, and sat. In silence she served them, then started, as Sandro lifted the fork to his lips. He heard her out, chewing thoughtfully.

'However bad it got, how could you make yourself believe it? That the one you had lived with for all that time, the love of your life, would just, just—leave you? Abandon you?'

Alarmed, Sandro nodded, trying to work out where this outburst had come from. He put his fork down carefully. 'Eat,' he said. 'It's so good. And you look worn out.'

It was true; Luisa was pale, her eyelids were dark and heavy. She made a sound of frustration, but she began to eat. It was the best strategy against Luisa's outrage, the threat of letting food spoil. She eyed him as she ate, but he saw her grow calmer. Then he understood; it seemed so long ago to him, but clearly not to Luisa.

'Oh, that,' he said impatiently. 'I know. I was never going to do away with myself, you know that.' Her eyes narrowed, dangerously. Carefully Sandro poured her half a glass of the very nice Brunello Pietro had given them. He had connections down in the Val D'Orcia; a nephew drove for one of the winemakers, who'd lost his licence. Luisa exhaled, took a sip of the wine, softened.

'You say that now, Sandro. I think you've forgotten.'

Maybe it was true; maybe he had forgotten. He'd certainly been in a state two years ago when the body of the child's killer was found, when questions started to get asked at Porta al Prato, and Sandro had decided to head off on his lone mission, like John Wayne. Knowing he would be out of the force when they found out what he'd done. When they caught up with him. Had he intended to do himself in? He'd be lying if he said it hadn't gone through his mind, but that wasn't the same thing. There was planning involved; you'd have to think of who found the body, how to manage it without too much mess. Or too much pain.

As if she knew what he was thinking, Luisa said, 'How would you have done it?' Her voice was rough; she was still angry with him for putting her through those twenty-four hours of worry, just for that thought passing through his mind. 'I wouldn't have done it,' he said quietly. 'I would never have done it.'

She said nothing. He shrugged, uncomfortable. Not pills, he said uneasily. 'Something very quick. Instantaneous.' She knew they were both thinking about his gun, police issue. 'But we're not talking about me, Luisa. I would never do it.' Her hand lay on the table, and for a moment he laid his hand on top of it.

What he did not add was that he would not have taken pills, but neither would he have filled his pockets with stones and walked into the muddy Arno below the shacks and tipped rubbish of the Lungarno Santa Rosa. Down in the muck with river vermin swimming over you. He would never have done what Claudio Gentileschi had done.

Pietro had called back, eventually.

'The guy was a serious depressive,' he'd said. 'I'm sorry, Sandro, we talked to the doctor. He fought it all his life; he must have just got tired of fighting.' Sandro heard him let out a heavy sigh. 'You know—the camps. He was in the camps, that kind of thing—well. I don't think they ever leave it behind.'

Sandro knew Pietro was thinking of that writer, who'd been in the camps, written about the camps, then thrown himself down the stairs in Turin forty years on. But Pietro's assumption niggled at him; no two men are the same, not even if they've survived the same horrors. He said nothing.

Pietro went on, earnest. 'Maybe something happened, some little thing, the straw that breaks the camel's back, who knows? Come on, Sandro; you know as well as I do. It happens all the time. Suicide.'

There'd been a silence then. 'First job, eh?' Pietro said, trying to buck him up. 'Nice one, Sandro, you're back in the saddle, anyway.'

They'd finished by making their usual arrangement to meet. Sandro knew Pietro was trying to convince him he'd got a future, but perversely it had the opposite effect; the kinder Pietro was, the more he remembered he could have lost his friend his job. For a whole day after Sandro had gone AWOL—with a loaded police gun—Pietro had scrambled to cover for him. Had lied for him; could still be disciplined for it, too, if anyone in the system took against him.

'I'm not saying people don't commit suicide,' said Luisa, now standing to clear the plates. 'I'm saying the ones they leave behind don't want to believe it. I'm saying that it's natural to deny it.'

Sandro nodded, but he wasn't sure if Luisa would say the same, had she met Lucia Gentileschi. They couldn't have been less physically alike—he thought this observing Luisa at the sink, her hair as black and glossy as when he'd first met her, her shoulders plump, hips wide and strong—but Claudio Gentileschi's widow was a woman in the same mould as Luisa herself.

'They *said* he'd killed himself?' he'd asked her as gently as he could, sitting there with her straight back in the room filled with pale November light. She seemed to be permanently bracing herself against something. 'You don't believe them?'

She took a while before answering him. 'I don't know,' she said at last. 'I mean, no, I don't, of course I don't believe them, that is my first reaction. I knew him, you see...' And at this her voice faltered, then recovered. 'They—you—didn't know Claudio.' She nodded. 'But I can see that perhaps, under the circumstances, I'm not thinking clearly.' Sandro saw her eyes, fixed on some point through the window behind him, intent. 'I have to be sure, you see,' she went on. 'I need to be convinced. Because I cannot—I can't...' She gave a little gasp, drawing breath in. 'I can't really stand to think that he was in pain. Or that he was frightened.'

'No,' said Sandro, feeling a tightness in his own throat. 'Of course not.' He still didn't know what she wanted of him. Lucia Gentileschi turned her head a little to transfer her gaze from the window at last to Sandro. He wanted to look away, as if from something very bright, but he did not.

She went on, determined. 'The police won't tell me that, of course; it isn't part of their job to find that out, I suppose they aren't like doctors, or priests. Or perhaps they think it wouldn't be good for me to know the truth.'

Despite himself, Sandro nodded minutely; he knew well enough how much was never told to relatives. His heart sank at the thought that he was being offered an opportunity to make amends, to handle it right, this time; the problem was, he had no idea if he could manage it. What if the truth was intolerable? But Lucia Gentileschi—he couldn't imagine ever being able to refer to her by her first name, or to use the informal, *tu*—was still looking at him, and now he could see that if anyone could handle it, she could.

'You see,' she said, 'he was missing for a whole day. Eleven hours unaccounted for. The last time I saw him was at eight, when he left our apartment to buy the newspaper; they said he died at about seven in the evening.' She paused; her eyelids fluttered. 'They found his body the following morning.' She took a sip of the water she still held in her hand, dutifully. All Sandro could think of was the night she must have spent without her husband; the first night alone in fifty years. How long it must have seemed.

And now sitting in his own warm kitchen and going over it again he understood what Luisa was saying; the night he'd stayed out, and those hours she hadn't known if he was alive or dead, would not be easily forgotten. He stood up and went to the sink and folded his arms around her from behind, warm and solid against his chest, and for a second he felt her lean back against him.

'So what are you going to do?' Luisa sounded distracted, as if the feel of his arms around her shoulders had reminded her of something else entirely. He set his cheek against her hair, breathing in her smell.

'I'm going to see her tomorrow,' he said. 'In her—their apartment.' He sighed, thinking of all the things Claudio Gentileschi's wife had told him, and the things he had deduced without being told. That he had been a proud man; an intellectual, an artist. A loving man, though not good at expressing himself. A man who'd had dark moods but had been good at controlling them. A man who'd known that he was losing his faculties. And then there were those missing hours, Gentileschi's last hours on earth, the absence that his wife could not ignore. 'I need more information,' he said. 'I need to find out about the husband, of course. And I need to find out about her.'

And as he thought of Lucia Gentileschi and what she did and did not know about her husband, he became aware of Luisa's hand on his, how cool it was in spite of the kitchen, and how she was not letting go as he would otherwise have expected.

'Luisa?' he asked.

'Darling,' she said, without turning her head to look at him, and he knew she was about to tell him something he didn't want to hear. 'I went to the doctor today.'

Chapter Six

WHEN IRIS WOKE the next morning, nothing was familiar about the room in which she found herself. Another kind of dark, strange place: but this was definitely not the Piazza d'Azeglio. Even in the dark she knew that; the bed was low and hard, the thin light was more diffuse, the smell was different, a spicy, unfamiliar scent. And it was warm.

Then she remembered.

Hiroko's flat had not after all turned out to be in the streets and streets of dull apartment buildings out past the station, but buried in a narrow alley beyond the big Victorian covered market. It had been a longish walk from the school, and it was dark by the time they got there.

Paolo—they seemed to be on first-name terms now, that hour with the police, talking about where the bag had been found, that terror she'd felt and he'd seen had shifted things somehow—had offered to escort her back to the flat in the Piazza d'Azeglio to get some things. 'I don't know, toothbrush, nightclothes?' he had said, seeming nervous, and she'd found herself feeling sorry for him. This kind of thing couldn't be good for the school, and she wondered what he would find to say to Ronnie's mum. She felt stunned, herself, unable to think.

They'd found a number for the Hertford house in Greve very quickly; it had taken the taller carabiniere, who Iris thought was the senior officer, a couple of minutes on his mobile. On autopilot Iris had found herself wondering if all foreigners

maybe had to register with the police, but then of course even if
you looked in the phone book, there'd only be one Hertford in
Chianti, wouldn't there?

It had been a moment's relief, to see the policeman's
face when the number came through, a breakthrough. The
carabinieri were both very dark-skinned, with stubbled chins
and black eyes and thick southern accents. The tall one wrote
the number on a piece of paper Massi pushed towards him,
squinting down his long nose. *'Artfoord,'* he pronounced
triumphantly, *'Ecco.'*

They existed, then, at least, these friends of Ronnie's
mother Serena in their castle. Iris wondered if it was a real
castle or if it too had been built out of glass and rotting wood
by an experimental architect. Probably the real deal, knowing
Serena and her Georgian farmhouse surrounded by yew
trees with the gallops running for miles; again Iris's stomach
churned, at the thought of Serena this time, and what she
would say.

They looked at her, then at Massi, then all three of them
looked at Iris.

'Should I do it?' she said, nervous to the point of hysteria.
'You want me to phone them?' At least she'd be doing something. Massi pushed the phone across the table to her, and the
carabiniere handed her the number.

At least it rang; the long Italian tone that never sounded
anything like a telephone's ring to her. It rang a long time; Iris
was about to put the phone down, feeling tears of frustration
pricking at her eyes, when it was snatched up and someone
shouted, *'Pronto?'* Her heart sank, it was Italian, and a thickly
accented, bad-tempered Italian at that. Female.

But Iris hadn't given up. *'Potrei parlare con i signori
Hertford per piacere?'* she got out, with some effort.

'Eh?' There was a cavernous, echoing sound to the voice;
Iris, holding tight to the receiver, imagined a baronial hall. If
this was a housekeeper she wasn't very welcoming.

'I signori Hertford?'

Massi gestured to her for the phone, but she persevered. '*E la casa degli signori Hertford?*'

Perhaps hearing the desperation in her voice, the housekeeper, or whatever she was, seemed to relent. '*Si,*' she said. '*Ma gli signori non ci sono. Sono in Inghilterra da un mese.*' And then Iris had given up, handing the phone dumbly to the long-nosed carabiniere.

They weren't there. The Hertfords existed, they had a house in Greve and therefore probably were Serena's friends. But they hadn't asked Ronnie out there for the week, nor even for a day, because they'd been in England for the previous month and were still there now.

After talking to the housekeeper for another five minutes, the policeman had hung up. The place was shut up for the winter, he said. There'd been no one there, no teenagers, no house parties, not even unauthorized ones. No Ronnie.

There was a silence, then Massi and the carabinieri talked among themselves about how to proceed. Massi seemed serious, but he didn't betray any panic, for which Iris was grateful. Ronnie, she thought, where are you?

As they talked, Iris listened but they talked quickly, and she found the accents hard. 'What—what do they think has happened?' she asked quickly, at the first opportunity.

'They're not sure,' said the director, carefully.

'I know that,' said Iris. 'But what do they think?'

'Iris,' said Massi, and she had the impression of being deflected. 'I think first we need to talk to Ronnie's mother. Perhaps—well, it's possible Ronnie may have phoned her. And then perhaps—well, other friends.'

'Yes,' said Iris, trying to stay calm, trying to be reasonable. 'Of course.' But the panic she'd felt at the sight of that fine dust in Ronnie's bag was still there; it wouldn't be held down. She forced herself to say it.

'But do they—they're worried, aren't they?'

And reluctantly Massi met her eye. 'Yes,' he said. 'It's four days. If Veronica's mother has heard nothing, either—well. I think they have to take it seriously.'

She was grateful for the way Paolo pretty much forbade her to go back to the flat on her own. 'If necessary, you can sleep here,' he said, and she could see he was worried, too. About her, as well as Ronnie. 'There is a fold-out bed in the office.' But Hiroko inserted herself into the conversation at that point.

'I have a bed in my apartment for visitors,' she said in her polite, quiet way. 'It's no problem.'

They had walked along the Arno in the dark, the lights coming on in the big, fabulous apartments overlooking the river. And then they'd turned north and dived into the maze of narrow streets and cold, dark façades heading off towards the station, with Hiroko leading the way as she took small determined steps, occasionally looking anxiously at Iris with her pale, closed face. The more she walked, the colder Iris felt, and she wondered if it was some kind of shock reaction. Florence had never seemed like a sinister place to her before, but now she was scared; every shuttered window, every heavy door, every overflowing dumpster looked frightening to her in the sparse streetlighting.

Now in the soft, warm gloom of another unfamiliar apartment, Iris stared at the ceiling in the dark. It had been stupid of Ronnie to go away with that bar owner, hadn't it? What had his name been? Josef. Ronnie'd hardly known him. But when she'd got back and gone over it all with Iris in the freezing kitchen with a cup of tea, Iris had to admit that some of what she'd felt had been jealousy. Because she didn't know if she'd ever dare to do such a thing.

The flat was quiet but not silent; as she lay still, not wanting the day to begin, Iris could hear small, measured kitchen sounds; things being put away, or set out, very carefully. She'd gone straight to bed the night before, apologizing, suddenly unable to keep her eyes open. Hiroko had pulled out the futon in her sitting room, showed her the tiny bathroom, and disappeared, and overwhelmed with voiceless gratitude Iris had fallen deeply and mercifully asleep.

Now, though, she could feel the beat of her heart accelerate as the anxieties clamoured to be heard. The first problem was marshalling all the facts. Iris had always been good at that, good at homework and revision and sorting out the essential from the insignificant, but here and now she felt as if her head was stuffed with cotton wool, her eyes swollen with crying. What else had the police said? They'd asked which other students on the course had known Ronnie. Traude and Hiroko had hardly even spoken to Ronnie since she'd been there; Sophia had twittered nervously to the policemen in her British Council Italian for twenty minutes.

'What did you say?' Iris had asked her.

'Well, I told them she enjoyed going out, you know, she had hundreds of friends, but I hadn't seen her with any—any special friend.' Sophia pushed out her lower lip, like a baby. 'Maybe I should have told them about Jackson? But they weren't—you know.' Her eyes opened wide. 'You don't think? Jackson?'

'No,' said Iris frowning 'I don't think so.' She hesitated, unwilling to decipher why she was resistant to the idea. 'Jackson was here yesterday, wasn't he? But there must have been someone. She wouldn't plan to disappear for days on her own.'

'Do you think so?' said Sophia. 'But at the party—if she had a boyfriend you'd think she'd have invited him to the party. Gosh, I would.' She looked pensive.

Sophia was living with an Italian family; even Iris had scorned the protectiveness of Sophia's mother, the curfew arrangements and Alice bands and pastel jumpers, the packages of food her Italian family sent her to school with. It looked only sensible now, she reflected, with a twinge of envy.

'And she can't have—been—well, abducted,' Sophia had said, as if it had only just occurred to her. 'Do they really think that? I mean that would be just—it would be—no! Don't you think maybe she's sitting in a swanky hotel with whoever he is and he's bought her a new bag and a new phone and she'll turn up tomorrow or something and she'll wonder what all the fuss was about?' Then she'd let out a hysterical sound, half giggle, half shriek.

For a second, Iris had let herself believe it. Why not? She imagined this boyfriend, with unlimited money for honeymoon suites and new handbags. Why wouldn't Ronnie have phoned, though? Maybe she wouldn't have; not just to let them know she'd lost her bag.

'Maybe,' she'd said.

Sophia had been at the Halloween party, hadn't she? But she hadn't stayed long; she'd been collected by the father of her Italian family, from the door, at ten. She'd been funny at the party, gazing round-eyed as Ronnie had strung some boy along; secretly, Iris knew, Sophia idolized her. 'She's so good at everything,' Sophia had said, watching Ronnie blow smoke out of the side of her mouth. 'Don't you think they think she's the best of us at drawing? I'm sure she'll get more into the end-of-term show, more than any of us.' And Iris had stared at her, wondering how anyone could be so deluded, even if Ronnie had developed a belated interest in doing well. Maybe it was because Sophia was so hopeless at it herself.

As she lay in the dim grey light, just remembering the conversation made Iris blush. What a bitch I am, she thought. It doesn't mean anything, just because Antonella put my drawing up on the wall. What makes me think I'm so great? Maybe Ronnie was good after all.

She heard sounds elsewhere in the flat and Iris's mind raced. She'd have to make that list. The name of the bar owner. She needed to talk to Jackson. To Sophia. To the police. Would she have to talk to the American boy who'd called her fat? And she needed to talk to Ronnie's mum, before she left for the airport, before she got on the plane that would bring her here, hysterical, furious, terrified. Unable to deal with any of it, Iris threw off the duvet, and headed for the kitchen.

Walking into the bright room, Iris realized she was wearing something of Hiroko's, a long grey cotton nightdress. It felt warm; the flat was warm; the table was laid with small white cups, a board with slices of dense brown bread, a Japanese teapot. It was so perfectly welcoming and ordered that Iris wanted to cry suddenly. She sat down.

'You sleep OK?' said Hiroko, appearing behind her in the doorway with wet hair. She made a gesture inviting Iris to eat, twisted her hair up in a white towel and sat down. 'The bed is hard,' she said apologetically.

'No,' said Iris, 'I slept amazingly.' And she realized it was true, like a log. No dreams, just a heavy blissful dark sleep, like crawling into a soundproofed cave. Maybe it was because they were at the back of the building, on the ground floor. She remembered Hiroko showing her a small courtyard garden through a long window when they arrived.

They ate for a while in silence. The bread was quite hard, tasting of bitter grains Iris couldn't identify, and the tea was yellow, with small flowers floating in it.

'Is this tea Japanese?' she asked. At home Iris drank her milky Indian tea by the bucketful, but she surprised herself by liking this; it was light and fragrant and somehow purifying.

'Chinese,' said Hiroko, smiling. 'Sorry. I can't find Japanese here.'

Iris took another sip, and with the unfamiliar taste in the warm, quiet, bright room, she felt something shift in her head, a pressure easing, just enough.

'What did the police say yesterday?' said Hiroko. 'What can they do? To find her?'

Propping her elbows on the table, both hands warmed around the cup, Iris said, 'They were going to check the hospitals, emergency admissions over this week.' She spoke normally, but she didn't feel normal. It was surreal. 'But they didn't call, did they? To say they'd found her?'

Hiroko moved her head slightly. 'No one called,' she said.

Iris nodded, feeling the tension build again.

'Then they'll try to trace the phone. If it's still got power, you can do that, they said. You can find out where it was before it lost power, too.' Had Ronnie even taken her charger? She'd been planning on being away a couple of days, hadn't she? Or she wouldn't have cooked up the trip to the countryside.

She kept the implications at bay. Don't think about that, she told herself, don't think about whether Ronnie still has the phone but can't answer it or recharge it. The thief—if there was a thief—took the phone; the phone won't lead us to Ronnie. 'And then they can check her bank account, to see if she took money out.'

'Before the bag—before she lost the bag?'

Of course, thought Iris, staring at Hiroko's smooth, clever face, saw her thinking it through. The cards were all still in the bag, so they wouldn't lead anyone to Ronnie either. 'But it might give them a clue,' she said. 'To her movements.'

Hiroko nodded.

'And then there's CCTV,' Iris went on. 'Cameras, in the streets.'

Hiroko nodded again, a little sadly. 'Not so many in Florence,' she said. And then, delicately as though this was the question she thought might be the awful one, 'And—where did they find the bag?'

And only then did Iris think about it, think properly. At the time she had only been relieved when they'd said, because it had allowed her to stop thinking about rabbit holes and burials.

"They found it in the Boboli,' she said. 'In the Boboli gardens.'

And on the only visit she'd paid to the big park that covered a hillside behind the Pitti Palace—a Sunday walk with Ronnie when the sun had come out and Ronnie's hangover had ebbed at the same time—Iris had seen that that soft grey-white dirt was everywhere. The dusty gravel paths left it on your shoes; it coated the hem of your coat, your skirt, your trousers. It had sifted down into Ronnie's bag, like sand in a swimming bag after a day at the beach.

'What are you thinking, Iris?' said Hiroko quietly.

And before she could find a way of stuffing it right down to the bottom of her bag of options and out of sight, Iris said, 'I think something bad's happened to her.'

❀ ❀ ❀

Luisa had made him get up in the end. Forty years of married life and he had always been the one to fetch her a glass of water in the morning when she was always parched and, besides, it was the secret of good skin.

Sandro lay under the quilt, unable to face it.

At eight she sat down on his feet, hard.

'I've got to get going in half an hour,' she said. 'We're dressing the windows today.'

He stayed where he was, immobile, face in the pillow.

'This was what I was worried about,' she said. 'Not the lump. Not the biopsy. Not the doctor. I was worried about you.'

He struggled upright, his stomach clamped hard like iron; it seemed to him that for all a lifetime's carrying a gun and arresting pimps and wife-beaters and drug-addicted street thieves, he'd never really been frightened by anything in his life before this. Luisa looked into his face.

'It's very small,' she said. 'I'm not afraid of it.'

There were so many things Sandro wanted to say, and he found he could not say any of them. I love you, would be a start. I can't live without you, although that would probably be the wrong thing to say, under the circumstances.

'OK,' he said. 'I'd better get going, too.' It was Saturday, but there was no point just sitting here, on his own. 'Can you do lunch? We could have a bite at the Cammillo.'

'Sorry, *caro*,' she said, sounding like she meant it, 'the shop's always so busy today.'

At the door he found himself with his arms around her, his face pressed against hers, his eyes squeezed shut.

'It'll be fine,' he said. 'We'll go together.' She pulled back, gave him a wild-eyed look. 'To the doctor's,' he said. 'We'll go to see the doctor together.'

❀ ❀ ❀

Lucia Gentileschi's apartment was much closer to the house than Sandro's office; the Via dei Pilastri was five minutes north of Santa Croce on foot. Her voice through the intercom was clear and steady and she buzzed him up with a firm hand.

It was a nice building, four hundred years old perhaps; the hall and stairway well kept, with retouched decoration on the vaulted ceiling, pink and grey, and a smell of wax and cleaning fluid in the air. Lucia Gentileschi opened the door to him before he even had a chance to ring, and Sandro found himself briskly ushered into a light and spacious sitting room, almost completely bare of ornament except for a tall candle, burning on a table.

Holding his coat in her arms, Lucia Gentileschi saw him looking at the candle flickering in the bright room. 'We light a candle for the dead,' she said. 'In the time of mourning.' She hung the coat up.

For a second he didn't understand at all. And then it dawned on him; the slight foreignness he'd detected in Lucia Gentileschi's manner, a huge eight-armed candelabrum in the window of the dusty little shop he'd passed, the street itself. The great green-domed synagogue, for God's sake, just around the corner in the Via Farini, never mind Ruth's Kosher Café; Sandro had lived in Florence for close to sixty years and had for all of those known that this was what you might call the Jewish quarter, if such things could still be said.

'Yes,' was all he said. 'Of course.'

Still on her feet, Lucia Gentileschi eyed him, small and fierce. You should meet my wife, he thought.

'You didn't know?' she said, with the ghost of a smile. Sandro gave an apologetic shrug.

'Good,' she said. 'I mean, it was one of the reasons the police made me angry. That they thought it was significant. Because Claudio was two years in a concentration camp, they thought it meant he was more likely to commit suicide.' Her pale eyes gleamed.

'Two years?' he said. 'How old was he?'

'Aged seventeen to nineteen,' she said, and Sandro bowed his head to hide his shame.

'We weren't religious,' said Lucia. She looked at the candle. 'At least, I thought we were not. There are some things that turn out to—to bring comfort even if you have spent your life finding rational ways to deny them.

'Would your husband have disapproved?' asked Sandro, nodding towards the candle.

She thought a moment. 'Yes,' she said, and smiled the smile again that had made her beautiful before. 'But he didn't like demonstrations of any kind, not saying...' She hesitated. 'Not saying one loved him, for example. Even if one did.'

She gestured at the long, low sofa, upholstered in dark linen, and tentatively Sandro sat. It felt strange to be interviewing someone without the benefit of uniform. He took out his notebook.

'Do you have the post-mortem report?' he asked. She reached towards the low table where the candle was burning and he saw that she had set it out ready for him, in a pale brown folder. Sandro opened it and scanned it. The yellow water of the Arno had been found in Claudio Gentileschi's lungs; some lesions seen in the brain consistent with late-onset dementia although this would be confirmed by a neurologist at a later date. There was some bruising that would have occurred at or around the time of death, but it was not definitive; it did not unequivocally indicate violence. He had been alive when he had entered the water.

There were photographs with the report, which was unusual. He took them out, looking up at Lucia Gentileschi. He found he didn't want to look at the pictures; perhaps two years out of the force had changed him more than he'd thought.

'I asked for copies,' she said. 'They were shocked, I think. But I insisted; I knew that I would need them if I were to—well. If I went to you. I had to pay for them.'

'Yes,' said Sandro, and he sighed. He looked again at the top of the post-mortem report, where the investigating police officer would be named. Gianluca Scappatoio; not a bad guy, but not a brain surgeon. I'll talk to Pietro, thought Sandro.

He looked at the pictures then, quickly. He had seen drowned bodies before; he expected the pallor, the swelling to the tissues. He could see that Gentileschi had not been in the water long because he still looked human. You could imagine him alive. A heavy, handsome man, short-cropped white hair and a strong Roman nose. There were photographs of bruising to one arm, and abrasions to the palms of the hands. He put them away.

There were photographs of the contents of his pockets—a wallet, a handkerchief, a set of house keys. A separate photograph of tiny white pebbles.

'Found in his shoes,' said Lucia. 'It's crazy, isn't it? Little stones. I don't want to know, or about the kind of waterweed they found clinging to his trousers.'

'No,' agreed Sandro. 'They must be thorough, though. Sometimes these things tell us something.' He paused a moment. 'No mobile phone?'

'If he'd had a mobile, I might have called him,' she said, her eyes faraway. 'He didn't like mobiles.'

'Didn't he?' he said. 'Tell me. Tell me about your husband.'

The conversation went on for two hours, perhaps more, and by the time they had finished Sandro felt quite done in. He had filled half his notebook. He knew the daily routine—the route he took on his morning walk, the swim at the Bellariva twice a week, winter and summer. The career he'd had as an architect in Milan and Verona before coming back here and settling in Florence with his own small practice.

'Government work,' said Lucia. 'Some restoration, some buildings for the *comune*. Nothing grand.'

'Did he enjoy it?'

'He didn't mind, in the end,' she said. 'He always wanted to build something wonderful and new, but he got too old. He got tired.' The lines in her face deepened, making her look old herself, and sad.

'Are these his paintings?' asked Sandro, pointing at one of the large canvases on the wall for something to say. They were abstract paintings, mysterious to Sandro. Large rectangular patches of mostly sombre colours—a dark purple like a bruise, rough, chalky white, the grey-green of church stone—that bled into each other.

'Yes,' said Lucia. 'He was a wonderful painter. But he stopped, oh, maybe ten years ago. Started the swimming instead.'

Sandro debated whether these were the actions of a man who took steps to keep his life on track; a man who modified his expectations. A man deserving of respect.

'The last morning,' he said gently, and she nodded obediently. 'Was everything normal? Was there anything—anything at all out of the ordinary?'

'No,' she said. 'Nothing. Absolutely nothing.'

So, thought Sandro, if anything happened to his state of mind, it happened after he left home.

'Do you have another photograph?' he asked gently. 'I think I'll need one.'

She stood up, crossed to a long, modern desk in the corner of the room; it had a scroll top and he watched as she sat at the chair, took out a key and opened it. He could see from the set of her shoulders that he had exhausted her. Inside the desk Sandro could see a neat stack of document folders and a box like the kind a shop would use for petty cash. She took a small envelope from one corner and withdrew a passport-sized photograph; she looked at it for a tiny second before holding it out to Sandro.

'I'm sorry,' she said. 'There are so many things—I didn't know how much there would be to do. His desk. His papers. The bank account—I have to set everything in order. And people come round, to pay their respects, people one hardly knows...'

'Yes,' said Sandro, turning away from that thought in his head, the thought of the practicalities of restoring equilibrium, with half your life taken from you. 'I should leave you in peace.'

'Do you have any children?' he asked, at the door. It was an impertinent question, which was why he saved it until last. Why should it make any difference to whether or not a man committed suicide? He himself had no children. But he wanted to know.

'No,' said Lucia Gentileschi, but her face was clear and serene as she said it, unclouded by grief or disappointment. 'We couldn't have them. It never mattered; we always said it ends with us.'

And Sandro found himself thinking of Luisa, whose face would have told a different story if she had been asked the same question.

'May I ask, Signora,' he said, knowing that he had to say it, 'why you are so sure that your husband did not take his own life?'

It was as though her pale eyes were looking right through him, to something far away.

'Because he would have taken me with him,' she said simply. 'He would never have left me behind.'

❊ ❊ ❊

On the pavement outside Sandro stood in the drizzle, suddenly unable to move for the sound of her words, beating like a pulse in his ears. Had he even thought of Luisa, when he'd made his own desperate bid to escape the mess he'd made? What was it that had saved him, then? Years of training, comradeship, duty, a certain doggedness, a lack of imagination? All and none; the truth was, he was afraid to remember that night. The precise quality of despair was a dangerous thing, and the instant at which there had been nothing and no one between him and the final step was not one Sandro wanted to summon up. But if he wanted to help Lucia Gentileschi, it looked like he was going to have to.

We are all afraid of being alone.

It was a declaration of love, and Sandro must prove it justified. He had felt the white light of her gaze as she'd said it. 'He would never have left me behind.'

Chapter Seven

For SOME REASON it took the ringing of the phone in Hiroko's apartment to remind Iris that of course there was no school, because it was Saturday.

'Do you want me to come with you?' Hiroko asked with concern, when she told her where she was going.

Iris told her she'd be all right. It was a gloomy old place, true enough, and she'd been grateful not to have to go there last night, in the dark, but the truth was, she wanted some time to herself in the Piazza d'Azeglio before Paolo Massi got there with the carabinieri. She felt a need to pace the apartment, to look at things that they probably wouldn't understand.

It had rained in the night, and the air was fresh. The streets were gleaming with puddles and amazingly empty, because it was Saturday, Iris supposed, and still early. She felt warm and clean from the long shower she'd taken at Hiroko's as she passed the red and grey ironwork of the big covered market where trucks were unloading; she saw a rack of meat carcasses wheeled inside up a ramp, and a man obscured by cases of artichokes stacked up in his arms. Life went on; it still looked like an orderly universe—not one in which people could just disappear.

It wasn't that she minded being on her own. She had been used to spending at least part of every weekend alone anyway. Ronnie was often no more than a hump under the duvet sleeping off a heavy night, or had been invited somewhere, lunch parties, bowling, skating. She'd even been skiing, one Sunday, with a group of Italian boys she'd met at the Zoe; they collected her in a flash SUV and whisked her off somewhere in the white-topped hills to the west, bringing her back at nightfall. There were so many people; Ronnie'd known so many people. Were they all...suspects? Iris thought wryly that it would be an awful lot easier for the police if she'd gone missing instead of Ronnie.

Was it unnatural, Iris wondered, the way she was feeling? It was as though somewhere in Hiroko's dim, quiet, apartment her brain had found a way of dividing it up, separating the terror of what might have happened to Ronnie from the puzzle of it. She went over and over it, until her head began to hurt.

Iris walked on, down a street lined with stalls being set up. Now the tourists were starting to drift in, clogging the road, and so she turned between two stalls to get to the pavement, a shaded, forgotten space where the shop-owners chatted on their doorsteps, as yet untroubled by customers.

Something had happened to Ronnie; she knew it the moment she said the words to Hiroko. She was hurt; she'd lost her memory; she was lying in a ditch somewhere, beside a road, after being mugged or hit by a car. Or worse; of course, it could be worse. Iris thought of the look on the stocky policeman's face; she didn't know the statistics, but probably he did, and his expression had said it all.

What had the story about going to the Hertfords' been a cover for? That was the first thing. And how had her bag got into the Boboli gardens? Iris thought of the place, which she had visited only once but remembered vividly; the narrow dusty alleys between high hedges, the neglected patches of overgrown woodland where the sun hardly penetrated.

A man, she thought; it had to be a man. Somewhere in the depths of her drawing satchel Iris's mobile rang; finding herself beside a wide stone bench on the corner of the Via Cavour, she dumped the bag down and rooted through it, swearing. Serena, she thought; Ronnie's mum, it'd have to be. But it wasn't.

'Iris?' The voice sounded panicked, and she didn't recognize it straight away; *withheld*, her phone said. 'It's me.'

Jackson. 'Is it true?' he said. 'About Ronnie?'

'She's gone missing,' said Iris bluntly. 'How did you hear?' The bench was damp and cold underneath her, and on the narrow pavement a family of Sri Lankans carrying checked nylon holdalls were trying to squeeze past between her and the row of parked *motorini*. She hauled the bag back on her shoulder and set off again, the phone to her ear.

'Someone in a bar,' he said, sounding evasive. 'This morning. Look—do you have time for a coffee?' Iris sighed, audibly, then she thought, Don't be nasty. It's not his fault. And then she thought, I need to talk to him.

'Sure,' she said. 'Only—well—later. Give me an hour.' She hesitated. 'Jackson, do you have any idea about this? Where she is? Because if you do...'

'I don't know,' said Jackson, but for a moment he sounded scared. 'OK,' said Iris. 'Come to the apartment. You've been there before, right?'

'Yeah,' he said, then, quickly, 'I brought her back one time, so, yeah.'

'The police are coming there,' said Iris. 'So maybe give it an hour and a half?'

'Police?' said Jackson. 'Jesus. OK.'

There was a pause. 'They'll probably want to talk to you,' Iris said. 'You know that?'

'Uh-huh,' said Jackson, uneasily. 'What do they think? Do they, like, have a theory?'

'Not really,' said Iris. 'I suppose there might have been... developments. I'll find out, won't I?'

'Look,' said Jackson, 'I—do you mind if we meet somewhere else? I don't really want to—I mean, I want to talk to you first. Before I talk to them.' There was a pause. 'The police kind of freak me out.'

Iris sighed; she didn't blame him. They kind of freaked her out, too; they seemed so alien, so dumb and dangerous in their uniforms, with their guns. 'Sure,' she said, 'OK.' She thought a moment, and something came to her.

'Let's meet at the Boboli,' she said. Where they found her bag, though she didn't say that to Jackson. 'Two o'clock, at the Boboli. At the Annalena gate to the Boboli.' The side gate; somehow she couldn't face the great expanse of forecourt in front of the Pitti Palace. There was a silence.

'OK,' he said. 'The Boboli.' He didn't ask why.

The Via Cavour was a wide, busy road, buses whistling and thundering, mopeds whining, the heavy-fronted palaces black with exhaust; Iris walked up it in a daze, thinking about Jackson. He was rattled. In a way it was a credit to him. She'd only ever seen him cool, supercilious, unfazed, not even when Antonella Scarpa was tearing him off a strip for being lazy, not even when Paolo Massi talked to him in that quiet, dangerous voice after he'd been out drinking at lunch, not even after three hours of vodka and red wine on the town with Ronnie and answering her phone for her at midnight, when Iris called to find out where she was.

She'd learned her lesson after that, never ask Ronnie where she is or when she's coming back.

'Jesus,' she'd hissed, stumbling through the door an hour later and waking Iris up. Sitting on her bed, 'Jesus, that was embarrassing. What am I, your kid?' And she'd started to laugh.

Down the narrow Via degli Alfani, left into the wide, quiet, lovely Piazza Annunziata, across the empty flagstones and right into the Via della Colonna where a gang of tall, noisy high-school kids were smoking among the bicycles, waiting resentfully to go into the big Scuola Superiore for Saturday morning classes. Iris came around them, musing. It couldn't just be some guy, she thought; she's never bothered with a cover story before.

Is she dead? Iris stopped as the thought popped into her head, and a high-school girl in a violet cashmere sweater blew smoke in her face without even looking.

No, thought Iris, moving off, glaring at the smoking girl, who ignored her. Assume she's not dead. Assume there's a point in all this. It began to rain.

And soon Serena would call; soon Iris would have to talk to her.

She let herself back in, through the big wrought-iron gate, into the cavernous lobby, around the jungle-green courtyard with its palm trees, into the rickety lift. As it drew her upstairs, she felt her stomach lurch. It had never bothered her before, coming back here alone, but today she was on edge, as if she didn't know what she would find.

❀ ❀ ❀

This was no good, thought Sandro, trudging down the length of the Via dei Pilastri with leaden limbs. He felt as though Lucia Gentileschi's grief—so pure, so palpable—had taken him over entirely, and he couldn't let it immobilize him. In an attempt to reassert normality he took refuge in the first bar he saw. It was a deep, narrow place, dark and warm, smelling of sweet dough; Sandro picked up a paper abandoned on a table just inside the door and went to the bar. He asked the fat barman if he knew Claudio Gentileschi; the man shrugged. Showed him the little photograph, and the man shrugged again.

'Seen him walk past,' he said, a little sourly. 'Maybe every day for the past twenty years. Doesn't come in, though.' He nodded towards the Duomo. 'He doesn't take his coffee around here.'

Strange, thought Sandro. That Claudio Gentileschi took his coffee elsewhere. Even if this wasn't the most salubrious bar in the city, the coffee was excellent, it was local and it was cheap. Strange, but, he supposed, not unknown. Perhaps he took his coffee at the Bellariva; Lucia Gentileschi had said that he used to leave for the swimming baths every morning at nine, sharp. Sandro frowned.

'Which way was he going?' he asked. The barman pulled his head back, perplexed. 'Every day when he walked past,' Sandro explained, patiently. 'Which direction?'

Again the barman nodded towards the hospital of Santa Maria Nuova, and beyond it the Duomo. The Bellariva, by any map, would have been the other way.

'See him coming back at all? Later in the day?' The barman shook his head, his expression darkening perceptibly, perhaps at the waste of his time although there were no other customers in the place.

Taking the hint, Sandro took his *caffè lungo* to the back of the bar. Before he got to a seat, his phone rang. It was Pietro, and his heart jumped at the familiar voice; the signal was uneven, buried away as he was in the back of the bar, tons of stone around him, and he moved back towards the light.

'OK,' said Pietro, and Sandro knew that if there had even been a hint of reticence or embarrassment in his former partner's voice, he would have given up then and there. But it was the same old Pietro.

'I can tell you what I could tell her, the widow,' he said. 'There was a full investigation, that is, Gianluca Scappatoio asked around, no one saw anything.' There was a pause, as if Pietro was looking down at some notes. 'They set up a sign asking for information, anyone who'd been along there, but there wasn't much of a response. The fisherman who found the body had only just arrived there and set up his gear when he saw it floating, by which time Gentileschi had been dead a couple of hours.'

He heard Pietro blow out through his nostrils, his way of expressing disappointment. 'Sorry, brother,' he said.

"Ah, never mind,' said Sandro, but he didn't hang up. It was like they were back in the car together, each thinking it through, each working through the evidence. Scappatoio, huh.

He could hear Pietro thinking on the other end, then heard that click of the tongue that signalled a conclusion reached. 'It's a funny old bit of town,' he said, thoughtfully. 'The Lungarno Santa Rosa. It's kind of...dead. A backwater; maybe he picked it for that very reason, so no one would see him, no one would try to stop him.'

'Maybe,' said Sandro, feeling defensive. 'Or maybe someone else picked it for him.'

To his surprise, Pietro didn't start to argue him out of that one.

'Listen,' was all he said. 'I've got to get going. Let me know if—well, if I can help any more, OK?'

'Well,' said Sandro, and Pietro was gone.

Feeling the chill of being alone again, Sandro got another coffee, sat down, opened the paper. *La Nazione*. 'Girl Raped in the Uffizi,' was the headline. Holy Mother of God, he thought, scanning the story. A cleaner, from Eastern Europe, raped by a builder from Naples working on the extension. *Madonna*. Outraged, he turned the page. Flood defences threatened, more rain forecast. But he wasn't looking because there were no good-news stories, were there? He closed the paper again, on a photograph of a girl, and absently stowed it away, although for a second the after-image of the girl's face—dark-haired, smil-ing—persisted as some part of his brain carried out a processing function. He needed to get his blood pressure checked, if things were going to go on this way. He paid for his coffee and set off to the east, and the Bellariva swimming pool.

It was a long walk, and he wasn't an eighty-one-year-old; Gentileschi must have been pretty fit, reflected Sandro ruefully, his own body creaking like an old house, a painful reminder of two years' idleness. Down the gloomy, high-sided canyon of the Borgo Allegri, along the Via dei Malcontenti to the river where the *viale* hit it, cars roaring around the ring road, day and night. Not a picturesque walk, even if it was home turf to Sandro; not a walk to lift the spirits. Not the glorious red dome, not the golden cloisters of San Lorenzo, not the pale arcades of the Innocenti; this was another Florence. Following the footsteps of a melan-choly sort twenty years older than himself, it was purgatorial.

The Bellariva was pretty quiet in November; Sandro himself could barely swim, and certainly would not have been seen dead at a public swimming bath. He liked the seaside, for a month once a year, liked a green-shaded sunlounger at one of the nicer bathing stations in Versilia, liked to stand with his feet in lukewarm seawater and watch the old men with their grandchildren in the waves. The Bellariva's ugly grey reception desk was another thing entirely, its discordant soundtrack of splashing and shouting, the dismal acoustics and the awful smell of bleach and stagnant water and old socks. Gloomily Sandro reflected that it would take a better man than him to endure this at nine o'clock every morning for the sake of his health. Only to develop Alzheimer's.

Sandro looked around himself incredulously, to try to understand; a woman of roughly Sandro's own age with improbably coloured hair, gold trainers and a duffle bag walked inside and past, flashing her membership card. Ah, the membership card: the *tessera*, that would be the key. He should have asked Lucia Gentileschi for it. The woman behind the reception desk—dead-eyed, with hair hidden by a kind of plastic bath-cap—looked at him with suspicion. He stepped up to the counter.

'I'm making enquiries,' he began, suppressing the failure of nerve he felt start up at the lack of his uniform, his ID, a warrant. 'Following the death of one of your members…'

The woman stiffened visibly at this, and oddly it was only at that moment that Sandro thought how strange that a man who came swimming every day of his old age should choose to drown himself.

'No, no,' he hastened to reassure her. 'Nothing to do with the club, simply…I am working on behalf of his widow, to trace—well…' Running out of options, Sandro took the photograph from his pocket. 'His name was Claudio Gentileschi; a member for many years.'

She frowned down at the picture. 'No,' she said.

'Excuse me,' said Sandro patiently, 'perhaps someone else—are you here every day? In the morning?'

The woman's mouth pursed; this was going against him, already. 'Five mornings a week,' she said. 'Since 1987.'

'And you don't recognize him?' said Sandro incredulously. Was she just being perverse? Five mornings a week in this place for twenty years, maybe she'd turned permanently nasty.

The woman—Eva it said, on her lapel—set both hands on the counter. 'I'm sorry,' she said with heavy finality, 'I don't recognize this man. What did you say his name was?'

He waited while she typed on a keyboard behind the counter, frowning at the computer. Tap. He saw the screen reflected in her eyes, data scrolling down. Tap.

Eventually Eva said, 'Via dei Pilastri?'

'That's him,' said Sandro; at least there was a single concrete fact between them.

She raised her eyes to his, curious at last. 'Well, he was a member. Was. He took out membership…' She leaned down to the screen, then back up. 'In 1997.'

'Right,' said Sandro, energized, 'so—'

She interrupted him. 'For one year only. It lapsed a year later. It doesn't look as though he used it much.'

'How much?' said Sandro.

'He came twice,' said Eva. Her eyes shifted to look over his shoulder.

Someone was behind him, a tall man with stringy hair and a beard waiting with his *tessera* held out for inspection. Sandro left.

Outside on the *lungarno* the traffic roared and screeched; Sandro crossed the road to enter the dingy grey park that ran along the river for a bit of space to think. There was a mist of fine rain in the air; more rain. He walked through the park, around the empty children's playground, to the parapet along the river, where he stopped. He leaned on the stone, looked up at the great hills of the Casentino for a glimpse of something other than grey and far off he saw it, a little cap of snow above the cloud.

All right, he thought, so he didn't go swimming every day at nine o'clock. Ten years ago or so, he took out membership, maybe intending to distract himself, do something useful, but he changed his mind.

According to the barman on the Via dei Pilastri, he didn't even come this way, and Sandro felt strangely reassured by this turn of events. He had hated the Bellariva and, besides, this wasn't the part of town he'd have put a man like Claudio Gentileschi, the modern apartment blocks, the smoked-glass penthouses along the river rooftops, the grey park, the traffic. He looked the other way, towards the city; he couldn't see the Duomo from here, but he could see the arches of the Ponte Vecchio, the cupola of Santo Spirito, the Cestello. That way, out of sight at the far end of the city and the far side of the river, was the Lungarno Santa Rosa, where Claudio Gentileschi had drowned three days earlier, the only other fixed point in his missing day.

If he didn't go swimming every day at nine o'clock, where did he go? What had happened, ten years ago, so that he needed to tell this lie, and where had he been going every morning since?

Giving in to his aching knees after the discovery that the eighty-one-year-old Claudio Gentileschi had not, after all, spent every morning swimming for the sake of his health, Sandro took the bus. He crossed the river to the Piazza Ferrucci and the stop, which he knew because it was outside the best *rosticceria* in the city, of the little electric bus that would take him meandering all the way to the Lungarno Santa Rosa.

❀ ❀ ❀

Odd, thought Iris as she let herself in, how the place felt completely different. Twenty-four hours, and everything had changed. It even smelt different; she tried to catch Ronnie's scent in some superstitious attempt to summon her up, but it was almost gone, overlaid by the smell of musty curtains, old wood and—what was it? Dead leaves, a smell come in from outside. She must have left a window open. She stood in the hall, feeling the draught; dropped her bag to the floor in the half-dark.

'Hello?' she said, feeling stupid even as she said it. 'Anybody there?'

Chapter Eight

THE JAUNTY ORANGE bus hummed and whined along the Lungarno Serristori, jolting through potholes, the rain off the river whipping at the windows. November rain, thought Sandro gloomily as he stared through the bleared glass, a whole five months of winter; something squeezed in his chest at the thought of the future. What will they say, he found himself thinking, caught somehow off balance, what will they say at the hospital? He closed his eyes briefly as too much detail flooded his mind—the consulting room, the bed, the monitors and drips and anxious faces. The doctor in green scrubs talking seriously as he and Luisa sat and listened.

The bus stopped by the bridge where the jewellers' windows were bright in the grey morning, a couple with umbrellas looking in. An elderly woman got on with difficulty, hauling a shopping trolley after her. Sandro got up to help her in, showed her to his seat. The buses were so tiny they were full after one stop; the woman shuffled past him and sat down, muttering something to herself. Another crazy one.

Luisa's mother had had breast cancer, but she had been old. Did that make any difference? And in addition it had not actually killed her, he remembered the doctor saying that to Luisa; it had been a sizeable tumour that she had never said anything about to anyone, as far as they could determine, but it had not spread. She must have been able to see it, the doctor had said gravely after her death from heart failure, kidney failure, everything failure, when had it been, ten years ago? Luisa's mother had been eighty-three, which had been a good age for a lonely old woman who had struggled to live on for fifteen years after her husband without really wanting to. But there are two of us, he wanted to say; we aren't lonely. What had Lucia Gentileschi said? It ends with us.

The bus turned away from the river, into the maze of the Oltrarno's streets that remained obstinately foreign to Sandro, the damp alleys with their smell of overflowing drains, the workshops, the dusty bars. It buzzed across the front of the Palazzo Pitti, which stood bleak and grey in the rain, the big sloping forecourt empty of tourists. It turned down the Via Mazzetta and across the Piazza Santo Spirito where the junkies huddled on the stone bench around the base of the Biblioteca Machiavelli. It juddered to a halt at the end of a ramshackle line of traffic, a rubbish truck, a delivery van, the *furgoni* from the market reversing out with their loads of cheap clothes and trestle tables.

The pavement was so narrow and the bus was canted so steeply into a pothole, he could have leaned out of the window to touch them, the junkies. They were pressed back, grubby hooded sweatshirts up against the rain, to get some shelter from the big eaves overhead. Grey-skinned, shivering, like rats forced up from underground; Sandro was glad he didn't have to deal with them any more. The one on the end looked like Giulietta Sarto had looked, before she cleaned up. So thin you could see every bone in her face, and the eyes yellow with alcohol and sunken. Ahead the lights changed, the traffic shifted; he thought maybe he'd ask Giulietta if she fancied a bit of lunch when this was done.

Sandro thought of Luisa's mother not telling anyone about the tumour, because she didn't want to be alone any more. She'd wanted to die. He thought of Lucia Gentileschi; would that happen to her? Was hiring him a delaying tactic, some kind of denial? Maybe it was, but he had the strong feeling Lucia Gentileschi would not be good at telling herself lies. And clearly there was an investigation to be carried out: Claudio Gentileschi's life had not been what it seemed

The bus skirted the front of Santa Maria del Carmine, right into the Viale Ariosto and along the old wall. He got out at the Porta San Frediano and within two minutes could feel the drenching rain soaking his shoulders. Against his better instincts he bought an umbrella from a Nigerian in a baseball cap at the traffic lights, wondering as he handed over his five euros what kind of trade the poor guy thought he'd find out this way, miles from the centre. Soaked through, too, with the thin jacket he was wearing. But he was cursing the Nigerian soon enough, as the umbrella's spokes buckled before he'd even got it up.

The wind blew straight down from the river; walking towards it, Sandro could make out nothing but grey, the rain slanting horizontally towards him so he could hardly see across the bridge. There was another of those hoardings, commemorating the flood: this one showed the Uffizi's long courtyard, drowned and empty and silent. November, 1966. There was more rain forecast for the next five days. Sandro peered over gingerly, looking down at the water, yellow with mud and swirling.

The parapet along the river here was waist height, and Sandro walked along slowly, looking along towards the Lungarno Santa Rosa, looking down. On the far side the church of the Ognissanti shone white in the rain among the big hotels with their shutters closed, low season, and a little further on, the black, leafless trees of the Cascine. The police station was out there; it wouldn't have taken them long to get down here and pull Claudio Gentileschi out of the water.

They'd found him in the evening, and he'd been in the water a couple of hours. A fisherman setting up at dusk had seen his back, half-submerged. Sandro could picture it as Lucia Gentileschi told him, sounded almost wistful, like a seal, she said, his big back in the waterweed, rolling over in the dusk.

Sandro wondered why he hadn't been seen earlier. It had been a bright day on Tuesday, people might have been out walking in the afternoon sunlight. He thought back to Tuesday morning, when he'd been standing idly in his office—office! That was a joke. Looking out of the window, at girls. Claudio Gentileschi had been somewhere between there and here, somewhere between the Via dei Pilastri—the synagogue, the shop with its dusty menorah in the window and notice offering a Sabbath meal to Jewish visitors—and the quiet, anonymous streets of the Oltrarno.

There had been stones in his shoes, Lucia Gentileschi had said, and she had produced a handful of gravel from a little lacquer box; *I asked for it*, she'd added with a puzzled look on her face as if she didn't know why she'd asked, or indeed why her request had been granted. Just a handful; there'd been more. What had that idiot Scappatoio been thinking of, giving it to her? But Sandro realized that he might not have been able to say no either.

White gravel, in a black lacquer box like a holy relic or a talisman. Not enough to keep a body down, though. Neither here nor there.

Sandro walked along the parapet, looking for a way down. He came to the old wall; this was where they drew the line in the property freesheets, 'San Frediano, Fuori Muro'—inside or outside the wall. Outside was beyond the pale. Nestling under the mediaeval stone were the remnants of a church, a glassed-in shrine and part of an arch; jammed up next to it were the pergola and Portakabins of the Circolo Rondinella, a social club. A tattered, handwritten poster on a wire fence advertised a ballroom dancing evening.

Pausing, Sandro looked through the link fence at the garden—more a yard than a garden—dripping plastic tables, the bare wire of the pergola; not enough room to swing a cat. He tried to imagine the couples turning slowly in here, the women in high-heeled dancing shoes. There was a meal and a drink included in the price, twelve euros; he caught himself wondering if Luisa would be up for it, and almost laughed. In the Portakabins behind the yard something moved, and then moved away.

Sandro stepped back, looked up at the wall; Claudio Gentileschi had been found the other side; the Lungarno Santa Rosa was *Fuori Muro*. Wrong side of the tracks. He walked away from the little social club and the shrine with its plastic flowers, feeling an odd kind of reluctance. His old partner Pietro said—and he had never given it much credence before—that San Frediano was the real deal, the survival of everything that was ancient and original in the city, never mind that it contained no palazzi, a bare handful of notable churches. So what if it had the Circolo Rondinella?

On the other side of the wall was a fenced stretch of sickly grass and stunted trees, then a children's playground. Gingerly—because there was always something suspect about a grown man entering a playground on his own, but it was the only way he could see of approaching the river—he came through the gate. Was this where Claudio Gentileschi had come?

It seemed monstrously unlikely; indeed it was laughable that Sandro had thought twice about coming in here himself. The whole place was surely so disgusting that no children would be tempted by it. The grass was scabby, no more than occasionally tufted mud, and it was marked by regular mounds of dogshit in various stages of decomposition; the slide was emblazoned with garish graffiti, the swings were broken. The weird rubber asphalt that surrounded each piece of play equipment was crumbling and eroded like an ancient carpet. Sandro crossed to the parapet; you couldn't get down here, either, in theory; the low wall was surmounted by another stretch of chain-link fence. He walked along it, eyes flicking to the ground so as not to tread in anything, then down to the river. Maybe it was not so surprising after all that no one saw Gentileschi until later; who would come walking here? Even on a sunny winter afternoon.

Behind him, back towards the wall where all he had seen had been the fenced-in trees, a ramshackle assortment of huts ~d sheds and sawn-off bits of old rusting containers clung slope, against gravity. They might have belonged to the b; huts used by the fishermen to store their tackle, in theory, though God knew what else, maybe weedkiller and demijohns of cheap wine and tools and junk. It was pricey to own or rent a *fondo*—a garage or cellar—in Florence, so the city was full of these little accretions, like antheaps, testaments to man's inability to get rid of his rubbish.

Sandro looked back, down river to the traffic over the Ponte alla Vittoria, ceaselessly moving in the rain. The panorama took in the black trees of the Cascine and the distant misted flatlands out towards the Viadotto dell'Indiano. The city's hidden hinterland, a place of drainage ditches and shanty towns where illegals scavenged along the riverbanks and *contadini* scratched a living from a handful of olive trees and sheep that grazed between the airport runway and the *superstrada*. Not a pretty view.

At the far side of the playground there was a small square of dark red asphalt with four benches and a good-sized holm oak. As he approached, Sandro saw three men sitting on the bench under the tree; although it was still in leaf, it did not seem to be providing them with much shelter. The youngest of the men-under thirty, anyway—was reading a comic book, holding the pages up close to his face, the drawstring around his hood pulled tight. He kept breaking off to look at his watch, as though someone was waiting for him somewhere. The other two had the darkened skin of rough sleepers, and through the thin plastic of a bag on the ground between them Sandro could see three one-litre cartons of red wine.

You would come here to kill yourself, if it was out of shame, thought Sandro with dread; if you thought you deserved less than nothing.

With reluctance Sandro approached the men. He began to speak, standing in front of them. He asked if they came here every day, if they had been here, for example, on Tuesday. If they knew this man. They gazed up at him with faces completely blank, though whether from drink or idiocy or something more like alienation, he could not have said. He held out the photograph of Claudio Gentileschi and the two drunks turned away quickly, mumbling insensibly, as if he were a mendicant himself, a beggar holding out one of those handwritten cards telling them he had no work and children to support.

The man with the comic book—or boy, it seemed from this close, although that might be the result of retardation; it could leave a grown man's features looking smoothed out like this— peered at the photograph, peered at his watch. He moved his head with a bobbing motion, then jerked it back and raised the soggy pages of his book even closer to his face, to blot Sandro out.

Sandro gave it ten minutes, standing there in the rain, talking at first but then just waiting. They ignored him stolidly and eventually he didn't know what else to do but turn away. He turned back. He fished a card out of his pocket and with a sense of futility held it out to the young man, the only one of the three offering him any hope as a witness. Without looking him in the eye, the boy snatched the card and carefully inserted it into an already stuffed wallet; as he did so, Sandro glimpsed perhaps thirty business cards: a pizza delivery service, a leather-goods shop, an optician's. And his own; Sandro Cellini, Investigations.

He walked on until he came to an opening where the wire had been torn back, and put his head through. Below the parapet was an uneven scramble down to a wide path that ran by the water's edge. Claudio Gentileschi had been eighty-one, even if he'd been fit for his age; might he have fallen, might he have gone in? After the filth of the children's playground the bank looked almost inviting; it was green with a mixture of grass and the invasive, alien plants that had colonized the edge of the water in the city, bamboo thickets and horsetail. Claudio Gentileschi could have fallen, Sandro supposed, but he would have had to roll a long way to end up in the water and the bank looked soft, with waterlogged red earth showing through the grass. It had happened here.

He turned to look along the embankment at the windows; who else might have seen? In the city, there's always someone who knows, who sees you.

The other side of the playground there was a run-down *ambulatorio*, some dull modern apartment buildings with balconies, then a row of older houses overlooking the river; none of their occupants would have seen down to the bank. The housing was all low-rise, anonymous and modest; on the other side of the river, the grand baroque facades seemed to stare it down with contempt.

It was the wrong time of year, anyway, for hanging out of your window and having a look at anything; certainly a good half of the shutters were closed today, close to lunchtime, as if it was just too grey, and the view of the river filling up with rain was just too dismal. Pietro had been right; this was a dead place.

There was a bar, though, set among the older houses; there was always a bar. The Cestello, named after the church. It looked like it did some business, too; Sandro turned to inspect it from a distance, his back against the parapet. The two big windows were misted with activity, a couple of dozen heads inside at least. Out on the pavement was a planking deck for summer drinking, empty of chairs now and the wood slick with rain. The scalloped edge of the awning, rolled in against the façade, flapped forlornly.

For a second Sandro felt again that shiver of reluctance at the thought of stepping up to the place and asking questions without the talisman of his badge to hold up ahead of him. It was at that moment that the rain, temporarily forgotten, chose to make its presence felt again; a gust blew the umbrella up and inside out, and it collapsed messily and irrevocably, a tangle of cheap metal and dripping fabric in his face.

'*Merda*,' muttered Sandro, because suddenly everything was wet, his shoulders, his thighs, even up his sleeve. With disgust he strode across the street, dumped the malign object in an already full litter bin and pushed open the door of the Caffè Il Cestello.

It was so warm and marvellously stuffy inside that Sandro managed immediately to forget that he was here to ask questions; his nostrils filled with the mingling odours of warm pastries and coffee and lunch. He made his way to the bar, where a glass cabinet contained sandwiches, cold plates of ham and mozzarella and some long roasting tins heaped up with prepared pasta, *all'amatriciana*; with spinach; with capers and tuna. This was where he should have been coming to get his lunch; Sandro calculated the distance between the river and his office and decided it was just right for a midday constitutional. On a dry day.

Clearly it was too busy to ask questions; the proprietor was running from one end of the long zinc bar to the other, arms raised to point at heads, to take the next order. Sandro waited his turn, ordered a plate of penne all'arrabbiata, and took it to a small table by the door that was miraculously empty. He looked around for a paper but there were none; only when he sat down did Sandro realize that he'd managed to abscond with the copy of *La Nazione* he'd started to look at in the bar in the Via dei Pilastri. Stuffed in his pocket, and damp but not actually disintegrating; things were looking up. With care he extracted the soggy newspaper from his jacket and unfolded it on the table.

The penne were delicious, hot with just the right amount of chilli and garlic, a good, oily long-cooked tomato sauce, plenty of parsley chopped nice and fine and fresh. Sandro savoured the dish, turning the pages, passing the report of the Uffizi rape. They had the man, still working bold as brass, as if he hadn't even thought he'd done anything wrong. Thought, maybe, that an immigrant girl, a Romanian or Latvian or whatever she was, would be too cowed to make a complaint. Hardly even thought of her as human, perhaps; that was common enough among psychopaths.

As he chewed, the burn of the chilli in his mouth joining forces with a simmering outrage, Sandro reflected that people thought of psychopaths as big characters, Hannibal Lecter types, evil geniuses, but Sandro had seen enough of them to know different. They could be smart, but some could be very stupid indeed; they were characterized by a lack, by something missing in the whirring, complicated brain, a cog gone, a reservoir emptied. Disinhibition, lack of conscience, amorality, there were names for it. Sandro thought of the *autopsia* on Gentileschi. The lesions on the brain in that big domed head.

He turned the page again, mechanically, and the picture jumped out at him, just like that. The girl.

Mesmerized, Sandro stared; how could he be sure, people might say, but he was. She stared out at him from the page in some photo-booth picture, long dark hair parted in the middle and streaked blonde down one side, pale northern skin bleached paler by the flash. There was the ghost of an insolent smile on her face as she stared back at whatever authorities had required her to take the picture.

He scanned the story, the headline, the secondary photograph of some personal effects, laid out on an evidence table, handbag, wallet, women's stuff. *Girl student missing since—* Tuesday. A student of the Scuola Massi in San Niccolò; at the school's name something chimed, far off, in Sandro's policeman's memory, but was silenced by a more immediate piece of information he had on the girl in this picture.

Because this was the girl he'd seen walking down the Via del Leone on Tuesday morning, which in turn was the same Tuesday that was the last day of Claudio Gentileschi's life.

Around him the bar seemed to have emptied suddenly.

Gently Sandro laid the newspaper down and stared without seeing at the rain-spattered glass. Why should there be a link? There was no connection between Claudio Gentileschi and this girl, this Veronica Hutton. No connection. He turned the paper over, her face down.

❀ ❀ ❀

Of course there was no one there. Of course not.

Iris dumped her bag in the dark, chilly hall and walked from room to room, turning on lights.

The apartment's lighting had always been as frustratingly unusable as the furniture; ancient standard lamps with frayed cloth-covered wire; huge, dusty chandeliers, half of them non-functioning, the other half fitted with low-wattage, energy-saving bulbs that barely illuminated anything. But as she moved through the place in that unnerving draught, this morning Iris found the dimness more than just annoying; it made her uneasy. Actually, it frightened her.

As the clutter of the long *salotto* emerged in the half-light thrown by the only two functioning candle-bulbs on the chandelier—the prickly sofa with wooden arms, the console tables topped with black marble, the huge gilded mirror—Iris found where the draught was coming from. She must have left one of the long windows ajar; she opened it fully, pushed back the shutters to let more light in, then yanked the window tight closed on the inside. She stood there a moment, looking out, trying to work out what was different. Same synagogue, same black ivy, same statues. But something was different.

Slowly Iris turned away from the view, trying to resist the creeping claustrophobia of the room, damask curtains and the heavy furniture around her. The flocked walls and the heavy-framed portrait that hung over the red marble fireplace, a jarringly modern—well, 1950s—study of their landlady. Iris felt a moment of panic, because how on earth could she go on living here without Ronnie? Even supposing—and she stopped right there. Even supposing they find her? Even supposing she's OK?

Iris stood very still, waiting for the panic to pass. Why had she wanted to come back here? She had wanted to look around, in peace. She waited, listening; she could hear the roar of the traffic around the Piazza d'Azeglio, and the conversations of birds in the garden, but the flat was silent, just as it had been yesterday morning. She was alone.

Iris knew she should look in Ronnie's room but somehow she didn't feel quite ready for it. A cup of tea, she thought, procrastinating.

In the kitchen she set the kettle on the elderly cast-iron cooker, checked the milk in the fridge. She even stood there a minute or two, looking at the fridge's contents for hidden significance; Ronnie's yoghurts, a piece of waxy-looking pecorino half out of its paper, three bottles of prosecco, an open bottle of champagne with a teaspoon in the neck. How long had that been there? She closed the fridge slowly, thoughtfully, set her back against the door, looking at the long stone drainer. Two shallow champagne glasses etched with a Greek key design from the cabinet in the *salotto* stood there upside down, dry inside.

It was doing something to her head, all this. Iris really couldn't remember if the glasses had been there on Tuesday morning, there was a kind of buzz between her ears, as of static, that stopped her thinking straight; panic, it'd be panic. She breathed carefully, in and out, and her head cleared, just a bit. Yes; she'd washed them up herself, on Tuesday evening. She remembered because she'd thought they'd found every-thing on Monday night, clearing up after the party. Ronnie'd been in a good mood at the end of it, a bit pissed, singing, wearing her little mask as she carried glasses in ten at a time while Iris washed.

They'd talked; what had they talked about? The boy who'd called her fat.

'You heard what he said, didn't you?' Ronnie had said, rough but anxious. 'Don't worry about it. He's just a pig.' She set down another load of glasses, extracting her long fingers. 'So many boys are.'

And then on Tuesday night Iris had found the two champagne glasses in the sink and had wondered how she'd missed them.

The party had been a disaster, hadn't it? The Halloween party. A random bunch of people, hangers-on, liggers, half of them hardly knew Ronnie at all, yet she'd still spent fifty euros on wine and crisps. But she'd been perfectly cheerful; she'd been happy, bringing in the glasses. She hadn't spent all evening buried in some guy's neck on the sofa, but she hadn't drunk herself stupid out of disappointment as a result, as she would have done at school. Had she grown up since then? No; Iris would have said definitely, not a lot. Why had she been so serene, singing to herself as she brought the glasses in to the kitchen?

Behind Iris the kettle whistled; tea bag, milk, chipped cup—all the grand crockery seemed chipped—and before she could find another reason not to, Iris walked out of the kitchen and through the dark red and black hall to Ronnie's room. She stood in the doorway, hands warming around the tea, looking. Not wanting to walk in and change things, as if it was the crime scene, right here. Because something was different and she was going to stand here until she worked out what it was.

It was like that game, Pelmanism, or whatever, remembering objects on a tray. Eye mask, Tampax, a book with its spine cracked on the floor, bed unmade. Knickers, two pairs.

The shutters were folded back; she couldn't remember doing it, but maybe she had. The room must have been light, because she'd looked around, so maybe she had. A stack of school materials on the desk, leaflets for the studio, the school, the gallery where eventually their work might go on show, if it could be sold. Iris felt like crying at the thought of that, Ronnie's little drawings, her sketchbooks. She picked one up and went through it; to her surprise it was full of drawings, and so was the one below it; Ronnie'd been working, after all. Pages and pages of architectural detail, railings, stone lintels, escutcheons, eaves; another with anatomical sections, stuffed birds. Homework.

Next to the pile was the computer; Iris blinked. Ronnie's laptop was turned off.

Iris felt the tea going cold in her hands, and she set the mug down on the floor, at her feet. Tentatively she stepped into the room, trying not to disturb anything. She stared at the laptop, its little row of lights all extinct; the battery was dead, which meant…She leaned around the back, trying not to touch it, and saw that the mains cable was not plugged in. She frowned. She didn't know how long a battery lasted but she'd be willing to bet it didn't last four days, so the thing must have been plugged in yesterday morning.

Iris thought of Ronnie's MySpace, the messages she'd scrolled down to find; had there been a message from someone who meant her harm? Tart, someone had called her; Iris had assumed it was a joke. Had there been any clue to where she planned to go, and who with? Because there would be a someone; Ronnie didn't like to be on her own, everyone knew that, there was always a gang, or a man, or at a pinch there was Iris. Not this time. She rubbed her eyes.

It could have just—come dislodged, somehow. Iris thought of the face that had half filled the screen, Ronnie's face, upside down with striped hair hanging across her cheek. Why would anyone pull the plug?

A bell rang, a strident, old-fashioned sound. The doorbell? It rang again, and again; it was the ancient telephone and Iris stumbled after the sound, suddenly wanting to be out of the room, kicking over the cup of cold tea, not stopping to mop up the mess.

'*Pronto?*' she said, then, too frazzled to contemplate a conversation in Italian, 'Hello?'

'Iris?'

For a moment, for a tiny joyful second as she heard the voice, terse, irritated, absolutely English, she thought, Ronnie, and everything fell away, all the panic, all the nightmarish, unreal world of clues and break-ins and Ronnie's bag with that dust in it. But it wasn't Ronnie, it was Ronnie's mother; it was Serena. The voice she had not been longing to hear but dreading.

'What on earth is going on?' said Serena. 'What is the bloody girl up to?' And all the nightmare came rushing back.

She was in Dubai, selling a horse. She kept telling Iris how long this deal had been in the making, and Iris kept trying to explain what had happened, everything that had happened so far, but either Serena wasn't listening or she didn't seem to be able to process the information. She just kept saying impatiently, 'For heaven's sake!' Iris found she couldn't go further, she couldn't actually say, look, this is serious. Because Serena was the grown-up.

'Well,' said Serena finally, her voice distant. 'Look, I'll get someone on to it. And I'll try to be there by Monday. She'll have turned up by then, safe and sound, you can bet your life on it.' There was a pause. 'Has anyone spoken to her father?' Iris didn't know; Ronnie's father lived in Scotland, as far as she knew. As far away from Serena—and by extension, Ronnie—as he could manage without going abroad, Ronnie said once, because he couldn't stand abroad. 'I'll speak to her father,' said Serena, and hung up.

Iris set the phone back down and sat there a moment. She stared out of the window, and then, because she was not thinking about it, she understood. The window she had had to close this morning—this window—was not the one she'd looked out of the morning before. The huge cedar had not blocked her view of the synagogue yesterday, because she'd been looking out of a different window; she couldn't have left this one open.

The cleaner? The cleaner came on Monday mornings and, besides, nothing had been cleaned.

It must have been open all along, and she hadn't noticed; it had turned colder, or windier, and that was why she'd noticed the draught. She stared at the huge window panes, each one two feet wide by four high, the window itself taller than a man. Outside the rain was coming down in sheets, drenching the glass.

Maybe it would clear up before she met Jackson. She had an umbrella; at least the Boboli would be empty.

Who hadn't been there, at the party? Who had Ronnie been talking to, hanging out of the window and murmuring into her phone, while the American boy who'd called her fat got drunk and stared at her, and the streaked-blonde twins whose names Ronnie couldn't even remember threw up in unison in the bathroom?

Jackson hadn't been there, had he? Ronnie'd just shrugged his absence off, as if it wasn't a problem; he's waiting in for a call from his parents, she said, time difference or something. And he wouldn't want them to hear the kind of background noise generated at a Halloween party full of freeloaders.

The doorbell rang, a long, insistent buzz, and Iris went to let the carabinieri in.

Chapter Nine

IT TURNED OUT to be so simple.

The Caffè Il Cestello was almost empty when Pietro finally got to his feet, stiff with the damp and the walking he'd done but mostly with age, and crossed to the bar. He asked for a coffee with a splash of Vecchia Romagna in it, and noted approvingly that the barman made it a generous one. He was a weary-looking man of about Sandro's age, with thinning, reddish hair.

'You've got a question for me,' he said, and Sandro laughed abruptly, embarrassed.

'Am I that obvious?' he said. 'I think I'm in the wrong business. You, too, for that matter.'

'I get a lot of practice, looking at people,' said the barman. He held out a hand across the counter. 'Luigo,' he said. 'I appreciate you waiting till we were quiet, that's all. You're a cop, right?'

'Not everyone bothers to look,' said Sandro, not denying it, extracting the photograph of Claudio Gentileschi from his pocket. 'I'm Sandro Cellini. Do you know this guy?'

'Yup,' said the barman without even seeming to look. 'That's Claudio. He's in here for an *aperitivo* most days. He lives around the corner somewhere.' He pursed his lips, frowning. 'Come to think of it, he hasn't been in for a day or two.'

Sandro kept his face still. Scappatoio should be shot; he hadn't even been in here to ask if anyone knew Gentileschi.

It was bizarre. Claudio Gentileschi came all the way over here every day for an *aperitivo*? Lives around the corner? The Via dei Pilastri was two kilometres away at least.

'Did—do you know anything about him?'

The barman shrugged. 'He's a private kind of guy.' Thoughtfully he passed his cloth over the metal counter in long swipes, straightened the long spoons in the sugar dispensers, ripped a stray paper napkin from the holder. 'I think he's some kind of artist. Painter?' And he shrugged; painters were ten a penny in this city.

'Yes?' said Sandro. Not an architect but a painter. Who'd given up painting ten years earlier, according to his wife.

'He hasn't ever said, exactly; doesn't give much away, Claudio. How do I know?' The man mused, arms folded over his apron. 'Something about the look of him, you know, he has that artistic style, keeps his hair quite long. The way he stares off into the distance, watching things.'

He turned away, scooped coffee into a filter, cranked it tight under the wide, gleaming Gaggia's row of spouts, set a cup below it. What would life be without that little routine? thought Sandro. Imagine living in a country where there was no barman, no Gaggia, no espresso cup? And for a moment Sandro saw the littleness of the world he inhabited, the props he leaned on daily for support; he felt his limitations like a room contracting around him.

Over his shoulder the barman said, 'Definitely a painter, actually. I heard him talking about it the other day, explaining some technique or other. Painting faces in a crowd, he was telling this kid, one of those student types.' He downed his scalding coffee with his back still to Sandro, then turned around again. 'Funny, actually, him coming in with the kid, 'cause he was always alone, Claudio.'

'Right,' said Sandro, jolted out of reverie and thinking furiously. Kid? What kid? 'And when—ah, when was the last time you saw him?' He saw the man's expression harden, turn wary and he knew he was going to have to tell him, Claudio's dead. Just not yet.

In his pocket his mobile shrilled; he picked it out and saw it was Luisa. He clicked it to voicemail as something went leaden in his gut. He took a sip of the *caffè corretto*, so far untouched, and it burned through his system. Not helping.

'Funny you should ask,' said the barman, nodding. 'I know exactly when it was. Tuesday.' He nodded, then something halted him. 'Hold on a minute,' he said. 'Something's happened to him, hasn't it? What's happened?'

'I'm afraid so,' said Sandro. 'But tell me, just think first. Was there anything about him that day? Tuesday?'

The barman frowned, sighed. 'Well, he was half an hour late for starters, maybe even forty minutes. And he was wearing a jacket under his coat; usually, he wears a sweater. Casual, you know. Bohemian.' He looked expectantly at Sandro, who let him go on. 'Claudio was regular as clockwork as a rule, came in at 12.30, had a whisky sour—like I say, he's never been much of a talker but he did tell me how to make them; said he learned in New York. Some bar in New York.' He paused, shrugged. 'Can't remember the name. Anyway. Lemon juice, bourbon, sugar syrup, ice. By 12.45 he'd be gone, had to get home for his lunch, he said. Only on Tuesday it was after one when he turned up. He asked me to set up two drinks, didn't want to wait. Drank them both, then looked at the clock, and asked for another one. By then it was almost two.'

'He was on his own?' said Sandro.

'In here?' said the barman. 'Yes. He was always on his own.'

'Except—you heard him talking to someone? About painting?'

'That's right,' said the barman slowly, 'you're right, he was in here with someone, that time.' He scratched his head. 'Held… loosened up, lately. Started talking.'

By this time Sandro could not disguise his eagerness. 'Who?' he asked. 'Man or woman? When was this?'

'Just a kid,' said the barman, 'they all look the same to me, the students, a kid. American boy.' Then, looking him in the eye, he said, 'He's dead, isn't he? Claudio.' And Sandro felt himself subside, ashamed. Because this guy had liked Claudio Gentileschi.

'He drowned,' said Sandro. 'I'm sorry. It looks like he took his own life.'

'*Merda*,' said the barman with feeling. 'Not the floater? Not Claudio?'

'Sorry,' said Sandro. 'I'm sorry.'

The man was suddenly grey with shock. 'They wouldn't tell us, someone went down when they fished the body out and asked but they wouldn't say anything. Had to be official identification first.' He shook his head, over and over. 'Poor old bastard.'

'And they never came to tell you? To ask?' Sandro spoke with disgust.

'Not until you,' said the barman. He looked over his shoulder for someone else to tell but the bar was empty except for the two of them. 'They put out a sign, asking if anyone had seen anything, but...' he shrugged unhappily '...I didn't know it was old Claudio.' He was still shaking his head. 'What a way to go.'

'Are you—sorry, but are you surprised?' Sandro asked gently. The barman, dazed, refocussed on him. 'Am I—?' He seemed lost for words, puffed his cheeks, let the breath out. 'You know, you wonder, how well you know people. No, I don't think I'm blown away, no. He looked like he carried a burden, d'you know what I mean? But, but—' and Sandro could see him scrabble to understand why he didn't see this coming. Rocking back on his heels.

'But he had a wife, didn't he? He had a wife? He wore a wedding ring and it had to be a wife he had to be home for.' And then the triumph turned to incomprehension as he gazed at Sandro, his faded eyes bloodshot with tiredness.

'Yes,' said Sandro. 'He did. He had a wife.' He wouldn't have left her behind.

The moment Sandro stepped outside the phone rang, and for a second he imagined that someone had been watching him, waiting for him to reappear. He stood under what shelter the awning provided and tried to make out what the voice was saying.

He didn't recognize the speaker, and in fact it was a strange, almost mechanical voice, speaking quickly, without the usual intonation. 'Cellini Sandro?' It was hurried. 'I thought he was going for a swim, the voice said, over and over, 'I thought he was going for a swim, aquatherapy they call it, in the hospital.'

It was crazy. 'Claudio,' Sandro said. 'You saw Claudio going in the water?'

'I thought he was going for a swim,' the voice said again. 'Only he was wearing all his clothes. Cellini Sandro, that's your name, isn't it?' And the penny dropped. Sandro looked across at the playground and there he saw the boy-man on the swing, looking across at him.

'Can dogs swim?' said the boy. Oh, God, thought Sandro, this is going to be tricky. Dogs?

'Did Claudio have a dog?' he asked helplessly.

'I didn't think he had one,' said the boy, sounding confused; this is getting us nowhere, thought Sandro.

'Can I come and talk to you?' he said.

'You are talking to me,' said the voice. 'This is talking, isn't it?'

Sandro wondered what was the matter with the boy—autism? Probably; he'd had dealings with it once or twice over the years. There'd been that boy who lived at home with his mother and occasionally escaped to ride the buses on his own and had to be brought home, twenty-five years old. Hated to be touched, couldn't look you in the eye.

'OK,' said Sandro. 'I want you to think very carefully. Was he alone? When he went into the water? Did anyone go down there with him? Did anyone—push him?'

'No one pushed him,' said the boy, laughing as if it was funny. 'There wasn't anyone. He was on his own. He came out of the bar and went to the river, all on his own. I thought he would take his clothes off, but he didn't. I thought they told him at the *ambulatorio* to do the therapy.'

Sandro heard him make a slightly panicked sound, a kind of grunt, and wondered if the boy might just hang up on him and run. He tried to think; he knew there was a physio department at the little *ambulatorio* because they'd treated Luisa for a broken ankle, years back. Whether it was still running he didn't know; there'd been cutbacks.

'Do you do the therapy?' asked Sandro quickly, to keep the boy talking. 'Do you go to the *ambulatorio* here?' It might be why the boy hung out down here; he couldn't think of any other reason anyone would come to the Lungarno Santa Rosa.

'They've finished with me,' said the boy, and he sounded angry. 'They said I couldn't come back. It wasn't the same nurse.'

'What do you mean,' said Sandro, 'not the same nurse?'

'The one talked to Claudio, after he came out of the bar, after his drink. She was telling him off. Not the same nurse. Not my nurse.'

'A nurse talked to him?' He looked across at the *ambulatorio*; he could see a tall nurse in green scrubs right now, smoking a cigarette.

'She put out her hand and he gave her something,' said the boy. 'Maybe he didn't want it to get wet. He dropped it in her hand.'

'Did they say anything?' asked Sandro. 'Did you hear what they said?'

'I saw their mouths move,' said the boy. 'Don't you remember?'

'I wasn't there,' said Sandro, close to despair, trying to be patient. 'How could I remember?'

'That's what she said,' the boy went on in his monotone. 'Don't you remember—that's what she said.'

She must have tried to help, thought Sandro. What would he have given her? His ID? A letter? Surely she'd have come forward?

'What did she look like?' He realized there was almost no point in asking an autistic person such a question. 'Is that her now?' he said. There was a pause. 'On the steps of the hospital?' he prompted. Craning his neck, he saw the overgrown boy get to his feet.

'No,' said the boy, 'wrong colour. That one's the wrong colour. I have to go now. I have to go now.'

'No,' said Sandro urgently and he pushed away from the wall. 'Come back—don't—please—' He ran to the kerb but had to pull back because a truck thundered by and when it had passed all he could see through the rain was a grey, huddled shape flying along the embankment away from him, too far to see, too far to catch, flying like the devil was after him. Poor kid.

Out of the corner of his eye he saw the nurse watching him; saw her flick her cigarette into a puddle and turn to go back inside. He hurried towards her. She was a tall girl. Wrong colour, mused Sandro, as he came towards her. So the nurse who spoke to Sandro was black?

'Excuse me,' he called after her. She turned back.

It took an hour in Personnel with a demoralized-looking temp behind a bare desk, almost half of which was spent trying to persuade her that he was who he said he was, and that he had a genuine request. He showed the girl (Ana Lukic, it said on her tag) the picture of Claudio, and asked, as circumspectly as he could, about black or Asian nurses. The good news for him—although not, he supposed, for the patients—was that the place was running on a skeleton staff, had been for months, and there weren't many names to check. The *ambulatorio* certainly had a deserted, run-down feel to it.

Ana Lukic had a computer, at least, so it didn't take her long once she knew what she was looking for; she even brightened a little. There were three black nurses and one Filipina; none of them had been on duty the day Claudio had disappeared. Wrong colour; how many gradations of skin colour would he have to consider before he could approximate what wrong colour might mean in the mind of an autistic boy?

'Do you have a physiotherapy unit here still?' Sandro asked as he stood to leave, more out of curiosity than anything else.

'We do,' said Ana Lukic defensively.

'All right if I pop up there?' asked Sandro. 'I think I remember where it is.'

There were plenty of cubicles; there was a woman pushing a wide soft broom up and down the aisle between them. But the place was empty. Eventually he found the office, where a middle-aged woman in a white coat sat by a window, smoking.

'They're closing us down,' she said, when he asked where everyone was. 'Moving all physio out to Careggi.' He asked the same question he'd asked in the office, trying to be delicate all over again, about black nurses. She frowned at him, perplexed. 'Why do you ask?' she said, and as Sandro stared at her coat in embarrassment it came to him. White coats. 'Are you a physio?' he asked, and she nodded, still frowning. The girl on the steps was the wrong colour because she was wearing green scrubs; up here they wore white. The medics the boy knew—they were physiotherapists, maybe, rather than nurses, but how was he to know the difference?

Sandro's elation subsided when he came up against a brick wall all over again. 'Well, I'll ask around,' the woman said, looking at the picture of Claudio, 'but I certainly didn't talk to him, and it's been just me all week.' She sighed. 'Was he the guy they found in the river?' Sandro nodded; he handed her a card and watched as she poked it into an overstuffed desk-tidy. 'I heard he had Alzheimer's,' she said with a shrug. 'Happens all the time. They wander off.'

Outside in the rain again and no further ahead, Sandro stood under the dirty concrete pillars of the *ambulatorio*, and stared across the road at the playground, then back towards the bar. Someone tried to help him, thought Sandro, that's something. And now at least he knew Claudio went into the water on his own. And he knew when.

And now he knew whose voice he wanted to hear.

Chapter Ten

WHEN LUISA ANSWERED, he could tell the shop was busy behind her, all those tourists come in to keep warm and dry, fingering the goods. He could hear the harried tone in her voice. 'I tried to call you,' she said.

'Are you all right?' he said, unable to keep the anxiety out of his voice. 'Sweetheart?'

'For heaven's sake, Sandro,' she said, 'it's not about that. I'm fine. You start calling me sweetheart in public I'm going to get into a terrible state.'

'So what is it about, then?' he said, trying not to sound petulant.

'I've got a customer for you,' she said, then, 'hold on,' and her voice turned muffled as she talked away from him. 'Giusy, can you do this lady for me? Just give me a minute.'

When she spoke again the quality of the sound was different and he knew she'd ducked into the stockroom, her voice muffled by shoe boxes and cellophane-hung party dresses.

'A customer for me?' he said stupidly, thinking he can't have understood. She must have been talking to Giusy, the deputy manageress.

'Yes, you,' said Luisa with impatience. 'Listen, it's all a bit mad. It's a client, a foreign client, didn't I tell you they'd come to you?' She paused then, 'Only this one called from Dubai, if you can believe that,' and Sandro knew she was considering her own indiscretion, but she hurried on. 'Anyway, I might have said to a few people, and one of those people might have been the Contessa Badigliani who has the place in the Piazza d'Azeglio—' and only then did she pause for breath.

Dubai? Sandro couldn't take it in.

Luisa was off again. 'Right. Have you read about the girl they're looking for?' she said. 'They found her bag in the Boboli, a Carabinieri case?'

The missing girl. Sandro squeezed his eyes shut in a futile, childish attempt to avert something, but Luisa went on. 'Well, she is—or she was—staying in Giovanna Badigliani's *piano nobile*. And the mother's all worked up, says the Contessa doesn't trust the Carabinieri, stuck out there in the desert.'

'Stuck?' said Sandro incredulously.

'Can't get back, not in a hurry anyway. I don't know the details.'

Sandro leaned back against the cold flank of the building. Thought of this woman in the desert, thought with resentment of the blazing heat, the empty skies. 'She needs someone to find out what's going on?' he said, reluctantly. 'Make enquiries. About the missing girl.'

'That's it,' said Luisa with relief. 'The mother doesn't seem to think—well, it's happened before; she's a live one, apparently. Just a matter of fielding the Carabinieri. I gave Giovanna Badigliani your number.'

'Right,' said Sandro helplessly. He wanted to run a mile from this complication; he didn't want to track down a runaway, he didn't want to butter up the Carabinieri, but mostly he just had a bad feeling about the whole business.

'OK,' he said, defeated because although he didn't believe in fate, he knew that there was no other word for it. He'd turned the newspaper over so he wouldn't have to look at that girl's face and some power beyond him had turned it back over and held it up to his eyes. He sighed, pulled the paper out of his pocket and made himself study it.

The girl, wide-eyed but sly, a typical pretty teenage girl, knowing her own power, or thinking she did. The photo of the school's frontage.

'She was at the Scuola Massi,' he said. 'How do I know that name?'

'*Caro*,' said Luisa patiently, 'do keep up. Badigliani'll have recommended them, she sends everyone there, the usual stitch-up.'

'But I'm sure I've heard of Massi,' Sandro went on, doggedly.

Luisa sighed. 'I don't know, *caro*. It's an old family.' She paused, then went on, grudgingly. 'A good family, I suppose, partisans, all that, the father ran a printing press through the war.'

'But do you know them?'

Luisa clicked her tongue, thinking. 'Not him. The wife— Anna? Yes, Anna Massi, not that we're on first-name terms. She comes into the shop now and again. It's always the good families of Florence that complain about how they can't move for the tourists in here any more; she's one of those.' There was a pause, and she lowered her voice a touch. 'You never know who might be in. That set, the old families, they wander in and out of here like they owned the place, expecting discounts.'

Sandro tried to summon up a picture of the couple; had he seen them in some social setting? Perhaps a newspaper photograph at one of the cocktail parties they held—for charity, of course—at the Palazzo Corsini or the Torrigiani gardens. He knew it quite likely had nothing to do with anything—why should it? But it seemed important; what he needed to get his bearings in this case. He was floundering, and he wanted a few facts.

'So what do you know about her?'

'Well, said Luisa; he could see her frown of concentration in his mind's eye. 'Anna Massi, *Dio*, one of those women, could be any age, the way she behaves, but she must be around fifty.' Then, grudgingly, 'Pretty, if you like that kind of thing. Dark-haired, big eyes.'

'The way she behaves?'

'She doesn't seem to care too much how she dresses generally'—Sandro smiled inwardly despite himself: in Luisa's book, this was a sign of mental imbalance—'only she's got a thing about shoes. She's always trying on completely ridiculous shoes. Only the other week she had the high-heeled grey suede, so impractical, and five hundred euros to boot.'

Sandro felt a twinge of pity for the woman, despite himself, under Luisa's watchful eye. And he didn't know how he could fit a shoe fetish into this, but five hundred euros was a lot of cash. 'The school must be doing well,' he said, absently, trying to work it out. 'Still, maybe there's a lot of money in art students.' He chewed on his lip; he knew he'd heard the name Massi before, and in connection with an investigation, too; the explanation was coming to him, but it was maddeningly incomplete. 'Are there—well, rumours? Of any kind? About the Massi family, or the school?'

He was close to giving up on this; it was a waste of time, a tactic to avoid doing what he dreaded, which was talking to the Carabinieri.

'A lot of people wonder how the marriage works,' said Luisa, thoughtfully. 'But they probably wonder that about us, too.' She laughed.

Sandro was thinking hard. 'I think it was the Guardia della Finanza,' he said, finally. 'I have a feeling that name, Massi, came up in a tax fraud investigation.'

'Whose hasn't?' said Luisa, impatiently. 'Sounds like a bit of a red herring to me, the girl's just run off with a boyfriend. Go see the Carabinieri, *Caro*.'

Sandro grunted. 'You're right, as usual,' he said, resignedly. 'I'll go right away.'

'That's all, then,' said Luisa, but he heard hesitation before she went on, hastily. 'And my hospital appointment's fixed for Monday. They called me.'

'That's good,' said Sandro as easily as he could manage. Although he was thinking, So quickly? They must be worried. 'Sooner's always better than later.'

'That's what I thought,' said Luisa, and he knew that she was lying, too.

❖ ❖ ❖

In the end, they didn't stay long. There was one carabiniere this time, the taller of the two she'd seen in Massi's office, and awkwardly Iris showed him through into the *salotto*. He stared around the room, ill at ease, while Paolo Massi, hands in pockets in the doorway, looked at him with impatience. She'd heard somewhere—actually, she thought it had been Antonella, holding forth over one of their sandwich lunches—that the Carabinieri had a reputation for being slow, for being recruited from impoverished areas of the south, and that everyone despised them. They had always seemed preposterously full of themselves to Iris, looking down their noses as they sat on their gleaming mounts in the Piazza Signoria, long riding capes perfectly draped over the horses' flanks. Preposterous but romantic.

This one seemed less confident; Massi had to speak for him, in the end, taking a step out of the shadows.

'There have been no developments,' he said, forestalling the question that perhaps he could see in her eyes. 'Maresciallo Falco would like to go over a few things with you.'

'In Italian?' asked Iris nervously, trying to translate her suspicions in her head; *I think someone has been here.*

'If you can manage,' said Massi softly, 'though I've come in case you need me.' She looked at him with gratitude. 'On a Saturday?' she said. 'Don't you...' But she didn't know how to phrase it. Don't you have a life?

Paolo seemed to understand. 'My wife is as worried as I am,' he said earnestly, and he did have the drained look of someone who hasn't slept. 'We—well, we haven't got our own. But she's so young. We're *in loco parentis*. We have to take responsibility. He put both his hands to his forehead.

So he did have a wife. Weirdly, Iris found herself feeling grateful that he had no children, grateful for his undivided attention. Unlike her own father; unlike Ronnie's either, putting as many miles as he could between him and his daughter.

The carabiniere cleared his throat.

'Look,' said Massi, holding up a hand to the man in apology, 'why don't you try in Italian? I'll—I'll keep out of the way, just call if you need me. OK?' He seemed uneasy.

'All right,' said Iris. 'But look—Mr Massi, Paolo. I think someone's been here. I think someone's been in the flat, I don't know why. Maybe—looking for something.' Even as she said the words she thought they sounded ridiculous, melodramatic.

'What?' said Massi, and he looked about him, as if the person, whoever it had been, might still be there. Whoever it had been. And Iris's heart gave a great leap.

'Ronnie,' she said. 'It could be Ronnie, couldn't it? It could be her, popping back? To collect clothes, or something?'

At the sound of her excitement, the carabiniere got to his feet and said something to Massi impatiently and Massi held up his hand again, backing off.

'OK, OK,' he said, 'I think we need to take this slowly.' And Iris sat down, Falco sat back down, and Massi retreated to the doorway.

Laboriously Iris began to explain.

Falco didn't seem particularly convinced by her clues—the computer, the window. He shrugged. She took the man through the flat, pointing out what she had seen; he made notes, occasionally scratching his head. In the doorway to Ronnie's room he stopped, looking around, peering inside the open wardrobe and as she followed his gaze Iris's excitement ebbed.

She'd had it in her head that Ronnie had met someone, was just taking off somewhere with some new man, and what she'd have come back for would be to pick up some more clothes. It had all seemed to slip into place, a non-nightmare scenario, Serena right all along, and Ronnie loved her clothes, it'd be just like her to pack a few bits—a capsule wardrobe, ha—and decide she needed more. The only problem was, they were all still there, the dresses hanging in the massive dark wardrobe, the stack of jeans on the shelves, the favourite purple cashmere sweater.

'Her passport?' the carabiniere asked. *Documenti?*'

Iris thought; where did Ronnie keep stuff like that? Her own were all together in an elastic band, health card, passport, driving licence, house keys for France, stowed carefully underneath a book in the bedside drawer. She frowned, thinking. Trying to visualize the last time she'd seen Ronnie do anything with her passport.

'It was not in the handbag,' said Falco, interrupting her train of thought. 'Did she keep it on her person usually? In this country you have to carry the documents with you.' His expression was one of unsmiling reproof.

'We tell them at the beginning of the course,' Massi said wearily.

'Ronnie wasn't used to that,' Iris apologized, to both of them. 'We don't have to do it in England.' She averted her gaze from Falco's look of faint disdain and tried to get back to Ronnie.

The hall table, the drawer, yes. She went into the hall with Falco close behind her, pulled open the drawer, and as she opened it and saw the NHS card she knew she'd been right; this was where she'd seen Ronnie stash the small maroon and gold booklet, saying she didn't care, it was going to get nicked if she took it in her handbag everywhere she went. Yes.

Only it wasn't there this time.

'Oh,' said Iris. 'This was where she kept it.' She felt a glimmer of hope. 'She must have it with her.'

Massi nodded briskly, agreeing with her, and she was grateful.

Falco just gave them both that impassive stare; Iris was getting used to it. Bored scepticism, to cover for the fact that he didn't have any answers either. Saying nothing, he crossed over to the computer, bent to stare at the dark screen and clicked his tongue in exasperation, leaned around the back and before Iris could say 'Don't!' he stuck the cable back in and stabbed a finger at the start button. Behind her in the doorway Paolo Massi's sharp intake of breath echoed her disbelief and she turned.

'But what if—? There could have been fingerprints!' she said, seeing the dismay in his face, knowing she was just guessing, that she knew nothing about it. 'Couldn't there?' Massi shook his head helplessly, looking past her at the policeman, and the computer screen, which remained resolutely blank.

The carabiniere looked back at them, unconcerned.

'I'll take it back to the office,' he said in Italian. 'We can get it working, we have computer guys who can rescue anything. Clearly we have to examine her emails, that kind of thing.'

'MySpace,' said Iris faintly. 'She had a MySpace page.'

'Of course,' said the carabiniere, but his haughty look didn't convince her he knew what she was talking about.

'Will you examine the apartment?' she said, and he made a gesture of ambivalence with his hands. 'Eventually,' he said. 'But I think if there was anything of interest—you would have seen it, yes?' She nodded uncertainly.

'Can I stay here?'

He looked at her curiously. 'Of course,' he said. 'If you want.' He sighed. 'Signorina March,' he said, 'perhaps we were hasty. We don't know yet that anything wrong has happened, do we? There is nothing in the Boboli, no sign of—ah, violence. No-thing. The Signorina Hutton—' he pronounced it 'Utton '—she is legally adult, yes? Adults disappear quite often, and then they reappear, she has her passport.' He shrugged.

Iris stood as obstinate as a child in front of him, her lips compressed. She knew when she was being told to stay out of something. She knew he'd looked around at the way they lived— slatternly, careless English tourists—and had made assumptions.

'But she lost her bag,' she said stubbornly. 'Or her bag was stolen. She would need money.' She saw the policeman's expression darken, and felt Massi's hand on her arm, touching her lightly.

'Iris,' he said, 'you will not get anywhere like that.' She opened her mouth to protest but between the two of them, outnumbered and alien, she suddenly felt like bursting into tears, or screaming. *Find her.*

'OK,' she said, squeezing her eyes shut so neither of them would see.

Massi saw the policeman to the door, the computer under his arm in the same kind of zipped plastic evidence bag they'd had Ronnie's handbag in when they'd come into the school. In the *salotto* Iris slumped onto the prickly horse-hair sofa.

'Do you think he's right?' she asked fiercely of Paolo Massi when he came back in. He looked pale; he turned his hands palms up, renouncing responsibility. 'I don't know,' he said, shaking his head. Iris felt like stamping her foot, sick of this fatalism crap, all this what will be, will be stuff.

'There is no point in assuming the worst, Iris,' Massi said haltingly. 'Try not to worry. We'll find her. We will.' He considered her for a moment, standing over her: 'Are you hungry? Come back and meet my wife.' She stared at him; she wasn't hungry at all. She looked at her watch: twelve. His voice was gentle. Suddenly Iris didn't want to be alone here, for all her acting tough, and she had two hours.

'I'm seeing Jackson this afternoon,' she said, and Paolo tilted his head back, looking at the ceiling.

'I wonder,' he said. 'I wonder about that boy. Do you think he knows anything about this?'

Iris stared at the floor. Jackson had sounded scared; what did that mean? That he did know something?

'I doubt it,' she said, not knowing why but wanting to do this on her own. Even if it wasn't safe, she wanted to do it.

'Come along,' said Paolo, a hand on her shoulder. 'My wife has made you some lunch.'

In the palm-filled courtyard the Contessa Badigliani was lying in wait for them, hair stiff as auburn candyfloss. She greeted Paolo Massi with elaborate surprise, holding out a hand covered in ornate rings, started going on in hushed Italian, something about how well his wife was looking.

They all know each other, thought Iris, not wanting to be so English and suspicious, but suspicious all the same. We're their meal ticket, aren't we? Do they like us at all? Now she was on the subject of Ronnie, and glaring at Iris as she spoke.

'I'm very worried,' the contessa said, wringing her hands rather theatrically, but she didn't sound it; she sounded cross. 'What has she done, this girl? Where has she gone?'

Massi said something soothing, but the contessa was having none of it; she threw up her hands, muttering about the mother, the police, dreadful to have the police on one's door-step and she wouldn't deal with them. She had clearly waited until the carabiniere was off the premises before emerging from her apartments. When Iris and Ronnie had arrived, she had explained to them that she liked the ground-floor rooms for their coolness in the summer, and their access to the garden for her little dog; behind her, through the door, Iris could see only deep gloom, and caught a whiff of damp. She felt a twinge of something like pity, an emotion she knew would enrage the contessa even further were she to express it.

In a sentence full of the usual formalities and courtesies, Massi murmured again and she turned away from them then, their cue to escape.

He had taken her to the car parked illegally on the piazza; it was at least fifteen years old, a dirty gold colour and surprisingly messy, piles of papers sliding off the back seat.

'I'm sorry,' said Massi, 'my wife's car.' He smiled stiffly. 'I don't have one any more; bad for the nerves, in this city.' It was months since she'd been in a car, Iris realized; it was weird. She'd forgotten what a confined space a car was. The rain was still coming down relentlessly, the elderly windscreen wipers flogging back and forwards as they drove through the big boule-vards of the northern city, unfamiliar to Iris.

The apartment was just beyond a railway line where the road went up, he said, to Fiesole, although the sodden cloud hung so low you could see nothing beyond the roof of the apartment block. It was a solid building, not ancient, not new; Iris settled on *fin de siècle* because it had solid stone detailing around the windows, and balustraded balconies, though what did it matter? She hoped no one judged her and Ma by the terrible architect's terrible concrete house.

'Why do you live here?' she asked as they entered a tiny, flimsy-looking lift, hoping she didn't sound rude; it was so anonymous, the wide and beautiful city all stretched out to the south of them, and Massi lived here. Massi looked at her, refusing to be offended, she thought; he smiled.

'It's a very popular area,' he said. 'Good for families.' The lift shrieked as if prompted, and jerked them upwards. 'Cool in the summer; we have to be practical, you see. Living here all year.'

Unlike you foreigners, he meant; by the time the hot summer came, Iris would be long gone.

The door opened before them; they must have been expected, thought Iris, but before she could think anything else, a dark-haired woman was on top of her on the threshold, long, thin, cool fingers stroking her cheek, amidst an outpouring of exclamations and endearments in Italian.

'Anna, Anna,' said Paolo behind her. And then they were inside and the door shut behind them.

Massi's wife stepped back at last and put a hand to Iris's cheek. 'Poor child,' she said, in Italian. 'Poor child,' and Iris retreated in alarm.

Anna, said Paolo again, and then, to Iris, 'My wife does speak very good English, actually. She's just very—emotional. She can only be emotional in Italian.' He said something in Italian to his wife then, something like, Don't. You'll worry her.

'It's all right,' said Iris, not knowing what else to say. Not surprising he kept his wife away from the school; she would certainly be a distraction. She looked around; the place was big and dark, like the Piazza d'Azeglio; it seemed wrong to her, she still couldn't understand a country where there was so much sun you needed to shut it out. Not today, though; through a tall curtained window she could see the rain gusting. It was only early afternoon but there were several lamps lit inside.

Anna Massi put a hand back to Iris's cheek again, and smiled. There was something unusual about her that Iris couldn't quite pin down; her hair was very black, but her skin was pale and she seemed delicate, in an old-fashioned sort of way. Even her clothes were old-fashioned, particularly for an Italian; she was wearing a woollen skirt that might have belonged to her mother.

'Sit, sit,' said Anna Massi, gesturing at the sofa before abruptly turning away to stare moodily out of the window. '*O dio*, this weather,' she said, flinging her arms around herself. 'The rain! Like the apocalypse, the global warming, don't you think?'

Iris kept quiet. 'Even Sicily,' Anna Massi went on, shooting a reproachful glance at her husband from the window. 'They say it's even cold down there.'

Paolo Massi grunted; looking from him to his wife, Iris thought he seemed quite different in her presence. It was strange to think of her own sudden self-consciousness with him, all that time ago, a whole twenty-four hours. Yesterday morning, when all she'd worried about was being told off for Ronnie not being there.

Anna Massi turned back to Iris, smiling. 'One can sometimes swim in Sicily at this time of year, the sea still warm, you know.' Iris nodded warily. 'Of course, I have too much to keep me busy here. Last week I accompanied pilgrims to a shrine near Treviso; imagine! The study of religions is my passion, not only Christianity, you understand. Also the ancients, Thebes, Peru...' She clasped her hands together at her breast. 'My passion.' Iris stared; she was a weird woman all right.

'She's lovely, isn't she?' Anna Massi went on to her husband in Italian, still smiling at Iris. 'Like a Botticelli, don't you think?' Massi did a funny thing of tilting his head back and looking at the ceiling, while Iris pretended not to understand, but as the blush rose inexorably to her cheeks she thought, It's OK. She's being kind.

The food had not been what she had expected, just like the apartment, just like Massi's odd wife; some meat, roasted to dryness, stewed vegetables, a jug of water. It was elaborate without being organized, as if Anna Massi actually had no idea how to cook at all. Iris told herself off; had she really thought that all Italians lived in picturesque old buildings and made their own pasta? They talked about nothing much, chewing their way through the tasteless food; they avoided the subject of Ronnie completely, as if Iris were a small child that needed to be protected.

'Are you enjoying the drawing course?' Anna Massi asked. 'Paolo tells me you're very talented.' Startled, Iris stared at him, fork in midair, then blushed, again. 'I don't think so,' she mumbled.

'Iris, said Paolo Massi wearily. 'Don't be ridiculous. You must know you're good.'

Iris thought of the drawing of Ronnie that Antonella had put up on the wall of the studio. 'Well, I am enjoying the course, yes,' she said, cautiously.

'You English are strange,' said Paolo Massi. 'So unlike the Americans. They never have a problem believing in themselves.' He seemed tired, suddenly, forking the food into his mouth without enthusiasm. Iris looked from him to his wife, feeling inexplicably sorry for him.

'Thank God for the Americans,' said Anna Massi, blithely. 'Look what a success the school has been, thanks to them. The gallery, the exhibitions—well. Aren't they what really made the difference, these last ten years?' She leaned across the table and took Iris's hand, impulsively. 'Oh, dear, you aren't offended, are you? It's just that the Americans have the money—and there are so many of them.' And she laughed; Iris joined in, not very convincingly, and Paolo Massi remained uncomfortably silent.

Would the Americans go on coming? wondered Iris. Was he worried, not just about Ronnie, but about the effect on the school? And immediately she felt ashamed; of course he was just worried about Ronnie. And, anyway, she thought stoutly, what's she talking about? There were only a couple of Americans on the course, and the studio could hardly be that much of a money-spinner; it couldn't be down to Ronnie disappearing if the whole thing died a death. She thought Massi's wife was rather peculiar and naïve, in fact, with her faith in the Americans, with her faith in the school.

After they'd eaten—and none of them ate much—and drunk some tiny cups of bitter coffee, Anna Massi had leapt up. 'Would you like to see the apartment?' she asked Iris, recovering some of her English. Taken aback, Iris agreed, and found herself led through the place, shown every corner of the big dark sitting room, which turned out to be full of ornaments, candles and mobiles and pieces of pottery—'Anna likes to encourage artisans,' Paolo Massi had said wryly, and Iris had just nodded, thinking, some of them maybe shouldn't have been encouraged. Worse than some of the stuff Ma's friends in Provence produced; far worse.

A big double bedroom with dark, heavy, furniture—'From my family,' Anna said haughtily—a completely ordinary bathroom with toothpaste stains in the sink and mismatched towels. Iris wondered if they thought all English people were obsessively interested in other people's houses, or if they just didn't know what to do with her. A small, white-painted room, with a single bed with a crucifix on the wall behind it and a big picture of Padre Pio or someone like him over a chest of drawers with more candles underneath it, like a little shrine. Iris had backed out of that room, but not before she had seen a nightdress folded neatly on the pillow and had understood that this was where Anna Massi slept. 'My back,' said Anna by way of explanation, before Iris could forestall her. She put a hand to the base of her spine and grimaced. 'I need the hard bed.'

Oh, God, thought Iris; what am I doing here?

'I think I'd better get off, now,' she said hastily, when they came back into the *salotto* where Paolo Massi looked up at them from his newspaper, tired and nervous. 'Really?' he said, looking at his watch. 'When are you—I'll take you, yes?' He glanced at the window; it was grey and gloomy for early afternoon, but the rain seemed to have eased.

'No,' said Iris quickly. 'I mean, thanks very much, but you've helped enough, the lunch, looking after me and everything...' Massi and his wife both protested at once, arguing with her, arguing with each other, but Iris held firm. She shouldered her bag and moved towards the door.

'Look, no, it's absolutely fine,' she said. 'I have bus tickets, it's stopped raining—well almost,' reaching behind her for the door, suddenly desperate.

She managed to confer a hurried kiss on Anna Massi's outstretched cheek and to avoid actually being rude in her haste, but once the door was shut behind her Iris fairly flew down the dank stairwell, dodging the claustrophobic lift and not even really taking a breath until she was out on the street with the beautiful cool rain falling on her cheeks and the fresh air in her lungs.

In less than a minute a bus lumbered towards her on the wide anonymous street, and climbing aboard it with ridiculous gratitude, like a child running out of a detention, Iris made her escape.

Chapter Eleven

SANDRO HAD SPOKEN to the mother.

Serena Hutton; the woman was a ballbreaker from hell. Christ only knew how much it had cost when she called him from Dubai on his mobile, as he made his way across from the Lungarno Santa Rosa towards the Carabinieri station. The Via della Chiesa had been too narrow for the delivery van to avoid splashing him, and as Sandro jumped back with the phone clamped to his ear, just too late, pressing himself against the damp plaster of the nearest wall, he had felt the filthy gutter water seep into his trouser bottoms, his socks, his shoes. Not that it made any difference by that stage; Sandro's morale was not high.

It was the thing he'd dreaded when he went private, the way she'd talked to him, issuing instructions as though he was a dog she was training. Even as a police officer, of course, people sometimes seemed rude in their distress, but this was different; this didn't look like anguish to Sandro. Serena Hutton had said she should be able to get to Florence some time the following week, Monday or Tuesday; he supposed that there was in fact nothing she could do, but still. Three more days, not knowing? Was it normal, in England, to shrug off your children this way?

She had barked instructions at him, bits of information, telephone numbers; in his pocket Sandro had the newspaper report so he was able to respond, he knew where Veronica Hutton had been studying, her age, he had a photograph.

'Has she done this sort of thing before?' he asked, 'Is this like her?' and immediately regretted it. A torrent of recriminations followed in botched Italian concerning the girl's school and their irresponsibility, from which he gathered that Veronica—Ronnie, the mother called her—had absconded from her boarding school for a weekend on one occasion. He further gathered that the mother had not actually lived with her daughter for more than a week since the girl was sixteen, what with school and holidays with wealthy friends here there and everywhere, and in fact she didn't know if it was like her at all.

'Look,' she said in English, 'I don't want any investigation; I'm not paying for any investigation. I've spent enough on that girl. She'll turn up. I just—well. The police seem to think they need a—a representative of the family. You'll have to do.'

And Sandro had had to put up with the woman's dismissiveness. He needed the business, he needed the contacts; if he upset Giovanna Badigliani, then Luisa would get upset and, besides, however much of a self-absorbed monster the mother was, a girl was missing.

Had he detected, below the bluster and the recriminations, a note of guilt in Serena Hutton's tirade? He hoped so, for the girl's sake. And for Lucia Gentileschi's sake he needed to put to sleep his ridiculous idea that Veronica Hutton's disappearance had anything at all to do with her drowned husband.

As he had stood there in the Via della Chiesa with his feet soaked, Sandro wondered if that was really what it was, just a ridiculous notion he'd got into his head. He had seen the girl on Tuesday morning, around eleven-thirty, walking through San Frediano, when by the limited evidence he had gathered, Claudio would also have been in San Frediano. Had she been walking towards the Boboli? She had been carrying her bag, certainly, so she hadn't lost it there yet, and going vaguely in that direction; quite possibly following the route he had taken himself, straight along the Via della Chiesa towards the Via Romana and the back gate to the Boboli.

So their paths might have crossed; that meant nothing. In his head Sandro turned over what the barman had said; Claudio the silent type with his regular habits, asking for his whisky sour and nothing more, so quiet they never guessed he didn't live around the corner at all, but over the other side of town.

Futilely Sandro had shaken out one shoe, then the other, but he hadn't set off again, only stood in the limited shelter of the jutting eaves of a deconsecrated convent where, he read, Sister So and So had devoted her life to the rescuing of the city's wanton girls. May she rest in God's peace.

She had not looked wanton, Veronica Hutton hurrying down the Via del Leone with her striped hair and her handbag slung over her shoulder; she'd looked pretty, anxious, eager; maybe a hint of a sharp edge to her, a tiny clue to what she might grow into, with a mother like the woman he'd just spoken to on the crackling line from Dubai. But, then, the older he got, the less ready he was to judge wantonness much of a crime anyway; look at poor old Giulietta Sarto, a life of prostitution was hardly a barrel of laughs, was it? Promiscuity—well, he didn't like it, it didn't make anyone happy, but the world was changing and there wasn't a thing he could do about it. Did he still want women to marry as virgins?

Damn, thought Sandro, on a tangent, he'd meant to call on Sarto at that women's health centre place, get her out to lunch.

He'd have to talk to Sarto about Luisa and her—her—he could hardly bring himself to say it, lump, even though lump didn't have to mean the worse word. He had looked at it when she raised her shirt in the kitchen, and for a second it *had* been just flesh, just another of the body's irregularities, the kind of thing you get used to as it all starts to sag and slide. And then in the blink of an eye it was something else; it was the future. It was waiting in queues at the clinic; it was having to wear a hospital gown that didn't close at the back; it was fear.

Luisa was the closest thing Sarto had to a mother, her own long since dead, consumed by drugs, Luisa the one waiting for her when she was released from the institution they'd kept her in after she was found unfit to plead. Giulietta Sarto would have to be told. The truth was, he wanted to sit down with and say it out loud to another human being. It might be cancer.

And only then did he push himself away from the wall of the convent in the Via della Chiesa and set off, for his hastily arranged appointment with Maresciallo Falco of the Carabinieri, soaked to the bone and naggingly aware of having shaved badly that morning. In the thin morning light of the bathroom they had shared for their whole married life, his mind had been on Luisa's expression as she left for work and not on his razor. Catching sight of himself in a shopfront, Sandro didn't look like a policeman, or an ex-policeman; he didn't even look much like a low-rent private detective. What he most looked like was a bum.

It had made it worse, not better, of course that he was an ex-officer of the Polizia Statale; it would have made things easier if he'd been one of the private detectives off the hoardings with their toytown badges, fresh out of college. The girl's mother should have looked one of those up in the yellow pages instead of talking to Giovanna Badigliani.

Of course, it would be a Carabinieri case; they generally handled that kind of thing, petty theft, burglary, and, besides, if the bag was found in the Boboli it was a no-brainer, as the Americans would say. The Boboli housed the big and beautiful station that was their Florentine headquarters, set above the orangery in its own iris beds.

He'd been there before. The Polizia Statale and the Carabinieri always acted in full co-operation. On paper they did, anyway. But even when he'd still been a policeman, in that building, among the southern boys with their cavalry officers' uniforms, dark blue striped with red, Sandro had never had any kind of leverage, no inside track. Now he'd told himself that he was representing the girl's mother, who could not be there and didn't speak a great deal of Italian anyway;

it was reasonable. And if they'd spoken to Serena Hutton already, there was the possibility that they'd be very happy indeed to deal with Sandro instead.

At least they had let him in. The young couple under an umbrella at the entrance to the Boboli, making their minds up as to whether it could be worth going in—were they crazy? Sandro thought perhaps all foreigners were just crazy—looked at him curiously as he stood there bareheaded, but the girl in the booth just waved him through. The trees dripped on him as he made his way up to the big villa, the cold hallway echoed with the sounds of traffic and rain, and the little pudgy-faced desk officer made a meal of searching for his name on an admissions sheet. Then made him wait in a pokey lobby outside the maresciallo's office for a good half an hour, because he was out.

When eventually Maresciallo Falco returned, he sauntered in past Sandro without looking at him, his gloves in one hand, a tall, dark-skinned, handsome man. There was something about the way carabinieri walked, Sandro decided. Put his back up. And the man was perhaps twenty years younger than him.

Falco disappeared into the office and a full ten minutes later Sandro was buzzed in. They didn't get off to a good start when without preamble Sandro said briskly, 'So, can we start at the beginning? Who found the bag?'

It was like pulling teeth. Falco looked offended and promptly disappeared again for another ten minutes, during which time Sandro suspected him of doing nothing more productive than getting a coffee. On his return the maresciallo reluctantly handed over a thin cardboard file—soon there'd be no paper files, reflected Sandro gloomily, it would all be on computer—which contained a copy of the report. Sandro glanced at it, noted that it contained the name of the woman who'd found the bag, Fiamma DiTommaso, forty-nine years old, an address in the Via dei Bardi. Otherwise known as the Cat Lady.

'It's all in there,' said Falco, obviously expecting that to be an end to it.

'Um—might I just ask a couple of questions, Maresciallo?' Sandro could hear himself, trying to be obsequious, and didn't like it. Falco sighed, explosively, but stayed where he was.

'Fiamma DiTommaso handed the bag in on Tuesday?' said Sandro.

'Tuesday evening,' said Falco, looking away from him and out of the window. 'Five o'clock.'

'What did she say, this Cat Lady? Anything useful?'

'She's nuts,' said Falco. 'She's only interested in her cats.' Sandro nodded, wondering how that little exchange would have gone, Falco and the Cat Lady.

'So she said nothing?'

'She did a lot of muttering about her cats,' said Falco tersely. 'I'm surprised she bothered handing it in at all.' He seemed ready to jump up and show Sandro the door if he said another word about the Cat Lady.

'OK, OK,' said Sandro, hands up. He paused, gauging the best way not to sound offensive with his next question. 'And you didn't identify the owner—didn't trace her to the Scuola Massi till Friday?'

Tight-lipped, Falco said, 'We assumed it had just been dumped by a mugger. It happens all the time.'

Sandro breathed out. 'Although there was money in the purse.'

Falco shrugged, holding Sandro's eye. 'Had to dump it before he got a chance to look inside. That happens, too.'

Sandro nodded cautiously.

Falco went on. 'And we conducted a full search of the immediate area.' He paused. 'Actually, that was when we found the card for the Scuola Massi.' He allowed himself a smile. Great detective work, thought Sandro.

'On Wednesday?'

'Thursday. Wednesday the visibility was no good.' Meaning, they had been hoping it would stop raining because they didn't want to get their uniforms all wet. Lazy bastards.

Sandro wrote it down, laboriously, feeling the man's eyes on his bowed head. 'Look,' Falco said impatiently, 'perhaps you would allow us to do our job.'

'Did anyone see Veronica Hutton in the gardens on Tuesday?' Sandro asked. 'Park employees?'

'We have put her photograph out to every employee,' said Falco, 'in the nursery, the orangery, the postcard shop, the Kaffeehaus, at each entry point, the maintenance workers, the stonemason...' He paused for effect; all right, thought Sandro, I get the message. 'But bear in mind that we only received a visual on her yesterday afternoon. And that Tuesday was sunny and the park was busy.' He spread his hands. 'So far, no one remembers seeing her.'

'CCTV?' asked Sandro quickly. 'There didn't seem to be anything in the report about CCTV. Have you got her on camera at all?'

'We're still processing the images,' said the carabiniere stiffly.
'But?'

Falco pursed his lips. When he spoke it was as though he was himself delivering an official statement to camera, in a monotone. 'There are two cameras in operation at present, at Palazzo Pitti and the Annalena gate. The Forte di Belvedere exit is currently out of use, and the Porta Romana camera isn't functioning.'

Sandro waited, and reluctantly Falco continued. 'So far,' he said, 'we have what we believe to be an image of the girl entering the gardens via the Annalena gate, at twenty-five minutes past eleven on Tuesday morning. Carrying her bag.'

'And?'

'We haven't managed to isolate an image of her leaving, as yet,' said the carabiniere, tenting his long brown fingers on the desk and frowning at them. 'But there could be various explanations for that.'

'She could have left by the Porta Romana gate,' Sandro said. 'Or—' Or she didn't leave at all.

'Or she might have been obscured by another departing visitor, or we might have missed her,' said Falco. 'As I said, we are still processing the images.'

'Of course,' said Sandro, knowing he was on borrowed time now, then casually, 'but there's been no sign of her in the gardens themselves? Since—since the bag was found?'

'No,' said Falco. He eyed Sandro with weary hostility. 'We've conducted a full search.'

They both knew that 'a full search' could mean anything from a cursory glance with a torch to a dozen men combing the undergrowth; Sandro suspected the former.

As if Falco could hear his thoughts, the carabiniere fixed him with a look. 'Of the immediate area and of the wider park. We have checked every tool store and glasshouse in the place. I told the girl's mother this.' He did not drop his eyes. 'She's not there.' He leaned forward, and Sandro saw genuine gravity in his eyes, for once. 'Look,' he said, 'this is my patch; this is my back yard, believe me, if she was—if she was still here, I'd know about it.'

She wasn't here, but she hadn't gone.

'You mean if she was dead?' asked Sandro.

Falco shrugged as if to say, You know what I mean.

'I'm sure the girl's mother's satisfied you're making every effort,' said Sandro with formality. 'I am sorry.' And indeed it did seem as though Falco had been doing his job; a ballbreaker like Serena Hutton could have that effect, he supposed.

Apparently mollified, Falco sat back in his chair, and when he spoke again he seemed almost conciliatory. 'Look, we've got the girl's computer,' he said. 'We're looking at that, too, for emails, that kind of thing. Networking sites.' Sandro nodded as though he knew what a networking site was. 'Anything?' he asked warily.

Falco frowned. 'Not so far,' he said. 'No boasting about a new boyfriend or a trip away, no emails from boys, no nasty stuff.' He shrugged. 'The other girl had an idea someone might have tampered with it, but apart from the battery being dead as a dodo, our computer guy said it was clean. If anyone did try to wipe anything off it, they didn't know what they were doing, was what he said.'

'Hold on,' said Sandro. "The other girl thinks someone's wiped it? What other girl?'

'The girl,' said Falco impatiently, 'the room-mate; I've just come from there. She thought somebody might have got into the flat, looking for something last night.' He shrugged. 'Personally I think she was a bit hysterical.'

Sandro cursed silently; why hadn't the mother given him a single useful piece of information?

'Right,' he said, 'you got a number for her?' Eyeing him stonily, the carabiniere shook his head. Sandro's heart sank; ask the mother.

'One last thing,' he said. 'Could I see the bag?'

❀ ❀ ❀

As he picked his way down through the iris beds in the rain, the towering bulk of the Carabiniere station above him, Sandro's gut churned. It had been the sight of the bag that had done it, scuffed and manhandled; the contents in their plastic. And the tiny stones, sifted with dust, at the bottom.

He'd stared at them; powder-white.

'I wonder, Maresciallo,' he'd said quickly, fumbling in his pocket, 'if I might make a request?' Falco leaned forwards a fraction, suspicious already. Sandro kept his tone grave and respectful. He produced the crumpled photograph of Claudio Gentileschi. 'If one of your men might have a quick look on that camera footage?' Falco took the photograph and glanced at it with a frown, handed it back.

'We're very busy,' he said. 'Who is this man?'

'It's a long shot,' said Sandro, finding himself unwilling to tell this man anything about Claudio. 'There may be no connection.'

Falco looked at him a moment from under hooded eyes, making him wait. Then he seemed to tire of the game, smiling briefly and without warmth. 'Very well,' he said, 'give it to Giacomini.' He nodded towards the door. 'On your way out.'

Giacomini was the pudgy-faced desk officer; he took the photograph with sublime indifference, photocopied it, returned it to Sandro, taking his time at every stage of the operation.

There'll be no image of Gentileschi, Sandro told himself, and there'll be an end to it. The tall blades of the iris leaves scattered more rainwater across his feet, and he shivered; Luisa'll kill me, he thought, and then he thought some more about Luisa herself. Which was why, when the little *telefonino* rang in his breast pocket he didn't hear it for a while. Luisa, wet feet, fever. The weather was clearing, a patch of late afternoon blue through the clouds, and what was that noise? He pushed his way out through the side gate and he was on the street.

It was Lucia Gentileschi; as though she was already a friend, he knew her immediately.

'Sandro?' she said, and even though her voice was as soft and controlled as always there was something else in it. Confusion; fear.

Instinctively he stepped back from the street, into the shelter of a shop awning; it wasn't the rain, which was easing now anyhow; Sandro hated talking into a *telefonino* out on the pavement. It always seemed wrong to him when he saw people standing in the street shouting their business—or someone else's—into a little machine and oblivious of where they were.

'What is it?' he asked. 'What's happened?'

He turned his back on the street and found himself looking into the shop window; not a shop as it turned out but some kind of gallery—half the greengrocers in the city had been turned into galleries, it seemed to Sandro. He must have answered Lucia Gentileschi more sharply than he had intended because inside the shop a woman was staring curiously at him, a large canvas in her arms. Hurriedly he stepped away, crossed the street.

'Can you come over to the house?' Lucia asked. 'I've found something.'

❀ ❀ ❀

'She's nuts,' said Jackson, with something like relief in his voice. 'The wife? Yeah, totally, totally nuts.'

There was a pause; they both looked through the wrought-iron gates, up the sodden gravel, between the leafless limes to where a fine mist of rain hung over the Boboli's avenue of cypresses. In the ticket booth a bad-tempered young woman in several layers of cardigan and a padded coat gave them a glance before returning to her magazine; the man who'd been standing bare-headed in the rain moved off, talking on his phone.

It seemed to be fine as long as they were talking about Massi and his crazy wife; Iris was suddenly in no hurry to ask Jackson what it was he was frightened of, or to mention Ronnie's name, even. She was tired of it, that leaden feeling of apprehension, the permanent state of anxiety: the constant question, where is she? The long bus ride through town, the smell of wet wool and raincoats, umbrellas scattering rain on her stupid canvas shoes: all this and not much of a night's sleep made her long only to forget about the whole thing. Made her wish she'd said she'd go back to Hiroko's, drink jasmine tea, wait for news. Not rush about in the rain, knowing she was going back to the Piazza d'Azeglio alone tonight.

Must call Hiroko, Iris thought. Say thank you. Monday morning, when they'd next all see each other, seemed a long way off. Would they really all be going back into the studio, sitting down to draw, as if nothing had happened?

'You OK?' said Jackson nervously. 'Look, are we going in there? Seriously?' He nodded towards the misted, dripping gardens. 'You don't want to?' she said, watching him for a response. He looked at her quickly, shrugged. 'Whatever,' he said, 'only, it's, like, pouring with rain?'

What had she expected to find out, by arranging to meet him here? She looked into his face in search of guilt, or understanding, but he just looked wet, and tired. 'OK,' she said. 'Let's find somewhere to sit down.'

'So when did you meet her?' she asked, as they squeezed behind a table in a narrow bar opposite the Pitti Palace. The place was full to steaming with disconsolate tourists; inside the door a tall stand was overflowing with umbrellas. Iris eased her shoulders out of her raincoat, and as she emerged from the wet nylon, shaking her head like a wet dog, Jackson suddenly smiled at her.

'I'm sorry?' he said, and Iris blushed. Again. When would she stop blushing, when she was forty or something? She knew if she dwelled on it one second longer it would go nuclear; it had happened to her once, on a bus in France when a nice-looking boy had tried to talk to her. Her face had felt like it had been scalded, the heat in her cheeks out of control, and eventually the boy had stopped talking and looked at her with concern instead. She squeezed her eyes shut; Ronnie, she thought, and the heat subsided. She opened her eyes.

'Massi's wife,' she said calmly. Did he think by doing that laid-back charming thing she was going to lose the thread? By smiling at her? 'When did you meet Massi's wife?'

'Duh,' he said striking his forehead. 'Oh, he invited me for dinner over there.' He grimaced. 'The food was kind of weird, too.'

Iris laughed, despite herself. 'Yep,' she said. She thought a minute. 'Was it just you? They invited over?'

'Yeah,' said Jackson, shrugging. 'I arrived early for the course, they thought I was all on my own.'

Iris remembered what Anna Massi had said about Americans having made their money for them; perhaps she'd told Paolo to invite Jackson over. It wasn't a pretty thought, but perhaps it was just practical, everyone in Florence made their money out of foreigners. The memory of the lunch lingered, stale and dismal; the Massis' big, gloomy, expensive apartment in an area perfect for families, even though they had no children. Perhaps Anna Massi was child enough all on her own, with her girlish laughter and her silly ornaments.

'*In loco parentis*,' she said, 'looking after you,' and Jackson eyed her with amusement.

'I guess so,' he said. 'I do know what that means, you know. Americans aren't all dumb.'

'No,' said Iris, smiling back, 'I didn't think you were dumb.'

'Why were you early for the course?' she asked on impulse, and his eyes shifted, opaque.

He shrugged. 'Nothing much else to do,' he said. 'My folks are busy, busy, busy.' He smiled briefly but she waited, wanting him to tell her more. 'They run their own business, luxury car, sales franchise.' He smiled wryly. 'Dull, huh? Twenty-four seven kind of stuff. Want me out of the way till Thanksgiving.'

'OK,' said Iris cautiously, feeling a little twinge of guilt. Ma was pretty much always there, wasn't she? Change the subject. She paused. 'I guess they feel responsible,' she said. 'The Massis, I mean. They don't have children of their own, so...'

Jackson gazed thoughtfully out of the window. 'Weird, isn't it,' he said. 'Who ends up with who? They're kind of a crazy couple. She said they were high-school sweethearts.' He shook his head in disbelief. 'D'you see that nun's room of hers?'

'Yes,' said Iris.

'Well,' said Jackson. 'You bet they don't have kids.'

Iris said nothing; the thought made her uncomfortable.

The waiter came over; the crowd had thinned and she saw that the place was slightly more upmarket than she'd have liked, the tables battered antiques, the waiter wearing a long apron and black waistcoat.

'Two glasses of champagne, please,' said Jackson carelessly, without asking her. She stared. 'I'll have a coffee,' she said, '*un caffè, per favore,*' more out of defiance than anything else, and a gesture towards staying sober because it was three in the afternoon and she wasn't used to drinking champagne then or at any other time.

The experimental architect used to produce champagne with a flourish in the Ventoux, if he came to dinner, which he did occasionally; perhaps Ma asked him for old times' sake or, God knew, out of misplaced gratitude for the crumbling house. And even Ma was impatient with him, on occasion, with his assumption that she was still holding a candle for him, and that he was bringing balm to her soul by turning up to eat their week's supply of food in one night. He would bring out the bottle, which even Iris knew was the cheapest stuff you could buy in the SuperU, as if it was Cristal, and press a glass first on Iris, with a knowing murmur. 'Isn't she growing up,' he'd say. Arsehole; or jerk, as maybe Jackson would say.

But the waiter brought two glasses of champagne anyway, and the coffee as well. His not to reason why, supposed Iris; maybe he thought that Jackson was going to drink both glasses. '*Grazie*,' she said, pulling the coffee over, and Jackson laughed.

'You don't like champagne?' he said, with that laid-back smile of his. 'Come on, Iris, everybody likes champagne.' She gave him a sharp look, conjuring up all her animosity for the experimental architect to maintain it, then gave in. She took the glass, and sipped. It was nice; very cold, so the glass had turned cloudy with condensation. Iris felt herself relax just enough, and she leaned into the padded banquette.

'Do you know this place?' she said. She didn't know why she didn't just get to the point, instead of making small talk, except that she didn't really know Jackson very well and she couldn't just jump in. Besides, she was curious and guiltily she realized that she was enjoying herself.

'Uh-huh,' said Jackson, looking around him. 'Could be, yeah. I think we've been here, one time.'

'We?' she said.

He looked at her consideringly. 'The guys,' he said. 'You know. The guys. Brett, and Alice, and Tracey and Bernard and Imi and Jonathan. The guys.'

Jonathan had been the one who'd called her the fat chick; Iris remembered the name immediately Jackson said it, like a brand on her skin, and she felt the heat rise to her cheek in response. Jackson was looking at her. 'I guess you don't know 'em, do you?' He sighed. 'Ronnie always said you had no money. No dough, no point in asking you, you'd get embarrassed.' He shrugged. 'Sorry.'

Iris swallowed. 'That's OK,' she said, shrugging. 'She was right, as it happens.'

'Yeah, but still,' said Jackson. 'I'm sorry.'

Iris saw that the cuffs of Jackson's sweatshirt were ragged, as if he chewed them, like a child.

'Jonathan came to the party,' said Iris. 'None of the others did.' And again Jackson eyed her with amusement.

'Yeah,' he said. 'He's got a thing for you.'

Iris froze, holding her glass at her lips. 'Don't be stupid,' she said, trying to sound like she didn't care, like this wasn't the biggest insult she'd ever heard.

'Whatever,' said Jackson. 'Actually, he does.'

'Why did he call me the fat chick, then?' she burst out, except that she knew straight away. There were boys like that.

'Because he's an asshole,' said Jackson, still looking at her. Suddenly his glass was empty; he lifted a hand to the waiter. Iris drained her glass too, stood it back on the table, light-headed. 'I can't pay for these,' she said. 'You know that.'

'Another two, please?' said Jackson to the waiter as if she hadn't spoken. At least he asked in Italian this time, even if it was with a terrible accent. The waiter nodded; in her light-headed state Iris wondered if she'd ever be able to talk to a waiter that way, as if it was perfectly normal to be drinking champagne at three o'clock on a wet November afternoon. It was the drink, of course, but she felt like crying, then suddenly she thought of Ronnie, that she should be here and that they didn't know where she was. Come on, she told herself, wake up.

'So why did no one else come?' she asked. 'None of—the guys?'

Jackson's eyes flicked away from her. 'Ah, well,' he said, evasive. 'Kids' stuff, Halloween. When she first planned it, y'know, it was all going to be great, we were going to go out on the town, do crazy stuff, dress up, break into the Boboli, do fireworks—' He broke off, frowned. 'Uh, her bag—Ronnie's bag, that's where they found it, yeah?' She wondered how he knew; except, of course, word got around.

'Yeah,' she said, warily. 'The Boboli.' The carabiniere had said something about the vineyard, could that be right? Was there a vineyard in the Boboli? A woman feeding cats had found it. She remembered the cats, one particular corner with plastic trays and a scattering of pellets, and a ginger tom curled up motionless in the sun.

The waiter delivered another two tall glasses, took away Iris's coffee cup. The place was emptying; through the big, steamed-up window it seemed that the rain had stopped.

'Uh, OK, the party,' said Jackson. 'Well, she seemed to lose interest, didn't, like, say come, you absolutely have to come. Talked about it like it was kids' stuff, just for the babies, like Sophia.' He smiled, far away.

It was true, Sophia was just like that, a big, pretty baby; spoilt, too. Since when, Iris wondered, had she got so world-weary herself? Had Ronnie done the Halloween thing as a way of including her, another baby?

'What were you doing instead?' asked Iris, without really thinking. Again Jackson's eyes flicked off and away from her. 'Some guy, some friend of Alice's mom's, has some place up in the hills, they were having a fireworks party, we got dragged along, kind of.' He looked back at her from under his eyelashes. 'It was fun, you know? But I do, like, feel guilty, now. We—well, I should have come over to Ronnie's, to see you guys.'

'Can't be helped,' said Iris quickly. 'It was fine, actually, she didn't seem upset.'

'No, I wasn't thinking of her, exactly,' said Jackson. 'I know she wasn't upset.' He took a meditative sip.

Iris felt something move into place in her head, a piece of a puzzle. 'You talked to her? After the party?' She thought of Ronnie hanging out of the big window at the end of the *salotto* in the dark, trying to get the best signal on her tiny silver phone. Talking to Jackson?

Jackson stared, his eyes turning dark; Iris heard the almost-accusation in her voice. She thought he was paler; he looked handsome like this, she thought, eyes properly open, serious. He was the one, wasn't he? Ronnie'd been planning to go away with Jackson. She scanned back through the previous weeks; how could she have missed it? She thought of how they'd been with each other, so casual, everything always just in a group, drifting off to bars with the guys. She felt angry, as if she'd been deceived, Ronnie pretending she was just playing the field when really there'd been Jackson, sweet, laid-back Jackson with his iPhone, her man.

Only there was something else to him, this afternoon; an edge to laid-back Jackson.

'Ah,' he said. 'Ah, you got me. Yeah, I guess I did.'

'She called you?' she said quietly.

Jackson whistled. 'Yeah,' he said, eyes narrowing. 'She called me.'

'So she called you that night,' said Iris, 'when you were up in the hills. At that other party.' Her voice was flat. What was she angry about?

'No, no,' said Jackson. 'Not then. Well, she could've called me then, only I didn't talk to her, I—I left the phone at my place, it was out of battery.' He shrugged, watching her.

She stared at him. Was he telling her the truth? Ronnie had certainly been talking to someone. She couldn't work out what he was telling her. Behind the bar a man with slicked-back hair was looking at them as he pretended to polish a glass.

'Look,' said Jackson. 'Do you think I'm lying, is that it? Do you think I've done something to Ronnie?' His voice was cool and level, and Iris sat, frozen, unable to believe it. Not Jackson. But there was something in the quality of his anger, some extremity.

'Well,' said Iris carefully, 'you've been a bit weird. About the police, and stuff. And you weren't in school on Tuesday.'

'Wasn't I?' he said. 'Maybe not,' and he shrugged again, still watching her. It was as if he was daring her to ask him more.

'So what did you get up to, Tuesday?' She tried to sound light, but they both knew it was serious.

He let out a deep breath.

'OK,' he said. He smiled warily. 'She didn't call me during the party, she called me Tuesday morning, the morning after.'

Iris saw those two champagne glasses on the drainer, the bottle in the fridge with a spoon in it.

'And?' she said.

'And, she said, she wanted to talk to me.' He leaned across the table towards her and spoke earnestly for once; now he wanted her to believe him. 'OK? She was real excited, you know Ronnie.' Almost imperceptibly Iris shook her head.

'You came over?' she said, and he shrugged, spreading his hands. 'You were going away together,' she said, her voice flat with the sense of betrayal she could not explain. She put her hands to her face, her cheeks burning into her palms. 'She planned this whole thing so she could go away with you.'

Jackson started shaking his head and laughing. 'No way,' he said. The sound of his laughter made her so angry she glared. 'Come on, Iris,' he said. 'No! Me and Ronnie? No way! No way!' It was almost comical, Jackson's expensive education, his vocabulary boiled down to a handful of words, but she couldn't laugh.

'Where is she?' she said quietly. 'Do you have a key to the flat, Jackson? Did you come into the flat yesterday, after—do you have her keys? Did you wipe her computer, because they took it, you know, the police took it, they'll be able to get into it.'

'You're crazy,' said Jackson, impatiently. 'Of course I don't have a key.'

'Where is she?' said Iris, doggedly.

'I don't know,' said Jackson bringing his fist down on the table. The glasses jumped and at the bar the waiter turned at the sound.

'I don't know anything about her computer. There was totally nothing between us, only friends.' She was beginning to learn that the angrier he was, the quieter his voice grew. She refused to be intimidated.

'So you came over to the flat, and drank champagne with her, when you should have been at school.' She could hear herself, scolding like a schoolteacher. 'And nothing was going on?' She stopped, something sticking in her throat. 'And now she's disappeared and you don't know anything about it?'

Jackson let out a strangulated laugh.

'I drank champagne with you,' he said. 'Is there something going on?'

She shook her head, wordless.

'Ronnie and I were friends,' he said. 'Yeah, I came over, jeez, it wouldn't have been the first time.' He looked over her shoulder into the distance and she couldn't tell if he was avoiding her gaze or just concentrating. 'We were just having fun, talking, stuff.'

'Stuff?' said Iris stiffly.

'Well maybe at the beginning—I mean, when we first got to know each other, uh—we fooled around a bit, come on. But it was never—anything. And Tuesday morning, she...' And again he shifted his gaze '...she just wanted an audience, I guess.'

All Iris heard was that they'd been more than friends, at the beginning; she and Ronnie'd only been here a month, the beginning might have been three weeks ago, not a hundred years. It felt like a hundred years to Iris. She breathed out. None of my business, she thought. Who she fools around with; except it is, now she's run off.

'So what did happen?'

Jackson folded his arms. 'You don't give up, do you? OK, here's the full deal. We had a drink, in the apartment.' He paused. 'Jeez, that place, gives me the creeps.' He grimaced; all right for you, thought Iris. I'm the one going back there tonight. 'She was happy. Totally happy. She even said one glass of champagne was enough. She said she didn't need it.'

'Did she say why?'

'She said she'd tell me sooner or later, but she couldn't say anything just now. A wind-up, I thought.'

Iris looked sceptical.

'Well, I guess I thought it was some guy, and she'd bring him along one evening, maybe he was some count or something so we were all supposed to be really impressed.' He sighed. 'I kind of pushed her a little, just to tease her, but she clammed up. Said she was going to do some painting, that's all. She was all fired up about painting, suddenly, said she'd been stupid, wasting her time, she really wanted to paint, after all.'

Iris snorted. 'And you believed her?' But then she thought, That MySpace page. The Leonardo drawings she'd posted, that dreamy stuff about being an artist. And she'd just thought, You've changed your tune, Ronnie. She became aware through the window of the long façade of a stone *palazzo*, a baroque doorframe, a cornice, a statue; the standard, beautiful Florentine view. Why not? Why shouldn't this place have got to Ronnie?

Jackson shrugged. 'Yeah, I know. Ronnie, working? No way, that was what I thought. But y'know, it's been going on a while. Tuesday, she showed me her sketchbooks, she's been working on the quiet, like she was going to surprise us all.'

'What did you think?' asked Iris, grumpily. 'About the sketchbooks?'

Jackson sounded uneasy. 'Well, she was trying, y'know?'

'If she wanted to get good, it's a shame she didn't work a bit harder, after all that eyelash-batting she did at Massi the first couple of weeks. He really put in the hours on her; he must have thought she was serious.' Iris could hear how she sounded, all pinched, like a schoolteacher, but it had been annoying, really.

Jackson looked bleary. 'Not at the school, she said. It was kids' stuff, she said.'

'OK,' Iris said. 'Let's say I believe you. So what was she excited about? Who *was* she going away with? Some kind of—painting holiday?'

Now Jackson looked really uneasy. 'I dunno,' he said.

'Right.' said Iris, and she made an effort to speak calmly. 'OK, I'm not making this up, this isn't all in my head. She told me she was going to stay with friends in Greve for a couple of days. Only the friends never invited her, they're not even there. I called them.' She looked him in the eye. 'So she was planning something for that couple of days. She had to be going somewhere.'

He looked away. 'With the new guy, maybe?'

'A new guy none of us has got a single peek at. This top-secret new guy—come on. You know what Ronnie was like, she couldn't keep quiet if her life depended on it.'

And they both stared at each other again. 'Maybe this guy was different,' he said thoughtfully.

'Come on, Jackson. Did she say anything about where she was going? Did you—did you leave with her? You never told me what you did, the rest of the day, did you?'

He shook his head. 'I left her there,' he said quietly. 'She said she wanted to do her face. Didn't want me looking over her shoulder.' That sounded like Ronnie, all right, hours in the bathroom and a rubble of open pots and dried-out brushes left behind.

'That's the last time I saw her.' He didn't say any more; Iris supposed she had to believe him.

The place was silent, outside the light yellow and soft. In front of them the glasses were empty suddenly, and the waiter was there; she shook her head minutely and he took the glasses and retreated.

And then Jackson was speaking again. 'There was a bag,' he said, reluctantly. '"There was—like an overnight bag, just in the hall.'

'A bag,' said Iris. How could she have been so stupid? There had to be a bag. 'So where's the bag now?'

Because it could explain everything, couldn't it? Ronnie could have all kinds of stuff in that bag, her phone, money, it could be why she hadn't bothered to be back in touch. And what if—her mind ran on, what if all this was an elaborate game, to throw them off the trail, to wind them up—Ronnie'd ditched the handbag because she had the other bag all along? One of Ronnie's little games. But—any number of questions jostled in her head, all those buts—still she wanted to go and look, now. Wanted to find that spot where the cats lay curled in the grey dust, sleeping in the sun; if there'd been another bag, a holdall, then they'd have found it, but still. Iris wanted to see that place for herself.

'Come on,' she said.

Chapter Twelve

ALL LUCIA GENTILESCHI'S composure was gone. She met Sandro at the door and he could see immediately that she was lost; she had not been prepared for this. This was what grieving was like.

'All right, all right,' he said gently, guiding her back into her own sitting room. 'Sit down.' He glanced around and the first thing he saw was the desk in the corner, its rolltop thrown back and drawers pulled open, a pile of papers strewn on the wide leather-covered surface where Claudio Gentileschi would have done his writing, signed his letters, paid his bills.

Lucia saw him looking. 'Yes,' she said, 'that's it, that's where I found it—' and she started up.

'No,' said Sandro, 'wait,' because he had a sudden vision of the self-contained Lucia Gentileschi throwing herself on the papers like some Indian widow on a pyre, soaking them with tears, hurling them around the room. He found he couldn't bear such a vision of chaos and disarray; this *was* what grieving was like.

'What did you find?' he asked gently, holding tight to her hand, as much to hold her there as to comfort her.

She looked about her distractedly, avoiding the mess at the desk; looked down at her hand in his. She sighed, and her shoulders dropped; her hand relaxed.

'Bills,' she said simply, 'I looked at the bank statements, and there were standing orders to pay bills I couldn't—couldn't understand. Every month not one but two payments to Fiorentinagas, to Enel, to—to the *acque*—to...'

She rose and fetched something from the desk, set it in his lap. The same computer printouts he received at his own expense from the Cassa di Risparmio di Firenze every month, full of maddening inconsistencies he then had to sort through himself—why have they charged me for this, what does that mean? In the end he always thrust them at Luisa to unravel. The figures swam before his eyes, and Sandro frowned to force himself to focus. She was right; this wasn't just bank chiselling, a few euros here and there for taking money out of the wrong cash machine, it was just as she had said, two of everything. Gas, water, electricity. As if he was running a parallel household; could there be any other explanation?

He looked into Lucia Gentileschi's face. 'Your husband always handled the bills,' he said. 'You never saw them—before.' And she nodded dumbly, her face somehow contracted with pain. She drew a swift breath.

'He had another place,' she said. 'Didn't he?' She held his gaze. 'Another life.'

Sandro stared down at the statements again, so as not to have to answer. Stared hard.

'There's no telephone bill,' he said, slowly, grasping at straws, but then he saw something else. 'These sums are tiny. Barely more than the standing charge, look.' He held the paper up to her and she winced, then steadied, and looked. She put her finger to the paper, running down the column, conceded a tiny nod.

'Small,' she said. 'Smaller than our apartment's bills, yes.'

'A fraction,' said Sandro, running his finger up to the other figure, and before he could stop himself, 'and there were only two of you. He leaned in to make sure she knew what he was saying. 'If the gas bill for you two is, say, a hundred and fifty euros, then this other bill, thirty, that doesn't support another human being, does it?' She stayed silent; he didn't know what she was thinking.

'Are you worried he had another woman?' he asked bluntly. 'That something might have happened with another woman that made him kill himself?' She stared at him unblinking. 'Did you ever have reason to believe he was unfaithful to you?' This was the standard phraseology; the answer was almost never to be trusted. Except in this case, he believed her.

'Never,' she said. 'That's why—well. I can't understand this.'

In discomfort Sandro stood up then, paced to the wide window, a single piece of glass. The rain seemed to have stopped, for the time being; above the rooftops to the west he saw a golden line of sun between banks of purple cloud, like a blessing, a reprieve. He swivelled, taking in the panorama, thinking of Claudio Gentileschi installing this wall of glass. You could see the greened copper dome of the synagogue, the backs of the vast piles of the Piazza d'Azeglio, the skeletons of trees in the gardens, the distant green and terracotta of Fiesole. Think.

He frowned a moment as something came back to him, some crazy thing the autistic boy had said. 'You don't have a dog, do you?'

Lucia Gentileschi looked at him blankly. 'A dog? No. Claudio was...nervous of dogs.'

'Look, Lucia,' said Sandro, leaning forward with urgency, 'this isn't a matter of another life, another...family. I don't know what it is, exactly, but we'll find out, all right?'

Again Lucia Gentileschi made that gesture of crossing her hands in her lap, calming herself. She opened her mouth, hesitated. 'Yes,' she said, and for a second allowed herself to close her eyes.

'Shame there was no phone bill,' said Sandro, thinking. 'In a way. If there was a number, we could trace—we could find this place. This—whatever it is.' But as he said it he felt a chill. Because they didn't know what they would find.

Silently Lucia Gentileschi got to her feet and crossed to a wide teak sideboard. She reached into a drawer and took out a plain metal ring holding three keys; they clinked as she lifted them for him to see.

'Wherever it is,' she said, 'whatever it is. I think these are the keys.'

❀ ❀ ❀

It wasn't until they got to the spot she was looking for, up under the low grey sky, that it occurred to Iris that this might not be a good idea. She thrust the thought down, concentrated instead on her triumph at getting up there, getting in past the woman at the gate who told them they only had forty minutes, then we close, who'd clearly not wanted to let them in at all. At making their way up here through the narrow, claustrophobic alleys, some of them almost dark, there was so little light left in the sky and the hedges were so high and overgrown.

Behind her all the way she had heard Jackson's laboured breathing; too many cigarettes, too many late nights. And it was when they stopped that the sound of his breathing worried her in a different way. It was suddenly, sharply, a reminder that she was alone here with him. Why had he come? She didn't know if he liked her or hated her.

When he arrived beside her, she turned away a little to look around, surveying the wide horizon. The city was laid out in front of them, red and grey, domes and loggias, hills in the distance and just along the horizon to the west there was a line of light coming out from under the cloud. Closer there were the backs of ordinary buildings along the Via Romana, built into the side of the gardens; a balcony here, a broken pane of glass there. Did their inhabitants slip out on summer evenings and have a quiet drink, the Boboli their private back garden? She leaned to get a better look.

'Iris,' Jackson said, and there was something in his tone that made her not want to turn and look at him.

'Mmm?' she said, fixing on the last of the sun.

There was a crackle of sound in the air suddenly, an announcement in Italian. Iris looked for the source and saw that there were loudspeakers fixed to tall poles here and there.

She listened, something about sunset; the announcement came again but was no more intelligible. She knew it must be something about the place closing, but when? She looked at her watch; they'd only been here ten minutes, maybe fifteen. No problem.

'What?' she said, turning to Jackson, more fierce than she meant to sound, to stop that stupid anxiety

'What are we doing here?' he said.

'We're looking for—we're looking for Ronnie,' she said. 'For her stuff, anyway. In case there's anything else.'

'It was here?' he asked, looking around. It needed work, Iris realized, to know whether people were telling you the truth or not. And probably experience, which she did not have much of.

'I think so,' she said, but she knew it was the place.

There was a horseshoe-shaped green amphitheatre behind them, terraced in box and grass; either end of the horseshoe ran into high-hedged alleyways, dark and narrow, and they stood at one of these ends, where three little rows of vines had been planted inside a box hedge. This was what she remembered, the vines, and the narrow, dark space between hedges where the cats had lain, curled in the shafts of sun, and there had been plastic bowls of food set out by someone. The woman who fed the cats had found the bag. The ground wasn't dusty now, it was soaked, and there were no shafts of sun.

Reluctantly Iris stepped out of the last of the green evening light, and into the dark between the hedges. Jackson was right behind her, she realized; she stopped, letting her eyes accustom themselves to the dark.

There were sounds, tiny drippings from the leaves; she could feel them on her face. Lower, lighter sounds still, the sound of leaves settling, something moving low and light among the undergrowth. She held her breath, but she could still hear Jackson's. 'Iris,' he said; his voice was in her ear, and without his face to look at she heard the panic in his voice just as she'd heard it on the telephone. She held up a hand to keep him quiet; they were here to look, even if he was scared. Even if there were still things he hadn't told her. Even—

Putting out a hand to pull a branch out of her way Iris felt another scattering of cold drops on her face and arm and let out an exclamation; below her line of vision something ran, over her feet. Cat. She knelt.

They seemed dense and solid, these hedges, but kneeling there, quiet, Iris saw that they were hollow inside, and no leaves would grow in here, in the dark. Of course; it was like that at home, in France, the scrub across the hillside below the house was scraggy and thin. It came back to her in a rush; hiding inside a myrtle bush, spiky and scented, she had been perhaps nine years old and hiding from Ma. Then it had been hot, the air full of insect sounds; she had seen a viper. Or perhaps it had been a stick, but it had still sent her running out, screaming, into Ma's arms.

Now Jackson was standing over her; she tried to ignore him. Looked along the ground, wishing she'd brought a torch, because she did have a torch, one of the things Ma had taught her, always take a torch, a penknife, a piece of cord, for tying stuff up, holding your suitcase together if a lock breaks. Good old Ma, who knew how to take care of herself after all, and Iris, despite all the disastrous men.

There were dead leaves everywhere, prickly, shifting and settling in the half-light, under the dripping. Except where there weren't any, a dry, bare patch further inside the hedge; on her knees Iris edged closer to it. Skirting a cat bowl in which a clump of swollen pellets floated, giving off an unpleasant smell. She swallowed, pinched her nostrils against the smell.

'What are you looking for?' said Jackson, his voice steely with impatience. 'There's nothing here. If there was, the police would have found it, wouldn't they?'

Iris snorted, thinking of that policeman casually stabbing at Ronnie's computer.

'Were you a MySpace friend?' she asked, over her shoulder. 'Could you access her page?'

There was another crackle from the loudspeakers.

'Sure,' said Jackson, wary. 'Come on, come out.' On all fours Iris looked across the gravel where there were no leaves; it was level, there were no bodies buried here, no overnight bags resting against the wiry trunks. She worked her way back again, on hands and knees.

'All right,' she said, putting a hand back on the ground to steady herself, the other hand up for Jackson to pull her up. Something sharp on the ground dug into the fleshy part of her hand and she exclaimed, pulling the hand up and overbalancing.

'Hey,' said Jackson, pulling her upright. He was surprisingly strong, both arms around her to stop her falling.

'OK,' she said breathlessly, holding the sore hand away from him. There was something funny in his expression, his face very near to hers. 'What is it?'

'I gave her this guy's number, a while ago,' said Jackson, abruptly. 'And that morning, when we were having our little drink, she said she was going to meet him. I had the impression that was her plan right after I left.'

'A guy?'

'A painter guy,' said Jackson reluctantly. 'I met him in some bar. Old guy.'

Iris frowned at him, not understanding. Ronnie wasn't interested in old men. 'Rich?' she asked. 'What do you mean? Famous?' She could just about imagine Ronnie being interested in that, in going away with someone like that. Just to say, afterwards.

Jackson let her go. Her hand was hurting, a splinter or a thorn still stuck in there; Iris rubbed at it without looking.

'I didn't know too much about him,' said Jackson. 'Only he could sure draw, he was down by the river there, with a sketchbook one time. I bought him a drink.'

'On the river? You mean on the Ponte Vecchio?' Iris was disbelieving; there was a string of iffy tourist artists set up down there; in fact, Florence was full of people sketching or painting or setting up easels.

'Further along,' said Jackson. He laughed, not very convincingly. 'I was checking out the wild side, one time. San Frediano, Santo Spirito. Off the beaten track.'

'Florence doesn't have a wild side,' she said, mocking. 'You're kidding.'

Uncomfortably Jackson said, 'Well, I was only looking. It's all kinda safe, over this way.'

'You mean you were looking for—ah, stuff? Um, dope?' She didn't even know the words. Jackson looked at his feet. 'Maybe,' he muttered. 'Nothing big time.'

'Right,' said Iris. 'With Ronnie? For Ronnie?'

'Nah, no, no,' said Jackson. 'She didn't—not really—she wasn't into that stuff. Maybe a bit curious.' He looked at her and sighed. 'This sounds worse than it is, Iris. A couple joints—I don't really—'

'All right,' said Iris impatiently. 'You know, it isn't any of my business, as long as you didn't get Ronnie into anything—' He was looking at her with a new look in his eyes; it might almost be unhappiness, or guilt.

'What?'

'Well, that's just it,' he said, 'I think maybe I did.'

'You went looking for—for dope and you found this painter guy? Was he also a drug dealer, the old guy?'

'No,' said Jackson with impatience, 'you're kidding, I mean, no way. We got talking on the river, he was drawing...' He hesitated, as if trying to remember. 'A bird, some bird down there in the water, a big white bird. Then before I knew it, it was like I couldn't stop him talking—he had real good English—like he'd been saving it up years and years, his life story.' He blinked; Iris looked at him, waiting. He went on.

Iris found herself listening. The old man seemed real to her; it was a good story.

'It got cold, y'know—this was just, like ten days ago, remember that day it turned cold?' Iris nodded.

'So I could see he was real cold, kind of blue, almost, and we went in this bar, by where he'd been drawing, and I bought him a drink. And he gave me his number, that was all.' He caught a look in Iris's eye, for which she was already ashamed. 'Nothing like that,' said Jackson coolly, as if something like that could have happened to him once upon a time. 'He was kind of strange but, y'know, I think he just wanted to talk. It was like he'd never talked to anyone before.' He looked at her earnestly. 'And his drawings—well. You think Massi's good? He's nothing. You had to see 'em. That's what I said to Ronnie.'

There was a silence. 'And then you gave her his number.'

'Yup.' He spoke defiantly. 'Monday. Look, he seemed fine to me, what was I to know? He was something. She took the number.'

'This was Tuesday?' He nodded. 'Tuesday morning, at your place.'

She'd run off with a painter? There was Lucian Freud, he was eighty-something, and girls threw themselves at him. Or—Jackson hardly knew this guy. He could be—crazy. She stared at Jackson. 'Have you seen him since, this guy?'

Slowly, Jackson shook his head. 'Don't you believe me?'

'I don't know,' she said. 'Do you have his number?'

'Should I call him?' he asked.

Duh.

She watched while he flicked through icons and data on the slick screen. He held the phone to his ear, his expression perplexed. She could hear a mechanical voice and Jackson passed her the phone for confirmation. There was the message she'd often heard but never quite understood, something about the number being unavailable or inactive or unreachable. She hung up; she could hear Ma's voice. *What kind of a cooked-up story is that?*

'Listen,' she said, carefully. 'You should tell someone. I mean, like, someone else. Tell the police.'

'Oh, yeah? The Italian police?' His voice was contemptuous.

'What is your problem with the police?' she asked. Between the hedges the light was draining out of the air and she couldn't really see his face properly, a pale oval with shadow pooling where the eyes should be. 'Have you been in trouble?'

'You know how easy it is to get a police record in the States?' he asked brusquely. 'Under-age drinking'll do it. I don't like 'em.'

She felt his resistance to her, and it had a weird effect. The prickly, angry Jackson roused her somehow, more than the laid-back, likeable Jackson. It seemed to her dangerous that he should have this effect, some kind of primitive, unstable thing, but she couldn't help herself.

'OK,' she said, quietly. 'But tell someone. Maybe tell Massi, first, yeah? He'll go with you, to the police, he's good, you know. He'll talk to them for you.'

'Maybe,' said Jackson. 'OK. Yeah, I will.'

In the fading light Iris squinted down at the fleshy pad of her thumb, still hurting her, and impatiently she pulled it out, whatever it was, held it up to her face. A shard of fine blue glass, a metallic corner.

'What *is* that?' she said, distracted. 'It looks like—'

'Looks like a bit of screen,' said Jackson with casual expertise, 'Someone's phone, I'd say. Like—hey—that colour—'

'Blue—Ronnie's phone's blue glass,' said Iris, dropping to her knees, groping for where she'd put her hand down the first time. 'There's other bits.' She scraped them up, splintered glass and plastic mixed with leaves, and not knowing what to do with them, she shovelled them into her bag, down there with the pencils and sketchbook and loose change.

The loudspeakers crackled angrily over their heads. 'Shit,' said Jackson, looking around, 'come on, look, the sun's down. Didn't she say something about sundown?' He tugged at her. 'Come *on*. Or we're going to be in here for the night.'

In the near dark Iris got to her feet, and she saw that he was right. 'I think we'd better run,' she said.

Chapter Thirteen

THOUGH THEY CAME back the way they'd come, in the near-dark everything was horribly different. They ran faster and faster, saying nothing, the gravel skidding under their feet the only sound. Iris felt as if she was in some sort of nightmare in which she was being chased, her heart in her mouth. The hedged alleyways and twisted trees of the big garden were suddenly full of dead ends and strange sounds and there was a kind of damp mist coming up, smelling of stagnant water.

Ronnie, thought Iris as she ran, chest burning, had Ronnie been here? Did someone bring the bag in here, some mugger? But he hadn't taken her purse, or her money, or her phone. Ronnie's phone had been smashed, with force, stamped into pieces. Someone had taken it and smashed it against a tree or a rock, until it was destroyed. Ronnie wasn't sitting up in any honeymoon suite; that dream was over.

What did people tell themselves, when their kids, their friends went missing? Did they cling on, like Iris was doing, to any story but the most likely one, that the person they loved was dead? Iris wanted to be alone, to look inside the bag, to sort through the pieces without Jackson looking over her shoulder. She forced herself to go faster while he panted to keep up, just a shape behind her in the dark. I could get away, thought Iris, could Ronnie? And felt grateful for once for her big lungs, her muscles, the muscles she'd learned to draw, tendons and hamstrings, her heart pumping.

The yellow lights of some windows appeared to their right, those houses backing on to the gardens, then the wide avenue lit yellow by streetlamps, and Iris realized that by sheer luck or gravity they had found their way back to the gates. She slowed, getting her breath back.

The gates were closed; a chain had been locked through them and a board had been put up against the plexiglass of the small ticket booth, but behind it there was a light still on. In a panic, Iris battered on the door, and the woman emerged, face like thunder. After a flurry of angry Italian she let them out, even more reluctantly than she had admitted them, banging on the sign and its clear instructions, last admission, the gates will be shut at sunset. She shooed them through the gate, clanging it shut behind them.

They stood a moment in the street, Jackson still panting. 'You're good,' he said, with breathless admiration. 'You're fast.'

'For a fat chick,' countered Iris, back against a damp wall as she leaned to get her breath back. She looked back at the gate, the dark trees the other side of it. A car passed; they were back in civilization, it wasn't even late. Beside them the window of a gallery glowed with light.

'Hey,' said Jackson, softly, and she tensed as she heard him shift into a different gear, after the running, the panic. She knew what he was going to say.

'You're not fat, baby.'

She hadn't expected that, though, not that word; it made her angry, and she pushed herself away from the wall.

'Do you call everyone baby?' she said, irritated suddenly, hands on her hips in front of him. 'Is that an American thing?' But he stood his ground, hands in his pockets, and looked at her. She could see his chest moving up and down.

'I don't,' he said quietly. 'Not everyone. Though I can't speak for all Americans, sure.'

'Sorry,' said Iris, hearing herself, like a sulky child. 'I just—'

'It's OK,' said Jackson. 'Baby.' She stared at him, then laughed, and suddenly his cheek was next to hers, his ribcage against hers and one of his hands was in the hair on the back of her neck, and she had no idea what to do.

Behind Jackson a car slowed, then bumped up over the kerb on to the wide pavement and with the engine sound so close he pulled away quickly, his cheek instantly gone from hers as if it had never been there, the hand gone from her hair, and Iris just stood, stupidly, mouth open.

The door of the car opened and a small woman with cropped hair climbed out, opening an umbrella as they stood there, and Iris laughed with disbelief, because it was Antonella Scarpa. Antonella, like the cavalry, come with her usual brisk efficiency to—what? To save her? To offer her a taxi service home? How did she know where to find them?

Antonella turned and saw Iris and made a sound that was almost a laugh back at her. Antonella Scarpa never laughed. Jackson, beside them, took a step back like a wary male animal straying into unfamiliar territory. As she saw the small movement of retreat Iris felt irrationally victorious, as if she and Antonella had won some kind of fight together instead of just bumping into each other in the street.

Then the passenger door of the car opened and Paolo Massi climbed out and the feeling was gone, as if it had never been. Iris just felt like some teenager whose parents had turned up early at the disco; deflated, angry, frustrated. Of course, Massi knew she was over here, he didn't think she could take care of herself.

'Ah, Iris,' he said uneasily, his surprise completely unconvincing. 'Of course.' And was ready with a cover story. 'Come to pick things up,' he said, 'from the gallery.' He nodded towards the yellow-lit window and for a second Iris thought he was making even that up, then she remembered, they'd been here the second day, to see finished work, the school's gallery. But, still, it was a cover story; Massi nodded to Jackson, who mumbled something, as much a guilty kid as Iris.

'Jackson's going home now,' Iris lied, and she was surprised to hear how clear and confident she sounded.

'OK,' said Massi warily. 'Would you like a lift, Jackson? Or perhaps you, Iris, too, I can take you, Antonella can manage here.'

Because, of course, there wasn't really anything to pick up from the gallery, was there? Massi had come to find Iris, maybe his wife had sent him, maybe she'd have to go back there and eat another terrible meal, and—No, thought Iris, no way.

'I'm fine,' she said, 'I've—got some stuff to do. Shopping, and stuff.' She improvised hastily. 'There's nothing in the fridge at home.' She wished she hadn't said that: the unfinished bottle of champagne haunted her.

'I'll walk with Iris as far as the river,' said Jackson. He went on earnestly, 'We'll be fine, Mr Massi.' And Iris saw Paolo Massi frown. He didn't trust Jackson, thought Iris. Was he right?

As they walked away, not hand on hand, not arm in arm, but stiffly keeping step on the narrowing pavement, Iris had to stifle a nervous giggle at the thought of Antonella and Massi staring after them. When they were out of sight, in the wide space in front of the Pitti, she stopped.

'Shit,' she said. 'Massi.'

'What?' said Jackson warily.

'You were going to talk to him. Tell him about the painter she was meeting, your Claudio, Massi might know him, we might—'

Jackson stopped at the sound of her voice. 'Yeah,' he said slowly, 'I guess I should do that. Only—'

'Go back,' she said. 'Go back now.' They were opposite the bar where they'd drunk champagne that afternoon.

'OK,' said Jackson. 'Only—I kind of wanted to come with you.' He ducked his head, looking at her from under his fringe, not cocky, not too cool, just waiting. Wanting her to say yes.

'I'm fine,' she said, knowing that she would have to turn her back on him and walk away in the next three seconds if she wanted him to go. She stayed where she was.

'Run and tell him,' she said. 'I'll wait here for you.' And she watched him go, fast as a track star suddenly in his tattered sneakers down the Via Romana. He had his jacket pulled around himself, head down, and Iris watched him go, terrified and breathless with longing at the same time.

Her phone bleeped, new message. It was from Hiroko.

I am here, it read, *if u need a bed again 2nite. The girls want 2 talk.*

But it was too late.

I'm ok 4 2nite, she punched back in. *Can we talk 2moro?*

Message sent, it said. Iris felt suddenly winded at the thought of what she might have agreed to, and as if to confirm the feeling there was a sudden rush of wind that fluttered all the awnings along the façade facing the Pitti Palace, a soft ominous patter that seemed to come up towards Iris from the river. And as Jackson reappeared, still running, the rain began again.

❊ ❊ ❊

The bank statements, then the keys; and that wasn't all. But no address.

'They were in the drawer,' she said. 'Just at the back of the drawer.' Sandro nodded.

'I didn't really look at them,' Lucia Gentileschi said. 'I tried them in the door downstairs, but they didn't work, I just thought, old keys. I don't know what I thought; it didn't occur to me that—'

'No,' said Sandro, 'but they're something. They're going to help us.' He held the keys up, one by one. A Yale key, for a street door; a front door key, E-shaped; a small key, such as for the small padlock often used for a letterbox. A standard set of keys, just like Sandro's own; just like any Florentine's.

Weighing them in his hand, Sandro looked across at the desk; he could tell from the particular kind of mess Lucia Gentileschi had left there that she had begun her search methodically, then had lost control.

'We begin again,' he'd said gently.

'You,' Lucia said. 'Could you do it?'

There was nothing personal in the desk; nothing at all. There were insurance policies—on the apartment, on both their lives—pension documents, one relating to employment in Verona, another in Milan; the pensions were tiny. That stopped Sandro short; how could anyone live on such a pittance?

Lucia arrived with tea.

It was very far from his usual thimble of heart-jolting coffee, but Sandro took the cup anyway, a wide, shallow bowl-shaped cup. She moved a small table in front of the low sofa and set down another cup for herself and he could see that it caused her pain, the sight of two cups.

Sandro took a sip and set it down, went back to the desk. He looked at the piles he had made, looked back inside the rolltop.

'Nice desk,' he said, thinking.

'Claudio made it,' said Lucia. 'Out of elm. The only thing he ever made, ten years ago or so.'

'Really?' said Sandro, awestruck, '*Mamma mia.*' He put a hand to the curved wood, the joints, leaned down and looked inside. Ten years ago, he mused, and then he saw it, in the back, a marquetry square of coloured woods that might have been just decoration, but why put it there? Inside, at the back, where no one could see it? He put his head inside the desk.

'It took him a year to make,' said Lucia behind him. Sandro contorted his heavy shoulders to get his hand inside and ran his fingers over the marquetry, different coloured prism shapes; pressed it. It gave, and clicked back against his hand; the panel moved. It opened. Sandro jerked his head back.

'What was that?' said Lucia quietly.

'It's a...' Sandro cleared his throat, 'there seems to be something else. Hidden. A secret compartment—these desks, perhaps...'

Lucia nodded, minutely. 'Please look,' she said.

He reached in. The compartment was about the size of a folded newspaper but no more than a couple of centimetres deep; it contained a brown envelope. Sandro looked at Lucia.

'Please,' she said.

In the envelope was a passbook for a bank account. A deposit account in the name of Claudio Gentileschi, opened in 1997 with an initial payment of 1,500 euros, in cash. Sandro flipped to the last page; the most recent payment had been at the end of August, for 1,000 euros. But what stopped Sandro in his tracks was the total, with interest, at the end of August 2006: 800,000 euros. Sandro stared at the figure. Mutely, he held it out to Lucia.

She stared, shaking her head. 'No,' she said, 'no, no, no. That's not ours. That's not our money.'

'You didn't know about it?'

'We are not rich,' said Lucia. 'We live on Claudio's pension, we get by.'

Despite himself Sandro shook his head, thinking of the tiny sums the pensions yielded.

'Where did it come from?' she asked. 'How did he get it?' Sandro shook his head, not really answering her, looking through the pages. Payments every two, three months, always in cash, always about the same sum. No outgoings, but it was a high-interest account, there would be a penalty for withdrawals, and standing orders not allowed. He would have had to have the bills paid from the regular current account.

'I don't know,' he said. He closed the book, looked at the front; not the same bank as the current account, the Cassa di Risparmio di Firenze, but the Banca Toscana. Opened the front page again; a branch in San Frediano, in fact, the one on the corner of the Via del Leone and the Piazza Tasso.

Had Claudio been blackmailing somebody?

'There wasn't anything—any compensation?' he asked. 'After the war? I know there were some reparations...' He paused, 'Anyone—from then? From the war, who might have wanted to help him?'

'No,' said Lucia, 'no reparations to us, but Claudio wouldn't have taken the money if there had been. He would never—never—never have—'

And as he looked into her fierce pale face, the wild thoughts Sandro had been entertaining about the Holocaust, lurid stories of blackmail and ex-Nazis, suddenly seemed silly and melodramatic, much too easy. And in the silence that followed Sandro heard the rain start up again, soft at first but growing, a rush of wind. Raindrops slapped with sudden violence against the wide expanse of glass that Claudio must have envisioned full of light, and Lucia turned towards him.

'He was killed,' she said simply. 'Claudio was killed because of this money.'

Sandro felt suddenly very cold, as if he would not get warm, would never be warm again. Regular payments, a bank account, as though Claudio had a job, behind his wife's back. But what kind of a job would he have to hide from his wife?

'You're shivering,' said Lucia, and she put a hand to his cheek; he flinched at the cold of her fingertips.

'I'm fine,' he said.

'You have a fever,' she said. She put a hand to his jacket and squeezed the fabric, 'You're soaked,' she said. 'Why didn't you say? You could have—could have borrowed—'

'I'm fine,' Sandro repeated, as if all other words had suddenly deserted him. He made an effort. 'Leave this with me,' he said, holding up the bank book. 'If you can give me the keys, too?'

With compressed lips Lucia plucked the keys from the table and held them up to him.

'It can wait until tomorrow,' she said. 'My husband is dead; it's too late for him. I won't be responsible for making your wife into a widow, too.'

Sandro tried to laugh, an exaggeration. 'You do have a wife?' she said, smiling, and he managed a smile back.

'I'll call a cab,' he said, to placate her. 'OK?'

❀ ❀ ❀

Outside on the street Sandro stood in a borrowed raincoat three sizes too large for him, and waited for a cab. Claudio Gentileschi had been a big man, and as he pulled the coat around him an image of that broad back rolling in the grey water came back to Sandro with a shiver that was partly fever, and partly the horrors.

The horrors had come on with full force after his first dead body, when he'd been twenty-four and attending the scene of a traffic accident in the Borgo degli Albizzi. Nothing lurid; a boy knocked down by a *motorino*, struck his head on the kerb and was dead within ten minutes. The life had just gone out of him, without a sound, and that night Sandro, who had been first on the scene, had lain in his bed rigid with the effort of not seeing, all over again, the pallor that had come over the boy's face, the horrible slackness in his limbs. And how the boy's mother had come running, still in her apron, awkwardly down the street.

He'd had to learn that there was a trick to dealing with the dead—with dead bodies, at least—that was learned gradually, with repeated exposure. One had to be methodical, and at all costs to consider the corpse as just another kind of matter, no longer animate. Respect was important, however; he'd seen men jeer at corpses—policemen and others, and once a woman, kicking the body of her dead, violent husband as she was being handcuffed—and such people, in his experience, never returned to full humanity. Cells died off, and could not be replaced. Sandro had instead developed a kind of impassivity, the mask of a stolid, imperturbable officer who could keep going when the younger ones had to go outside to vomit.

Luisa used to say to him, long ago, 'I can't talk to you when you've got that face on.' He hadn't really understood what she meant; he'd thought, then, that it was exactly what was required; they weren't paid to have feelings.

But it wasn't some sort of technique, it was a trick, all along, an illusion; the girl's death fifteen years ago had proved that. Doggedly Sandro had passed information to her father, collating, photocopying, posting as efficiently as a machine, and all the time a connection had been loose, fizzing away. The feelings hadn't gone away; out of sight, they'd mutated into something altogether harder to manage. The horrors. In the rain

Sandro pulled the coat tighter, binding himself to stop the shivering. He realized that he wasn't sure what to do next.

Something bleeped in his pocket: a new message. Although Serena Hutton didn't grace him with any kind of message at all, in fact, only the name, Iris March, and a complicated mobile number with a foreign prefix. His heart sank at the thought of calling this English girl; not even twenty, probably, no Italian, she'd be immature, hopeless, idiotic. He pressed dial, and held the phone to his ear. It rang three, five, seven, times; he was just about to hang up when it clicked and he heard an English voice say, nervously, '*Pronto?*'

His taxi was now approaching down the narrow street; holding the phone against his ear with his shoulder, Sandro held up a hand. He climbed in, at the same time introducing himself, and hoped he didn't sound too out of it. All he wanted was a nice warm office and a secretary to connect him, but it wasn't going to happen, was it?

He put a hand over the receiver; 'Piazza Tasso,' he said to the driver. He'd promised Lucia Gentileschi he would go straight home. Sorry, Lucia, he thought, then took his hand off the receiver.

'Should I speak in English?' he said, with dread. He didn't know if he was up to it.

'It's all right. Italian is all right.'

Iris March sounded jumpy, on edge; he remembered that the carabiniere had called her hysterical. Sandro could hear background noise, men's voices talking, traffic sounds. Was she with some gang of friends, off out on the town?

This was useless, he thought; afterwards he was terrified by how close he had come to hanging up, and not hearing what Iris March had to say. But then she said, 'I'm so glad you called, I didn't know what to do.'

There was something in her voice that spoke to him—humility, directness, desperation—and the image he'd had of this girl fell away. Poor kid, he thought, and then it all came tumbling out, half in Italian, half in English, something about the missing girl's boyfriend, about a plan to leave the city, and then he couldn't believe what he was hearing. He wondered if he was more addled than he'd thought.

He made her repeat it twice; the name, twice.

'He's called Claudio, we think,' she said down the crackling line. 'An old man called Claudio.' And a fit of shivering almost took him at that moment, a shock reaction. He pressed his lips together while she spoke. 'We tried the number Jackson had for him, but there was no answer. There was that message you get, *in questo momento non e raggiungibile—*'

'A mobile number?' asked Sandro, and waited while she turned and said something to another person. In the background he heard a radio and he understood immediately that she was in a taxi too. He thought of their two taxis hissing through the wet night streets, towards their separate destinations, and he felt the fever rising in him.

She was back. 'Yes,' she said, 'a mobile.' There was another pause, then she read out the number to him. It would be dead as a doornail, wouldn't it, Claudio's mobile; Sandro wondered where it was, because it hadn't been on his body. She went on. 'He—this guy could have been the last person to see her, couldn't he?'

'And you have no idea where they were meeting?' Sandro felt a desperate longing for witnesses, sightings. Let it be far away from the Boboli, let someone have seen Claudio shake her hand and wave her goodbye, alive and well.

'I'm not even sure—well, no,' she said, sounding downcast. 'It's just—a kind of hunch, you know? Do you think we can find him, this Claudio?'

'Listen,' Sandro said carefully, 'I think it would be a good idea to have a meeting.'

This girl was the only person he had encountered so far who seemed to be worried about Veronica Hutton's disappearance; why did she also have to be the only one to make the connection between Veronica Hutton and Claudio Gentileschi?

'Maybe you're busy tonight?' he said, but even as he said it he knew it would be a mistake to do anything but go home and sleep; he was almost grateful when she said, after a long pause, 'Um, well, tomorrow morning would be better.'

'Sure,' he said. 'I'll call you. In the morning.' Suddenly, the morning seemed a long way off.

He gave her his number, concentrating hard on not letting his teeth chatter. He fished in his top pocket for the *tachipirina* he always kept there for headaches and dry-swallowed a couple. 'Don't worry,' he said, keeping his voice gentle. 'We'll find her.' And he heard her swallow a sob.

He fell back on the worn leather seat of the cab, ridiculously exhausted by the mere effort of the conversation. The car rolled on through the streets that gleamed in the sheeting rain; when eventually they drew up on the corner of the Piazza Tasso and the Via del Leone where Claudio Gentileschi's bank stood, it was coming down so relentlessly and with such force that it bounced back up off the flagstones, like hail.

The bank was a hundred metres from Sandro's office: if he'd set up there a month earlier, he might himself have seen Claudio Gentileschi going in and out. It was closed; wearily Sandro looked at his watch; six-thirty now, of course it was bloody closed, what did he expect? He realized that he had had some idea of standing on the pavement outside it and watching, waiting for the gut instinct that had always served him well to tell him which passer-by might recognize the crumpled photograph of Claudio Gentileschi he had in his wallet.

But the streets were deserted in the rain, and slumped, feverish, in the back of the cab Sandro felt as if every skill he'd learned as a policeman, every instinct he'd developed over thirty years, had deserted him.

'This it?' said the cab driver over his shoulder, startling him back to himself.

'Ah, could you,' Sandro grappled with the situation, 'give me a minute?' Then added, 'Wait there.' The driver shrugged, tapped the meter. 'Fine by me,' he said. 'Take your time.'

Sandro stood outside the bank's dark windows and peered inside. There were close to a million euros of Claudio's money in there, in this dingy little back-street branch. He pressed his back against the façade in a fruitless attempt to stay out of the wet; this was the place, though. These humble San Frediano streets were Claudio's secret life. This was his bank, the Cestello was his local; his other place must be somewhere around here.

His *telefonino* rang again; he thought he should go to his office and dry out, but he found he couldn't move. With fumbling fingers he retrieved the phone and found himself talking again to the pasty-faced carabiniere he'd spoken to on the way out of the station that afternoon.

'The old guy?' said the carabiniere without preamble. Giacomini was the desk-officer's name, thought Sandro blearily, how come he could remember that when everything else was fuzzy? 'The one you asked me to look for on the CCTV?'

'Yes?' said Sandro, his heart sinking; it was like opening an envelope you knew contained bad news.

He was right. 'Yup,' said Giacomini, 'found him all right, that was some hunch.'

'And?'

'In, at the Annalena gate, 11.20.'

'Out again?'

Nope,' said Giacomini. 'Not so far. But he could've—'

'Yeah, I know,' said Sandro with a heavy heart. 'He must have come out of the Porta Romana gate.' Because he did come out, that much they knew. What he'd wanted was proof Claudio had left the Boboli alone.

'Looking like, sort of blank, he was, on his way in,' said Giacomini, musing. 'On another planet.'

'Yeah,' said Sandro. 'He had Alzheimer's. He felt a surge of empathy for poor Claudio, like some big wounded bull elephant blundering through a habitat turned hostile, his world growing unrecognizable around him. Would that face tell him anything? That he'd had some kind of brainstorm, and had abducted or hurt or killed a young woman, then concealed her body? He thought of the gardens, all those woodstores and toolsheds. Or taken her off with him, to his other place? Taken her back to the bolthole his wife had known nothing about, until now.

'Can I come in and get a look?'

Giacomini sighed. 'Not tonight,' he said, 'no way, I'm off in twenty minutes. Monday morning?'

Monday morning? Monday morning will be too late, thought Sandro, because he was in full possession of the knowledge, dull and sinister, that every hour that passed, every minute, made it less likely Veronica Hutton would be found alive. It was how it was, with abductions; it was how it had been when Lucas Marsh's daughter went missing from that swimming pool nearly twenty years ago. And just as he had on that occasion, he had to fight the despair that rose in him, the nagging voice that said, It's too late already. You're wasting your time.

As if he heard something in the silence, Giacomini sighed. 'How about I email you the stills?' he said. 'You'll have given us your email address? Can do that, wouldn't take a minute.'

Not about to admit that computer technology was too much for him at the best of times, Sandro gave in. 'OK,' he said. 'Sure.' He needed help, and he appreciated the hand the man was holding out to him. 'Thanks.'

As he hung up, Sandro caught the cab driver's curious gaze at him up through the window, open for the cigarette he'd lit. He felt the shivering rise up again, and struggled to control it in front of the man. He looked away, trying to will a miracle. An answer.

Across the way, the scrubby grass of the Piazza Tasso contained another children's playground; though this one was newer, it looked just as dismal under the shroud of rain. On one of the swings the hooded figure of some large child swung back and forth monotonously in the pouring rain, while his frail-looking mother bent over him, trying to persuade him home.

He needed help. As he stared blindly at the scene, suddenly Sandro felt entirely overwhelmed. Lucia's silent grief; the nagging terror for a missing child; the brute intractability of the facts, of hidden money and secret apartments and lost handbags; he was drowning under it. And the biggest, blackest wave, rising far out to sea and rushing towards him, was Monday morning, and a tiny lump in Luisa's breast: his breast, his pillow, his beloved.

I am afraid, he thought. I am afraid of death.

For a moment it seemed to Sandro that it was simply too much for him: he would send the cab away, stand in the rain like a vagrant until he dropped and someone else could take over.

As he stared, the woman at the swing straightened and came away from the intractable child and through the rain Sandro saw that it wasn't a child, but a young man, holding a comic book up to his face. And as the woman hurrying towards him raised her hand, trying to get his cab, that she wasn't anyone's mother. It was Giulietta Sarto.

'Sandro?' she said, dashing across the road.

'Do you know him?' said Sandro, staring at the young man on the swing, wondering if he was delirious.

'It's the funny kid,' she said, impatiently. 'Comic-book Boy, everyone knows him, Jesus Christ, Sandro, look at you!' She took both his shoulders in her hands.

'What was he talking to you about?' he said, wondering if he was making sense.

'Oh, dogs, asking me about a guy I know—well, I guess we both know him—keeps asking if he's got a dog. The kid's obsessed, but he's harmless. He's worried about the goddamn dog, I tell you, there is no dog, I don't know what he's talking about. What I'm worried about is you, Sandro. What the hell are you up to? You're soaked to the bone.' She leaned in closer, staring into his face as she used to when she was in rehab, and they'd told him it was because she had to relearn the idea of personal space. 'You're not well.'

Sandro found he didn't have it in him to agree or not. He did feel very odd.

'This your cab?' she asked, and the driver answered for him, 'Get on with it, I can't hang about all day,' flicking his cigarette away into the gutter.

'I'm taking you home to Luisa,' she said, and before he could argue she opened the car door and shoved him inside.

In the warm dark of the cab, the radio burbled, about the rain, and an anniversary. In the Casentino a mudslide had buried a small hamlet, and above Lucca a weir had collapsed under the weight of water; the president of the republic would be visiting the stricken village.

Sandro heard the driver snort. 'Lot of good he'll be,' he said. The voices continued, an old *contadino* talking about 1966; a government spokesman brushed him aside, talking over him. Flood defences were holding, he said with weighty assurance, the rain should ease overnight, although more was forecast in the morning. Tomorrow there would be no repeat of November, 1966.

Flood defences holding for the time being; no, repeat, the rain should ease—the words went round and round in Sandro's head, absolving him. The defences were holding.

'Tell me about Comic-book Boy,' he mumbled to Giulietta Sarto. 'I think I'd like a proper introduction.' From the expression on her face he could tell he'd stopped making sense.

❀ ❀ ❀

At three in the morning by the small, leather-bound clock on her bedside table—the clock that Ma had given her when she'd gone away to school at thirteen—Iris raised herself on her elbow, leaned across Jackson's humped shoulder beside her in the narrow bed, and whispered.

'Jackson?' Then, louder, 'Jackson?' He made a noise, still asleep.

'I want you to go,' she said, in her normal voice, and waited, her back against the wall. After a minute Jackson sat up beside her, alert in the moonlight but not all there, still actually asleep even as he answered her.

'OK,' he said, unquestioning, fumbling for his trainers. ''Sssa time?'

'Late,' she said, and he just nodded.

'OK.' Now he was awake.

He swayed as he stood over her, shoes on, belt buckle undone. He felt in his pocket for his keys; she heard them jingle. 'You all right?'

'Mmm-hmm,' said Iris, meaning to say, of course I am, but not able to find the right words, the right tone. He leaned down towards her but she turned her face away so he got her cheek. She felt his dry lips brush it.

The door closed behind him but she could hear him on the stairs, then the street gate rattled and clanged, a deep silence settling like fog in his wake, filling the flat's dark corners.

Even though the whole point of telling him to go had been that Iris would get some sleep, at last, with the clang of the gate her thoughts set off again. She wondered where he was going back to, at three in the morning. She didn't know where he lived, or who he lived with; she knew he could get angry and he had a police record in the States, and she knew he had an iPhone, and that was about it. She knew what his skin smelled like, now. What have I done? she wondered.

The detective guy had called as they were getting into the cab on the way home. Sandro Cellini. She had felt Jackson next to her as she spoke into the phone, listening intently as she tried to remember to say everything that was important. She'd felt breathless as if she was being interviewed, more nervous than when she'd been speaking to the carabiniere earlier; it all seemed so absolutely hopeless. Searching for needles in haystacks, old painters called Claudio in a city full of painters, looking for Ronnie's mystery man when he could have been any one of dozens of playboy Italians in blazers, American college boys in Bermudas or even a sculptor with his own studio.

When Jackson could have made the whole thing up, because she only had his word for it. And Jackson had been the last person to see Ronnie.

She told herself the detective was taking it seriously, though there had been long silences on the phone; maybe he was writing it all down. She had to believe in him because he was their last chance, Ronnie was slipping through their fingers and only

Sandro Cellini could catch her. She hoped he had been writing it all down. She had felt Jackson's long, cool fingers slip between her own as she spoke.

When he had spoken the detective had sounded tired; he really should talk to her, face to face, he'd said. They had agreed on tomorrow, both of them reluctant but they didn't really have any choice, did they? What could they have done in the dark, worn out? A whole, long night, wherever Ronnie was, whether she was inside or out in the rain—and Iris had to stop that train of thought. It wasn't cold, Iris told herself, it was wet but not yet cold. Not winter yet.

Although if she was dead, she wouldn't feel the cold. Iris saw the rain falling on a cold cheek, streaking the brown and gold hair across Ronnie's dead skin, in undergrowth. Perhaps it was too late; she had said goodnight and maybe the detective, Sandro Cellini, had heard the despair in her voice because he had said, 'Don't worry.' Then he'd added, 'We'll find her.'

She had held Jackson's hand the rest of the way back in the taxi but it had been Sandro Cellini's words that had stopped her feeling alone. Until they had arrived in the Piazza d'Azeglio, that was, and Jackson had paid the cab, and they were inside the deep dark of the apartment, alone together and both holding their breath for what would happen next. And then she had stopped thinking about Sandro Cellini, or Ronnie, or anything at all.

Afterwards, of course, it had all come rushing back at her, in the darkness, and she began talking, quickly, out of guilt.

They had been crushed against each other on the narrow bed as she talked into the darkness, Jackson silent beside her.

'You wouldn't have fixed up for Ronnie to meet this Claudio if you'd—well, if you thought there was anything funny about him. Would you?' Her voice was small, pleading.

There was a silence. 'Look, Iris,' he said, with resignation, 'I don't know, that's the truth. I mean, sure, I wouldn't have knowingly put her on to some old creep—I didn't think he was a creep. I liked him a lot; I thought Ronnie'd be blown away by him.' His voice was hollow.

'But?'

'But you never know about people, do you? Not really.' He sounded low and tired and desperate.

Iris took his hand, under the thin cover; she knew she should just leave it, they both needed the rest, but she couldn't. 'And what about the boyfriend?' she said. 'I don't understand why we didn't know anything about this boyfriend? Why didn't she tell anyone about him?'

There had been a silence; beside her Iris felt Jackson fighting sleep.

'Maybe it's just none of us would have known him,' he had said eventually, 'so no point bragging.'

'And why didn't he come to the party, then? She could have showed him off.'

'Busy guy, maybe.' His voice had been drifting by this point. 'Some place else to be.'

And he had rolled away a little, and was gone, holding her hand tucked under the dead weight of his arm. And Iris had stayed awake staring into the dark, while things made less and less sense. Until at three she had given in.

And now she was alone, and there was something else to think about, she realized. How much time had it taken? Iris had no idea. Not long at all, then a long time lying awake. She couldn't imagine ever doing it again.

He's gone, now stop thinking, Iris instructed herself. And fell instantly asleep.

In the pre-dawn sky beyond the tall, shuttered windows, the cloud rolled down again, and softly the rain began to fall.

Chapter Fourteen

'YOU SAT BOLT upright,' said Luisa, setting the water glass down carefully on the bedside table, 'and you said, that's it. I've got it, you said.'

Sandro groaned, and raised himself on an elbow to drink the water. He found he was very thirsty. 'I don't suppose I said what it was I'd got, did I?'

It had seemed like a very long night; under the influence of the fever Sandro felt as though he'd travelled enormous distances in his sleep. He felt completely drained of energy, but the fever was gone.

They'd got back to an empty apartment. Giulietta Sarto had done everything, paid the cab, fished in Sandro's pocket for his key, got him upstairs and shoved him into the bathroom while she brewed some potion up for him of sticks and leaves and ginger. He had heard her rooting through the cupboards as he stood under the shower, trying to get warm. She told him Luisa had given her the recipe for it, good for fevers. Giulietta had had a lot of fevers after rehab and the halfway house, during the six months she practically lived with him and Luisa. Listening to the hiss of gas under the pan and the clatter of cups, Sandro had twice opened his mouth to tell her that Luisa had a hospital appointment on Monday, but the words would not come out.

While he drank the disgusting concoction Giulietta had scolded him. He'd protested that he had two jobs on now, he couldn't afford to stay at home just because of a bit of rain. He had fumbled with the words, and the more robust he tried to sound, the more defeated he had felt. He hadn't thought it would be like this, he'd tried to tell her. It was a different kettle of fish being in a police force; he thought of Falco, delegating, a whole team to send off here there and everywhere, not to mention all the comforts of a police station. He was on his own, and on the outside.

'It'll look different in the morning,' Giulietta had said. 'Come on.'

And there were things he had wanted to ask Giulietta, too, he knew that, only he couldn't think of what they were right now, and as he'd tried Sandro had found himself falling silent at the table.

By the time Luisa's key had turned in the lock Sandro had been past worrying about what she would think, he had only wanted to see her. His teeth had chattered as she leaned down close to him and felt his forehead and his chest, clicking her tongue in exasperation. She had felt around his neck for swollen glands, interrogated him as to sore throats and chest pain but he had just shaken his head. 'I'm fine,' he'd croaked.

'No, you're not,' Luisa had said, fishing for *tachipirina* in a drawer, pouring him a glass of water and then another, rubbing his arms with her strong hands to stop his shivering. Giulietta had stood in the corner, but Luisa hadn't told her to go, and after he had climbed into bed and felt the paracetamol uncramp his aching body, he had heard their voices in the kitchen, talking too softly for him to hear. And then he had fallen asleep.

'Did you tell her?' he said now, upright in the bed and looking at Luisa in her Sunday morning outfit, white towel gown and big soft slippers, hair sticking straight up.

'I showed her,' said Luisa defiantly, folding her arms across her soft white front.

'You showed her—it? The—the—' The word stuck in his throat. 'How did she take it?'

Luisa snorted, 'Giulietta? She was fine.' She shook her head at him.

'People worry, you know,' she said. 'They think they don't want to look directly at things, because they're frightened. But the more you know, the less you worry. The more you know, the more you can just—get on.'

Sandro leaned back on the pillows, exhausted by her logic.

'That's why it's harder for you than it is for me,' Luisa said, plumping herself down on the bed, a breath of her clean sweet smell reaching him. 'It's why you got ill. You can't do anything, you start to just—burn up from the inside. I know you.

'I thought this job would be good for you,' she went on. 'I'm sorry, it's my fault, piling it on, that missing girl...' She looked tired suddenly. 'I didn't think.'

'No,' said Sandro sharply. 'Stop it. Of course it's good for me. It's work, isn't it? It was just...' And he paused, trying to pull his thoughts together. The night's fever seemed to have churned everything up, all the possibilities he'd found himself considering yesterday, the names and connections and leads, and now they'd been left scattered at random in his head, like junk.

He sighed. 'It's different, being on my own,' he said wearily. 'Without Pietro.'

'So call Pietro,' said Luisa, getting to her feet. 'Get help. For heaven's sake, *we'll* help, Giulietta and me.'

'I spoke to the room-mate last night,' he said, and it came back to him with a dull impact, like being thumped in the chest. 'The missing girl's room-mate.'

'And?' Luisa looked at him warily.

Sandro compressed his lips, let out an explosive sigh, and told her.

'What?' said Luisa incredulously, sitting back down. 'She thinks the girl was meeting Claudio?' She shook her head. 'Ah. Not good.'

'What's your theory?' he asked with dull resignation.

Luisa set her hands on her hips and regarded him. 'The worst-case scenario? Claudio Gentileschi met the girl, made a pass at her or worse, hurt her or worse, then walked into the river and killed himself out of remorse.'

She brushed her hands against each other in a cleansing motion. 'Don't look like that, like a dog that's been beaten. That's the scenario you haven't wanted to look too hard at, isn't it? Because you like Claudio Gentileschi's wife, number one, and by extension, you like him. You don't want to believe he's capable of such a thing.'

Sandro gazed at her with something approaching awe. He swallowed. 'I would have to be very sure of that scenario before I took it to the Carabinieri,' he said. 'Or to Lucia Gentileschi, or indeed to Veronica Hutton's mother, even if she is a ballbreaker.' He passed a hand over his head in despair. 'But you're right. From the minute I knew they both went missing on the same day, I thought, what if?'

'It's like cancer,' said Luisa, and he didn't blink at the word. 'Being afraid of it doesn't make it more or less likely to be real. It's either true or it's not; the thing to do is have a close look at the facts, then act accordingly.'

She got to her feet. 'Try to prove he did it,' she said. 'Don't keep trying to prove he didn't.'

Obediently, Sandro swung his legs out of bed; they felt like jelly. Luisa set her hands on her hips. 'Because I don't like my theory any more than you do, and I think we have to find some holes in it, yes?'

'Yes.'

'And Giulietta's coming over to check up on you in less than an hour,' said Luisa as she turned her back on him. 'So if I was you I'd get up and start looking better, or else.'

They sat across the table from each other with a little stack of paperwork between them. The police photographs, statements and post-mortem report on Claudio's death; the thin cardboard file Falco had given him on Veronica Hutton's disappearance; the battered copy of *La Nazione* which included the report of the discovery of her bag.

Luisa put some sweet cake from the bar on a plate, set a pot of coffee on the iron stand and poured a cup for Sandro. He sipped cautiously; in his newly purified state, it had a kick like a horse.

'I wish we had it—more narrowed down,' he said. 'If only there was another sighting of her, if only we knew where she was supposed to be going. The room-mate said she'd planned something, had a cover story that she was going to the country to stay with friends, only it turns out the friends are in England. The room-mate thought maybe it was going to be a romantic couple of nights in a hotel, I don't know—the lakes, somewhere—'

'Wherever,' said Luisa, impatiently. 'So where's this guy now? If she didn't turn up? Why hasn't he been asking questions?' She wrote again. *Boyfriend?*

'Of course,' said Sandro slowly, 'one reason he hasn't been asking questions is that they're together having their romantic break. She's alive and well and drinking spumante on some hotel terrace somewhere.'

'Yes,' said Luisa drily. 'That would be nice. Even if it did make us all look idiots, running around chasing our tails. No.'

Sandro put his head in his hands. 'We have to assume the worst.'

Luisa sighed. 'Yes, I suppose we do.' She frowned. 'So the boyfriend could be panicking. Keeping his head down.'

'It's possible,' said Sandro, nodding.

'Or it could be him. Isn't it usually someone you know? Most women killed by their boyfriends? Or their husbands?'

'Yes,' said Sandro, 'only this relationship, if it ever existed, seems to have been so top secret no one has seen hide or hair of the guy.' He puffed out his cheeks. 'The Carabinieri have even been through her emails, all that stuff.'

'So we're back to poor old Claudio, suspect number one.'

Luisa reached across the table for his hand. 'Call the room-mate,' she said. 'Fix up to see her. Like you promised. Check out the place they live; you might find something about this boyfriend they've missed.'

Reluctantly, Sandro dialled. It was strange; it might be Sunday morning but for the first time since he'd left the force, Sandro felt like he was getting to work. He wondered if it was always going to be like this, from now on. Irregular hours, and

Luisa acting as his foreman, cracking the whip. He didn't alto-gether hate the idea, but a part of him was relieved when the metallic voice told him Iris March's number wasn't available. It was the bastard thing about Florence, mobiles going in and out of signal, blocked behind stone palaces and towers. It would never be a modern city.

Luisa looked frustrated. 'Damn,' she said. 'Well, on to the next thing, let's work without her, for the moment. Come on. Let's say the girl was meeting Claudio Gentileschi; where?'

'Boboli,' said Sandro straight off. 'Obviously. She was on camera coming in through the Annalena gate at 11.25; he'd come in five minutes earlier.'

'Right,' said Luisa thoughtfully. Public, but not public; not an entirely safe place for a girl to arrange to meet a man she didn't know. 'Her friend Jackson knew him,' said Sandro, in mitigation. 'And he was eighty-one, for heaven's sake.' Luisa pursed her lips judiciously.

'Strong guy, though,' she said. 'Big guy. She wasn't to know that.'

He conceded defeat. 'Yes.'

'I'm playing devil's advocate, *caro*,' said Luisa, a hand across the table on his forearm. 'On the plus side, he came out on his own. And there's been no—body found in the Boboli.'

'No,' said Sandro, feeling a stirring of hope, almost imme-diately crushed. 'But the Boboli is full of hiding places.'

'And the Boboli's heaving with state employees,' said Luisa, 'wardens, gardeners, school leavers, old men looking for a quiet place for a sit down. They'd have found her.' She paused. 'And your theory is a man with dementia, an ordinary guy, has managed to hide a girl's body so well no one has found it?'

Sandro stayed quiet, trying not to smile. She was so smart.

Luisa went on, 'What do I know? But they usually find dead bodies fairly quickly, don't you? You, the police, I mean?'

Sandro nodded. 'If not premeditated. And you're right, not many people have the right…temperament. To hide a body.' The glimmer of hope kindled again; hope made things harder, in some ways. 'She might have been alive when he left her. He—or someone else—might have put her somewhere. While they thought what to do.'

Luisa nodded. 'That happens, does it?' She appealed to him. 'You mean, by some random person?'

'Or by the boyfriend,' said Sandro, reluctantly; it seemed too much to hope. 'It's the cock-up theory, you know; things go wrong—the victim is a witness, perhaps, to wrongdoing, very often has been raped for example, and it's a short-term measure, shut them up.'

He considered. 'In rape cases, there's a motive for keeping them alive, but in fact most people have a strong resistance to killing. There are cases where victims are confined, held against their will for weeks, while their abductor tries to work out what to do. There was that old man in Abruzzo, last month, locked a child in his garden shed because he'd—exposed himself to her.'

They both fell silent then, thinking of another old man. Luisa was the first to speak.

'D'you think Claudio might have done that?' she said reluctantly. 'Gone a bit loopy, locked her up somewhere, then, I don't know, forgotten where he'd put her?'

Spoken out loud, it stopped Sandro in his tracks; he put a hand out towards the keys on the table and closed them in his fist. 'It's possible,' he said slowly. 'But Lucia Gentileschi says there's never been any trouble at all in the marriage, say, with other women. Nothing. They were everything to one another.' The keys dug into his flesh.

'And you believe her?'

'She's an exceptional woman,' said Sandro. 'She's like you; she's completely straight, not the kind to deceive herself. If there'd been trouble she'd have told me, and I'm pretty sure she'd have known.'

'OK,' said Luisa. 'Let's assume that he wasn't a womanizer; to make a move on a girl young enough to be his granddaughter—great-granddaughter—would have been completely out of character.'

'Alzheimer's does funny things to people,' said Sandro, reluctantly.

'But he wasn't at that stage yet, from what I understand. Just getting a bit vague. Not at the stage when he thinks—and I know this is what's going through your head—he's still nineteen himself, and Veronica Hutton's in his league.'

'Maybe not,' said Sandro cautiously. 'But—he had the means. He had the place. There was this other life.'

'What?' said Luisa. He told her, all about the keys, the payments for gas and electricity and water.

'An apartment to—take women to? Or something?'

Sandro tried to look at the facts; he thought of the barman telling him about Sandro's regular habits, how he never talked to anyone as a rule, how he came in for his whisky sour on the dot, always alone. 'I don't think so,' he said cautiously. 'No money spent on heating the place.'

The only sound audible was the rusty tick of the clock.

'A—a bolthole, then.'

'It would be good to find it,' said Luisa carefully. 'I think—it might rule him out.'

'Yes,' said Sandro, not saying the obvious. Outside in the street an argument erupted, along with a honking of horns. 'We need to find the place.'

Luisa wrote. 'And then there's the last sighting of Claudio,' said Sandro. 'Around one-thirty, late for lunch.'

'The barman?' asked Luisa, frowning. 'No, the nurse, the autistic boy saw him talking to the nurse?'

Sandro had forgotten he'd told her about the nurse. She was sharp.

He nodded. 'And then the boy saw him disappear down the bank. That nurse must have tried to help. Maybe she'll come forward; it's only been a few days, really. Maybe she said something to him.'

'Maybe,' said Luisa.

He had his head in his hands again, in an effort to remember. It seemed hopeless, trying to interpret what an autistic boy thought he'd seen, or heard; the world must look so different to Comic-book Boy. Who else had called him that?

'Come on,' said Luisa gently, 'Giulietti'll be here in twenty minutes. What's the plan?'

'Ask her about the boy,' he said. 'Giuli knows the autistic boy. She was talking to him last night. Or did I dream that?' He sat up. 'I remembered,' he said, astonished.

'What?'

He concentrated. 'In the night, when I thought I'd solved it. I must have been delirious. It was all to do with the autistic boy and the art school, I dreamed him at the art school, working as an assistant. But...' and he held up a finger '... it wasn't all nonsense. I remembered where I'd heard of the school before, the famous Massi family. What was it you said? About the wife?'

Uncomprehending, Luisa stared at him.

'That she had a thing about shoes?' she said. 'Always trying on crazy high heels?'

Sandro frowned. 'And went away without buying?'

'Actually no,' said Luisa. 'You wouldn't know it to look at her but I think that woman must have a wardrobe just for her shoes. Though where she gets the money...'

'Yes,' said Sandro slowly. 'That's it; you said, the school must be doing well. There was some kind of investigation, only I don't remember the details. A few years back, the Guardia di Finanza looked into the business. Thought they were doing a bit too well, considering it was just a little art school.'

'And?'

'I can't remember,' said Sandro frustrated. 'It wasn't a police case. The Guardia don't involve us unless they have to, obviously.' He frowned. 'I guess they didn't have enough evidence; the school still seems to be going.'

He thought there was just a trace of scepticism in the look Luisa gave him. 'Could be nothing,' he said apologetically. 'I mean, it could be just the standard operation for fleecing foreigners, couldn't it? Plenty of money in art schools.'

'Could be,' said Luisa, and he sighed at her cautious tone. At the sound, she said, 'But it's something, isn't it? A bad smell, always worth going after the source of the bad smell.' A third note went down on the paper, Massi. 'Plus, of course, you really should have talked to him already, about the girl. *In loco parentis*, isn't he?'

There was a silence. Luisa stood and began to clean out the coffee pot and refill it. They'd had that little pot since they were married, though it had been through a couple of dozen rubber seals; he watched her run the tine of a fork around the seal, fill the base up to the valve and build a little mound of coffee, the Vesuvio as they called it in Naples, her hand cupped around it to stop the coffee spilling. Women should be put in charge of most things, he reflected. She spoke to him over her shoulder.

'So why don't you go and talk to someone there? Better than sitting on our hands, isn't it? Call Pietro. Call the guy himself, dammit, call Massi.'

'But it's Sunday,' he said, losing hope almost immediately. 'I'll call the school tomorrow. I guess he'll talk to me.'

Luisa gave him a look.

'You bet he'll talk to you,' she said. 'He's responsible for that girl, and if you can't get hold of the room-mate...I'm sure I can get hold of his home number—Badigliani'll have it, but why not try the school, anyhow? You've got nothing to lose. And if I was married to that woman, I'd go to the office on a Sunday, too.'

'I'll call Pietro, first,' he said, giving in. He went into the sitting room they never used and dialled his old friend from the stiff, slippery silk of the sofa they never sat on. What Pietro said was interesting. But Sandro wasn't going to rush this one.

'I think I will call the school after all,' he said to Luisa, who beamed her encouragement from the sink. At least all this is keeping her happy, he thought.

But as Sandro took out his phone again, it was already ringing. On the other end Iris March was breathless.

'You tried to call me?'

But before he could say anything she went on. 'You have to come over,' she said.

Chapter Fifteen

IRIS HADN'T EVEN been looking, when she found it. Or at least, she'd only been looking for a raincoat, and despite all her best intentions she had been thinking about Jackson, wandering with cold feet through the apartment in the flat, grey morning light. Catching sight of herself in the huge spotted mirror in the *salotto* and inspecting herself, to see if she looked any different.

She'd woken at eleven to see that it was raining again, relentless, falling straight down and blurring the view, the green dome and the distant hills of Fiesole. It was as if Florence was getting a whole winter's rain in one week. She stared out at it, and shivered. *What did you think you were doing?* she heard Ma scold. *You're all I've got. I don't want you pregnant before you've even started. You hardly know him.*

Iris thought of how Jackson had been, all yesterday; his fist banging down on the table, the sudden coldness, the evasion. The busy parents in Vermont with their luxury car franchise might as well have been aliens for all they had in common with Ma, pottering about the galleries in Aix, trying to make ends meet. And there was the police record he wouldn't tell her about, and the afternoon after he'd said goodbye to Ronnie—or so he said—when he hadn't come to school. He had avoided telling her about that, too.

I like him, Ma. She tried the phrase out in her head. It sounded lame; the kind of thing any number of girls said.

You hardly know him.

I can't stay your baby for ever, Ma. Iris put her head in her hands.

Her phone bleeped, somewhere in the flat. It took her a full five minutes to find it, and she was ridiculously breathless when she saw the words, *New message; read now?* She opened it.

You have one missed call, and then the number. Damn it, thought Iris, that bloody signal that comes and goes, wiped out by a draught or a passing bus. Then she looked at the number and recognized it as the detective Sandro Cellini's and felt slightly less alone; she wasn't sure if that was a good thing or not. She needed to stand on her own two feet. She decided she would get dressed and call him.

There was another message, though; Hiroko. *Maybe today?* it read, plaintively.

All right, thought Iris guiltily, maybe today, hell. She needed to get out, and suddenly the thought of the dim, scented apartment and Hiroko's anxious face was an oppressive one. She flipped the phone shut.

She looked back at herself in the big rusted mirror. There were shadows under her eyes, that was all. No older, no thinner.

Slowly Iris got dressed, staring through the window at the rain; her clothes weren't up to it, her coat still damp from yesterday. The rain seemed to have a special quality of wetness, hyper-drenching. She thought there might be some kind of mac in the big hall cupboard. This was heavy, ancient, made of carved black wood. There was a door at either end and a central panel; one door opened on a cleaning apron and a stack of candles, the other on a row of clattering hangers and a smell of mothballs.

Then she saw that the central panel contained a small knob of blackened brass, almost indistinguishable from the carved rose around it. It was stiff, but when she yanked hard it opened, and suddenly there it was. Innocent as anything, a plain black nylon holdall; a weekend bag, packed and ready to go.

It was heavy; Ronnie never had been good at travelling light. Iris tugged at the straining zip and there, sitting on top of a brand-new and expensive watercolour set, was a long rectangle of printed card; Iris pulled it out carefully and looked at it. It was an effort to process the information it contained, at first: a first-class return air ticket to Taormina, Sicily, leaving at 15.40 on the evening of Tuesday November 1.

Fifteen-forty? She'd have had to head straight there, practically. Even Ronnie'd have needed to check in by two.

A return. Ronnie had been due to fly back to Florence on Friday afternoon; she should have landed at three, in the rain; she would have been back in the flat at around the time the police came looking for her at the school, with her bag. Only she never caught the flight in the first place. Alive or dead—and at the thought Iris's stomach lurched, as if she was really understanding it for the first time—Ronnie was still in Florence. And as it lurched there came a guilty stab of relief, because Jackson had been telling her the truth; there had been a bag.

Then, as she stared down at the ticket, what Iris thought was, this is what he was looking for. Whoever had come to the flat had been looking for this bag. He'd been through the flat and found nothing; he'd tried to wipe the computer, and he'd gone. He had her keys, that was how he'd got in; he knew where she lived.

Could it have been a double bluff? Could Jackson have come to the apartment looking for the bag, and, having failed to find it, covered his tracks? Suddenly it was as if that draught was blowing through the gloomy flat all over again; it was as if there was whispering in its dark corners.

She fought panic, rooted to the spot in the dark chill of the hall, and then it came to her that she wasn't alone. There was someone. 'Don't worry,' he'd said last night, like the father she'd never had. 'We'll find her.' She took out her phone and called Sandro Cellini.

❀ ❀ ❀

Luisa stood in the warm ticking quiet of her own home and wondered what she would do when all this was over. Tomorrow still seemed a long time away: the appointment at the breast clinic at Careggi; the bus she would take to get there; the argument she would have with Sandro about whether he should drive her.

The parking was madness at Careggi. Stupid to take the car, this wasn't an emergency.

Sifting through the papers on the table, the photograph, the newspaper cutting, Luisa put them away in the brown file and slotted it into the big tote she took to work. Giulietta would be here in a minute, and there were things to do. She could sort this Scuola Massi business out, for a start. She reached for the phone book.

It turned out that Luisa had been right, of course; Paolo Massi did spend plenty of time in the office, whether it was to get away from his wife or not. Plenty of men did, she supposed. Dottore Massi wasn't on the premises when she called—Luisa explained the situation instead to a stern-voiced woman who told her warily that she was his deputy, Antonella something—but he would be in the studio later.

'May I make an appointment for Mr Cellini to speak with him?' said Luisa, inhabiting the part of tough secretary with enjoyment. 'Yes, of course, it is Sunday, I understand that, but clearly this is a matter of some importance.' She waited while the woman blustered to indicate offence, mild outrage, suspicion, and finally capitulated.

'Twelve o'clock?' she suggested, looking at the clock. Sandro had left at eleven; twelve would give him a chance of some lunch, afterwards, maybe with her and Giulietta. 'That will be fine.' She hung up, and texted Sandro with the details.

The doorbell shrilled furiously; Giulietta. Only Giulietta Sarto leaned on the bell like she wanted to wake the dead.

'The bird has flown,' Luisa said as she opened the door. 'Sorry about that, Giuli, but you know what he's like when he's on a case.' It was a nice thought, Sandro back on a case.

She smiled broadly into Giulietta's exasperated face, and reached behind the door for her coat. 'I thought we might go for a walk instead.' Giulietta, already dripping as she stood on the threshold, now looked at her as if she'd lost her marbles. 'Boboli, I thought.'

❀ ❀ ❀

The Piazza d'Azeglio, of course, Sandro knew of old, its massive blackened façades and the old families nursing their declining fortunes behind them, but Iris March came as a surprise.

There was a light on behind the door to Giovanna Badigliani's dismal ground-floor apartments, but Sandro walked straight past, having no wish to waste time with the poisonous old creature. At the clang of the ancient elevator grille as he reached the first floor Iris March opened her door and they were face to face.

The first thing he had not expected was that she would be beautiful. The city was overflowing with nice-looking foreign girls, he was used to them: pretty teenagers with streaked hair and bare arms and youth on their side, but beautiful was something else. Her broad, pale face, her freckles, her big, light eyes that slanted at an odd angle to the long straight nose, the width of her white shoulders like a Greek marble from the sea bed; the girl standing in front of him was in a class of her own. It occurred to him that not everyone would find her beautiful, but Sandro was glad Luisa wasn't there with her beady eye to note how he fumbled for the first words he had to say to Iris March.

He spoke in the best English he could manage; it might be clumsy, but it somehow covered his awkwardness.

'Miss March? I am pleased to meet you, finally.'

As she led him impatiently inside the big cold dark hallway, Sandro had time to tell himself to grow up and find his tongue. And then when she pointed at the ticket lying on top of the holdall, Iris March's beauty was forgotten entirely. This meant something more urgent.

'She'd have had to be at the airport at two,' he said, and Iris March nodded eagerly.

'Yes,' she said, 'that's what I thought. It means—'

'It means we know that whatever happened to her happened between 11.25 and, say, one o'clock. When she'd have left for the airport, assuming she was going to call back here for the bag.'

'One-thirty, maybe,' said Iris March, and that was another unexpected thing about her, the precision. 'She liked—likes to cut things fine.' He guessed at the meaning of that phrase, accurately.

'OK,' he said, moving through the door into the *salotto* where there seemed to be some light at least and gesturing to her to sit down. His phone bleeped; message from Luisa. He put it away without reading it.

'Have you looked through it?' he asked. 'The bag?' She nodded.

'Clothes,' she said. 'A painting set. Washbag. Passport.' She faltered.

From her stricken face he could see that where he had taken the presence of the ticket instantly as something useful, narrowing down the timescale of Veronica Hutton's disappearance, to Iris March it had meant something else. It meant that this was real, and that there had been some kind of holiday, romantic or otherwise, planned by Iris's friend but now there was proof that she had not made it. She was not sitting on some terrace sipping spumante.

Sandro removed the clothes from the holdall carefully, stacking them on a small table in the thin light of the vast, cold *salotto*. A faint perfume rose from them. He looked at the passport photograph and saw the ghost of a knowing smile. The painting set was brand new; he lifted it out and held it in his hands. A long flat tin of watercolours; Iris March leaned over and took them from him, turning them over reverently in her hands. He looked in the washbag and saw toothpaste, toothbrush, a blister pack of contraceptives marked with the days of the week. He didn't need to look to see that the last one she'd taken would have been Tuesday, at the latest. Carefully he replaced everything, except the passport and the aeroplane ticket.

'I'll take these to Maresciallo Falco,' he said. 'To the police,' and Iris March compressed her pale lips.

'Can't you...' She bit her lip.

'I have to,' he said, with resignation. 'They have the authority, to contact the airline, to talk to them about passenger lists.' She bowed her head. 'They have the resources.'

'OK,' she said, 'if only they didn't take so long. They seem to take so long. They don't tell me anything.' Sandro hesitated.

She watched him closely while he impersonated the police officer he had once been, on the phone to Alitalia. He asked for the names of no-shows or cancellations on those flights; the operator, initially cooperative, stalled. Patiently he listened as she got up on her high horse, talking about passenger confidentiality.

'Perhaps you could call me back,' he suggested politely. He gave her the mobile number and then, as an afterthought, gave her Pietro's number, at the station. He could tell she was on the point of questioning his authority 'You could fax them to him?' he pleaded; she made a noncommittal sound, typical of petty officials everywhere. He held out no hope, however; the man might have flown separately. Or there might be no man, or he might be some Sicilian who'd be meeting her there. It was a mess.

'Don't think so,' said Iris slowly, when he asked her, any boyfriends from down there, the south, anyone she'd hooked up with. She struggled to remember. 'Mostly it was American boys,' she said. 'None of them was serious.'

'You need to think,' he said, taking both her hands without thinking. 'Let things settle, you know, in your mind, and there will be something. Some clue, something. You have the mind, you have the eye for detail.' He really believed it, too.

She looked back at him, pale and serious, and nodded. Self-conscious suddenly, he let her hands drop.

Sandro stared at her, willing her to understand, to come up with a single piece of solid proof. There had to be a mystery boyfriend. Otherwise the only suspect was Claudio.

'She wouldn't have gone on a trip on her own,' said Iris March, shaking her head, then, with growing confidence, 'it's just not the kind of thing she did; too lazy. I'm sure there was a man.'

He chewed his lip; it had to be faced. 'You think Veronica was meeting someone called Claudio, though.'

'Well,' said Iris, looking bewildered, 'you don't think he could be the boyfriend? As far as I understood—if he really exists, well, she'd only just met him. She hardly knew him.'

'Tell me what you know about him,' said Sandro carefully.

She nodded reluctantly, then spoke in a low voice. 'Someone—a friend, our friend, Jackson, he was close to Ronnie, he says he met this guy in a bar and told Ronnie about him, how he was a genius, really—' She broke off.

Sandro, who had been nodding in recognition, said, 'What is it?'

She stared at him. 'You believe me? You believe—Jackson? You think this guy exists?'

Jackson must be the boy Claudio had been seen talking to, by the tired red-headed barman. Sandro nodded. 'Oh, yes,' he said unhappily. 'He's real.'

She looked as if a great burden had been lifted. 'Oh,' she said, exhaling. Sandro wondered what this Jackson was to her; he was pretty sure the boy didn't deserve her.

Taking out a photocopy of the photograph of Claudio that Lucia Gentileschi had given him—it had pained him to see the original getting dog-eared—he held it out. But Iris March was shaking her head.

'It's not him?' said Sandro, feeling a great leap in his chest.

'I never saw him,' said Iris. 'You'd have to ask Jackson.' Sandro sat back, swallowing his disappointment.

'Where is this guy?' he asked. 'This Jackson?' And saw a flush appear as bright and startling as a rash on the marble neck.

'I don't know,' said Iris. 'That is, I'm not sure, somewhere in the city, I've got his number—here, have his number.' She fumbled for her phone, and he saw the flush rise as she bowed her head.

'All right,' said Sandro, putting out a hand to stop her, 'it's not that crucial, I—well, I'm pretty sure it's the same guy.' She relaxed, took a closer look at the picture. Her colour subsided.

'Is he Jewish?' she said, as if remembering something. 'He looks Jewish.'

'Why do you ask?' said Sandro carefully.

Iris frowned. 'Jackson said something about the guy he met learning to draw in the camps, in the war. He said the old guy told him the story of his life, pretty much. So he is Jewish?'

'Was,' said Sandro.

'What?' said Iris March, suddenly paler than he would have thought possible.

'He's dead,' said Sandro. 'It seems he walked into the Arno, an hour or so after your friend Ronnie was last seen.'

Chapter Sixteen

IT TURNED OUT be a very long walk.

'A bit of wet won't kill us,' Luisa said, watching Giulietta Sarto for a reaction, and quietly pleased to see Giulietta's likeable, weatherbeaten monkey face grinning back at her as they set off in the lee of the houses of the Via dei Bardi. It wasn't so bad if you kept close to the wall, and they'd kitted themselves out with waterproof boots, raincoats and a pair of sturdy umbrellas.

She'd be forty this year, not a girl any more. 'Tough as old boots, me,' Giulietta said, and her face was alive with interest. 'So what's the story again?'

They came past the Palazzo Pitti and the main entrance to the Boboli, where a dismal huddle of elderly women in pac-a-macs milled indecisively at the ticket booth, and set off down the narrow winding length of the Via Romana. The huge park loomed up behind the houses to their left, grey-green through a mist of rain. As they walked, Luisa pieced the story—two stories—together and saw Giulietta struggle to make sense of it. They came past the neglected façade of the natural history museum, a shuttered up greengrocer's, an antique shop, a restorer, a dumpster still unemptied from the night before, overflowing with pizza cartons. Everything seemed abandoned, dead in the rain.

They stopped across the road from the gate, huddled in the inadequate shelter of a shopfront. Behind them a girl was dressing the window, rigging light fittings up over a bed with a velvet spread and heart-shaped cushions. The new trend towards Sunday opening hadn't affected Luisa yet; she thanked God Frollini was holding out against it. She gave the girl a smile through the glass.

'Dunno what Sandro's take on this is,' Giulietta reflected with cheerful practicality, 'but I'd say when girls go missing, it's about half and half.'

'Half and half?' said Luisa curiously, her attention drawn away from the girl and her window display.

'I mean half the time they're just murdered, straight off, and dumped.'

Luisa looked at her stony-faced and Giulietta grimaced apologetically. 'I mean, I'm talking about street girls, here,' she said. 'Not your art student types, but it could be the same, couldn't it? We're not that different.' She shrugged. 'Except if she's got money.'

'And the rest of the time?' Luisa managed. She didn't want to know. Giulietta took Luisa's hand and Luisa felt how cool the thin fingers were in the rain, the poor girl's circulation shot to pieces with diabetes.

'Maybe you don't want to know,' said Giulietta, and Luisa smiled wanly. She went on. 'But look at that guy, in Germany, was it, kept a girl prisoner for years, didn't he? Of course, it's not years, mostly, but weeks.' She hesitated. 'They do tend to be nutters, though. The ones that keep 'em alive.' She made a face.

There had been cases, Luisa knew that. Girls—pretty much always girls—kept in cellars and sheds and outhouses. Somewhere the man could visit, somewhere private. There had been rooms built underground, for the purpose; she remembered a case in the newspaper of a man who'd abducted a couple of young girls and kept them in a soundproofed cellar. Only he'd been arrested for some minor offence, got a couple of months in prison and the girls—the children—had starved to death. Luisa pulled her arms around herself in the rain, because Claudio Gentileschi had a bolthole he kept secret from his wife, and he'd gone to his grave without telling anyone where it was.

'What I'm saying,' said Giulietta earnestly, taking her by the elbows, 'is never say die, though. I think that's what I'm saying.'

They both laughed the same small grim laugh, and in the window the girl looked up at them. Giulietta gave her a little wave, and they stepped out of the awning and crossed the road. As they approached the gate Luisa registered that the gallery opposite them and to the left of the entrance was called the Galleria Massi.

'Ha!' said Luisa, pointing.

'What?' said Giuli.

'Must be something to do with the school,' said Luisa, 'the great Massi empire.' The window was dark; she frowned and turned her head from the gallery to the back gate of the Boboli, practically next door.

'Sandro says the girl was last seen heading in here,' she said slowly. Through the little window in the park's gatehouse a young woman in glasses and several layers of clothing was hunched over a book.

'Caught on camera,' said Giulietta drily, and pointed up to a place on the wall where a camera was mounted. Luisa would never have noticed it but, then, she had never had to hide from anyone. She followed the angle of the lens, pointed at the gate-house and a little beyond, into the Via Romana.

'It's a big place,' said Giulietta. Through the iron gates the gardens looked deserted; a broad gravel path led up between yellowing lime trees. Beyond that stretched darker foliage, holm-oaks and cypresses, and through their canopy the roofs of several buildings were visible. The orangery, greenhouses, stores, sheds. Odd bits of building work behind screens of corrugated iron; once you started looking at it, thought Luisa with dismay, the place was one big building site.

They showed their residents' passes; the girl barely glanced up as they came through before pushing up her glasses and returning to her book.

'But someone might have seen her,' said Giulietta robustly, and took Luisa's arm. 'We can ask, what've we got to lose?'

But there was no one to ask.

Arm in arm under their umbrellas they doggedly traversed the alleys and avenues in the rain, down past the shuttered orangery, its knot garden looking ragged, around the fountain where the orange trees had been removed for winter, and then under the huge semi-circle of plane trees, up the wide cypress avenue, all deserted. They zigzagged back up again slowly, up behind the jumble of mismatched rear façades looking down into cramped courtyards, the storerooms of shops, up until they were level with shuttered bedrooms, then roof terraces.

They reached the rose garden and saw that even the porcelain museum, once some Medici princess's summer house and the favourite of old ladies on rainy Sundays, was shuttered up for restoration. Luisa stared out across the olive groves to San Miniato, the little church she loved more than any of the others. As she stared she became aware that the downpour was easing up, but still no one appeared.

They came down from the rose garden, on the point of giving up when they passed a low plastered building with a terracotta roof where a light was on. Giulietta peered inside, through the half-glazed door. An elderly man in overalls was sitting at a table under a bare light bulb, staring at the wall. They knocked and after staring at them for a long minute he got to his feet and came to the door holding a cup between his hands.

Hesitantly Luisa produced the battered newspaper cutting and showed him the picture while Giulietta turned her back and stared down the avenue. She obviously thought this was daft. The old man frowned and shook his head for what seemed like a good ten minutes. Then he said, 'No. But the Carabinieri already asked all about her. Crawling all over the place.' He grimaced. 'Tuesday there was a bit of sun, I was busy cutting the bay, clearing up the mess people make. I never saw her.' He sighed again. 'And I've had enough, the bloody Carabinieri asking blooming questions every five minutes.' He flung an arm out. 'Look at the place. You can creep from one end to the other without being seen, if that's what you want. People get up to all sorts, and don't get caught.'

Luisa nodded; he was right, of course. As a child she'd played endless games of hide and seek herself in the Boboli, in the dusty shade of the old hedges. If you knew the place, and were determined, you could stay concealed for hours. She looked past him, past the potting shed that was his domain. Right there, for example, she could see a hole in the hedge and darkness beyond; a shortcut or a secret passage for children.

'Clearing up mess?' She spoke lightly; it was half an attempt at sounding sympathetic, half curiosity. 'Was there any particular mess that day?'

The old gardener grunted. 'I'd say.' He fell silent and Luisa thought that might be all she'd get, but steadying himself against the doorjamb he took a step across his threshold. She wondered how he managed to do the job, as he seemed almost as dilapidated as his shed, but once he was in motion he improved. He strode across the gravel path and pointed down the slope towards an empty pedestal, about waist height, just opposite the avenue down to the Annalena gate and with a thick hedge half surrounding it.

'Lovely terracotta urn,' he said. 'Some idiot knocked it off, smashed it to pieces. Three hundred years old, had survived all those frosts. Stupid foreign kids, jumping out of the hedge and not looking where they were going.'

'Did you see them? What time was this?'

'If I had, I'd have walloped them,' he said, with another scowl. 'Heard 'em, mind you. I was finishing my *merenda*, around twelve, twelve-thirty. Bloody great crash, and a girl shrieking in English. Or German.'

Despite herself, Luisa raised her eyes to heaven; surely even an old misery like this would know the difference? And if only he'd been quicker on his feet. Unfortunately the old man caught her expression, and their time was up. 'That's it,' he said. 'I've had enough of people like you.' And the door slammed shut behind him.

Giulietta stuck some gum in her mouth, considering the closed door. 'She must have got out again, somehow,' she said thoughtfully. She pointed down towards the gate and they wandered back as far as the empty pedestal. 'Maybe it was her knocked it off, that what you're thinking? In some kind of a struggle?'

Luisa bent and picked up a piece of terracotta from among the gravel. The hedge was relatively dense around the pedestal, but as she straightened she saw that a hole had been torn through it out of sight, and fairly recently; behind the hedge was an extended stretch of dark, stunted wood, leading uphill. Someone might have come out here, hidden behind the urn- only they came out too suddenly, and knocked it off. Then they'd have had to make a break for it pretty quickly; down towards the Annalena gate, for example.

Luisa sighed, frustrated. 'Sandro told me there was no footage of her coming out again.' She slid her arm through Giulietta's. 'Up,' she said. 'Let's get some height.'

At the top of the wide cypress avenue they turned and looked back down.

'Plenty of ways out,' said Giulietta. Her eyes darted across the expanse of trees, bordered by houses, the *viale* to the south, the higgledy-piggledy rear façades of the Via Romana to the west.

They folded their arms and fell silent. Below them the city lay under a blanket of cloud and drizzle, around them a bewildering number of paths led away through the dark green hedges.

'Gawd,' said Giulietta, scowling at the rain. 'This weather.'

'Yes,' said Luisa, but she wasn't really listening. The view across the soft green drizzled hills to the glinting facade of the little church seemed to have imprinted itself on the inside of her eyelids. 'I don't want to die,' she said suddenly and definitely.

And all at once Giulietta's scarecrow arms were around Luisa, then she sprang back, as abruptly as she'd bestowed the embrace. 'You're not going to die,' she said, hugging herself angrily. 'Don't say that.'

'Well,' said Luisa.

'You're not,' said Giulietta with certainty, and for a minute or two they stared at each other, before Giulietta broke the spell. 'Are we meeting Sandro for lunch, or what?'

'You hungry?' said Luisa, who realized that she hadn't felt hungry for days.

'Starving,' said Giulietta, cheerfully. 'Isn't there a bar in this dump?'

'Yes,' said Luisa, trying to remember the route.

'Here,' said Giulietta, and there was a signpost, Fountain of Neptune, it said, Forte di Belvedere, Vineyard, Kaffeehaus.

Vineyard? Luisa pondered the word; someone had told her about the vineyard.

'Why's it in German?' complained Giulietta. 'Kaffeehaus?'

Luisa shrugged. 'I think it's modelled on something Austrian, you know,' she said. 'They go in for coffee houses, cake and all that, whipped cream.'

Giulietta brightened. 'All right,' she said grudgingly. Luisa remembered the struggle it had been to get her to eat a slice of bread, once upon a time.

As they came past the little row of stunted vines en route, Luisa spotted something that stopped her in her tracks.

'That's it,' she whispered, pointing.

'What?' said Giulietta, impatiently.

'Shh,' said Luisa.

'Cats?' said Giulietta, not bothering to lower her voice. Because under the hedge beyond the little vineyard there were four or five cats in shades of grey, as if bred to the shadows, clustered around a bowlful of food. They made soft mewling, growling sounds as they competed for space. They didn't seem to be bothered by the presence of humans.

'It's where the girl's bag was found,' Luisa said. Behind the vineyard, Sandro had said.

'Cat Lady found it,' she went on, thoughtfully. Giulietta snorted.

'Loony, more like,' she said, and Luisa put a finger to her lips. Giulietta followed her gaze; there crouched behind the hedge and opening a family-size tin of veal and liver was a woman in a cheap transparent mac, hood over her thin hair, bare legs in German sandals. She seemed almost as oblivious to the observers as her cats were.

Repelled by the woman's appearance, Luisa struggled for sympathy. What made a woman behave like this? Out in the rain, feeding cats. Thwarted maternal feelings? The need to be needed. Judge not, lest ye be judged. Sandro needs me, she thought, and found herself wishing he needed her less.

'Hello?' she said and the woman turned her head sharply, in that instant echoing the half-feral movement of a cat's head at the bowl. She scowled.

'Are you—um...' and Luisa searched her memory for the name, came up with it in triumph, 'Signora DiTommaso? Fiamma DiTommaso?' Cat Lady. 'Are you the one, found the bag?' The woman glared at them and turned her back, shovelling empty cans and Tupperware and spoons into a hessian sack and then, before they could work out what was happening, had set off at a lopsided scurry between the hedgerows and was gone.

'Hey,' shouted Giulietta belatedly. 'What's the rush?' She turned to Luisa in frustration. 'Bloody hell,' she said.

'It's all right,' said Luisa, thoughtfully, 'I've got her address.' And she patted the bag slung across her body.

Giulietta looked at her admiringly. 'You're doing this properly,' she said.

Luisa looked her in the eye. 'I'm not going to let Sandro fail on this one for lack of a bit of back-up,' she said. 'It's his first job, since—well. All his life he's been too proud to ask for help, or advice, and look where it got him last time; chucked out of the police, even though he saved two lives that time, if we count yours. A life's work, and all he was trying to do was the right thing—but that's not always the point, is it?'

She was ranting; Giulietta was looking almost alarmed. 'All right, all right,' she said. 'I just meant, you're good at this stuff, that's all.' But at the sight of the woman's disappearing back Luisa felt weary, suddenly, and it showed.

'Come on,' said Giulietta, taking her arm. 'Kaffeehaus, this way.'

The elegant little building did have the odd Viennese touch, plush comfort to counteract the desolate look of the empty terrace where tables and chairs had been stacked to be put away for the winter. Inside it was cosiness itself; a small wooden bar and a curved bay window facing out across the city with little golden chairs set at round tables. Behind the bar a stout middle-aged woman in an apron and an elderly bowtied and waistcoated barman observed their entrance, possibly the only customers they'd had all week. Luisa felt revived just by the smell of wood and fresh coffee. She plonked herself at a table, and when Giulietta went to get two cups and fished in her ragged purse for coins, for once she didn't remonstrate.

Giulietta took her time, rattling off questions at the old barman's back while he made their *cappuccini*. While she waited Luisa took out the folder, a touch damp but intact, and withdrew the newspaper cutting.

When she got to the table with two brimming cups, Giulietta said, 'Cat Lady's got a screw loose, is their opinion, though she used to teach anthropology at the university, so I suppose she can't be stupid. They say she's here every morning, regular as clockwork, feeds the cats and talks to them, eleven till twelve-thirty, sometimes comes in here and asks for a glass of tap water at twelve thirty-five or so before she goes off home clanking like a rag and bone man with all her cans and forks and whatnot.'

A woman of regular habits, thought Luisa, musing on the similarities between Fiamma DiTommaso and Claudio Gentileschi. Cautiously she sipped the cappuccino; she was fussy about her coffee, and if it was made with longlife milk she wouldn't drink it—but it was good.

She set the cup down. 'Did you ask them about Tuesday?'

'Hmm,' said Giulietta. 'She was feeding the cats Tuesday lunchtime, says Roberta.' She nodded at the elderly woman, who gave her a stiff smile. 'Didn't bother with coming in for her glass of water, though. Which was odd, as she's a bit obsessive about it, and it was a nice warm day, Tuesday.'

Something or someone upset her routine, mused Luisa. Scared her off?

'They were both working? Did you ask them about the girl?'

Giulietta nodded, plucking the newspaper cutting from Luisa's hand; Luisa let it go, because there was something else she needed to check. She withdrew the carabiniere report. 'Says here that Cat Lady brought the bag in at five,' she said thoughtfully. 'Not midday.'

'That her?' said Giulietta curiously, peering at the grainy photograph of Veronica Hutton. 'Doesn't look dumb. Looks like she knows her way around.' She peered at the bag. 'What else you got in there?'

'Nuh-uh—' said Luisa, holding up a finger. 'One thing at a time.' Giulietta snatched up the cutting with a pout, and flounced to the bar with it.

Luisa turned and looked away, out through the big bay window at the red roofs in the drizzle, the windblown umbrellas on the terrace below them. In the back of Luisa's mind an idle thought began to form, but it did not have time to take shape before Giulietta was back, plonked next to her and rummaging through the bag.

'They'd already seen the photograph,' she said, holding the buff folder aloft. 'What have we here?' Luisa shook her head, and held out a hand for the folder. Thanked God she'd left the postmortem photographs of Claudio Gentileschi back at the flat. Giulietta was tough, but not that tough.

'This isn't a game, Giuli,' she said.

'No,' said Giulietta, sheepishly. 'Sorry.' She put the folder down.

Luisa sighed. 'You can look,' she said, and after a moment's hesitation Giulietta pulled the folder onto her lap and opened it. She stared, stared so hard Luisa followed her gaze to the dog-eared photograph that was clipped to the top of the folder.

Reverently Giulietta tugged the photograph from its resting place and held it up.

'Giuli?' said Luisa. Giulietta's face was slack, afraid.

'It's never him?' she said. 'The suicide? Not our Claudio?'

'Our Claudio?' Luisa took her hand. 'What do you mean?'

'Our Claudio,' said Giulietta, slowly. 'Lives next door to the Women's Centre in the Piazza Tasso. Our Claudio.'

Chapter Seventeen

As SHE CLOSED the door behind Sandro Cellini, Iris suddenly felt completely wrung out. She'd known immediately that she had seen him before. It had taken her a second or two to place him but then there it was; the dejected-looking man who had been standing bareheaded in the rain, at the gate to the Boboli gardens. And with familiarity had come a sudden rush of relief; the relief of not being alone, the relief of finding out that Jackson had been telling the truth and that therefore when she had believed him—and by shameful extension when she slept with him—she had not been making the most stupid move she'd ever made. Just the relief had left her feeling like a jelly even before Sandro Cellini had told her the old man was dead. She sat down.

He'd taken out his mobile and looked at it, just to cover the shocked silence. 'I'm sorry,' he'd said, 'I've got to go.' He looked thoughtful. 'I'm going to talk to your teachers.'

'Teachers?' she'd said, alarmed. 'You mean Paolo Massi?'

'Who else is there?' he'd asked, curiously, and she'd explained to him how it worked, about Antonella Scarpa, and studio visits and life classes. He'd seemed to take it in, nodding intently, but he was obviously in a hurry, now. He apologized again; shook her hand. 'Contact me,' he said. 'Please. If anything occurs to you.'

She'd liked him. Grumpy, suspicious Sandro Cellini, with his notebook and his way of looking at her under his eyebrows, impatient and solicitous at the same time. It had been weirdly comforting, having him in the flat, watching him look around curiously at the stuffed eagle in its case, the mounted antlers and the tattered gold damask curtains, then his look returning to her, Iris, with something like respect. That she could live in this weird Gothic set-up, without freaking out completely? She'd liked him, but even with him on the case, it wasn't looking good, was it? And now he'd gone Iris felt the place reassert itself around her, settling and creaking.

The old man Ronnie'd gone to meet had been found dead; what was worse, it looked like he'd committed suicide. The conclusion was logical.

The doorbell shrilled, startling Iris on to her feet.

It was the contessa, on the landing. She was wearing a curious kind of housecoat.

'Ha,' the old woman said with hostility. 'Another visitor?'

Iris folded her arms, not budging from the threshold to let her past. 'Signore Cellini,' she said, as icily polite as she could manage. 'I think you know him?'

'His wife,' said the contessa with a contemptuous sniff. 'I know the wife, a shop woman. I give her number to Mrs Hutton.'

'So you know,' said Iris, 'that he's trying to find out what happened to Ronnie. To Veronica.'

The old woman inclined her head. 'He didn't come to ask me,' she said, her mouth set in an ugly line.

'Do you have anything to tell him?' Old bat.

'How can he know, if he doesn't ask?' She sniffed again.

Something occurred to Iris. 'On Friday night,' she said, 'did you see anyone? Did anyone call?'

'Anyone, what do you mean, anyone?' said the contessa, her eyes like a small, suspicious animal's.

'I think someone was in the apartment on Friday night.'

The Contessa Badigliani drew herself up. 'Absolutely negative,' she said. 'Do you think I would allow any stranger into my house? My concern for security is paramount.' Her creaking, antiquated English made her sound mad.

Iris looked at her, because there was something about the way she said it. 'Not necessarily a stranger,' she said. 'Did anyone come here?'

The old woman puffed herself up. 'This is my house,' she said. 'I admit whom I wish. And while we are speaking of these things, I do not permit the visits of young men, who leave in the middle of the night.'

Iris froze, furious; she expected the blush but it didn't come. Slowly and deliberately she closed the door on the Contessa Badigliani's nasty old face, then rested her back on the door. Behind her there was an outraged muttering, some threatening Italian, a silence, then the clang of the elevator door.

Iris got her bag, her keys, her phone. She texted Hiroko: *on my way.*

She called a cab.

❀ ❀ ❀

Sandro noticed straight away that no expense was spared at the Scuola Massi. The entrance was in a narrow, pretty street between the church of San Niccolò and the peeling burnt-orange stucco of the Palazzo Serristori. It was one of the highest-priced areas of the city, and the most picturesque, even in the November rain. Perfect for making a good impression on foreign visitors, as was the façade of the school, which was newly painted in rich ochre, the *pietra serena* around windows and doors wire-brushed and pristine, and the brass nameplate gleaming.

When he had come blearily to the phone that morning, Pietro hadn't had much to say, or at least not on the subject of the investigation into the finances of the art school.

It had been inconclusive; there were country properties that had aroused suspicion but none of them were in Massi's own name; the school did well, every course fully subscribed, some students even came back for several years running, three of the big American universities used the place exclusively. The art school enjoyed goodwill, because the Massi family had that record during the war, the father printing leaflets in his cellar for the partisans. Of course they were doing well, and if the Guardia didn't dig too far down to investigate whether all those students actually existed, well, they were a busy bunch. A huge corruption case had erupted while the investigation had been going on, half the officers had been transferred to it, and the whole thing petered out.

'Plus,' Pietro had said almost as an afterthought, 'it was a woman denounced him to the Guardia.'

'So what?' Sandro had said.

'Come off it,' Pietro had said. 'You know what that means. Ex-girlfriend, spurned lover, whatever. Ulterior motive.'

'They know that for sure?'

Sandro could picture Pietro's world-weary shrug. 'She started as a life model for the school then started doing bits of work for him, and I believe it might have turned into something more, very briefly. I gather he's rather attractive to the ladies.'

'Ah,' Sandro had said, filing this little nugget away for possible future use. Gossip never quite counted as fact, but it sometimes led somewhere, all the same.

'Did you have any feeling, though,' he had asked Pietro, 'for whether they had cause for the tax fraud investigation?'

'I don't like the man,' Pietro had said. 'So I'd have pursued it.'

The woman who let Sandro in—Antonella Scarpa, as she introduced herself with a firm, dry handshake—struck him as exactly the kind of woman a jealous wife would select as a secretary, for example, if she wanted to keep her husband out of trouble. Crop-haired, handsome enough, slight but severe in her white coat. She reminded him of something or someone, but he couldn't think what. A police technician, maybe, with that serious look; then again perhaps he was recognizing a type, clever, tough, hard-working: balls of steel, gender notwithstanding. The archetypal Italian female.

'The director is not here yet,' Scarpa said. 'He thinks perhaps five minutes? The traffic is bad on the *viale*, with all the rain.' Sandro grunted in sympathy.

As the woman led him inside, through the stone-vaulted entrance hall where uplighters shone on a series of—even to Sandro's untrained eye—exquisite engravings of Florentine landmarks, he remembered where he'd seen her before. He was good like that; the memory would always click into place, in the end. He'd seen Antonella Scarpa only yesterday, hanging paintings in a gallery in the Via Romana.

'You've got a gallery space, too, am I right?' he asked casually, and Scarpa turned to look at him over her shoulder.

'Yes,' she said politely, as if talking to a prospective customer. 'We exhibit students' work there at the end of their course.'

'Is it also run commercially?' he asked. It was surely too grand a premises just for student efforts.

They had come to a small lobby with low seating and she gestured to him to sit down.

'Yes, of course,' she said. 'We sell. Can I offer you a cup of coffee?'

While she fetched the coffee, Sandro tried to think of a way of putting her at her ease. Five minutes wasn't much time to extract information from a tenaciously loyal and fiercely discreet employee—and even in the few moments he had had to observe Antonella Scarpa he had registered these characteristics—but it might bear fruit.

'Have you been with the Massi school for long?' he asked, by way of preamble.

'Eight years,' she said. So she arrived the year after the tax case. Is she in love with Massi, thought Sandro, and doesn't know it herself? Eight years as a married man's sidekick. He didn't have to ask if she had a family of her own, because she was here, wasn't she? On a Sunday. He looked around; there was a wall of glass beyond which he could see a vaulted studio space; it looked as though she had been halfway through setting up easels around a podium.

'Do you usually work Sundays?' he asked, and she shrugged.

'Now and then,' she said. 'It's hard to get things done with all the students here.'

Cluttering up the place, thought Sandro; maybe she's really interested in the other side of the business. 'What kind of art do you sell?' he asked. 'In the gallery?'

Standing with arms folded while he sat, she looked at him curiously. 'Do you—excuse me—' she said, 'do you know anything about fine art?'

Sandro shrugged, smiling amiably. 'Not really,' he said. 'Humour me.'

Scarpa looked at him sternly. 'We source original drawings and engravings of the Renaissance for international dealers,' she said, 'for the most part American and German, although increasingly we have some Russian clients,' as if reading from a rubric. 'And we are dealers for some contemporary painters and conceptual artists.' She mentioned a few names, which he noted, but Sandro had never heard of any of them. Conceptual art, as far as he knew, was a matter of pigs' heads and wrapping the Ponte Vecchio in tinfoil; was there money in that?

'I must come and have a look,' he said. 'Would that be permitted?' It seemed to him that Antonella Scarpa's attention sharpened at the request.

'I'm sure,' she said warily.

'Maybe this afternoon,' mused Sandro, as if to himself. Was she being professionally tight-lipped, protective, or something more? 'A bit of a treat for a rainy Sunday.' And he smiled at her.

'Well, you'd have to talk to the Direttore about that,' she said with alarm, and in response to that hint of panic in her voice he resolved that that was precisely what he would do, although whether out of a desire to cause trouble or sound detective instinct he couldn't have said. And then on cue the grating sound of an iron key in the heavy lock interrupted them.

Paolo Massi was handsome in the Florentine patrician manner, and Sandro took an immediate dislike to him, from the hand he held out, unsmiling, to the wings of distinguished dark and silver hair, to the deepset green eyes. Sandro gave the offered hand the briefest of touches.

'I want to be every help I can,' said Massi earnestly, ushering Sandro into his office, which was on a mezzanine floor up a flight of iron stairs. From where he sat Sandro could see out through the studio space and into the courtyard beyond, where some large gardenias in pots were dripping in the rain. Sandro imagined the space full of bowed heads, eager foreign girls labouring away at their easels.

What did they come here for, these girls? Romance? Escape from the parents or the school, a bit of instant growing up?

'Of course,' he said, not thinking, to Paolo Massi. He transferred his gaze from the studio to the interior of the man's office; another row of beautifully framed pictures, pages from a mediaeval manuscript of some kind. A desk with nothing on it but a photograph in a silver frame, of the wife. A bit of a beauty, dark hair and eyes, fine nose; Luisa had been right.

'What do *you* think's happened to her?' asked Sandro, on impulse, as if confiding in the man, 'because the police and the mother don't seem to be all that worried, so far. They seemed to think it would be characteristic of the girl to—well, just bunk off for a bit. Have something of an adventure.'

Aren't you worried? he wanted to say. What if some lunatic's got her in his cellar? Massi looked down his nose. Sandro wanted to shake him by the throat.

'I just don't know,' said Massi eventually. 'I suppose we have to consider the fact that harm might have come to her.' He looked grave. 'But isn't there the hope—I mean, there's still the hope that it could be some—man? That she's gone off on some holiday?'

Sandro nodded noncommittally. 'Do you think that would be typical? I mean, did you get to know her at all?' he said mildly. 'Did you get that impression of her, that she was wild?'

Massi looked at him, and sighed. 'I can really only talk of her as a student of art,' he said. 'I can tell you that she wanted to be good but she wasn't used to hard work. She liked to enjoy herself; she was impulsive. One day she wanted to be a great painter...' and he spread his hands '...the next she wanted to stay awake for twenty-four hours drinking with strangers.' He hesitated. 'It's not uncommon.'

He seemed to be trying hard.

'So you think she was impulsive enough, what, to just run away?'

'There are so many students,' he said, spreading his hands. 'You know, she seemed a nice enough girl. Many of them are impulsive, or lazy; they are very young.' There was something studied, Sandro thought, about his cool manner; distancing himself already, he thought, in case of any bad publicity.

'I bet they cause you any amount of trouble,' said Sandro, trying to sound sympathetic. 'Not turning up, that kind of thing.'

'It happens,' said Massi curtly. 'We make every effort to keep attendance good.' There was a silence during which Sandro heard the rain pattering on the glass roof of the studio's extension. He hoped Luisa and Giulietta were under cover somewhere, whatever Luisa was up to. Then he thought, what am I doing here? Trying to work out if this man's defrauding the state? Not my job.

His job was to ask about Ronnie.

'Where were you, then?' he asked, 'the day she was last seen?' He didn't even know why he asked the question, except that he didn't like Massi, he wanted to provoke some reaction. 'You were here, I suppose? Didn't you ask where she was?'

'No, I wasn't here,' said Massi, frowning ominously.

'You were away?'

'I was hanging a show,' he said. 'I've been there most of this week. Taking down an exhibit of installations we had for the beginning of term, so that we could begin to hang the students' work.'

Sandro brushed the information aside, refusing to show that he had no idea what an installation was, and got to the point.

'Were you alone, on that particular day?'

Massi stared at him, then laughed. 'Are you asking me for an alibi, Mr Cellini? I mean, isn't that a matter for the police?'

'I asked if you were alone,' said Sandro calmly. 'I was a police officer myself until fairly recently, if that makes any difference.'

Paolo Massi swivelled on his chair and looked down through the glass wall into the studio space. Following his gaze, Sandro could see Antonella Scarpa looking back up at them, hands in the pockets of her long white coat. Was it just that he'd seen her before, in the gallery, or was it something else about her that bothered him? And without any conscious decision on Sandro's part, in his head the old machinery of professional suspicion began to turn. He couldn't hurry it, it would tick down in its own time until it decided: was this little itch of doubt something, or nothing?

'Early retirement?' Massi asked coolly, interrupting his thoughts. 'From the force?'

Sandro ignored him. 'So you were alone? All day?'

'As a matter of fact I was not,' said Massi through gritted teeth. 'Not all day, anyway.' He drew himself up in the chair, fine-boned, aristocratic; Luisa should be here, thought Sandro, to give her verdict on this man, as he was no longer able to control his prejudice.

'Dottoressa Scarpa came over to see me, in the morning,' he said. 'To give a hand; there was a lot of work to do. The students were visiting a potter's studio at that time, so she was able to come away.'

Sandro nodded just slightly. 'She was with you from what time until what time?' he asked.

'An hour and a half? I really can't remember the exact timing,' said Massi, frowning. 'My wife arrived. She brought me lunch.'

'That's nice,' said Sandro. The wife arrives, the other one leaves. 'Does she do that often?'

'Whenever she can,' said Massi. 'We like to eat together.'

'And you were in the gallery the whole day?'

Massi nodded. 'Yes.' He smiled politely, patiently, as if he could spend all day having this kind of conversation. A man used to dealing with clients.

Suddenly Sandro was itching to get out of this place; what was the point of winding the man up when they didn't even know what time the girl went missing? When the lead he should be following was the possibility that Veronica Hutton might have set off that morning to meet Claudio Gentileschi? He hadn't the shadow of a doubt that this Paolo Massi was capable of defrauding the taxman—he was clever enough, and arrogant enough. As for dishonest enough, well, who wouldn't cheat if they could get away with it?

As Massi led him out Sandro slowed his pace, to have one last look around. It was beautiful, certainly, very tasteful, the dark wooden work tables, the creamy plastered vaulting, the displays of old etching equipment and even an antique printing press; perhaps the very one Massi's father had kept running through the war. An old family, a good family; but perhaps family didn't count for everything.

'I hope you find her,' said Massi at the door. 'This is all very difficult.'

There seemed to be nothing but bland sorrow in the man's voice, and Sandro felt frustrated and tetchy. He waited until they were at the door before casually putting in his request to visit the gallery. That afternoon.

He wanted to cause maximum trouble, he had to admit it, out of bloody-mindedness. But the gallery was bang next to the Boboli, wasn't it? And Massi was a smooth operator: if he gave him any room for manoeuvre, Sandro would end up seeing nothing more than he'd seen already.

'I don't think so,' said Massi. 'Really, on a Sunday afternoon? Why?'

The man's disdainful tone meant that it was now impossible for Sandro to back down.

'We need to cover every angle,' he said mildly. 'Actually, I really must insist. I'm sure I don't need to remind you that I am the appointed representative of the girl's mother.' He didn't add, Who pays your wages, too. 'And she would want to know you were offering every co-operation.' He saw Massi's jaw tighten, and felt a tiny flare of satisfaction that he'd managed to get the man's back up.

'Five o'clock,' said Massi shortly. 'You know where it is?'

I do, thought Sandro, and Massi held the door open for him without ceremony, and he was on the street again.

And for a moment Sandro just stood there, breathing in the clean, wet air. For the moment the rain had stopped, but the sky was low and black overhead, and in the Sunday quiet Sandro could hear the great thunderous rush of the river, the other side of the crumbling ochre bulk of the Palazzo Serristori. About six or seven metres up on the palazzo's great flank Sandro's eyes rested on the familiar small rectangle of stone; a commemorative plaque common so close to the Arno. Engraved in it was a horizontal line, and above and below the line ran the words: *On 4th November 1966 the Waters of the Arno Arrived at this Point.* And forty years later, thought Sandro as the din of the water drummed in his ears, Lucia Gentileschi walked into my office.

As he came out of the Serristori's massive, dilapidated shadow and into mobile range Sandro's phone bleeped. Impatiently he patted himself down, with no idea where he'd put the damned thing. He located it in his back pocket. *Message waiting*, it said; he jabbed at it, managing to press the wrong button and send the message back to the inbox. It would be Luisa, asking him where they were going to have lunch.

He weighed the phone in his hand thoughtfully; the image of the old printing press came to him. Claudio would have liked that, he'd thought. The beautiful old machine, with its partisan pedigree. There was a connection here somewhere, though he was doing no more than groping in the dark for it. With the phone in his hand, instead of checking the message he dialled Lucia Gentileschi.

Her voice had lost the crispness it had when she first came into his office, and Sandro imagined that she had slept badly. He was brisk, because he knew she didn't want sympathy.

'Did you—did you and Claudio know someone called Paolo Massi?' he asked without preamble. 'Runs an art school?'

'Ha.' She made an odd sound, a kind of surprised laugh. 'No, actually,' she said. 'We didn't know them. Not personally.'

'You know of them, though? The family?'

'They were among those who came around to pay their respects,' said Lucia. 'Well, his wife did, on Friday evening; I was just about to start going through Claudio's desk. We hardly knew them but, then, death brings funny people out of the woodwork, doesn't it? Ghouls.'

'There was some connection?' Sandro didn't quite get it.

'Everyone knows about Massi Editore,' said Lucia, and there was a note of scepticism in her voice that interested him.

'Go on,' he said.

Lucia sighed, 'Well, the old man, Matteo, he ran that press through the war, printing propaganda for the partisans. That was the myth, anyway.'

'You don't believe it?'

'Oh, I'm sure,' she said, 'the old man was decent, I'm sure he was. But the younger—well, let's say Claudio and I disagreed over the son.'

'You knew him?'

'No,' she said patiently, 'not really, not at all.' She hesitated. 'Well, we did meet him once, ten years ago and more, at a reception at the synagogue.' She sighed. 'We were bullied into it, in a nice way; a reception for the friends of Israel, the righteous gentiles, you know the kind of thing. We steered clear of it, as a rule. Anyway, he was there. The young Massi.'

'You didn't like him?' Sandro tried to sound neutral.

'I did not. I thought he was a fraud, a self-righteous young man, using his father's name to get on. Ambitious.'

'But Claudio saw things differently?'

'Well,' said Lucia, sadly, 'it was the kind of thing we disagreed on. I was tiny during the war, you see; I couldn't understand, as he understood, the value of partisanship.' She sighed. 'And I couldn't call him a sentimental old fool. At least, not too often.'

Things shifted in Sandro's head, but did not quite take shape; a good sign, though, the shift. It meant something; there was a connection.

'Are you all right?' he enquired gruffly.

'I'm all right,' she said. 'Thank you, Sandro. I'm not sleeping so well, that's all.'

'I'm sorry.' He hesitated. 'Lucia,' he said, 'I don't think it'll be long. I think—I'm getting close. To the truth.' And it was true; what he did not say was that the truth might not bring her any peace at all.

'Yes,' she said with weary gentleness. 'Just come to me with an answer next time, Sandro. Instead of a question.' And, softly, she hung up.

If it was a rebuke, it was of the mildest sort, but it stung. Chewing his lip, Sandro scrolled back to his inbox with impatience. But what he saw stopped him in his tracks.

We've found Claudio, the message read. *Piazza Tasso.*

It had come in close to an hour earlier, at about the time he had entered the Scuola Massi.

Chapter Eighteen

THE BELLS WERE ringing all across town as the taxi took Iris over to Hiroko's. As they skirted the huge, alien, green and white bulk of the Duomo, its belltower was clanging as well, a deep, ominous sound. Italian bells were different, always more of a funeral toll than a peal. A queue of tourists had already gathered, waiting for the faithful to come out so that the unbelievers could go in and stare. Nothing more awful than a rainy Sunday; Iris knew how pissed off Ronnie would be.

Even as she thought it, though, Iris understood that Ronnie was beginning to lose shape, in her mind; forcing herself to wonder, what would Ronnie think, now, was just a last-ditch effort to stop her disappearing altogether.

They were waiting for her at the door; Hiroko held her lightly by the shoulders for a minute, then let her go, while Sophia hopped excitedly from one foot to another in the warm, dark, jasmine-scented apartment. It seemed to Iris as if she'd last been here drinking Hiroko's tea a hundred years ago, but the place welcomed her back in. She collapsed on the low sofa and took off her shoes. Her feet were wet from waiting on the pavement for the taxi because she hadn't wanted to stay inside the flat a moment longer. She hadn't even wanted to wait in the courtyard, in case the Contessa Badigliani might run back out and grab her with her ringed claws, but the ground-floor apartment had been dark behind the linen-hung door; perhaps the old snoop had gone to Mass.

'So?' said Sophia. 'Is there any news? Anything?' Iris's heart sank.

'Not exactly,' she said. She needed to gather her thoughts.

Quietly Hiroko opened the French windows into the patch of soaked courtyard garden, and the sound of the rain came in, with the fresh air. At least it wasn't bitterly cold; Iris couldn't help thinking that mattered. Although it would get cold soon enough, wouldn't it? It was November.

'I couldn't stay at home,' said Sophia, 'I mean, with my host family, sitting around the table for hours and hours eating lunch.' She rolled her eyes. 'Sundays go on forever.' Iris just looked at her, wondering what Sophia's Italian family thought of her and her friends: free-range foreign children roaming the planet, too jaded for Sunday lunch.

As her eyes adjusted, Iris saw that all around the room were hung charcoal sketches that must be by Hiroko, they were so unmistakably Japanese in influence; long bodies made up of a few fine lines. They made her think of someone—Matisse? She thought of her pencil drawing that Antonella Scarpa had put up, and for a moment she longed to be in a studio somewhere, on her own, trying to do something as good as this.

Sophia was going on. 'I wanted to come over last night, but Hiroko said you weren't around.'

'No,' said Iris, hesitating. 'I was—um—I was with—I was talking to Jackson, yesterday.'

Sophia's eyes were wide, but for once she didn't say anything.

'He's got this theory,' she said reluctantly, 'that Ronnie went off to find some painter. Some guy Jackson met in a bar.' She pulled out her phone, in case there was a message from Jackson, a reprieve. No signal, it said. She put the phone away.

'Oh, yes,' blurted Sophia, 'Jackson told me about him, too.'

'Really?' said Iris, taken aback. Sophia flushed, perhaps, thought Iris, at her sceptical tone. 'Sorry,' she said. Sophia looked like she might be about to cry; Iris hadn't realized she was so wound up by all this.

'You didn't believe him?' interjected Hiroko mildly.

'I didn't know what to believe,' said Iris. 'Though it looks like it's true, after all, doesn't it?' She shot a glance at Sophia. 'It's—it's just—well, it was him I wasn't sure about. Jackson.' She shook her head, all the doubts returning. *Think*, Sandro Cellini had said, hadn't he? *You have the eye for detail.*

She bit her lip and went on, their eyes on her. 'Jackson's not what I expected; I always thought he was so laid-back, you know, in school. He—he seemed very strange yesterday. Angry.' She hesitated, trying not to think of the time when he had stopped being angry. She went on, blurting it out, all the stuff that had been sitting there at the back of her mind, because even if this Claudio existed, it didn't let Jackson off the hook, did it? Not completely.

'And he told me he saw Ronnie on Tuesday morning. He admitted that; only he wouldn't tell me what he was doing for the rest of the day.' She looked from Sophia to Hiroko, and back, pleading. 'He wasn't at the potter's place, was he? Did he turn up in the afternoon?'

'I don't think he did,' said Hiroko, troubled, turning to Sophia.

'I left after the pottery thing,' said Sophia in a small voice. Guilty; Sophia was always a fair-weather student. 'Before lunch.'

'I think he wasn't there in the afternoon,' said Iris, dully.

'But why?' asked Hiroko, puzzling over it. 'What motive would he have, to—to do anything to Ronnie?'

Iris felt a burning in her eyes. 'I don't know,' she said. 'Sex? I don't know anything about—all that.' Meaning, sex, or jealousy, or passion, or rage. All she knew about was the sick sensation in her stomach at the thought of last night, and how out of her depth she was.

'Did you sleep with him?' asked Hiroko, and the question in her soft singsong voice didn't seem intrusive. It was almost welcome.

'Yes,' said Iris, feeling cold, suddenly, as if she didn't have enough clothes on. How could she have done it? She felt Hiroko's hand on her shoulder.

'Come on,' said Hiroko. 'It is not the end of the world, that's what you say, isn't it?' She hesitated. 'It's something people do. We all do.'

In the muffled dark of her hands Iris heard Sophia make a stifled sound. She looked up.

'But I don't even know if I can trust him,' said Iris, hating herself for the whining note in her voice. 'He wouldn't tell me where he'd been, would he?'

'On Tuesday afternoon?' It was Sophia. Iris nodded, bewildered at her new tone, which was defiant, almost truculent.

'Well, you can't trust him,' said Sophia, and her face was red. 'But he wasn't with Ronnie.'

'What do you mean?' said Hiroko.

'He was with me,' said Sophia, and burst into tears.

Iris stayed very still, and said nothing. She became aware that Hiroko was watching her. 'I will make some of my tea,' said Hiroko, and when no one said anything she left the room on silent feet.

Sophia's crying petered out eventually, while Iris concentrated on the sounds of Hiroko in the kitchen. Reluctantly she put out a hand. 'Sorry, Sophia,' she said cautiously. 'I didn't know.'

Sophia sniffed and shook her head. 'Jackson said there was no need to make a thing about it.' She rubbed at her eyes with the back of a hand. 'I wish I was at home,' she said miserably. 'Don't you? I want to talk to Mummy.'

Iris felt ancient. 'Come on,' she said, edging closer to Sophia, nudging her arm.

'Don't you miss your mother?' said Sophia, still sniffing. Iris sighed.

'She's got enough on her plate,' she said. *Of course I miss her.*

She pulled her bag onto her knee; there was a pack of tissues in there somewhere. She pulled one out and handed it to Sophia, who blew her nose loudly.

'You haven't called her at all?' Sophia said curiously when she was done, the tissue a crumpled rag in her fist. 'Not even with all this?' Her pretty nose was very red, and her big, puppy-lashed eyes had almost disappeared with crying. All the same Iris found herself thinking, she could understand, really, why Jackson would want to sleep with Sophia.

'No,' said Iris.

It would worry her, wouldn't it? And she'd said, don't phone.

Hiroko came back in with a tray, and set it down on the table.

Sophia swallowed, and nodded, taking the tea. In silence, each took a sip; Iris was the first one to speak. 'So,' she said cautiously, 'um, when—on Tuesday, when did you and Jackson—what—where were you? How long was he—um, with you?'

Think, Sandro had said, and it came back to her, Tuesday. They'd all trooped off to the potter's studio, stuck up on a hillside towards Fiesole, only of course not Jackson or Ronnie. Antonella had grumbled a bit about Jackson; Iris had already told her lie about Ronnie. It had been a short minibus ride and the potter had turned out to be an elderly American woman with an eccentric house, a pool inlaid with her own mosaic, a terrace overloaded with pots painted with peacocks and fish and geckoes. Antonella had taken them there then said she'd be leaving and they could do their own thing, afterwards, as long as they were back in school by one-thirty for the afternoon session. She herself would be there earlier. She'd remembered Sophia clapping her hands together at that, and getting a glare from Antonella.

'We went to his flat,' said Sophia, looking as though the tears might bubble up again at any moment. 'I—we were there the whole afternoon.' She swallowed.

'What time did you meet him?' Iris tried to remember; once Antonella had gone—about ten-thirty? Earlier?—the session with the potter had lost momentum somewhat. She'd begun demonstrating her techniques of painting on terracotta and had seemed oblivious to who was or was not still there. Students had drifted off, started looking around her garden.

Sophia looked guilty; 'I left at midday,' she said. 'Well, maybe even a bit before. I went to his place.'

'Where does he live?' said Iris, feeling stupid.

'Oh, he's got a big place,' said Sophia, brightening. 'All to himself. On the Piazza Signoria, didn't you know? Overlooking the Uffizi, actually.'

'Was he there when you arrived?' Trying not to think of how much money that meant Jackson's parents must have; one of the most famous views in the world. Iris could hear herself, steely.

'Yes,' said Sophia, like a nervous child.

'What's his place like?' she found herself asking; heard a bitter note in her voice.

'Messy,' said Sophia, with an unhappy attempt at a smile. 'There always seemed to be a pizza box under the bed.'

Ugh, thought Iris. Sophia looked at her imploringly, her eyes brimming.

'No, I didn't mean—' Impatiently Iris burrowed in her bag again, but the tissues seemed to have disappeared and all she came up with was the watercolour set that had been in Ronnie's weekend bag. How had that got there?

'Ah!' It was a soft sound, and it came from Hiroko; she put out a hand to the box of paints and without thinking Iris surrendered them. 'They're Ronnie's,' she said.

Sophia sat up, and leaned to look, too. 'Zecchi,' she said. 'They're the honey-colours from Zecchi, 150 euros for a set like this, forty-eight colours. Don't you remember the visit to Zecchi? Massi told us, if you want the best, you should buy these. She wrinkled her nose. 'I had to buy the Windsor and Newton travel set, because Mummy said it was a ridiculous waste of money.' She frowned. 'Don't remember Ronnie buying anything. She seemed bored.'

'It was the first day, wasn't it?' said Iris, 'she wasn't in love then. And that was when the solution popped into her head, as simple as that. It—he—had been staring her in the face.

'I have the small set,' said Hiroko, bobbing her head, 'Forty-five euros. They are the best.'

Iris held out her hand for the paints, and got to her feet. 'I'm going to see Jackson now,' she said.

❀ ❀ ❀

The Women's Centre in the corner of the Piazza Tasso had a
dirty yellow façade with peeling stucco and a smoked-glass door.
Peering through it, Luisa could see posters, warning against
HIV and hepatitis and unprotected sex, in various languages,
a row of plastic seating, a scuffed reception desk. This was the
place Giulietta was so proud to be working in; she had beamed
as she indicated it to Luisa. And Luisa did admire her, even if it
was not in a way she could express. 'Great,' she said.

But they weren't here to visit Giulietta's place of work. It was
next door they were interested in; Claudio's other life, his bolthole, his hiding place. All of a sudden, Luisa was reluctant. They
looked up at the grubby frontage, no sign of life, all the shutters
closed. Beside the battered front door were six bell-pushes; no
brass nameplates here, but an accretion of punch-tape or faded
paper strips stuck down with yellowing sticky tape one on top of
the other, half the names out of date, probably. Gentileschi did
not figure among them; that would be too much to hope for.

'We should wait for Sandro,' said Luisa, taking out her
phone and staring at it in vain. They'd shot out of the Kaffeehaus,
down the wide cypress avenue and out at the Porta Romana.
Even as they emerged Luisa thought, trying to make some kind
of route map in her head, if it was Claudio, hustling the girl out
here on the quickest route to his bolthole, that smashed urn was
right out of his way. They came out on to the busy ring road then
round to the Piazza Tasso. It had been perhaps forty minutes
since she'd texted him this time but they weren't really into this
texting thing, her and Sandro. He might not be picking them up
at all, for all she knew.

She looked at Giulietta for confirmation. 'Don't you think?
He should be here.'

Hunched in the drizzle, Giulietta shrugged, shifting her
feet impatiently. They turned their backs on the door and stared
out into the rain.

It was not the kind of place you'd expect to find a respected architect, thought Luisa; it was an ugly little square, and the buildings were all alike, two or three storeys, grubby with fumes from the *viale* that ran along the south side. In the centre was a battered and graffiti'd kids' playground ringed with stunted trees, empty save for a bullnecked dog, lowering its haunches on to the scrubby grass and staring at them balefully as it did so.

'I like it down here,' said Giulietta defensively, as if reading Luisa's thoughts. 'It's real.'

Luisa nodded without agreeing; Giulietta had spent her childhood in a prostitute's walk-up on the Via Senese, a mile to the south, so it might even look pretty to her. And although Luisa knew Sandro was coming around to having his office down here—she'd found it for him, after all—she reserved judgement. It felt irretrievably malign to her, down at heel and resentful. And behind them, overlooking this grim little place, was Claudio Gentileschi's secret place. With growing apprehension, she turned back to face the door again.

'OK,' she said.

'We can ring all the bells,' said Giulietta promptly, raring to go. 'I'm always doing that when I can't find my key. People don't mind. Well, some of them do—but—'

'There's no need for that,' said Luisa with a calmness she didn't feel. 'I've got the keys. And out of her bag she pulled the envelope containing the cuttings and reports and, at the bottom, the keys she'd dropped in at the last minute, because it was better to have everything together.

Giulietta stared, shook her head in disbelief. 'You had the keys all along.'

'I wanted to wait for Sandro,' said Luisa, not meeting her eye. Not wanting Giulietta to know she was frightened. And suddenly she was very frightened.

At first the Yale key refused to go in, but she knew she wasn't off the hook, it was just her stupid hand. Giulietta guided it in, and they were in the hallway. Narrow, poky, and bare; a heap of junk mail in the corner and the smell of unemptied bins.

'What floor, d'you think?' whispered Giulietta.

'I'll try the first,' said Luisa, because surely no one could live at street-level in a place like this, with barred windows and no light. It would have to be the *piano nobile*, although that was a misnomer if ever there was one, and she guessed the back rooms, for peace and quiet and a better view than that squatting ugly dog. And she was right; the wide flat square key slotted in, Luisa pushed against the sprung lock, turned, and it opened in front of them.

Braced in anticipation of a sound, pleading, scuffling, shouting; for the ugly traces of violence or abuse or imprisonment, Luisa held her breath. But there was nothing. The place was empty, of humanity at least.

As Luisa stood, Giulietta came in beside her, and together they took it all in. It came to Luisa that she stood there as a substitute for Claudio Gentileschi's widow; that she was looking at this place, her dead husband's secret life, through that woman's eyes. Had she been betrayed here?

If it was, it wasn't the kind of betrayal Luisa recognized. This was not a love-nest, or a bigamist's cosy second family set-up.

It was a single, large room and, against the odds, it was beautiful. Even on this grey, terrible day, it was full of a pale northern light. And as for the more common kind of betrayal, well, there was no bed, to start with. There was a small sink in one corner, beside the single large window; the sink seemed to be very dirty, spattered with something, and there was a cheap white cupboard fixed to the wall above it; a single, fluorescent pink Post-it note stuck incongruously to it. A tall wooden contraption Luisa didn't immediately recognize leaned, folded, against an ancient, filthy sideboard. The old red cotto of the floor was as spattered as the sink, and papers lay about underfoot, as if a wind had blown in at the window and sent them flying, only the window was closed. In the corner opposite the sink stood what looked like a huge dead tree branch, scraps of silvery dried leaf clinging to it. What kind of place was this?

Giulietta let out a short laugh and pointed at the branch. 'I saw him dragging that up here,' she said. 'He found it on the riverbank. He was always scavenging down there. It was, like, his world.' She fell silent.

'Why?' said Luisa, still trying to make sense of the place, the combination of disarray and abandonment. Had someone been living rough in here, squatting? Her phone rang.

'I'm in Piazza Tasso,' Sandro said. 'Where are you? What the hell's going on?'

Chapter Nineteen

TAKING ONE LOOK around the filthy room, Sandro began to laugh, but it wasn't a happy sound. 'God, I've been stupid,' he said, and he saw Luisa frown at him. 'It's a studio,' he went on patiently. 'This place was his studio, where he came to be a painter.' He squatted, and scraped with a nail at the spatter marks on the floor. 'It's paint. What did you think it was?' Luisa shook her head, still pale.

'I didn't know what to think,' she said sheepishly.

Sandro sat back on the battered floor; there was nowhere else to sit. Outside the tall window the sky was a grey so dark it was almost black; he realized that by now he had almost ceased to notice the rain. It might never stop.

'Keys,' he said, holding out his hand, and Luisa dropped Claudio's keys into his palm. Something about the action set up that ticking again at the back of his mind; he looked down at the keys, trying to work it out. Hand out, keys dropped in.

Front door key, Yale key, key to the postbox. He frowned, thinking of the pile of mail on the floor. No postbox.

'This is a, a what d'you call it, then,' said Giulietta, gingerly attempting to unfold the easel that was the first thing Sandro had seen on entering the room.

'Easel,' said Sandro. 'Is this it, then? Just the one room?'

'Far as I know,' said Luisa. 'No doors leading anywhere else, anyway.'

Sandro weighed the keys in his hand thoughtfully, then put them in his pocket.

He did a 360-degree turn, slowly; no keyholes or padlocks to be seen. He leaned down and picked up one of the dusty sheets of paper scattered around the floor. He'd thought they were blank, scrap paper blown around the place by a draught but in fact the one he was holding was what looked like the beginning of a drawing of a woman's head, no more than a few lines in a kind of fine reddish chalk. A woman with her hair pinned up, something familiar or ancient about it. The pose, maybe.

'He was good,' he said, not really thinking because if he thought about it he would have said, How the hell would I know if it was any good? I'm a policeman. Ex-policeman. But it seemed beautiful to him. It was something he'd like to have on his wall, even unfinished.

'I don't understand,' said Luisa. 'Why would he keep this a secret from his wife, though?'

Sandro sat back against the wall and looked at her; as so often happened, Luisa had got straight to the point. 'No,' he agreed, 'it doesn't make sense. Unless, well, some men have the need for, I don't know, compartments in their lives, something just for themselves...' He ran out of steam under the look she was giving him. Why would he keep a painting studio a secret from his wife, who admired his work?

'Ow-w.' Giulietta had pinched a finger in the easel. Painfully Sandro got to his feet. Luisa was already there, holding the thing while Giulietta extracted her digit, wincing. She looked like a drowned rat in a borrowed mac three sizes too big for her; underneath it Sandro could none the less see she'd got dressed up a bit, for Sunday out with him and Luisa. Fine little dysfunctional family they made; poor Giuli.

He sighed. 'No,' he said. 'I don't see why it should have been such a big secret, ten years here. It's not like Lucia's the kind of woman to call it a waste of time, art.' It didn't make sense.

'You don't think he brought women here, then?' said Luisa dubiously.

'Models?' said Sandro. 'Maybe.' But he couldn't imagine it; the place reeked of solitude to him, one man's lonely presence.

'Well, if he'd been bringing women up here we'd have known about it, don't you think,' Giulietta interjected, rubbing her finger. 'No one at the Women's Centre would have had any time for him if he had. He wasn't that kind of bloke.'

Sandro nodded, looking at the door of the filthy old sideboard that had swung open, released when the easel had moved. He knelt to look inside. At first it seemed empty, and then he saw something in a corner, thrust out of sight. It was a small stack of sketchbooks, four or five of them, green cloth board covers dark and greasy with age.

Opening one gingerly, he saw that every page was covered with drawing. And not just any drawing; it was so dense and detailed that every centimetre of white space was filled, with line after line, crosshatching and shading and here and there small splashes of colour; it somehow made him think of a tattoo. A row of bunk beds and a face like a bony gargoyle's peering out from under a thin blanket; a skeletal figure naked to the waist in ragged trousers, washing at a bucket. Like a tattoo of scenes from Dante's *Inferno*, page after page after page of the wretched, of devils and goblins in human form, in serge uniforms or paupers' rags. He closed the book, feeling the greasy covers between his hands, and thrust it back into the pile.

'Drawings from the war,' he said, catching his breath; he felt as though he'd been holding it since he'd opened the small book. This was what Iris March had said, wasn't it? When he'd told that American boy the story of his life in a bar, of drawing in the camps. God only knew how those sketchbooks had survived the war and made it back here, to lie unopened in this secret compartment in Claudio Gentileschi's life.

He fished in his overcoat pockets and found a plastic bag. He put the books inside carefully.

Luisa looked at him, aghast. 'Can you do that?' she said.

He shrugged, beyond caring. 'I'm going to give them to his wife,' he said, shortly.

There was nothing else in the sideboard. 'So if he's been holed up here painting and drawing for ten years,' said Giulietta suddenly, 'where's all the stuff? Because we've only seen those sketchbooks so far, and they're sixty-five years old.'

She was right, too. Sandro looked around but there was nowhere else to store anything but the sideboard. It had two wide drawers above the cupboard; the first one he opened contained two boxes of paints, a wooden one containing tubes of oils and a tin of watercolours, a box of charcoal, a bunch of sharpened pencils held together by a rubber band. He noted that the paints came from the same shop as Veronica Hutton's pristine box of watercolours. What did that mean? It might mean only that Zecchi was the best place to buy paints.

The second drawer contained a stack of Zecchi sketch pads; all apparently unused, some with their pages even uncut. But when Sandro lifted out the last one he saw that underneath it was a small pile of loose sheets. They were all versions of the drawing he'd found loose on the floor, only these were different; they looked old. Ancient, in fact, even older than Claudio's wartime sketchbooks, their paper soft and brown with age. He held them up.

'Still,' said Luisa, taking the drawings and inspecting them, 'ten years' work? And these don't even look like he could have done them. They look, I don't know, like Michelangelo or something. Could someone have come and cleared the place out? Some landlord?'

Distracted by Giulietta, who as Luisa spoke had crossed to the window to peer inside the cheap melamine cabinet that hung lopsided over the sink, Sandro did not immediately consider what she had said.

'Say that again?' he said, absently.

'What's this mean, then?' said Giulietta, interrupting at just the wrong moment. She had pulled off the dayglo pink Post-it note and was holding it up. 'It says, KH, 11.30, 1 nov.'

'KH?' said Luisa. 'Her surname begins with H, doesn't it? And K's got to be foreign, we don't have the K.'

'Hutton,' said Sandro distractedly. 'But she's not K, she's V, Veronica, Ronnie for short.'

Luisa was looking at Giulietta. 'He was going to the Boboli to meet her,' she said suddenly. 'KH, Kaffeehaus; the Kaffeehaus at the top where we were this afternoon. He'll have put it up there to remind him, especially if he was, you know, getting forgetful. He'll have come here at ten, just like he did every morning, pottered about, she phoned him, he put that there to remind himself.' She pointed down, and on the floor Sandro saw an ancient Bakelite phone. Claudio didn't have a mobile, did he? If only he hadn't been here when she'd called.

Giulietta had put her oar in now. 'So why hadn't they seen him, or the girl for that matter? At the Kaffeehaus?'

Luisa thought a moment, screwing up her face as she did when she was making an effort to remember something, and the sight of it made Sandro stop fretting over whatever it was he'd wanted to ask her, and just look at her.

'Maybe she never turned up?' she said, dubiously. 'Or maybe—well, I did think...' She hesitated. 'Something did occur to me when we were up there—' And she stopped, and illumination spread across her features. 'The umbrellas,' she said triumphantly, 'the terrace. Tuesday was a beautiful day, they would have had customers out on the terrace. They'd have had extra staff, for the terrace, might have been laid off when the rain started. Wouldn't have known about any of this.'

'Right,' said Sandro, holding up a hand. 'That's good, that's something, they met on the terrace, we knew they had to meet somewhere. We can get hold of that waiter—tell you what, you two can get hold of that waiter, but please, before you say anything else can you tell me again?'

He had Luisa's attention at least, although she was looking at him as though he was mad.

'Can you please repeat to me,' said Sandro, trying to sound as calm as he could, 'what you said before? About his work.'

'That they were—that they looked too old, the drawings looked too old for him to have done them? That the landlord might have cleaned the place out? That's what it looks like to me.'

Sandro held the sheaf of papers up to the pale, grey light. 'Too old,' he murmured to himself; rubbed a finger along the foxed edge of the vellum.

'You don't think—they're stolen? Could they be valuable?' Luisa was peering over his shoulder at the drawings, and he could feel the warmth of her breast against the back of his arm.

Slowly Sandro shook his head, thinking of the money. Regular payments into that bank account. 'Not stolen, at least not exactly,' he said.

'Then what?'

'You'd have to take them to an expert to be sure,' he said cautiously, 'But...' And he passed the flat of his hand over the worn surface of the paper, held it up close to his face, the reddish sepia of the faded ink, the worn edges. 'But I think they're faked. I think they're high-quality, beautiful, almost undetectable fakes.' Sorry, Claudio, he added silently, even though there was a part of him in awe of the skill. They were beautiful.

'And his wife never knew a thing,' said Luisa.

'He couldn't have told her,' he said, thinking of Lucia Gentileschi's small, upright figure, hands folded in her lap. 'Maybe he wanted to make sure she had enough, after he was gone.'

What was she going to say, when he told her? He ducked his head, not wanting to meet Luisa's clear, outraged gaze, as if he was Claudio himself, found out, and she Lucia.

But before she could speak his phone rang; Sandro pulled it out, promising Luisa with his eyes that whoever it was, he'd get rid of them. Only it was Pietro, ranting.

'Why the hell's Alitalia faxing me passenger lists on a Sunday lunchtime? Sort yourself out, Sandro, get yourself a secretary, and a badge, for the love of God.'

Sandro let him simmer down. There were six or seven no-shows on the outward-bound flight to Sicily, and of those names one also cancelled his flight back to Florence on the Friday.

'My God,' said Sandro, when he heard the name. 'So it was him.'

❀ ❀ ❀

He had seen them go into the house, Claudio's house. He had been on the swing. The swing in Piazza Tasso was better than the ones on Lungarno Santa Rosa, it was new and wide with a rubber seat made out of an old car tyre; on Santa Rosa they were narrow and hard. And mostly broken.

Even though he was getting wetter and wetter, Tomi felt comfortable on his swing, and his mother let him out even if it did mean he came in wet because it made the day go more smoothly, that was what she said. He had tried to explain that to the skinny woman he liked, last night, when she tried to get him to go home.

His name was Tomi—for Tomasso—although he knew that they called him Comic-book Boy. He wasn't any good at remembering names himself so Comic-book Boy seemed good enough.

Tomi preferred it when it wasn't raining, obviously, even if he was having difficulty remembering a time when it hadn't been raining. But it had been sunny when he had seen Claudio go down into the water, hadn't it?

They'd been in there twenty-eight minutes by the under-water diving watch his mother had given him for Christmas last year. Claudio was dead, Tomi knew that much. He wasn't stupid, but he just didn't want to think about it. Tomi had been going to wait for them to come out again but he decided he would go over to Santa Rosa, anyway. His mother had said that if he took his long raincoat with the hood he could stay out until Nonna came over, which would be at four-thirty. And he wanted to check on the dog. If it *was* a dog: he hadn't even seen it yet.

He got off the swing. Lupo Alberto had to be rolled in a plastic bag and stowed in his pocket; Tomi had a hundred and thirty-five books of the adventures of Lupo Alberto, that hapless farmyard wolf, and he kept them in a plastic box beside his bed. Even Lupo Alberto seemed to make his mother angry, sometimes, or at least it made her angry when he laughed too loudly on the bus with her, while he was reading.

It was Sunday, so the bar was not open. During the week Tomi went in there to buy small tins of sweets at the till, and the barman was almost always nice to him. Once what he had thought was a euro was a foreign coin but the barman took it anyway. It took Tomi a long time to get across the road because there was traffic; a fire engine with the siren going went past and splashed his trousers below the raincoat; it was going out towards the Viadotto dell'Indiano. Tomi stared after it on the embankment where he stood beside the Circolo Rondinella, looking for smoke, but perhaps it wasn't a fire, perhaps nothing stayed on fire in this rain. On the TV his mother had been watching fire engines rescue people from a mudslide.

There was no noise from the dog any more. Had someone come to take it away? Claudio never had a dog himself, not that Tomi knew about; Tomi wondered if he'd mind about this one being kept in his special place. If Claudio had had a dog, Tomi would have certainly asked if he could take it for a walk sometimes. The dog he had heard yesterday, and the day before, was not being walked. Tomi supposed it might be a different kind of animal; it had been dark when it was put there, late on Wednesday night, bundled out of a car in the dark, and the sounds it had made were not familiar to him. Toto and Patak had drunk so much they were asleep, each on his own bench, and so he'd gone to the swing under the trees, looking at the branches being swept downstream in the dark. He'd seen a car pull up, and he'd kept very still.

It was getting dark now although it wasn't four-thirty yet; the lights were coming on all down the river along the embankments, flickering yellow. Yesterday the lights had come on just after lunchtime because of the rain, it had been so dark; yesterday he'd heard whatever animal it was, if it wasn't a dog, banging against the side of the shack. You couldn't hear it just walking along the river, you had to know where to look.

Tomi leaned over the embankment wall beyond the Circolo Rondinella to get a better view, and he got a shock. The water was so high it had covered all the grass where Claudio had gone down. In his wallet Tomi still had the card that the man had given him, Cellini Sandro; he wondered if Cellini Sandro would be interested in the dog? Often, when he tried to tell people things, they ended up walking away, and his mother told him he'd gone on too long, they weren't interested.

The lower shacks were completely submerged, and he could see a plastic sack bulging to get out where boards had been splintered by the river pressing against them. Tomi thought about the animal inside and jerked his head back. I'd like to go home, he repeated to himself. It was what Mama had told him to say, if he got into trouble. I'd like to go home now, please.

Chapter Twenty

THEIR FACES, REALLY, staring at her, expecting something of her, had sent Iris out of there. Hiroko's calm, symmetrical features, on which Iris could never discern even the ghost of emotion, and Sophia's prettiness blurred with crying and the onset of a monumental sulk.

'You're going where?' she'd said. 'You're going to see *him*?'

Outside, the sound of the rain seemed to have been turned up, a dozen different kinds of percussion, pinging and clattering and rushing as it streamed down relentlessly. Iris had felt as if she was drowning in the big, dimly lit rooms of Hiroko's apartment, as if she was underwater. And she needed to have it out with Jackson.

'There's something I need to ask him,' she'd said.

And there was a question she had for Jackson, but the guilty truth was that even as they all sat there talking about Ronnie's watercolours and that small but blinding moment of revelation about Ronnie came to her, part of Iris knew she could use it as a way of going forward with him. Getting in a room with him, shouting, accusing, looking him in the eye, at least so she could know for once and for all whether she could believe a word Jackson said.

She wanted to see him, simple as that. Was this what it was like, then, this boyfriend, girlfriend thing? It felt more like a big steel trap; a great heavy thing Iris had to drag around with her, or else gnaw her own leg off to escape it. Like

Ronnie's bag, weighted with useless ironmongery, hurled into the undergrowth.

'On the north side of the piazza,' said Sophia reluctantly, 'seventeenth century, or so Jackson says.' This contemptuously. 'His flat's on the first floor, got a big balcony overlooking the Neptune statue. There's a restaurant on the ground floor called Medusa, or something.'

Even in the downpour, its flagstones running with water, the piazza held tourists under a sea of black umbrellas; a queue stretching out from the massive stone stronghold that was the Palazzo Vecchio, a gaggle of them looking at the plaque where Savonarola had burned at the stake. Not much chance of burning anyone today, thought Iris. The sky was charcoal grey overhead, and low like a great tin lid. In the distance there were sirens.

Following Hiroko into the kitchen to say goodbye, Iris had been feeling obscurely guilty about having accepted her hospitality when she'd needed it, only to turn her back on the girl now she needed to be alone. In the corner of the room was a small television tuned to a news channel, turned down low; there'd been a camera lens blurred with water and footage of a mudslide somewhere in the Alps. Hiroko had turned away from Iris to turn the sound up, which Iris had at first taken as the cold shoulder, but then she realized Hiroko wanted to hear what they were saying.

'They're talking about it being another 1966,' said Hiroko. 'Do you know? The flood, when all the cellars filled up, all the archives were destroyed. Art students came from all over the world to help clean up.'

Standing now facing the long grey porticoes of the Uffizi, Iris imagined she could almost hear it above the distant sirens, the rushing of the river. There was something biblical about the quantity of it. What had Anna Massi said? Like the end of the world? 'O dio,' she'd said. 'Like the apocalypse.'

It had even been raining in Sicily, she'd said. But surely even in Sicily it rained in November? What had she meant?

Iris had reached the restaurant called the Medusa, named, she registered, after the statue of Perseus standing opposite it on the far side of the piazza under the Loggiata dei Lanzi. A delicate little figure, poised on one foot, holding up the gorgon's head by the hair.

Above her she heard the sound of a window opening, and leaned back to look upwards. Forearms appeared on a stone balustrade, hands; she heard him clearing his throat. The underside of a chin; if she took a step backwards she'd see his face.

Instead Iris moved to the door. There were only two bells; she pressed them both. Jackson's voice when he answered was blurred and indistinct, but he buzzed her up.

'I know who it is,' she said, coming past him into a big, beautiful room with a coffered ceiling, filled with watery light. The windows were all open, and it was cold, but you could see along the rusticated flank of the old civic palace all the way down to the great arched windows at the far end of the Uffizi, the windows that overlooked the river. As she spoke defiantly, Iris tried not to think about what that expression on Jackson's face had meant, just at the sight of her on his doorstep. Before she'd said a word.

Surprise? Panic? Hangover? They'd drunk wine and some grappa last night, as well as the champagne in the afternoon; enough to give anyone a headache.

'I know who Ronnie was going away with.' Iris wanted to get a reaction out of him. 'I know who the man was.'

'Really?' he said, blinking. 'How do you know?' Iris almost felt sorry for him, he seemed so unprepared, somehow. What kind of world did he live in, where you slept with one person, then another person, and none of it made any impression?

'I worked it out,' she said, dumping her bag on a massive slab of wood that, like some mediaeval refectory table, ran along the back wall of the room. It held a bust of a blind-eyed Roman noble, gazing out at the Palazzo Vecchio, and an empty pizza box. She rooted through the bag, flinging things out of it.

'You want a coffee?' he said, rubbing his eyes. She shook her head fiercely. Jackson took a bottle of water that stood on the refectory table and planted himself in a chair by the window.

She held up the box of paints, took long steps over to the

window and held them up in his face. 'These,' she said. 'Ronnie went out and bought these, for her little trip.'

'OK,' said Jackson, warily. 'They're good paints.'

'They're the best, according to Sophia.' Was it her imagination, or did he shift a little at the mention of her name?

Iris went on. 'But one hundred and forty-five euros? She wasn't that rich. Who did she want to impress, buying the biggest set of the most expensive paints from Zecchi?'

Jackson shrugged. There was another hard chair opposite him, and angrily she sat in it, leaning forward, elbows on her knees. He watched her.

'And going to talk to painters? Kind of private tuition?'

Realizing for the first time that she would have to tell him that Claudio was dead, Iris stopped abruptly and stared away from him out of the window. Something was going on in the Uffizi's long rectangular courtyard; a rank of carabinieri were moving people backwards into the main piazza, cordoning something off. The sight stopped Iris in her tracks; she thought of the sirens she'd been hearing all day: too many of them, and the gathering chaos in the streets she'd walked through. What were the police doing out there? It must be the rain, she thought, and for a surreal and horrible moment Iris imagined that in all this upheaval, somehow Ronnie might be uncovered, some mudslide or tidal wave might sweep her wet, cold body up into the light. Was she accepting that Ronnie was dead? She stared, unblinking, out of the window.

'Yes,' said Jackson, impatiently. 'And she'd asked Massi, too, hadn't she? Extra work.' He frowned.

'Who would have been too much of a bigshot to come to her Halloween party?' Jackson looked uneasy. 'Apart from you, I mean,' said Iris, wearily refocussing on him, overwhelmed with the hopelessness of it. 'She told me, after the party, that she'd had enough of boys, they were useless. So she found herself a man.'

'A man.' He swallowed. Whether he thought of himself as a boy or a man, she didn't know. So she went on, leaning to look up into his face.

'Who was she flying to Sicily with that afternoon?'

'Sicily?' said Jackson slowly. 'Someone was going to Sicily, I remember that—'

'I found the overnight bag,' said Iris. 'It had her ticket in it. She was supposed to be coming back Friday evening, only she never got the flight.'

'Sicily,' said Jackson again, 'I heard—Antonella—'

Iris barged on. 'And who could have got into our flat, looking for that overnight bag, anything that would link her to him? Who tried to sabotage Ronnie's computer? Who knew I wouldn't be there Friday night? Who could have got past old eagle-eyed Badigliani? Because you certainly didn't, when you left at three o'clock this morning.'

Jackson looked down at his feet, murmured something.

'What?' said Iris, impatiently.

'You could have let me stay,' he said, and when he looked up at her there was an almost wounded look on his face. She bit back what she wanted to say to him. It could wait.

'So who?' said Iris. In her pocket her phone shrilled; it was Sandro Cellini.

'It was your Massi,' Sandro said, before she could even speak. 'Your teacher; she was having an affair with your Director. Paolo Massi's name was on the outward-bound flight, he didn't show; and he cancelled the return, the same day, Tuesday. But he would have been on the Friday evening flight.'

'Yes,' said Iris, 'I'd worked it out,' realizing he might not believe her, talking to Sandro but looking at Jackson. 'Can I call you back?' She clicked the phone shut.

'You know how I know it wasn't you?' she said to Jackson, softly. A couple of months ago, a couple of days, she'd have had to endure the furious blush, to fight back tears, but her face felt as cool as marble.

'I thought it might be you, because you wouldn't tell me what you were doing Tuesday afternoon. And you were so weird yesterday, so angry. Only I know now.'

'You do?' said Jackson, and it was his turn to feel the brick-red burn rise up his cheeks.

Go on, thought Iris, triumphant and miserable at the same time. Shame on you. 'I talked to Sophia,' she said.

'Oh,' said Jackson dully, and in that moment Iris lost the taste for it.

'It doesn't matter,' she said, and it really didn't. Ronnie was what mattered; disentangling this whole mess was what mattered.

'So,' she said. 'Do you know? Have you worked it out?'

Jackson spoke carefully, his flush disappearing as quickly as it had come. 'Massi was planning a trip to Sicily last week, because I overheard him telling Antonella,' he said. 'He told her he needed to go and see a picture dealer.'

In some remote corner of her calculations, Iris registered, there was a place for Antonella, wasn't there? But she didn't have time to think about that now.

'It was him,' she said. 'Yes. Sandro—the detective—he called the airline. Massi was booked on the same flights.'

'Wow,' said Jackson, awestruck. 'So you were right. Wow.' He stood up, brushed his hand through his hair. 'That's—wow. I mean, how does that fit in? I mean—Massi, why didn't he…?' He stopped. 'Huh. Well, I guess he wouldn't say, would he? If she just didn't turn up for the flight? He must have thought, shit.'

Iris said nothing, seeing Jackson, focussed for once, putting himself in Massi's shoes.

He was nodding. 'He must have thought, no one needs to know. It doesn't mean—jeez.'

'So he's kept quiet all this time,' said Iris, 'even though he had—at the very least, what they'd call crucial information about her disappearance?'

Jackson looked uncomfortable. 'I—well, I can kinda see how it might pan out. The longer you went without saying anything—I mean, it would be his job, his wife, on the line, wouldn't it?'

He stopped, and stared at her. 'You think he did it? Did—something to Ronnie?' He looked incredulous, shaking his head. 'Massi, and rough stuff? Nah.'

She frowned: although she now hated Paolo Massi, Iris could see Jackson had a point. 'I'm not sure.' And because there was Claudio, too. The old painter.

'You want that coffee now?' said Jackson. 'I'm sorry, only my head just isn't working without it.'

Iris gave in, knowing she was just putting it off. 'OK.' And she needed a coffee, too. What time was it, even? When had she last eaten? She didn't know.

The kitchen was narrow and dark, lined with expensive wooden cupboards. This wasn't an apartment where the tenants were expected to cook anything. She stood in the door, and he handed her a cup, American coffee from a percolator, tasting bitter and watery.

'Jackson,' she said at last. 'Your old painter.'

'Yeah, right,' said Jackson eagerly, 'Claudio. I mean, where does he fit in?'

'Sandro thinks she did meet him. That morning.'

'Right,' said Jackson faltering.

'You liked him, didn't you?' said Iris.

'Liked?' said Jackson.

'He died,' said Iris.

Chapter Twenty-one

'BUT HOW MUCH further does this take us?' asked Sandro, despairingly. He put his head in his hands on the crisp white tablecloth. Luisa tutted.

'Get some food down you,' she said. 'It's nearly three o'clock and none of us has eaten since breakfast. No wonder you can't think straight.'

They were at Nello, the last place in the world where despair belonged. Sandro couldn't believe he'd forgotten about Nello; a tiny little hole-in-the-wall trattoria, it had been the place he and Luisa always used to come when they were first courting. He'd long assumed it had closed down; he should have known better, because places this good never closed down.

Luisa had let Sandro call the girl, Iris March, to tell her—she's got to know, he said, come on—but the minute he'd hung up she'd taken charge in the pale clear light of Claudio Gentileschi's abandoned studio.

'You're white as a sheet,' she said. 'Don't think. Don't do any more detecting, I forbid it. You need food.'

And obviously Luisa had not forgotten about Nello at all, because after they'd locked the sad, empty room up carefully behind them, with an unerring instinct Luisa had frogmarched them around the corner—around the corner, from his new office!—and there it stood, after all these years. Nearly three on a Sunday afternoon, and twenty years since they'd last been here, but the old *padrone*—still in charge, his eyebrows a little wilder, his moustache a little whiter—had greeted Luisa as though it was only yesterday.

At Nello you didn't even order, food just arrived. While they waited Luisa called the Kaffeehaus; and of course it turned out that, yes, she'd been right, they'd still had the tables and umbrellas up on Tuesday, it had been a beautiful day. Sandro heard her cajole someone into giving her a name and number for the waiter who'd been working the terrace. He saw her get her little gold propelling pencil out of her handbag, and the dark red diary she'd bought every year since he'd known her, and write it all down.

Without even pausing for breath, Luisa called the number, and Sandro heard that she had all the right words available to persuade the waiter that, yes, maybe he'd call by for a coffee with them, he wasn't working today.

When she had secured her result Luisa put the pencil and paper away, and beamed at him. Sandro felt perhaps more useless than he had ever felt in his life.

'You're hungry,' said Luisa. Then, as if the chef had somehow been privy to the entire exchange, all at once risotto with pumpkin was at the table, a basket of bread, wine and water. The world reasserted itself.

Sandro's plate was nearly empty, it seemed, before he drew a breath; Giulietta had already finished hers, although Luisa was taking it slower.

He fished in his pocket for his own notebook and stub of pencil. 'So what have we got? She was having an affair with her teacher, was planning to go off to Sicily with him that afternoon only he says he was in the gallery the whole day. And as far as we know the last person to see her was still Claudio.'

'He was meeting her at the Kaffeehaus at 11.30,' said Luisa. Laboriously he wrote it down. 'So we need to talk to the waiter who was working the terrace,' and she looked down at her notebook, 'Beppe. Who should be along shortly.' She prodded at her risotto.

And we need to talk to Cat Lady. She ran off like a scalded cat herself, and there's something funny about that timing, if you ask me.

'What?' said Sandro.

Luisa poured herself a glass of wine and sipped it slowly.

'She handed the bag in at five, but she's only ever there at lunchtime. By one, one-thirty, Veronica Hutton was already missing, wasn't she? She'd failed to turn up for her flight. My guess would be, the bag was chucked into the bushes at the same time Veronica Hutton was—what? Attacked? Abducted? And Cat Lady might have been a witness.'

'No love lost between Cat Lady and the Carabinieri, that's for sure,' said Sandro, writing.

Abducted? She must be still there, he thought; that was what was giving him the headache. The Carabinieri can't have searched the place properly; Veronica Hutton must be in there somewhere. Because how the hell would you get her out, kicking and screaming? Holding a gun to her back under a raincoat, like in the movies? Could Claudio have calmed her down, got her to walk out with him through the Porta Romana gate? Everything in him resisted the thought that Claudio had had anything to do with her disappearance.

But if she was still inside the Boboli, she'd have to be dead. This was what he had not wanted to think about, and he said as much.

As if reading his mind, Luisa went on. 'So assume he, or whoever, got her out of the Boboli? There's the other gate, the one without the camera. And if you know the place, well, no doubt there's any number of alleyways. There was an old lady I used to know whose garden was behind a hedge down at the Porta Romana end and if she ever fancied a stroll in the park she just popped through.'

Raising his head from the page he was writing on in an attempt to process this information, Sandro saw Luisa pour more wine. Was it his imagination, or was she just pushing the food around her plate? 'Eat up,' he coaxed, and she gave him an impatient look.

'And what about Claudio, then?' she said. 'I know you; you don't want to talk to Cat Lady exactly because she might have seen the whole thing; she might point the finger at your beloved Claudio.'

Sandro looked away, because she was right. 'If I was still in the force,' he said slowly, 'we'd assume the boyfriend did it.'

'And only the wife as alibi,' said Luisa. 'That gallery's very near to the Boboli.'

'The sidekick from the school was there, too,' he said reluctantly. 'Antonella Scarpa.'

Luisa stroked her cheeks thoughtfully. 'We saw the place,' she said. 'This morning. Galleria Massi. He could have been in and out of the Boboli in ten minutes, no one the wiser, couldn't he? You haven't even spoken to the wife yet.' She turned to Giulietta. 'Wasn't there a shop right opposite? She'd see any goings on?'

'He was very quick with his alibi,' said Sandro. 'And I didn't believe any of that, about his wife always popping down with a bit of lunch for him.' He frowned. 'Particularly if he was supposed to be at the airport at two.'

'Yes,' said Luisa, sitting up straight. 'That's true. I bet she was never there at all.'

'I'm supposed to be meeting Massi down there in a bit,' said Sandro thoughtfully. 'I'd really like a look in that place, his gallery.'

The old *padrone* was at the table, with the bill.

'Caffe?' he asked, and as Sandro was about to answer emphatically in the affirmative, there was a discreet creak and the restaurant's door opened. A slight, faintly seedy-looking individual slipped inside, darting a sheepish glance at the darkened kitchen and the *padrone*, who was bristling at the after-hours intrusion.

'Beppe?' Luisa intervened quickly. The waiter from the Kaffeehaus.

'Four coffees,' he said, reluctantly, because he had the certain feeling that this camp, skinny, apologetic little man had come to bring him bad news.

❀ ❀ ❀

Iris thought he'd be upset, but she hadn't expected this.

'I don't know why I'm crying,' he said, hopelessly, wiping his eyes with the back of a sleeve. 'This is stupid. I hardly knew the guy.' Iris didn't know what to say; it was almost as if he was crying for himself.

'I can't believe he'd do that,' Jackson went on, 'walk into the river like that. He was such a—such a great guy, he—he was full of stories, y'know? Talking about his wife, and shit—' He swallowed, stopped, cleared his throat. 'Sorry. I mean, I liked him. How can you be so wrong about someone? He'd had such a life.'

'Jackson,' said Iris gently. 'You only met him once.' He stared at her.

'I guess I did,' he said, dully. 'I did feel like I knew him, though.'

Was that Jackson all over, though, thought Iris, just jumping from one fascinating new person to the next? Yesterday Sophia, today Iris; it didn't make her angry, even.

Looking at his crestfallen face, Iris hardly knew how to say it, but she felt she had to. 'What if he'd done something— I don't know, by accident, to Ronnie. Or if his illness—he had Alzheimer's, Sandro said.'

'Oh,' said Jackson, blowing his nose on the tissue she got for him. Her last one; Sophia'd had the rest.

'Alzheimer's,' said Jackson, sitting back on his chair. They were in the window again, although below them the piazza seemed deserted now. 'I guess Alzheimer's explains anything, does it?' He frowned.

'I don't know anything about it,' said Iris honestly. 'It seems to be a pretty bad deal.'

'He drowned?' said Jackson. 'You don't think she could be—he could have taken her with him?'

'Into the river,' said Iris, as that image returned to her, of Ronnie rolled over in the river, caught in branches, turned face up under the rain by some tidal bore. 'I don't know.' She forced herself to consider. 'Wouldn't they have—found her by now?'

'Massi did know him,' said Jackson suddenly. 'Knew Claudio, I mean.' He frowned. 'Or his wife did, said something like that. When I went back to ask him? Um, last night?'

'Last night?' She felt the flush threaten. The truth was she'd forgotten that bit. Standing in the Piazza Pitti waiting for Jackson to run back to her, and the rain had started up again. She'd told him to go back and say something to Massi.

'Did he say he'd tell the police?'

'He said I should give them a statement myself,' said Jackson. 'He said it was a really important piece of information, but he was kinda insistent it should come from me.' He made a face. 'I guess he's right, too. I guess I do need to talk to them, eventually.'

'Did he know the guy was dead?' she asked curiously.

'Well, if he did, he didn't mention it,' said Jackson, frowning again.

'They were still in the gallery? When you caught up with them?'

Jackson nodded. 'It was dark in there,' he said slowly, 'but the car was still parked, up on the pavement. So I knocked, and I looked in the glass and there was a light on, right at the back. They must have been having some kind of big discussion because they didn't hear me at first then I knocked again. Massi came and let me in, and Antonella stayed out the back, putting stuff in boxes, there's some kind of a storeroom and a yard out there. The gallery's weird, it goes back so far it's like a tunnel. We only saw the showroom, didn't we?'

It seemed a hundred years ago, that first week, when Massi had showed them around the gallery, telling them this will be where we show the best work produced on the course. A big room with downlighters and dark red walls, Massi's own massive seventeenth-century desk in the window, artlessly strewn with engravings and heavy art books. He must like sitting there, she remembered thinking, like some Renaissance noble, some patron of the arts.

Jackson went on. 'He turned on the lights when he saw me; they've put up some of the work already, did you know that? For the show?'

'I wonder if Antonella knows,' said Iris, not thinking about the end-of-course show, imagining instead the tunnel with

Antonella standing at the far end, in the shadows. 'You know, for a second the other day I did wonder if there was something going on between her and Massi.'

'Antonella?' Jackson sounded disbelieving. 'No way. It's just the work with her.'

'They spend a lot of time together,' said Iris. 'How could she not know? Didn't you say he told her he was going to Sicily?'

Jackson shook his head. 'I don't think she cared, one way or the other. I think all she cares about is the art, and maybe the business. She polishes that damn old printing press every five minutes, she stays late doing his books. I've seen her.'

There was something about the dismissive way he said it that annoyed Iris. She realized she liked Antonella; or had liked her, anyway. What was wrong with caring about the art, anyway?

'I wonder what he said to her, when he didn't go to Sicily after all?' Iris puzzled. 'She never said anything to us about Sicily.' In fact, she had told the class almost nothing; none of their business why he was going to be away for the week. Or why he was back earlier than expected. 'She just said he was hanging the show.'

'She does what she's told,' said Jackson. He sounded contemptuous.

'Not always,' said Iris, angrily, thinking of the line drawing of Ronnie that Antonella had stuck up on the wall in the studio. And then the obvious explanation came to her. It wasn't really any good at all, was it? What if Antonella had put Iris's drawing up there to make a point, to show Paolo that she was a woman, after all, not just his workhorse, and that she knew what was going on?

'Baby,' said Jackson, cajoling, putting out a hand.

'No,' said Iris, and she flipped his hand away, and got to her feet. All of a sudden she felt so overwhelmed with fury and disappointment that she couldn't look at him; she stalked away from the window, stiff-legged, to the door. She didn't even know who she was furious with: Antonella for being a fool after all, Massi, Jackson, Sophia; even Ronnie. With herself.

'Why don't you do something useful and speak to the Carabinieri, like Massi told you?' she said as he stood there in the window, shoulders slumped. Iris knew she should be kinder but he was occupying too much room in her head, and she wanted to be on her own. There was stuff she needed to do—well, one thing in particular—and she wanted her space back to do them.

'Where are you going?' said Jackson. 'What have I said now?'

'This is serious,' Iris said angrily. 'If your friend Claudio did something to—did something with Ronnie, then there's a chance they might be able to find her. The Carabinieri have to start doing something; we can't do this on our own. It's ridiculous.'

'Can't you come with me?' said Jackson.

The pleading note in his voice made Iris want to slap him. She reached abruptly for her bag and managed to drop it. It emptied itself out, a mound of sweet wrappers and receipts and Tampax, and as she knelt to sort through it Iris felt the flush come back, like an old enemy, scalding her face. 'Damn, damn, damn,' she muttered.

He was on his knees beside her, helping her; 'I'm all right,' she said, scooping stuff up in her hands and dumping it, dust and old envelopes and her purse and—and what were all these little bits of glass and junk? Iris sat back on her heels.

'Hey,' said Jackson, reverently, peering into his cupped hand. 'Hey, what's this?'

'Give it to me,' said Iris, and thinking it would be a tampon or something and he'd be trying to embarrass her, she grabbed.

'Hey, hey,' said Jackson, and there was a new note in his voice, curious, excited. He held it up between thumb and forefinger. 'Look.'

It was a tiny rectangle of plastic, scuffed and dirty, a centimetre by a centimetre and a half, with a gold square inset, and a minuscule circuit board.

'It's a—it's a—' Now she remembered, the blue glass from Ronnie's phone, the scraps of plastic she'd scooped into her bag yesterday.

'It's a sim card,' Jackson said it for her.

She raised her head. 'It's Ronnie's sim card?' she said, disbe-lieving. In the silence that followed as they stared at it the cold wet air outside seemed to be full of sirens, and then another sound, closer, and more urgent. Someone was battering at the door downstairs. They crossed back to the window and leaned out, looking down.

A man in a fluorescent tabard, face upturned, was yelling something up at him in Italian. Jackson looked at Iris blankly for help.

'I'm sorry,' she said in Italian, leaning down. 'What was that?'

'*Diluvio*,' said the man. 'There is some flooding.'

'The Arno?' asked Iris. 'The river?'

The man shrugged, his face slick with water. 'Maybe,' he said. 'Maybe soon,' and he pointed. At the foot of the building, grey water was bubbling up through an iron drain cover. 'Is better if you evacuate,' he said. 'Is temporary.'

Jackson held up a hand. 'Sure,' he said, nodding with eager politeness. 'Five minutes, yeah?' The man shrugged, already turning away; further around the piazza Iris saw other fluo-rescent tabards moving from door to door. At Rivoire, the big flashy bar on the corner, the tables and chairs had gone, and boards were being placed across the ornate threshold.

Turning back to Iris, all Jackson's plaintiveness was gone, and he was as excited as a small boy. 'If we've got her sim card, it's, like, we've found her phone.'

Iris stared at him blankly.

'You can put it in another phone,' he said, 'well, actually, not mine, the iPhone—um never mind,' he finished as he saw her impatience with the technology that had once made him seem so nimble. 'Gimme yours.'

Iris handed it over and deftly he slipped off the back, the battery, slid out its sim card, wrapped it carefully in a receipt from the pile of junk still on the floor and handed it to her. He slipped the new card inside in its place, carefully, laboriously put the phone back together and they stared at the screen, waiting.

Then there it was, an unfolding logo, an icon. Jackson punched the air; 'Not even blocked,' he said triumphantly.

Iris stared at the tiny bit of Ronnie, glowing up at them.

'See who she was calling, the night of the party,' she said. Wanting final confirmation that it was him, not Jackson, not some bar owner on the other side of town—not her mother, though fat chance of that. She wanted to know who Ronnie had been talking to when she looked so dreamy and happy leaning out of the big window in the Piazza d'Azeglio.

Jackson was humming to himself, his fingers flickering over the keypad. In his element. *Call info*, it said and he handed it to her.

She flipped back down, two, three, four days ago—31 October, Halloween, was what she was after, eleven thirty-three p.m., on the left a little arrow to denote a call out. Paolo, it said. She went to the address book; Paolo, an Italian mobile number. Yes.

When Ronnie had been hanging out of the window on the phone to someone who had made her smile all evening, all night, all the next morning, she had been talking to Paolo Massi.

Not finished yet, though. Iris flipped to the next day, up; 1 November, nine-ten, Claudio; nine-twenty, Jackson. She called Claudio to fix their meeting, then Jackson to get him over, to see if he'd guess, to tease him, only he didn't guess, did he? They had a glass of wine and she sent him on his way. At ten-forty she had been back on the phone to Paolo; calling him to make last-minute arrangements?

Then nothing.

Jackson was at her shoulder. 'Try missed calls,' he said, leaning across her. Concentrating, Iris nodded. Outside someone was shouting again. 'Go and look,' she said, distractedly. 'Tell them we're coming out.' He was gone.

Missed calls; Iris. A lot from Iris; she was working backwards this time, from today, yesterday, Friday; Iris, Iris, all Iris. All those calls Iris had made, that niggling anxiety when she heard, *The number you are calling is not in service.*

One from a girl they'd known at school, Joey, on an English landline, one from Jonathan, the boy who'd called Iris the fat chick. Just random, bored calls, Iris imagined, if she'd answered they'd have said, Hey, Ron, what's up? What ya doin? I'm bored. But, still, only two calls? Iris felt suddenly sad for Ronnie, who didn't have so many friends after all.

None from her mother.

And none from Paolo; not then. Iris scrolled down further, and there they were, 1 November, three calls, one after the other, 12.03, 12.05, 12.06; urgent calls, that had gone unanswered. All from the same mobile Ronnie had called at the end of the Halloween party; only this time, Paolo was calling her, on the day she went missing, over and over again.

'We have to go,' said Jackson, from the window, pulling on a jacket. And they went.

Chapter Twenty-two

THE RAIN BEAT on the roof of the car and Sandro sat inside, listening, alone. He needed to be on his own, to get things in the right order.

Luisa had known that; it was one of the many good things about Luisa, that she could read the runes. 'Come on, Giuli,' she'd said briskly to the girl, hauling her to her feet. 'Let's make ourselves scarce. Let's go find Cat Lady.' Giulietta had been going over it all again and again until Sandro's head hurt. 'So it *was* him?' she said, after the waiter had left.

All Sandro could think, his heart going down like a stone, was no, no, no. But he had no reason to doubt what Beppe DiLieto had said.

Sure, he was a dubious sort, but, then, seasonal waiting staff always were, drifters, barely employable. Watching the man talk, Sandro had noticed that DiLieto's eyes were a different colour, one a faded grey-blue and the other yellowy hazel; there was a breed of cat, he dimly remembered, with the same combination. It lent him an otherworldly air. The hands shook a little, he combed his thinning hair over, he was on the camp side but that was neither here nor there, waiters often were. He'd been decent; he'd come all the way over to Nello on his day off, hadn't he? When Luisa called, and never mind if a whole season of unemployment yawned ahead of the man now the rain had come.

Sandro was sitting in the car on the Via Romana, outside the gate to the Boboli, parked between two dumpsters, opposite

244

the darkened window of the Galleria Massi. Through the grey skein of pouring rain he could see the dark stretch of woodland; he stared up at it, as if willing it to give him an answer, but it gave nothing back.

There had been a time, such as the occasion he'd gone looking for a murderer in a godforsaken corner of the city's outskirts between highways and electricity substations and trailer parks, and had found him there, that Sandro had had a spark of instinct for a terrible place. He was a rational man, but he couldn't quite shake off his primitive belief that violence left its mark behind it, as if somehow it turned the air bad. From this stretch of green alleys and ancient trees, though, he felt nothing.

The rain battered out its tattoo on the car roof; you have no time left, it told him, no time to lose. No time to sit here waiting for that worn-out old instinct to finally kick in and say, here. Somewhere across the street a light went off.

What was the hurry? The girl was almost certainly dead by now, if she hadn't been dead for days, hastily buried under the dust and gravel on the hillside above him. They'd find her eventually. It was the answer he'd been avoiding for days, since he saw that photograph in the paper.

They'd showed it to Beppe DiLieto and his face crumbled, just a little, with self-reproach. 'I know,' he said, 'I should have said something earlier, shouldn't I?'

No need to ask why, or where he'd been when the Carabinieri had been asking questions—from the moment Beppe DiLieto, scarecrow-thin, lifted his tremulous hand to correct Sandro's order, four coffees, to say, 'And I might have a little something in mine, if you please,' you could see that he was a bit of a drinker. Laid off for the winter and crawling home with a box of cheap booze, he'd only resurfaced to go back to the supermarket, probably; what would he be doing reading newspapers?

Sandro had been patient with him, felt a tug of fellow feeling for a man long past his best. He let him drink his coffee that was more grappa than coffee, then beckoned for another one. The old *padrone* had looked mistrustfully at Beppe DiLieto, but Luisa had given him a pleading smile. 'A favour,' she said, 'just another fifteen minutes?' and he relented, though when he set DiLieto's little cup down it rattled disapprovingly.

Then at last the trembling hand was still, and the coffee gone. He gazed into the dregs, his two-coloured eyes watery.

'I served them, yes, I served them,' DiLieto began. 'It was a beautiful day, I think I was serving five, maybe six tables on the terrace when he arrived. He arrived first, you see; she came about five minutes after. The other tables were mostly Americans, one Japanese couple.'

All foreigners, thought Sandro. No Italian would sit outside in November, even if the sun was shining.

'I was surprised when he sat down,' said the waiter, as if he'd read Sandro's thoughts, 'because it wasn't that warm. Of course, when she arrived—the situation was clearer. When I saw that she was English.'

'What did you think of them?' said Sandro, curiously.

'What did I think?' DiLieto sighed. 'I don't know if I...' He wrinkled his papery forehead in an effort to retrieve what he had thought. He nodded and when he spoke it was with care. 'I thought at first he was a grandfather, or a more distant relative, even a guardian, perhaps. And she was a foreign girl who had to be polite to an old man.'

Fair enough, thought Sandro, I can live with that. But DiLieto went on.

'Of course, after—what happened, that went out of the window.'

Here it comes, thought Sandro. 'What do you mean?' he said carefully. 'Do you mean—the newspaper report? So you did see it in the paper, about the girl?'

Beppe shook his head, 'Not really, I mean, I might have glanced at it, but I didn't realize it was that girl. No. I meant, after what happened, later. What he did to her—I mean—'

'Take this step by step, please.' Sandro felt hope ebb away. He prompted; 'You served them.'

Again DiLieto seemed to be making an effort to be methodical. 'He had a small glass of Four Roses.' He paused. 'And she had a glass of champagne.'

'Huh,' said Sandro, thinking, at eleven-thirty in the morning? And before he could stop himself, 'That must have been expensive.'

'He paid,' said DiLieto, and Sandro nodded; a gentleman.

'Did he—seem to be prompting her to take alcohol?' he asked.

Slowly DiLieto pondered. 'I wouldn't say so,' he said. 'She seemed to be full of high spirits, it seemed to me that they were drinking because they were celebrating. Almost as if—well, young couples on holiday do it, honeymooners.' His eyes were distant, as if trying to recall an occasion on which a morning drink was innocent.

Iris March had said that Veronica Hutton had already had some wine before she left the apartment, hadn't she? She must have been close to drunk, after a third, maybe a fourth glass?

'Did you hear any of their conversation?' said Sandro.

'Snatches,' said the waiter, still distant. 'You know, I had other tables to serve.'

'But you heard some of what they said?'

'Yes.' He hesitated. 'That was when—the last table, the one next to them, I—this woman sat there and she took her time ordering, so in fact I did hear what they were saying then. They were talking about art.' He frowned. 'Yes, that's true, they were talking about art. She was getting out a sketch book to show him, very innocent.'

He spoke resentfully, as if the innocence was an affront.

'But in fact not innocent?' Sandro prompted him. The hand was trembling on the table again, but Sandro didn't want to buy him another drink, not yet.

The waiter seemed to have shrunk into himself at the table. He shrugged. 'Florence is full of old men who take advantage of young women, by talking to them about art,' he said. 'You know this. She was full of excitement, she'd had a bit to drink.'

'And he—what?' Sandro wanted at all costs not to lead this man with his questions. 'He took advantage of her?'

'He wasn't in a rush to do it,' said Beppe DiLieto, in a voice rich with disillusion. 'I was there long enough—the woman who—the woman on the next table wanted a camomile, she said, then wasn't sure if she wanted lemon, typical Florentine artistic sort of skinflint. And he got out his own sketchbooks, showed her some of his stuff, was telling her about the commissions he'd had. He paused. 'I lingered a bit, because I thought they might want another, while I was there.'

'And you wanted to be sure of the kind of man he was?'

DiLieto shrugged. 'I wanted to see which way it would go, yes. Because he didn't strike me as that kind of guy, to begin with. Just goes to show.'

'She was—she's a pretty girl, isn't she?' Luisa said quietly.

'Yes,' said DiLieto, 'I suppose she was. And she had her hand on his arm, maybe that's what did it.'

'Did what?' Sandro wondered what effect that might have on him, under the influence of a glass of whisky, on a bright November morning, when the end of his life had just come into view.

'That's how it goes, I've noticed,' said Beppe. 'Give a girl a drink, she loses her bearings a bit. She was excitable, anyway.'

On her way to meet her lover, thought Sandro. He was refusing to believe all this; he needed to be more objective. He pushed on.

'So she put her hand on his arm. And then what?'

'I was on my way in to get the orders,' DiLieto said, 'and that's when he made his move.' He was sitting back in his chair, fleshless as a ventriloquist's dummy under the cheap suit.

Sandro saw Giulietta shift in her seat, but she didn't say anything. They were keeping pretty quiet, for once, the women.

'What move?' Something in Sandro's mouth tasted sour.

'Touched her up,' said DiLieto. 'A hand in the wrong place. She might have given him a peck on the cheek, and he misinterpreted it.'

'Might have?'

'Well, I did see her lean up and put her face near his, like she was going to give him a kiss, when she had her hand on his arm. Just as I was going back inside.'

Sandro leaned in. 'What did you see, exactly?' He was clutching at straws. 'Sounds like it was her making the move, not him.'

DiLieto had that funny, sad, watery look in his eyes. 'I wasn't going to hang about staring; we get all sorts doing all sorts in public, American honeymooners are the worst. None of my business.' Out of the corner of his eye, Sandro saw Luisa nodding.

'Perhaps not,' said Sandro. Around them the empty restaurant was hushed and dark; outside the light was almost gone under the leaden sky.

'And a peck on the cheek, well—I can't say I thought anything of it. Except—

'Except I just caught a look of something on his face. Like he'd gone blank, like he wasn't sure who she was, or who he was. Then I went inside.'

He sighed, reluctant, dragged himself on. 'But he must have made the move just as I turned my back because the next thing I knew there was a great racket behind me, one of the chairs went over—and they're cast iron, you know, weigh a ton, the devil to get back up. So I came back out and the camomile tea lady was on her feet and shouting, saying how disgusting it was, shouldn't be allowed, filthy old man, get your hands off her, she said.'

Sandro's tired brain grappled hopelessly with it, the worst-case scenario, and surrendered.

'And then?'

'And then the girl ran off, down the alley towards the vine-yard, and he went after her.'

'But no one intervened? No one stopped him?' Giulietta spoke at last, her face ashen, although Sandro didn't know if it was in horror at what nice old Claudio had done, or a story of her own she was reenacting.

DiLieto turned towards her, his face crumpled with shame. 'It all happened so quickly,' he said. 'And then they were gone and I was left with my tray and a camomile tea, no lemon and the barman shouting at me because they hadn't paid.'

'What about the other customers?' said Sandro, despairing.

'Well, the camomile tea woman, of course, she had a go, set off after them—she was the type—but they were out of sight, she wouldn't have caught up with them, would she?'

'Hold on,' said Sandro, 'hold on—who was she? This camomile tea woman? What did she look like, where did she come from?'

Beppe looked uncomfortable. 'I can't—I can't really remember that well, you know? I was looking at the old man and the girl while I was taking her order, if the truth be told. She was wearing something over her head, scarf or something. Sort of a duster coat, light-coloured. Arty Florentine type, like I said; I only got an impression.'

'Italian, then,' said Luisa quietly. Beppe turned to look at her, and nodded. She looked thoughtful. 'Did you get the impression—did she know either of them, the girl and the old man? Or vice versa?'

The waiter began to shake his head, then stopped, and shrugged. 'Well, the girl had her back to her but, you know, I did see the old man look across at the woman, when she was giving me her order, sort of bewildered for a second. Like he might know her from somewhere, he just couldn't be sure.' He scratched his temple. 'And with the scarf—well. There wasn't much of her to see.'

'She didn't come back?' She must be on camera somewhere, thought Sandro, but without much hope. Their solitary witness.

Beppe shook his head, grey in the face. 'And the rest of the customers—' he sighed, 'well, they just looked the other way, foreigners, on holiday. Perhaps they thought we are all like this, Italians, always shouting, making drama. I just got on with clearing off the tables. I wasn't to know...' and he drew in a breath. 'The expression on the old man's face, though, when the girl leaned over and kissed him.' He put a hand to his own face as if he might find it there, and Sandro saw the tremor. 'He looked bad.'

'You should ease up on the drinking,' he said softly, and saw panic in DiLieto's eyes.

There hadn't seemed any point in going on torturing the man after that.

'You've got my number?' the waiter kept saying to Sandro. 'Anything I can do, you can call me?' Sandro knew with leaden certainty that DiLieto would call him again, possibly at regular intervals for the rest of his life, when he didn't have the price of a drink. He'd patted him on the arm, slipped him ten euro. 'Wouldn't mind talking to that camomile tea lady,' he said, more to comfort the man than because he had any expectation. 'If you spot her in the street, say.'

'Will do, *maestro*, will do,' said DiLieto, with dismal gratitude, and they let him go. It had been awfully quiet, after he went; they'd slid out of the restaurant, the *padrone*'s farewell a great deal more muted than his welcome. Luisa overtipped, out of guilt.

'So what's next?' Giulietta had said cheerfully, on the street outside Nello in the rain. Was this like a game to her? All Sandro had been able to think of was that he had to tell Lucia Gentileschi what he'd discovered. Then he remembered that he'd been supposed to meet Paolo Massi at his gallery and suddenly he was filled with rage at the man, the smooth, greedy fake. Anger that he should have been directing elsewhere, no doubt, but of all the characters he'd encountered in the preceding three days, it was Paolo Massi that was drawing his anger.

'I'd better go and talk to Lucia Gentileschi,' he said, mentally booting Paolo Massi out of the picture.

'Do you think that's wise?' Luisa had asked, her head tilted like a bird's. 'I mean, what can you tell her? What did he actually see?'

'It happened, though, didn't it? Claudio lost the plot and groped a girl. Even if Beppe didn't see it, there was a witness;

witnesses, no doubt, a whole terraceful. God knows who might come forward when—well. If it turns into a different kind of investigation.' He shied away from saying the word, murder. 'And I don't want Lucia to hear it from them.'

Luisa persisted, bravely. 'But it's a bit of a leap from a grope to—I don't know, doing away with the girl?'

He put his face in his hands. 'There were dark places,' he said, 'in Claudio's past, in his mind, too. We don't know what he might think, where he might think he was.

'If only we could find her,' he said. 'Alive or dead.' He looked up. 'She's out there somewhere.'

'So give yourself a bit more time,' said Luisa gently. 'Talking to Lucia won't get you to her.' She smiled faintly. 'And are you going to just let Massi off the hook? Because if you don't go and stick pins into him, I will. If he'd come forward when she didn't turn up for their rendezvous instead of just scuttling off home to his wife and saying nothing, then we'd be in a very different position now, wouldn't we?'

Sandro looked at her with admiration; she was a slow-burner, all right, Luisa, his little glowing furnace of a wife, but she sent out sparks. He felt one of them kindle and take. 'You're right,' he said. 'You always are.'

So now she and Giulietta were off to the Via dei Bardi on their wild goose chase after the mad old cat lady, and he was sitting here in his parked car staring at the Boboli, as if it was going to tell him all the answers.

Sandro shifted his gaze, and found himself staring instead into the darkened windows of the gallery, where Paolo Massi had spent all day working. There in the window was a desk, a great ostentatious carved thing, right in the window so that everyone could see the great man at his labours, and he in turn could amuse himself by watching the passing trade.

Luisa was right; he needed to get Paolo Massi in front of him. He'd seen men like him before; a slimy little wife-batterer from Prato who'd had an alibi for the time his wife was pushed down the stairs; a businessman who'd paid a market-stallholder to kill his wife for the insurance. He'd nailed them both, and others like them, because if there was one thing Sandro knew how to do, it was take a liar and shake him upside down until the truth came out.

Why did he hate Paolo Massi? Sandro felt his adrenaline rise as he surrendered to the feeling. Massi, so apparently high-minded, so noble-looking, but underneath it all, only interested in money. And sleeping with his students too, it seemed. But mostly money. Pietro hadn't liked him either, and neither had Lucia Gentileschi. Only Claudio had been taken in by him, it seemed; they must have had some kind of relationship, however sporadic—why else would Massi's wife have called on Lucia with her condolences? Poor Claudio.

Why couldn't it have been Massi, not Claudio, up there molesting Veronica Hutton? In his head Sandro assembled a makeshift series of events, the girl finding out about another woman, perhaps, and threatening to expose his affair with her, threatening to bring the business down? The business he'd snatched back from under the noses of the Guardia? But he'd been in the gallery all day, even if she'd probably walked right past it on her way to the Boboli. Had that been why she came through this gate? Now, that was an interesting idea.

But there was the wife and her alibi; would she lie for him? There was Antonella Scarpa. Somewhere in his head a clangour set up, of things wrong, things discordant.

His train of thought was derailed as a fire engine roared past, so close in the narrow street that the car wobbled, then another; and it dawned on Sandro that he'd been hearing the blasted things for hours now, in the distance while they'd sat in Nello, but closer now. The clamour of the fire engine bells, police sirens. What was going on? Wearily Sandro pushed open the door and climbed on to the pavement.

Up ahead the fire engine was stuck in the narrow canyon of the Via Romana. Behind the fire engines a car in the pale blue livery of the Polizia Statale had come to a halt; ahead the fire engines had been held up by a truck up on the pavement, and someone was sounding a horn with relentless aggression. Sandro walked the few steps to the stationary police car, leaned down and tapped on the window. He didn't recognize the man who turned an expressionless face up to him from the passenger seat.

'What's going on?' he asked humbly. 'All these sirens.'

The man looked away from him, through the windscreen, and seeing that they weren't going anywhere condescended to answer. 'There's some flooding,' he said warily. Sandro ducked his head further and saw that he recognized the officer beyond him at the wheel, vaguely, what was his name, Roberti? Alberti?

'Commissario Gioberti?' he said tentatively, and the man turned his head, gave a microscopic nod.

'They're closing the bridges,' the senior officer said curtly. 'A part of the weir at Santa Rosa has disintegrated, washed away. Water's coming up under the Uffizi and they're trying to pump it out, and the Rowing Club's under water.' He expelled a breath explosively. 'Hope you're not in a rush to get home, Cellini, because you won't get back to Santa Croce tonight, not unless you can call up a helicopter.'

Ahead of him the truck lumbered off the pavement and the fire engines lurched ahead; the two policemen in the car turned their heads away and his interview was terminated. Closing the bridges? Stuck in the Oltrano, south of the river? He tried to get his head around the idea, and didn't know where to start. He called Luisa.

❋ ❋ ❋

When Iris emerged on to the Piazza Signoria, Jackson close behind her, it was as she'd never seen it: completely deserted. On the far side a temporary barrier had been set up across the entrance to the great galleried space of the Uffizi.

'We could go to your place,' said Jackson hopefully. 'No danger of flooding there, huh?'

'Oh, no,' said Iris, shaking her head. 'I've got stuff to do.' And ignoring him she got out her phone, removed Ronnie's sim card, wrapped it, replaced it with her own. Laboriously she tapped in a message while he watched, then she put the phone away.

'Who was that to?' he said, and she frowned.

'None of your business,' she said.

'Listen Iris,' said Jackson, and this time he wasn't cocky or wheedling or angry, just desperate. 'Don't be that way. If this is about Sophia—I—she—she wasn't anything. We were just—'

'Just fooling around, yeah,' said Iris, angry more than anything because he thought she cared. He thought all this was about Sophia. 'Why don't you tell Sophia that she wasn't anything?' She folded her arms across her body. 'Look,' she said, relenting, because why would she even let him think she was angry? She wasn't angry. 'Look, can't you understand that this isn't about that stuff? It really isn't. We're in a mess, this is too serious for us to be just playing around trying to be detectives. There are things we know that the police should know, simple as that.'

'They look kind of busy,' said Jackson, nodding towards a Carabiniere vehicle parked under the statue of Neptune, an officer leaning on the side under a military raincape and talking urgently into his radio.

'You're making excuses,' said Iris. He looked at his feet.

'OK,' he said quietly, 'I'll go,' but she went on as if he hadn't spoken.

'And I know that whatever her mum thinks, Ronnie's probably dead...' and although she planned to say it in that casual, hard way, she found she couldn't, and she had to swallow. 'But we need to find her. I need to find her. She's my friend.'

Jackson looked up at her, his face frozen with reluctance. 'I still think it would be better if you came with me,' he said stubbornly.

'I think maybe you should take the sim card, too,' she said, ignoring him to fish in her purse for it.

'Jeez, no,' said Jackson, alarmed. 'How'm I going to explain that? Oh, I just found it lying around? They're going to think I had something to do with it.' She looked at him patiently.

'Jackson,' she said, 'come on. You can't go on running away. I—I've got my stuff to do. Take it.' He took it.

'Are you going to be OK?' he asked, ducking his head. 'I don't think you should go on your own.'

She held up the message she'd sent. 'Sandro'll meet me there,' she said. 'He's a good guy. Look, you take his number, yeah?' His shoulders lowered in defeat, Jackson took out his phone, no longer so magical to Iris, and tapped in Sandro Cellini's number.

'So you know where the Carabiniere station is, yes? At the Boboli?'

'OK,' he said, hands shoved in his pockets, scruffy backpack slumped over his shoulder, grungy waterproof, hair already plastered flat under the rain. Iris almost felt sorry for him. 'I'll call you?' he said quietly. 'Later?'

'Maybe,' she said, and he sighed. As she watched him trudge away she infuriated herself by thinking, He probably hates me now. Bossy bitch. Can't be helped.

❀ ❀ ❀

Jackson didn't look back to watch her go; he wanted her to believe in him. It made him feel more—resolute, was that the word? Just to look ahead. He turned off the darkening and empty Piazza Signoria towards the Via Por Santa Maria, the main drag from the Ponte Vecchio to the Duomo, to head across the bridge.

Only there was a police barrier, and the other side of it, where the Piazza Signoria had been deserted, the Via Por Santa Maria was thronged, as packed as a cattle pen. He reached the barrier and was allowed past, though he had no idea how he was going to get any further. Wondering what the hell was going on, Jackson felt his blood stir; this was something after all? This was a challenge. Jackson worked his way to the corner, with a lot of apologizing for his backpack; it was more or less dark by now, and the rain was still coming down. He had to fight his way through umbrellas and as he made his painfully slow progress he could tell that the crowd was half excited, half turning to frustration and anger. '*Cazzo!*' he heard an Italian man grumble, as Jackson trod on a foot, and an angry face turned towards him.

'Sorry, sorry,' he said, 'gee, sorry.' He looked left, down towards the Ponte Vecchio, and saw that it was empty, the passage blocked. It didn't make sense. He could see a carabiniere on a horse, upright under the rain in a raincape, and thought hopelessly of his mission. They really were kind of busy just now, weren't they? Could there be another Carabiniere station this side of the river?

Someone must have heard his American English, because at his elbow he heard a voice say, quietly, 'They've closed the bridges.' He turned his head.

'Some kind of precaution,' said Sophia, six inches away from him. Her face was washed out, he thought, like she'd been crying, but she looked steadily at him. The Japanese girl—Hiroko?—was standing next to her. They looked at him, unsmiling, his judge and jury.

'Right,' he said humbly. 'I've got to get to the Carabiniere station, or some kind of police station. Iris—we found some things out.'

'It's not going to happen, Jackson,' said Hiroko, and he thought, clutching at straws, that he heard the trace of kindness in her voice. 'We heard on the radio the Uffizi was flooding and we came down to see what we could do.' The crowd jostled them, but Hiroko held her ground patiently. 'Look around you,' she said. 'Who's going to have time to listen to you?'

'I've got to get to the police station,' said Jackson stubbornly, and for the second time that day, he felt like crying. Only this time he didn't.

'Let's get out of here,' said Sophia; her voice was different, wasn't it? Grown-up. 'We can't do anything stuck here. Let's find somewhere to sit down, and you can tell us, instead of the Carabinieri.'

'OK,' said Jackson, giving in. 'Why not?'

Chapter Twenty-three

STILL SITTING IN the dark, Sandro reflected that this was the most familiar of situations to him. Sometimes alone, sometimes with Pietro, inhabiting the warm seclusion of the patrol car almost as if it was a chamber of his own brain, and thinking. This was where the girl went in; he'd seen her pass below his own window on her way here on All Saints' Day. He'd stood there wondering if it had been a terrible mistake, who did he think he was, setting up on his own, his life was over and he'd better admit it, and there she'd been running past with her whole life ahead of her. Or so she'd thought: Veronica Hutton.

Was it a terrible mistake? For a moment Sandro felt an awful tug of longing, for Pietro to open the car door and climb in beside him just like nothing had happened; to say, like he always used to, *Where to next, capo?* And he knew that tug when it came; it was the very thing he'd been dodging since his father had followed his mother to the grave close to fifty years before. It was grief, and Sandro was on his own with it.

Where to next? Sandro gripped the steering-wheel of the stationary car as if he thought it might take him somewhere of its own accord. Think. What had he learned, categorically, over the previous forty-eight hours? That he was afraid of death. That Veronica Hutton had been here.

There was at least incontrovertible proof of that, not merely the word of an alcoholic barman, on the camera suspended above the Annalena gate.

Sandro leaned back, hands still on the steering-wheel, and gazed sideways out of the car window. Had it been a thrill for Veronica Hutton, to pass so close to where her lover was working? Was she thinking only about the time they would be alone together? Or was she planning how to charm the old painter into giving up his secrets, his gossip, his history, so she could just casually impress Massi with her insider's knowledge?

Another fire engine drew alongside, slowed to get past, sped on. Sandro fretted; where was Massi? He decided to tell Luisa what was going on, while he waited.

The line crackled as it rang, and not for the first time since the rains began and he started investigating Claudio Gentileschi's last hours on earth, Sandro had the overwhelming feeling that something catastrophic was in the air, literally. Flooding; chaos; everything coming apart at the seams. Claudio Gentileschi a fraudster, a faker, a molester of young women, a killer. But Luisa sounded cheerful.

'It won't kill us,' she said simply. 'We can sleep on Giuli's floor, we can stay with my aunt Alice in Galluzzo, we can book into a hotel, for heaven's sake. It's hardly high season. And, anyway, you know what they're like, it's probably all just an exaggeration.' She tutted. 'I mean, whoever heard of them closing all the bridges?'

Was she enjoying this? He didn't mind if she was. 'Massi hasn't turned up yet,' he said. 'Maybe he's stuck on the other side. I'll be here.'

'OK,' said Luisa. 'We're nearly at the Cat Lady's place.' She took a breath. 'Hope she's at home.'

'You're not tired, are you?' said Sandro, anxiously. 'You're feeling all right? You're dry?'

'I'm fine,' said Luisa. 'I've got my boots, my raincoat—I'm looking forward to pinning this Fiamma DiTommaso down, if you must know. I told you she did a runner when I tried to talk to her in the garden?' There was a pause, and Sandro grunted. Luisa did sound OK; she probably needed to take her mind off—things. 'Giuli's looking after me, anyway,' she said. 'I don't need you.'

'Should I pick you up?' said Sandro, helplessly. Luisa laughed. 'How you going to do that?' she said. 'If they're closing the bridges, the only way to get anywhere's going to be on foot. We'll come and find you.'

As he hung up, out of the corner of his eye he saw a whole golden window of light extinguished, and he turned his head to look. Opposite the Galleria Massi was a shop that sold carved and gilded light fittings, a window display with a scarlet silk-spread bed and boudoir lighting, now dark; as he watched a stocky woman came out and reached up for the iron shutter to the window to close up. She had a defeated look about her; she must be struggling, thought Sandro, if she's got to come in and open the shop on a November Sunday. Hold on, he thought, didn't Luisa say something about the shop opposite? Hold on. He climbed out of the car.

'Evening,' he said, and she looked at him, keys in hand and the shutter half-down.

'Yes,' she said suspiciously. Sandro briefly considered a story about needing a wall sconce before dismissing it. He merely nodded across the street at the gallery. In his pocket the damned phone pipped at him, again; he ignored it. How could a man think straight with these bloody things firing off messages every five minutes?

'The Galleria Massi,' he said, gesturing across the road. 'D'you know him? Paolo Massi?'

She snorted. She was strongly built, a small workhorse of a person, with thick dyed blonde hair and a watchful air that Sandro liked. 'I know him,' she said. 'Or at least, I watch him mess about with that place, if that counts. You can get to know someone that way, I suppose.'

'Don't like him much?' said Sandro, and she inspected him more closely.

'Not much,' she said. 'What business is it of yours?'

He gave her the swift outline of an answer, a private inves-tigation, involving a student of Massi's. She nodded. Gabriella, but he could call her Gabi, she said. With a sigh she removed her key from the shutter, leaving it up, pushed the door to the shop open again, flicked the light switch. 'Not as if I've got anything else to do,' she said. 'After you.'

From here you could see more of the dim interior over the road, he noticed; far down at the back of a shop some kind of security light was on.

'I only asked him to put some flyers in the gallery,' Gabi said indignantly, 'and said I'd reciprocate, and he acted like I was some kind of street trash with my hand out.'

'Is he there every day?' She tossed her head. 'When it suits him. He runs a school too, doesn't he? He comes down here to play at being a bigshot, or when he has some student show to put up, like last week.' She peered through the glass. 'At least, I think that's what it was; this one must be pretty special. A lot of to-ing and fro-ing all week.' She looked thoughtful. 'God knows where he stores all that crap, when it doesn't sell. Probably takes it to the dump.'

As she spoke they were standing at her desk—like Massi's, it was stationed at the front of the shop, just inside the door.

'You like to get a good view of the street?' he asked.

'Of course,' she said. 'Who wants to hide away at the back? And it deters shoplifters. Even he likes to look into the street.' She nodded over the road.

'Ever been inside his shop?' Sandro asked.

'You mean gallery,' she corrected him, curling her lip. 'I'm a shopkeeper, he's a—a patron of the arts.' She pursed her lips. 'Just the once, asking that favour; he made it clear he wouldn't welcome another visit. I thought it was full of rubbish, modern stuff, student exhibitions, hardly worth the storage space. I'd like to know how he makes a living.' She tapped the side of her nose.

'Got any ideas?' It occurred to him that Gabi might be the woman who sold him out to the Guardia; never mind discarded lover, more like retail envy. In this day and age, it was money over sex, every time.

She was talking angrily, staring across the road. 'Well, the nice shiny SUVs with German plates don't go away with pigs' heads in formaldehyde and student artwork, do they? They get their stuff out of the back room in beautiful hand-made portfolios.'

Sandro took a step nearer to the window, the germ of something taking shape in his mind. What had Antonella Scarpa said they sold? Renaissance drawings, that kind of thing?

'Tuesday,' he said with an effort, trying to tie this thing together, to get back to facts. 'Massi says his wife came down, to have lunch with him. Could that be right?'

'Wife?' Gabi snorted again. 'Which one?' Sandro started back at that, and saw her sourly mischievous expression.

'Only joking,' said Gabi. 'She's not his wife, is she? The bossy little Sardinian woman, the *Sarda* with the short black hair. Not his wife, even if she acts like it. Antonella Scarpa, thought Sandro. Gabi went on. 'She's down here often enough, that one. If I was his wife I'd—well, I wouldn't like to be his wife, put it that way.'

'So she—the real wife, I mean—you're saying she wasn't here on Tuesday?'

'Actually,' said Gabi, wrinkling her brow, 'Tuesday? I'm not open Mondays so, yes, I came in Tuesday, All Saints or not. Funny thing is, I think you could be right, she was here Tuesday, old number one wife.' She unfolded her arms, her face relaxed as she pondered. She laughed. 'I remember now, because it looked like she'd come down to take over from number two wife.'

Antonella Scarpa had been here for a couple of hours in the morning, Sandro remembered him saying that. Massi. Hiding behind his women.

Gabi seated herself at the small desk, as though re-enacting her working day; set her chin in both hands and stared through her rain-spattered window across the grey street.

Sandro found himself holding his breath, although he wasn't quite sure why; the stocky little woman was so intent, suddenly.

'He arrived first,' she began, slowly. 'Bright and early, for him, I remember wondering if today was the day, only the student show's always on a Saturday. He had a coffee in a takeaway cup, let himself in. He was…' she frowned. 'Let me think, he had something with him, more than the usual—he often has a document case or such like. Tuesday he had—what was it? He was having difficulty with the door, what with the takeaway cup, carrying it all. More like a weekend bag type of thing, fancy designer one. He went straight in the back, and left it there.'

Sandro followed her gaze, fixing on the glow of the security light visible at the back of the gallery. Once his eyes adjusted, he could see that it illuminated a wall of storage, and a door out to the back.

'Then he came back to his desk, sat right down, didn't really move.' She smiled to herself. 'Sometimes I just stare at him, waiting for him to give in and meet my eye, but it's like I don't exist, you know? He was on the phone a bit, then did some paperwork.'

'And Antonella Scarpa? His assistant? When did she arrive on the scene?'

There had been something about Antonella, thought Sandro, hadn't there? Tougher than him, by a long way. A worker, tenacious, prickly. How did she feel about being number two wife? Number three, maybe, after Veronica Hutton.

Pursing her lips, Gabi pronounced, 'She turned up, oh, must have been ten? I'd nipped down the road for a coffee myself around then, and she was arriving just as I was letting myself back in.'

'Was that the only time you left the shop?' he asked.

Gabi looked at him, affronted. 'It was,' she said with dignity. 'I bring myself a sandwich, generally. No such thing as a lunch break, these days.'

'And when the wife arrived?'

She frowned again, concentrating hard. 'An hour or so later? Eleven, eleven-thirty sort of time?'

'A bit early for lunch,' mused Sandro, half to himself. And a bit of a coincidence, anyway, if the wife hardly ever went down there, for her to turn up just out of the blue.

'Lunch? I didn't see much sign of lunch,' said Gabi, chin still in her hands. 'Not then, anyway, too early for lunch.' She frowned. 'I think she went out a bit later, when I was eating my own lunch, half one or so. First off, though, she saw number two wife off the premises pretty quick, literally took her place, rolled up her sleeves and got down to messing about with the pictures, like she was his assistant now. Fireworks, I'd say. Surprised to see her wasn't in it.'

'Oh yes?' said Sandro, carefully.

Gabi laughed to herself meanly. 'Whatever they were saying to each other, between the three of them, they scared off the only customer I've seen put a head around that door in months, poor thing ran off like a scalded cat.'

'And Scarpa left then? The Sardinian woman? At around—' he tried to sound casual—'eleven-thirty?'

'She did. Around then, yes. Although I had a customer myself at that point. It was a good day, Tuesday, the sun brings 'em out, you know.' At which they both gazed into the street, the sun a distant memory. A car drew up slowly on to the kerb opposite, two figures seated in the front.

'So you weren't looking over the road?'

'Oh, yes, I kept an eye,' said Gabi. 'I was interested, by then, you know? There's days and days go by, sitting here, and they don't often put on that kind of a show. Half the time the place is closed.'

'Thing is,' said Sandro, aware that this was the six-million-dollar question, 'Massi says he was there all day. Says his wife can vouch for that, she was there all day with him.'

Gabi grimaced. 'Well,' she said reluctantly, 'I got to say, he really was there the whole day, I can see him, you see, at that desk. Though they left a bit early, around four. I saw them locking up, the full works, shutters down. You'd think they had a couple of Leonardos in there instead of some student sketches.'

'And he couldn't have, say, slipped out for half an hour, while you were serving?'

This was getting too far-fetched, wasn't it? So it was no surprise when Gabi shook her head. 'Well, no,' she said with regret. 'Sorry, *caro*. He was sitting at that desk like she'd glued him down; she was out the back somewhere, she didn't reappear for a while, then when she did she went off in the car and came back with a sandwich bag, and he was there the whole time. He didn't even go out into the yard for a smoke; I've seen him do that, when he's under pressure. A couple of minutes? Well, possibly. But not half an hour, not even ten minutes. Nope.'

Across the road the couple climbed out of the car; they'd been sitting there like they were having a lover's tiff, but then Sandro saw that they weren't a couple but Paolo Massi and Antonella Scarpa.

Gabi stood up, and folded her arms back across her chest. 'Looks like number two wife's back in charge, hey,' she said.

❀ ❀ ❀

The Via dei Bardi, where Fiamma DiTommaso supposedly lived at number twelve and which was usually the most tomblike of streets with its high stone walls and deep gloom, found itself in noisy chaos. Cars were backed up in the rain and people smoking angrily on the pavements.

The two women edged along the narrow thoroughfare under the gardens of the Costa Scarpuccia, which were banked up and held in place by an ancient and bulging wall.

'They're closing the bridges,' said Giulietta, helpfully, to a man standing under the dripping foliage, as they skirted him. He scowled, more at the world, thought Luisa, than at Giuli. The world's not so bad, she wanted to say, even the rain on her face seemed a kind of blessing, even the chaos and the flooding were better than nothing.

They trudged on towards their goal. Most people who lived on this street were very wealthy indeed and the façades were well maintained, but there were pockets of poverty and dereliction. Lead-blackened plaster, cheap and shabby windows, disintegrating stonework. They were everywhere in the city, rent-controlled buildings where the landlords were trying to starve their stubborn, ancient tenants out by refusing to carry out repairs or modernize the properties. Sometimes they held whole families of immigrant workers, revealed only in summer when their ground-floor shutters would be thrown open in the gasping heat to expose a wall full of bunk beds, like a termite mound exposed.

Fiamma DiTommaso's place, unsurprisingly, was one of these. It was at the foot of the Costa Scarpuccia, which made sense; the wild triangle of garden supported by its crumbling wall was home, Luisa knew, to another colony of cats; you couldn't walk up the Costa Scarpuccia without tripping over a dish encrusted with rotting food.

It wasn't that Luisa didn't like cats, she told herself. She had nothing against them, even if they did make her sneeze; she could see that a nice well-fed animal curled up on an old lady's balcony could be a source of comfort in old age or widowhood. But en masse, the itinerant packs of half-wild ones, slipping through the shadows of the Boboli, shying from human contact, all shades of camouflage, grey and tabby and tortoiseshell? Downright spooky, and unhygienic to boot.

But, then, she realized, even before Fiamma DiTommaso finally allowed them entry to her own den, there was something half-feral about the woman herself.

They rang the doorbell, and predictably enough there was no answer. They stood in silence, watching the façade; on the first floor the shutters were so warped that they curled outwards from the wall like a stale sandwich. There was someone behind them, watching.

'Please, Signora DiTommaso,' Luisa called. 'It's either talk to us, or to the police, isn't it? Give us a chance?' Behind her on the pavement a woman in her car, stuck with engine idling, put her head out of the driver window and gave them a curious look. Behind the shutters there was a shifting of light and then, abruptly, the front door opened.

'Inside,' hissed Fiamma DiTommaso. Even in the hallway there was the overpowering reek of cat. Luisa sneezed.

It was two rooms on the first floor, one leading off another. There was a sink at the back beside an ancient electric cooker, and a crude cupboard in one corner that must, Luisa deduced, constitute Fiamma DiTommaso's facilities. No cats were actually in evidence, although the blanket that had been thrown over a small sofa was thick with silvered hairs.

Fiamma DiTommaso was wearing thick-soled sandals, despite the season, from which thin, bare, sun-spattered legs protruded, voluminous, gathered cotton trousers, and a faded sweatshirt. A thin scarf was wound around her head. DiTommaso was a name as old as Massi or Badigliani but this woman had taken a decidedly different route in life—no lipstick, no handbag to match the shoes: no greed. Despite a distaste born of the decades she had spent striving for elegance, to her surprise Luisa found herself admiring the woman.

It was impossible to say how old Fiamma DiTommaso was. Perhaps fifty, perhaps sixty; not far off Luisa's own age.

'Sit down,' she said, and gestured towards the hairy sofa. Luisa sat, and even before her behind came into contact with the blanket she could feel her nose and throat swell in response to the allergens.

Gingerly Giulietta sat down beside her; if anything she seemed more uneasy than Luisa. Looking around the sparse, dismal flat—one of the walls was in fact bare of plaster and showed exposed brick—Luisa realized that it probably resembled more or less every miserable, condemned squat and prostitute's walk-up in which Giuli had spent her formative years. There were small touches of home—a framed photograph over the sink, a can of coffee, a small Buddha in front of a cheap mirror.

Fiamma DiTommaso had her arms folded tightly across her grey-sweatshirted chest; she was thin, under all that voluminous cotton, Luisa saw. 'Just ask what you want to ask,' she said, her voice rusty, as if she didn't use it much.

The flat was dark, the shutters closed. A single lamp was lit, with a dim bulb, beside the sofa. Luisa kept her voice gentle.

'It's about the girl,' she said, surprising herself by beginning that way, but it was true, wasn't it? 'The girl you saw, the girl who threw her bag away.'

'Who says I saw her?'

'When did you find the bag, Fiamma?' asked Luisa.

'Evening time,' said Fiamma DiTommaso, a little too quickly. 'Handed it straight in, didn't I? Took it to the pigs at the Carabiniere station, though I got no thanks for it.'

Pigs; the woman was an old radical, that was it. 'How did you find it?' Luisa asked, patiently.

'Just lying there,' she said stubbornly.

'It must have been dark,' said Luisa.

'Closes at four,' Giulietta butted in, 'the park. Not usually there that late, are you?' Luisa looked at her, looked back at DiTommaso; there were similarities, weren't there? For a second it seemed to Luisa that DiTommaso might be Giuli's mother, if Giuli's mother weren't dead. She let Giuli go on. Good cop, bad cop, was that the phrase?

'You found it at midday, didn't you?' said Giulietta, as calm as if she'd thought this all out beforehand. Perhaps she had. 'You took it home, thinking you might take the money, because you're not exactly loaded, are you? And it wasn't as if you'd stolen it. Finders keepers.'

DiTommaso stared back at her sullenly, and said nothing.

'What made you bring it back?' said Luisa gently. 'It's all right, we're not the police, are we? Not going to tell them, either, if we can help it. But the girl—the girl's gone missing. Did you know that? We don't know if she's alive or dead.' There was a silence. 'What made you bring it back? Did you start to think? Was there something you saw, or heard?'

'You could help us find her,' said Giulietta. 'You could save her.'

'I didn't see anything,' said DiTommaso, at last. 'I only heard, I heard them shouting.' Her jaw set, mulish, like a child's. 'I didn't take the money, did I? I brought it all back. I was going to tell 'em, the pigs, the bloody police, only they treated me like—like I was dirty.'

Luisa nodded; she felt ashamed. 'I understand,' she said. 'You're not dirty. You can tell me, can't you?'

For a moment she didn't know which way it was going to go, but then DiTommaso sank down on to the sofa and made a soft clucking noise. From nowhere a huge tomcat appeared and leapt silently on to her knee. 'All right,' she said roughly. 'I'll tell you.'

Chapter Twenty-four

SANDRO DIDN'T KNOW what he was going to say until he said it, although at least he had the instinct to say nothing at all until they'd let him through the door.

Massi had clearly brought Antonella Scarpa along as back-up; typical, Sandro thought, as they busied themselves nervously around the lock. Hiding behind a woman. The security shutter was a wire mesh, he noticed; was this because they intended the place to be a showroom, a kind of advertisement? No point in hiding the wares from the public.

Massi was complaining about the traffic; Sandro kept the information that the bridges were going to be closed to himself. He had turned up, at least, the great Direttore; Sandro's ineradicable instinct for fear told him the man was very nervous: what had changed? Sandro had forced him out of his comfort zone, was that it? But this was his gallery.

'It's kind of you,' was all Sandro said. 'I don't think this will take long.' When he had made this arrangement, he marvelled, he had had no idea, none at all. But now he was here, now he could smell the air in this place, he knew he was on to something.

A row of lights flicked on, downlighting the dark-coloured walls, which were a kind of deep maroon. It was very cold. It occurred to him that they were practically underground, set back into the hillside, the great cold weight of earth and rock above them.

Buying a little time, Sandro walked along the row of framed work, some ink drawings of architectural detail, charcoal, a couple of oils that seemed to him to be poorly executed, but what did he know? A drawing of a girl lying on her back, reading a book; he stopped in front of the picture.

He turned.

'You know a man called Claudio Gentileschi,' he said. It was not a question; they both gaped at him under the sepulchral lighting. He focussed on Paolo Massi.

'You met him a little more than ten years ago, at a reception at the synagogue, to which you were invited because your father was considered a friend of the Florentine Jewish community.'

'I'm sorry.' Paolo Massi seemed belatedly to recover his tongue. 'Ten years ago? I—I—I have no idea what this has to do with, with your investigation.'

'Claudio Gentileschi died on the same day that Veronica Hutton disappeared.'

That would have to do; it seemed to have the effect of relaxing Massi, just fractionally. He inclined his head; it occurred to Sandro with the weight of inevitability that Paolo Massi was very happy for him to draw the obvious conclusions from that simple fact.

'Ten years is a long time,' he said with an attempt at a smile. 'But the name is familiar, yes.'

'Gentileschi's widow says your wife called on her,' said Sandro. 'To pay her respects. On Friday night.'

Massi's smile was a little fixed. 'My wife is very proper in these matters,' he said.

'But there had been a continued connection, obviously,' said Sandro. 'Between your family and theirs?'

Massi opened his mouth, and closed it again.

Reaching up to a hook beside the door to hang up her coat, it was Antonella Scarpa who spoke, over her shoulder, as if casually.

'Claudio Gentileschi has sold the occasional piece of work through us, Paolo. Don't you remember? He is rather a good artist, some beautiful drawings.'

Slowly Sandro turned to focus on her; he didn't believe a word of it. She slotted her arms into the sleeves of another of her white work-coats, her uniform. She was prepared.

'His own work?'

'What do you mean?' said Antonella Scarpa, and he saw through her in that moment, standing there looking severely at him, hands in her pockets, trying to bamboozle him.

You're good, he thought, you're good; is it love, or is it business, that makes you so good at lying for him? Across her shoulder he saw, through the window and out across the dark street, Gabi silhouetted in the window of her own shop, staring at them.

'What I mean, Signorina Scarpa,' he said, extemporizing, 'is that I have information to the effect that for ten years Claudio Gentileschi has not merely been supplying you with the odd beautiful piece of his own work, as you put it. He has been a one-man production line of high-quality faked drawings, for you to sell on to your international customers. Your Germans, your Americans, your Russian billionaires with Riviera properties to furnish and money to launder—you must have been very happy indeed with the fall of communism, no?'

'You're talking nonsense,' said Antonella Scarpa, calmly. 'This is pure fantasy.'

Sandro held her gaze. 'You thought you could put anything over on them, ignorant Russian peasants, did you? Well, let me tell you, when they find out that you've been cheating them, you'll find out there are certain things those Russian peasant oligarchs are very good at indeed.' He withdrew the flimsy cardboard folder from his bag and took out one of the drawings he'd lifted from Claudio's studio.

'You weren't scared of the Guardia di Finanza, were you? Bet you were pleased with yourselves when you saw them off. Scared now?'

'They found nothing,' said Massi, faintly. 'There was no evidence of any—of any impropriety.' Scarpa shot him a glance, and he fell silent.

'He was a good man,' said Sandro, surprised by the fervour in his own voice, as he defended Claudio. 'How did you talk him into it?'

Paolo Massi looked back at him, his jaw slack and weak, no longer the great patron of the arts, the Svengali to any susceptible, pretty student. No, thought Sandro, we haven't even got to that yet, have we? The girls. First things first. He stayed calm.

'I expect you used your father's name, didn't you? The old printing presses kept running through the war, the Jewish connection. With perhaps a hint of how he needed to make sure his wife, who was so much younger, would be taken care of after he'd gone?'

Helplessly Massi put out a hand for the drawing but Sandro pulled it back. 'Even if we can't trace all the Renaissance drawings you've sold over the past few years, one or two should be enough, don't you think?'

Sandro moved on. 'Are they out at the back?' It felt as though he might almost have been speaking in tongues; it all came tumbling out, guesswork, improvisation, but even as he said it he knew it made sense.

'Is that what you're keeping there, the work you cleared out of Claudio's studio, before anyone else knew he was dead? Pity to waste that investment you've been making in him all these years, and where are you going to get work of this quality?' He held up the faded sepia drawing, Claudio's life's work. 'A pity to waste it.'

And how did they get in? To Claudio's studio? Could Claudio have given them a key from the beginning, proud, private Claudio? Wouldn't that have seemed like they owned him?

But as the inconvenient questions posed themselves he noticed that Antonella Scarpa had moved to position herself between him and the door at the back of the gallery, down under the security light that he had watched from Gabi's shop. He flicked a look back across the road towards her, his only ally, but the shop was dark now. Gabi had gone home.

'I'd like a look in there,' he said, easily. 'If you don't mind?'

'And if we do?' said Antonella Scarpa. He almost admired her; she had guts, at least. The fierce little *Sarda* in her white coat.

'Well,' he said, 'I'm sure the police could persuade you, couldn't they?'

'I think they're busy just now,' said Massi, sneering; Sandro observed him try to puff himself up, like some creature trying to make itself appear larger when threatened.

And with the two of them motionless and blocking him in in the near-dark, Sandro was just beginning to wonder what he would actually do if Luisa and Giuli didn't turn up—or even if they did, would they be a match for these two?—when Massi's telephone rang. And everything changed.

❀ ❀ ❀

'No way,' said Sophia, her eyes wide. 'Oh, my, God. No way, Jackson.'

Too chastened to feel more than a tiny twinge of satisfaction, Jackson just nodded. At least this was an improvement; as they'd walked to the bar Sophia's eyes had been fixed on him, switching from silent reproach to sullen anger and back again. Couldn't blame her, could he? *Sorry, Sophia*; he tried it out in his head, but it sounded pathetic. So he said nothing at all until they were out of the rain, and then he told them.

They were in a bar Jackson had never been in before, a back-street place that was long and narrow as a corridor, nowhere to sit, mirror along one wall dripping condensation and a shelf under it to rest your coffee on. The air was fusty with the odour of damp wool but ahead of them Hiroko had calmly threaded her way through the packed bodies and made a space. Jackson fetched coffee, struggling with the Italian, but nobody in this place spoke English.

'So, Jackson,' said Hiroko, placing herself square in front of him. 'You have talked to Iris?' He got the apologies out of the way, he seemed to have spent the day stumbling over his words what with one thing and another, while they stared him down. And then he came to it.

'She thinks it's Massi Ronnie was going away with,' he said. 'Actually, she knows.'

'No way,' said Sophia, round-eyed.

Hiroko remained silent, waiting for his evidence.

'I don't like him,' she said quietly when he'd finished— or almost finished. 'I never liked him, from the beginning, too much fake. And he actually does not know so much about painting; he dated two of the Uccello drawings wrong, and the techniques of the mediaeval, he knows nothing, Antonella knows more than him.' Jackson stared at her; quiet, polite, attentive Hiroko, had been thinking this all along?

'Only this is not evidence,' she said patiently. 'The Zecchi colours, the trip to Sicily—well, I agree, there is some kind of evidence, but in a—in a court of law?'

Jackson fumbled in his pocket, in a panic; could he have just stuck it in there? Had it fallen out?

'Here,' he said. 'Look? Here?' They stared at the tiny square of plastic. 'Anyone got a phone?' he asked, and Sophia took hers out only she seemed to have an iPhone all of a sudden, just like his. He looked at her; she bought it because of me, he realized, and they cost twice as much here. Ah, shit.

'No good,' he said apologetically, bringing out his own, 'y'know, locked? Both of 'em. No way you can get around the contract with the iPhone. Stupid, huh?' He tried to smile at her, but ducked his head before she could glare back. Hiroko set her own phone on the counter, a modest, scratched little number. 'Yeah,' he said enthusiastically, 'yeah, great.'

Calmly she slid off the back, held out her hand for the card, slid it in over the contacts, replaced the battery, turned it on. The screen opened.

'Message,' said Hiroko, pointing to a small icon in the corner. Answerphone message?'

'Yeah, OK,' said Jackson, itching to get his hands on the phone but not wanting to muscle in. Hiroko handed it to him wordlessly. Call info, missed calls, down, down, and there he was. He held up the screen.

'Paolo,' said Sophia, sceptically. 'Well, it's not as if it isn't, like, about the third most common name in Italy or anything, is it?'

Hiroko gave her a soft look of reproof. 'You just have to telephone the number,' she suggested. 'And then we know.' Jackson handed her the phone. 'You,' he said. 'You do it.'

❄ ❄ ❄

Iris stopped outside the apartment building, soaked to the bone. She'd had to walk all the way, because something was up with the traffic—no buses, no taxis, nothing. She didn't know if she'd even be able to remember the way, but she was here.

At the crossroads a drain had burst, bubbling up through the grating like a geyser to meet a torrent pouring down the Via San Domenico from Fiesole. As she made her way through it the thought occurred to Iris that this was more than just another traffic screw-up, it was a full-scale natural disaster. Ma might be watching it on television; I could call, thought Iris, with longing. After; I'll call after.

Looking up at the building's grim façade, she thought that it would be warm inside, at least. She didn't want to start this thing by asking for something dry to wear, but what the hell. Too late now. She leaned on the doorbell, hard.

Chapter Twenty-five

GIULIETTA KEPT ASKING her how she was as they walked, half ran, back along the narrow streets in the dark. 'You OK, darling?'

And looking at her anxiously. 'I'll be fine,' Luisa said, through numb lips. 'When we get there.'

The traffic seemed to be moving, slowly, though it was still chaos; at the end of the Via dei Bardi they came out on to the river. To get to the Via Romana they could have gone over the top from the Costa Scarpuccia, up the steep, steep hill and back down on to the Via Guicciardini, but Luisa had just shaken her head when Giuli pointed up there; she felt breathless enough as it was.

Nothing to do with the damned stupid lump, she told herself, the breathlessness. It was to do with what she'd just heard.

'We should call Sandro,' Giulietta had said, straight away they came back out on to the street.

'No,' she said. 'Let's get over there, now. It's ten minutes, and I want him in front of me.' And she took a breath of the blessed cold wet air, her nostrils still itching and full of that terrible stink of tomcat.

Not dirty, though, she reminded herself, Fiamma DiTommaso wasn't dirty; what was dirt, after all, but matter in the wrong place? Luisa, proud housewife, had never imagined herself even thinking such a thing. Fiamma DiTommaso might be an angry, eccentric old woman, but she was sane. And she had an excellent memory.

'I was minding my own business,' she'd said fiercely, clutching the cat, hunched over it on the sofa. 'Setting out the dishes, clean dishes every day. I wasn't looking up, just setting them out then pouring the pellets in, when I heard these footsteps running, skidding, they were, down from the Kaffeehaus. Might have been kids, they're always hurtling around the place scaring the cats. Only the sound of the footsteps was louder, the breathing was heavier. And she was crying, and it wasn't a child's crying, nor yet quite an adult's neither.'

'Nineteen,' said Luisa, not even sure if she'd spoken out loud, thinking of the sound of a terrified nineteen-year-old crying. All the daughters in the world cry out for their mother when they're frightened. Luisa had cried out for her own, once or twice. 'She was—she's nineteen.' She swallowed. 'You couldn't see a thing?'

Fiamma DiTommaso shrank at that, defensively. 'I'm not lying,' she said.

'I know you're not,' said Luisa, looking her in the eye. The woman held her gaze suspiciously a moment then seemed to relax.

'I was concentrating on staying very still,' she said. 'I'm not always welcome there, you know. People don't understand.'

'No,' said Luisa.

'I saw shapes, through the trees,' said DiTommaso. 'The girl was wearing jeans, I could see her legs in the tight jeans. And there was an old man, only, well, he was staying out of my line of vision, I could hear him kind of shuffling, like he didn't know whether to stay or go. There was a woman in a kind of white coat, long, below the knees.'

'Right,' said Luisa, trying to imagine such a thing. An Italian woman wearing a white coat in November? Beppe DiLieto had said something about a headscarf—and a—had he said duster coat? It must be her.

'*Leave me alone*, the girl was saying. *Get away from me*. And sobbing, like a child.'

Fiamma DiTommaso frowned down at the floor. 'Then it was the woman. *Dirty old man*, she said. *Dirty, disgusting old man, what stories have you been telling her?* Then the girl said, again, *Leave me alone*, she was crying, *Get away from me*. All over again, terrified.'

She looked up from the cat then, eyes wide and blue, like some kind of Cassandra seeing into the future for a second. 'And then the old man said, *You heard her, leave her alone.*' She paused, still gazing up. 'Poor old man, his voice was trembling, like he was frightened himself. *Leave her alone, you terrible creature*, he said. *What's she done?*'

'I don't understand—' Giulietta had leaned forward at that. 'Who was attacking who?' She turned to Luisa. 'I thought the waiter said Claudio had been groping the girl?'

'It was the woman,' said Luisa softly, not knowing how she knew, but she knew. 'The woman in the white coat. She set it all up; Claudio would never have laid a finger on that child. Beppe never saw it with his own eyes, did he?'

Fiamma DiTommaso went on as if she hadn't spoken, rhythmically stroking the huge dusty cat on her knee. It set up a loud purring. 'Then someone's phone went off, and the woman said, *Give it to me, give it to me, you little b—*' And DiTommaso broke off, biting her lips shut on the word. She took a breath. 'There was some kind of struggle. Between the jeans and the white coat, I heard these horrible angry sounds, and something smashing, bash, bash, bash against a tree. Then the bag came flying over, through the trees, and landed right in front of me.'

'So it wasn't him,' whispered Giulietta reverently. 'Sandro was right. I knew it couldn't have been old Claudio. Old Claudio wouldn't have hurt a fly.'

DiTommaso turned her head slowly to look at Giulietta. 'Is that his name?'

Luisa opened her mouth to say, *Was*, but closed it again. Giuli nodded.

'It seemed to me like the woman had hold of the girl, at that point,' said Fiamma DiTommaso. 'Otherwise she might have come after the bag, she was furious when the girl did that. Their legs were very close together, the woman in the long white coat and the girl in jeans; that woman must have been strong.'

'Not if she was angry enough,' said Luisa, half to herself.

'She started shouting things at the old man, then. He was trying to leave, maybe he was going to get help, because I didn't think he would have left the girl like that otherwise.'

Fiamma DiTommaso was pale now, as if with the realization of her own small share in the guilt. Doggedly she went on. 'The older woman said, *Don't you dare leave.* She said, *I'll tell them you touched her, you dirty old bastard, I'll tell them, you did touch her, didn't you? What will your wife say?* Then she seemed to think of something. *Oh, sorry, your wife's dead, isn't she, don't you remember?*'

She paused, frowning. 'I didn't understand that, because if your wife was dead, you'd remember, wouldn't you? It's not something you'd forget.'

And then Luisa had said, her heart heavier than she could remember it, 'I don't know.'

Nearly there, thought Luisa as they came out on to the river, the home straight, down past the Palazzo Pitti—but then the sight of the river stopped her in her tracks.

The water looked black in the dark but she could hear it roar; my God, she thought, it's high. On the banks opposite she could see under the yellow glow of streetlighting that the Rowing Club's terrace was under three metres of foaming water and above it a row of fire engines were parked under the great arches of the Uffizi. Closer, the seething torrent was almost filling the arches of the Ponte Vecchio, and a boat that had been moored under the bridge was no more than matchwood, no more than debris among all the rest, great branches from the Casentino, planks washed away from jetties and shacks further upriver, like the contents of some gigantic nest. Like the nest of some vast untidy bird.

'Jesus,' said Giulietta, tightening her grip on Luisa's arm. 'Let's go.'

But ahead of them the road was almost blocked by a great crowd at the foot of the Ponte Vecchio, a crowd of rubberneckers and innocents, scattered across the stationary traffic, surging and clamouring against a barrier where ten or fifteen policemen stood with arms folded.

'How the hell are we going to get through?' said Giulietta, and at her side Luisa suddenly felt so weak all she could do was sit down, there and then, on the streaming pavement.

'Luisa,' said Giulietta, on her knees beside her, and Luisa could hear the alarm in her voice.

She took out her phone and pushed it at Giulietta. 'Text him,' she said. 'Text Sandro.'

❀ ❀ ❀

The moment Paolo Massi answered his phone, Sandro knew he was guilty.

The colour drained from his face as he stared down at the device's tiny screen, while it continued to ring. He looked from Antonella Scarpa to Sandro, then put the phone to his ear and said, 'Veronica?' His voice was hollow with fear.

Not shock, not anger at the trouble the girl had put them to, not joy that she was still alive, after all, but fear. As if he'd seen a ghost.

'Veronica?' he said again and this time it was with a hideous kind of false jaunty surprise that fooled no one.

Sandro lunged for the phone and snatched it from him before he had a chance to protest. 'Hello?' he said sharply into the handset. 'Signorina Hutton? Hello? Who is this?' But the line was dead. Sandro closed his hand tight around the telephone, whipped it behind his back, out of Massi's reach. Out of the corner of his eye he made sure of the whereabouts of Antonella Scarpa, under the light that led out to the back. She seemed rooted to the spot.

'It was you,' he said, looking at Massi. 'It was you, wasn't it?'

Looking hollow-eyed and unshaven under the down-lighters, the man tried a laugh, and Sandro took a threatening step towards him.

'Don't even start,' he said. Massi took a step back, so he was right up against the wall, next to the drawing of the girl on her back.

'Is that her?' he asked, coming up close to the picture's glass. 'Who chose the drawing? It looks like Veronica Hutton.'

Nobody said anything. Sandro shifted to face them again. 'I don't know how you did it,' he said to Paolo Massi, 'but you know she's dead, don't you? You know where Veronica Hutton is, because you put her there, and now you're afraid she's got out, she's come back to haunt you.'

'No,' said Massi, 'no—' white as a sheet '—she's not dead, it wasn't me, I was here the whole time, at my desk the whole time, anyone can tell you. It wasn't me—it was her, it wasn't me—'

In his pocket Sandro's own phone bleeped—again? Messages. How could he look at messages now? But it could be Luisa. His stomach took a lurch; he should never have set them off on their own. He felt a moment of awful indecision; he saw the three of them shut inside this red-walled cavernous space, and Massi and Scarpa just waiting for his concentration to slip. Outside the rain and the traffic receded, as if they belonged to a world to which he might never return.

Sandro reached inside his jacket to put Massi's phone in his pocket, and took out his own, slowly, deliberately. He clicked on the touchpad with his thumb and then frowned. Two new messages. First message, received, *porca miseria*, an hour ago, from Iris March.

Going over to see Massi, meet me there?

To see Massi? Had she been at the school? What had they done with her?

He raised his eyes from the screen and saw that they were still there, where he'd left them. Antonella Scarpa's face was frozen in an expression of absolute denial.

And from Luisa, two minutes ago. *It was the woman in the Kaffeehaus,* it read. *The woman in the white coat. On our way.*

And there she was in front of him, Antonella Scarpa in her uniform. Her white work-coat.

'What was that?' he asked Paolo Massi. 'Did you say it was her?'

And he turned to Antonella Scarpa.

'You did it for him, did you?'

She was sallow with fear. 'Paolo?' she said, but Paolo Massi didn't meet her eye.

'The woman in the white coat?' He gestured at her overall. 'Seen at the Kaffeehaus? And Gabi over the road says she saw you leave; you were the one that left. You left, didn't you, at just about the time some mystery customer stuck her head around the door? Gabi says you scared her off, you and Signora Massi. What did she come down for, then? Come to tell him she'd found out about his girlfriend—how did that happen? Was it the hotel called about their room, something like that? Or maybe she knew all along, she just came to make trouble.' He stuck his hands in his pockets. 'My guess is, Veronica Hutton wasn't the first student he'd slept with, was she?'

Antonella Scarpa's eyes were dark pools; she stood her ground.

Sandro went on, 'And then suddenly there she is in the flesh, the girl: Veronica Hutton, sticking her head around the door and biting off more than she can chew?'

Scarpa just shook her head.

'That must have been the last straw, mustn't it? Eight years of playing second fiddle to his wife and then he starts knocking off nineteen-year-old girls under your nose? Under both your noses? Did you think, Little whore? Did you rush off after her, did you follow her up to the Kaffeehaus and see her talking to Claudio Gentileschi, him spilling all your secrets? Was it money, or was it sex? Or was it a bit of both?'

Antonella Scarpa seemed to have lost the power of speech.

'Come on, defend her,' said Sandro, turning to Paolo Massi. 'If you were a real man you'd find something to say. Where would you be without your little powerhouse here? She gave me a nice spiel about the company this morning, she stood guard over your reputation like the little *Sarda* terrier she is. She was going to cover for you all last week while you pretended you were in Sicily, talking to dealers.' He paused for breath. 'It must have killed her to think of it all getting flushed down the pan because you couldn't keep your trousers buttoned.'

But Massi just shook his head dumbly. Sandro turned back to Antonella.

'It'll be on tape,' he said calmly. 'Even if the crazy old cat lady can't be trusted to ID you, the waiter will, and you'll be on film, they're sending me stills from the camera, probably sitting on my computer right now, waiting for me. You kicked up a fuss in front of waiters, customers, pretending Claudio had touched her—why? Just to stop him talking? Just to get the girl away from him—she must have been scared when she saw it was you under that headscarf.'

He took a breath; he mustn't stop now; he had to follow this to its conclusion.

'They must have thought you were crazy; no wonder they just tried to get away from you. And then, of course, you had to go after them; you had to finish it. You just lost it, didn't you?' He saw a tiny flush come to her sallow cheek; was this woman the type to lose control? You could never tell. He had to keep going.

And then the last piece of the jigsaw fell into place, and he could nail her. The woman in the white coat, holding out her hand to Claudio Gentileschi.

'And then you followed Claudio down to the river. How did you know where he'd be? Did you meet him there, sometimes, in his favourite bar, to talk business? So you knew where he'd go, you followed him down there and waited until he came out of the bar, the woman in the white coat that a witness...' He had to pause again, breathless. 'That a witness thought was a nurse. At one-thirty that afternoon, on the Lungarno Santa Rosa. You held out your hand for his keys, because you didn't want all that beautiful work to go to waste, and you told him—something. Something that pushed him over the edge.'

And Sandro folded his arms, felt a furious kind of pity almost choke him at the thought of poor Claudio, bewildered and bamboozled, two glasses of whisky on an empty stomach and a pretty girl. What did Scarpa say to him, in that state? She'd have thought of something.

And though Paolo Massi remained silent, an expression of idiot blankness on his face, Antonella Scarpa had found her tongue.

'No!' she said, flying at Sandro. 'No, no, no, never, no.' He held up a hand and gripped her wrist before it made contact. But the face she held up to his was not what he had expected. There was no hint of an admission, no hint of shame; had he underestimated her? He had not thought that she would lie.

'Where did you put her?' he persisted, though with Antonella Scarpa's refusal to capitulate he felt an unexpected and terrible ebbing of his courage. His belief teetered; was this her? Beppe DiLieto's camomile-drinking artistic Florentine? Arty—in her white painter's coat. He couldn't stop now, could he?

'It's what gets all murderers, in the end,' he said. 'The disposal of the body.' And her face turned a shade paler in the yellow light at the words.

He stood square on to her as she stood her ground in the doorway. 'I want to see what's out there,' he said, nodding over her shoulder to the dull oxblood sheen of the door under the security light. 'Open it.' And she stood aside.

❀ ❀ ❀

Hiroko hung up. 'It is him,' she said. 'Paolo Massi, that is Ronnie's Paolo.' She looked thoughtful. 'He sounded very frightened, I think.'

'Frightened?' squeaked Sophia, 'you mean—'

'If he has her caller ID,' Hiroko said, shrugging without finishing her sentence. 'He thought I was Ronnie calling.'

Jackson felt suddenly sick. 'Iris was going over there,' he said.

'Over where?' said Sophia.

'To see Massi, she texted the detective guy to meet her there.'

'At his house?' Hiroko said.

'I guess,' said Jackson. 'Yeah, the house. Jeez, d'you think she'd—well, I hope he's there. The detective guy. I hope she's not there on her own, it's just like Iris to go in, y'know, head first. She's really got it in for Massi.'

'Do you blame her?' said Hiroko.

'Guess not,' said Jackson. There was a silence. A television set on a bracket over the bar was showing the front of the Uffizi, and a fireman pumping out water, no more than a hundred yards from where they were sitting. Hiroko was looking down at her mobile with a thoughtful expression. The bar was still heaving and as hot as a sauna, Sophia was gazing at him with cloying hopefulness, and Jackson suddenly wanted to get out of there.

'Her answerphone messages have come in,' Hiroko said, pressing a button and holding the phone to her ear.

'Yeah,' said Jackson, thinking that he should have gone with her. 'Yeah, you said. Guess it'll be a whole bunch of people saying, *Where the hell are you?*'

'Not this one,' said Hiroko, holding up a hand to quiet him. She put the hand over her free ear to listen. 'Received, Tuesday, 1 November, twelve twenty-eight p.m. This one is from Massi.'

Chapter Twenty-six

THE APARTMENT WAS even darker than she had remembered, though of course it had merely been a gloomy afternoon the last time she'd seen it, and now it was actually pitch dark outside. As she entered the cavernous *salotto* the ornaments and mobiles and dreamcatchers Iris remembered from her previous visit swayed and gleamed and tinkled like so many airborne mechanical insects.

Anna Massi had sounded delighted to hear her through the crackle of the intercom, had let out a fluttering exclamation of pleasure. '*Prego, prego,*' she'd said, not attempting English, and buzzed her through the door emphatically.

It had not been until she'd been there ten minutes, set down on a sofa that trapped her like quicksand in its spongy depths, that Iris realized, to her despair, that Paolo Massi wasn't at home. Anna Massi had filled the time with one polite question after another, offering her wine and cake and tea, and stroking her hand in her own cold one. For a second, agonizing at the waste of time getting out of here politely was going to involve, Iris imagined herself blurting the whole thing out to Anna Massi. It was stifling in the apartment; Iris couldn't understand how the woman could have cold hands, and she didn't enjoy the stroking.

She shifted uncomfortably, and the sofa sucked her back down. Anna Massi was talking about her pilgrimages, Santiago di Compostela, Lourdes—'You know, I have witnessed so many miracles' and 'I walked a hundred kilometres to Santiago'—

holding out her slender hands as though in modesty, and Iris reflected in a distant corner of her brain that she could not be as delicate as she looked. Now she was asking Iris about Stonehenge, of all places, and its mystical significance. She moved on to the pyramids, and then it was extraterrestrials, all in the same monotone.

'Excuse me,' said Iris, interrupting her. 'But when will your husband be back?'

Anna Massi finished her sentence as though Iris hadn't spoken, but there was a shift in her expression, a hint of displeasure. She smiled at Iris, but the smile didn't reach her eyes.

'Oh, heaven knows,' she said, waving her hand vaguely. 'He's working with that Scarpa woman, always working. She makes him do too much. He's at the school, or the gallery, I forget.' Her fine head was tilted to one side, and she was smiling sadly. 'He's a martyr to his students, I do hope you appreciate him. Last week, he was in and out of there, just preparing for your little student show, so busy, I had to even help him myself.'

She allowed herself a small smile. 'He values my contribution. He needs me, you see. He is helpless without me. Sometimes I understand this.'

Iris gazed at her, repelled.

'This is a true marriage,' she continued, gazing past Iris at the teeming window with a vague smile on her face. 'It is a matter of sacrifice, compromise, working side by side, shared interest.'

Something rose up in Iris as she thought of Ma, whom she hadn't spoken to in a month, bent over her drawing board, trying to keep warm in her terrible house, trekking to Aix to tout her watercolours around the galleries. The thing that rose up in her was violence, a desire to thrash around this horrible spiderweb of a room and bring all the hanging, tinkling things down. A desire to bash a rock down on this woman's head, or worse.

And before she could stop herself she did say it. 'Your husband was having an affair with my friend Ronnie,' she said, very clearly and deliberately, in English. 'Your saintly bloody husband, and now she's dead. She's dead.'

❀ ❀ ❀

Antonella Scarpa had relapsed now into a stony silence, although it turned out later she was only biding her time. She pushed the door open in front of him and Sandro took a step through it knowing that once beyond it he would be in a position they were always advised against in police college. No exit, never mind no mobile signal, hidden from the street. But that was why he was in here, wasn't it? He was stepping into the pit laid for him, and he knew it.

She'd been here. He knew it even before he saw the evidence, he could smell it in the air. Not her perfume or her sweat but something baser, earthier, more primal, like the smell of a beast in a trap. The dismal smell of abandonment he'd detected in the desolate playground on the Lungarno Santa Rosa, where Claudio had walked to his death believing he need not go on living.

It looked ordinary enough. The space narrowed as it went back, barely room for him and Antonella Scarpa together. On his left a wall of shallow drawers for documents or plans—or drawings, as it turned out. Scarpa said nothing as he took one out, then another. 'Claudio's work?' he said, but she remained silent. Exercising her right, even though he wasn't a police officer any longer, no rights had been read. 'We'll soon find out, you know,' he said.

Slowly he turned; behind him on the wall opposite the drawers was a cupboard, an awkward wedge shape in the angle of the low vaulted roof; a key stuck out of the small lock. He turned the key, pulled gently at the door, dropped to his knees to peer into the confined space and that was when he smelled it. His more rational side told him it was probably the damp coming up from under the hill, but the side of him that believed in offering up a muttered prayer now and again knew it was something else too. The cotto floor was scuffed with dusty foot-marks, a scattering of tiny white stones and on the brickwork to one side of the door a single tawny hair was caught, dyed caramel blonde, dark at the root, long. Ronnie. He stood, face to face with Antonella Scarpa, and offered up the hair to her, on the palm of his hand.

'No,' she said, and her voice wobbled.

They were standing up against the end of the space now, and another door, cold against his back. He could see past Antonella Scarpa back into the red womb-space of the gallery and Paolo Massi hovering uncertainly beside his ornate desk. 'There's no point in trying to run for it,' he called down the narrow canyon of the corridor. 'Where are you going to run?'

Scarpa didn't even bother to look back. 'Let him run,' she said in a low voice.

'Not what you expected, huh?' said Sandro.

'I expected nothing,' she said. 'I work for him.' She spat the words again 'I. Work. When I am asked to move things, I move them, to take the students to a pottery demonstration, I take them, to organize life models, I organize. Work. I don't love him, I don't even like him.'

'So it was work,' said Sandro, and he felt some edifice he had built begin to topple. 'It was Claudio telling her all about his forging techniques. You killed her for that.' But his blank voice betrayed his doubt.

'It was not me,' said Antonella.

He jerked his head fiercely in the direction of Paolo Massi. 'He said it was her. You were seen.'

'If anyone saw me anywhere near the girl,' she said deliberately, unafraid now, 'they were mistaken.' She held up a thumb. 'Number one. I never, ever wear my coat outside the gallery or the studio; like a uniform, I take it off, when I leave.' She shrugged. 'Maybe someone who likes to pretend they are a worker, who wishes to appear as though they have a job instead of hiding in their apartment or buying shoes, maybe that kind of person would wear a uniform on the street.'

He stared at her; who was she talking about? She flipped up the index finger to join the thumb. 'Number two. Look at your camera stills, if you like, look at the whole day; I did not go into the Boboli, that camera did not see me. Ask your witness, if your witness really exists; I went the other way; I went back to the studio, where I had told the students I would be from twelve-thirty if they needed me and we would begin working at half past one.'

'Half past one,' repeated Sandro dully.

'So when your woman in the white coat was on the Lungarno Santa Rosa, I was in the studio with seven, no, eight students, doing tracings of the various proposals for the front elevation of Santa Maria del Fiore.'

'But he said, "It was her",' repeated Sandro.

'Another her,' said Scarpa, and pushed open the last door, behind him, and a security light sprang into live, blinding white around a tiny yard. At the back of the yard was a rusty gate, and beyond the gate a steep and overgrown path, that led up into the Boboli. 'Not me,' she said.

Behind them in the gallery something was happening.

❊ ❊ ❊

Jackson pressed the phone to his ear, hunched in an effort to hear every word over the din in the bar. The metallic voice repeating, *Received, Tuesday, 1 November, twelve twenty-seven p.m.* Then some heavy breathing. Then Paolo Massi, his prim, correct English hurried and jumbled.

Where the hell are you, Ronnie? Where? I've tried to call but you're not answering, call me back please. I'm sorry I couldn't talk when you came to the gallery, you could see—I don't know how she knows, but she knows. My wife is in the gardens. My wife is coming to find you. Ronnie? Ronnie? Just call me—my wife, she's—just call me.

Chapter Twenty-seven

TOMI WAS VERY close to being frightened, in the dark, with the sound and feel of all the water under his feet, but he had ways of controlling the fear; one of them consisted of the rolled-up copies of Lupo Alberto in his pocket, and he could feel their comforting pressure against his leg through the cloth. He had other things; his small stash of business cards, he liked to look through them and repeat the names, and try and make sense of the businesses they represented. Recycling Executive, for example, Social Care Assistant, Private Investigations. That calmed him. His wallet with the cards in was inside his pocket.

Mamma thought he was on his computer in his room; that was good, because it meant she wouldn't call him and interrupt his thinking. 'Where are you? It's raining again.' Wouldn't remind him of all there was to be frightened of, out here.

He'd thought he wanted to be at home, but he'd found he couldn't settle, not to his comic books, or his model-making, or his computer games. He had waited until she was settled in front of the television, then he had opened the front door very, very quietly; he had done it before, you had to use both hands, one for the handle, one for the key.

He needed to rescue the dog; the thought of the water pulling, pulling at the place where it was locked up did something terrible to his head; the thought of the shed breaking away from the bank and being washed down the river did something terrible, the thought of the dog scratching at the door as it tumbled down the river to the sea.

Tomi had got through the broken mesh surrounding the Circolo Rondinella's terrace; he had moved across the tarmac under the dripping pergola and was in among the little cabins at the back. He didn't know if he could go any further; he could hear the water rushing, rushing, roaring underneath him. There was a police barrier further up the Lungarno Santa Rosa to stop people coming close to the river, but they hadn't seen Tomi, who had already been inside it. Already inside the Circolo Rondinella, which was how you got to the jumble of little sheds, only the problem was he didn't know how to go any further. Tomi had not thought that this would not be solid earth; he had not understood that all it was held up by were posts and some concrete poured into the sloping bank here and there, everything held up by everything else. He had not thought what would happen when one brick was removed from the bottom of the wall, or more than one. He thought perhaps it was too late, now.

The water was like a huge animal; Tomi squeezed his eyes shut, trying not to think of what animal it might be, a black roaring thing, a tremendous black snake, an eel with huge teeth, lashing underneath at whatever it was that held it all up. He had not dared to look over the parapet at it on his way down here. He took a step, then another.

Tomi had reached a kind of narrow corridor, a wooden landing between two thin cabin walls when it happened, the whole thing shuddered and creaked; he saw the vertical line of a Portakabin shudder and shift in front of him, as he had seen the corner of a room do when caught in a small earthquake in Calabria with Mamma. Tomi took hold of a kind of fence post behind him, part of the pergola, and hung on for dear life.

His mobile, squeezed from his pocket by Lupo Alberto, fell to the boards with a clatter and he stared as it slid away from him across a surface no longer horizontal. Sliding down the post with his hand, he reached for it, only for the whole platform to take another lurch, down towards the river.

❀ ❀ ❀

Prompted by the commotion, Sandro had lunged out of the narrow space and back into the dark, downlit gallery to find Luisa and Giulietta in the street doorway, blocking Paolo Massi's exit. Massi had one arm between them as he struggled to find a way past and out on to the street, but they stood firm.

'Hold on, there,' said Sandro quietly. 'I haven't quite finished with you.' He held up the long caramel strand of hair. 'Recognize this? It's all we need, you know. This is what the police call hard evidence.' Paolo Massi stopped struggling, perhaps aware of how undignified he looked.

'I have no idea what you are talking about,' he said haughtily.

Sandro heard Antonella Scarpa's footsteps behind him.

'Signore Massi,' she said over his shoulder, dangerously calm. 'Tell him that you know I had nothing to do with this.'

Massi attempted to look down his long, straight nose, but his mouth moved stupidly, a foolish, guilty grin. 'Antonella,' he said weakly, 'I'm sorry.'

Scarpa turned to Sandro, holding herself very straight. 'The fakes—well, you call them fakes. They are beautiful. I knew about the fakes, I knew Claudio Gentileschi, I was the one to take him his money, every few months, in his studio. It was business, and if some corporation in Stuttgart or Minsk has a beautiful drawing that happens not to be entirely authentic, no one really suffers.

'Is she the woman in the white coat?' Luisa interrupted without ceremony, eyeing Scarpa. 'I thought she'd be bigger.'

Slowly Antonella Scarpa flipped one button undone on the white coat, then another, slid it off her small shoulders and hung it up on the hook by the door.

'Tell them,' she said, looking at Paolo Massi. 'Tell them what was the first thing your beautiful, jealous wife did when she arrived at the gallery last Tuesday? Tell them why, the next day, you told me that I would not be needed to help in the gallery that night, as had been planned? Was it because Anna would be helping, the devoted wife?'

Massi said nothing. 'The first thing she did when she saw me, on Tuesday morning, was to take down a white coat from the hook,' said Antonella. '*Paolo won't be needing you any more*, she said, and then she put the coat on herself.'

Standing very straight, Scarpa pointed a finger at Massi, skewering him. 'Let your wife pretend she hasn't a jealous bone in her body. Let her pretend her mind is on higher things, her retreats, her pilgrimages, her theories about the ancient gods. Not her ridiculous obsession with shoes, no one is allowed to mention that, just as no one is allowed to mention her ridiculous suicide attempts or those screaming rows you have, regular as clockwork in the office, after the end of every course.'

Only then did she take a breath. Luisa and Giulietta were gazing at her with something like respect.

'So it's not her, then?' said Giulietta. 'I could have told you that; she's a Sardinian through and through, no one could call her an arty-farty Florentine. Wasn't that what the waiter called the woman at the Kaffeehaus? Listen to the accent.'

She was right. He'd been right about the coat, only the wrong woman had been wearing it: not Antonella Scarpa, but Anna Massi. And there was something else. Sandro held up a hand and turned a moment to Paolo Massi.

'Your wife went to see Lucia Gentileschi, didn't she, on Friday evening? To offer her condolences? Or to find out how much the widow knew? Lucia hardly recognized her. And then the Gentileschis' flat is just around the corner from the Piazza d'Azeglio, isn't it? And on Friday night, when Iris March had been persuaded by you to spend the night elsewhere, someone let themselves into that apartment, looking for something? Someone, perhaps, who wouldn't have worried the old contessa; a woman of good family, paying a call?'

Taken by surprise, Massi seemed unable to speak.

'A shame she didn't know enough to know that you don't wipe a computer by just turning it off. And she underestimated Iris March, too; she's clever enough to know when someone's been inside her place.'

Iris March, he thought, and the name triggered a tiny alarm in his head—where did you go, Iris March?

But Antonella Scarpa was talking again, as if he hadn't spoken, staring only at her employer, daring him to contradict her.

'So she put on my white coat and said something to—to him, smiling sweetly in that way she does, about Alitalia calling for confirmation of Signore Massi's flights to Sicily, did he wish to be seated next to his companion, whose flight had been paid for with his credit card?' She smiled thinly. 'I expect she was as angry about him paying for the girl's flight as anything else, wasn't she? And then what happened? I'd had enough, I was at the door ready to go because, God knows, I had enough to do at the school. And then she appeared at the window. Miss Veronica Hutton.' She folded her arms across her chest. 'And then it all really went wrong, didn't it, Paolo?'

Massi had slumped to the chair at his ornate desk by now, though no one really bothered to look away from Antonella Scarpa to consider him.

'Why didn't you tell anyone you'd seen Veronica Hutton come to the gallery that morning?' said Sandro quietly.

Scarpa barely even shrugged. 'Loyalty?' She grimaced. 'Stupid.' She frowned. 'But I thought it was nothing, a coincidence. I knew he wasn't capable of killing her, hiding her. Not him.'

'And her?'

Scarpa gazed at Sandro, pale, cropheaded, like a defiant, angry child. She spoke carefully.

'I didn't see her go, not out the back into the Boboli; it didn't occur to me. But I did notice on Thursday, when they allowed me back to help in the gallery, that the gate had been used. It's never used, I thought the lock must have rusted up, but when I went out the back into the courtyard on Thursday because it had started to rain and there were packing supplies out there getting wet, I saw it was ajar. I didn't understand it, at the time.'

She paused, and when she spoke again her fierceness had returned. Despite it all, Sandro found he liked her fierceness. 'And it would have been just like her to keep her white coat on. Look at me, a serious person. A worker. Money-grubbing, me? Jealous, me? But if you'd seen her, spitting at him when the girl ran off again, you'd have said she wasn't just jealous but crazy.'

Antonella Scarpa contorted her face, hissing in imitation of her boss's wife. Sandro could imagine how the woman must have treated her, all these years. *'Is it her? It's her, isn't it?* And she flew at him. It was embarrassing, to tell the truth. That's when I left.'

'Where was Anna Massi, do you remember?' he asked softly. 'When you went? Was she still in the gallery?'

Antonella Scarpa's small white oval face was turned up towards him, clever, thoughtful. 'Inside, yes.' She nodded. 'Paolo was saying, it's all right, she's gone into the Boboli. Then Anna turned her back on him, and was stalking off. Towards the back of the gallery. In her white coat.'

Sandro looked at her. Proud, and desolate, and telling the truth. Antonella Scarpa had nothing left to lose. He put one last careful question to her.

'You've known Anna Massi a long time.' She nodded, just barely. 'And if, say, she heard Claudio talking about the work he did for the Massi family, in detail, to the girl who was sleeping with her husband?'

Scarpa tilted her head. 'Yes,' she said. 'She'd be capable of killing them both. Anna Massi would be capable of anything.'

❀ ❀ ❀

In the dark, and the wet, and the chaos, the screaming of sirens all around him, Jackson stood at the door to Paolo Massi's apartment building and looked up. He couldn't remember which floor the apartment was on, or which direction it faced. First floor? There seemed to be lights on the first floor, very dim.

Iris was too sensible to come here on her own; he'd seen her send that message. But what if Sandro Cellini never got it? What if he was trapped on the other side of the river, what if he was in a traffic snarl-up?

Leaning on the bell again, MASSI, Jackson held it down for longer than was reasonable, longer than could be ignored. And again.

He knew she'd come here; he was sure of it. It seemed to Jackson that for the first time in years his brain had been kick-started into working properly, right now; it could be adrenaline, but he knew it was because of Iris. Because she needed him to be clever right now. She'd come here, first of all because he'd seen her heading north up the Via Calzaiuoli, second of all because it was a Sunday and she'd assume Massi was at home, not anywhere else, and third of all because she couldn't have crossed the river even if she'd wanted to.

But there was no answer.

❀ ❀ ❀

Anna Massi had laughed that girlish laugh, straight off, when Iris said it. They were both on their feet now.

'Oh, you silly girl,' she'd said. 'Did you think I didn't know?'

Her English was good; her husband had been right. She seemed like a different person; her eyes glittered. 'Do you think she was the first?'

Inside the dark apartment Iris heard the squeal of the street doorbell, but she couldn't move. 'Sit down,' said Anna Massi, and there was something in her voice that made it impossible for Iris to disobey. She sat; Anna Massi settled herself decorously beside her.

'She was a stupid child. Imagining she was an artist's muse, no doubt!'

And she laughed again, only this time Iris heard it differently. It was as though the sound had brought something into focus in her frantically calculating brain. She's crazy, she thought, and then she thought of Giovanna Badigliani; saying to Paolo Massi, 'Your wife was looking well,' in that knowing way. Telling him that she knew his wife was unhinged; telling him in the same breath that she'd seen her.

'It was you,' said Iris. 'You came to the apartment. You unplugged the computer.'

And Anna Massi had tilted her head on one side, black-eyed and curious as a bird after a worm, and Iris, mesmerized, felt the cold hand creep back across hers but could not look down at it.

The laugh had turned breathy. 'A wife protects her husband,' she said.

Iris had a hand to her mouth. 'What do you mean?' she whispered. 'What have you done?' It was as though she was in a dream, and wanted to scream but no sound came out.

A new edge entered Anna Massi's voice; a kind of petulance. 'She should not have been there. She shouldn't have come to the gallery and showed her silly face to me.' She laughed. 'Paolo tried to stop me going after her but he didn't understand. I cannot—there are certain things I cannot allow.'

'You mean, as long as you didn't have to know,' said Iris, falteringly. 'As long as he was—discreet.'

Anna Massi gave her a long, considering look. 'The woman from Alitalia who telephoned, even she knew; she was laughing at me, asking me if I thought they should be seated together. Of course, I had to speak to him: I had to go to the gallery.'

Eyes wide, Iris kept silent. The gallery beside the Boboli. 'And then she was there, waving through the window. Paolo ran out to get rid of her, but I'd seen her. He told me she'd gone, into the Boboli. And when I came into the gardens, through the back of the gallery—ha! There she was, walking just in front of me, up the hill. Then it was simple, I had only to follow her, and then, when she arrived at the Kaffehaus to meet that foolish old man,

I simply sat behind them. She didn't know me—and he couldn't remember if he knew me or not!'

She laughed unpleasantly, leaning in towards Iris, and then Anna Massi's stealthy hands were on her again, just bones, light and cool. Iris kept very still. It had come back to her, too late, that Anna Massi was strong; hadn't she walked a hundred kilometres on her pilgrimage with a forty-kilo pack? And now the woman's thin, cold hands were closing around Iris's wrists in a grip so tight it was inhuman, like wire. She wanted to scream, Where is she? Where is Ronnie? But she had to wait.

'Old man? What secrets?' Iris didn't understand. Something came to her. 'She was meeting a painter. Claudio someone.'

'Claudio Gentileschi.' Anna Massi made a little pout. 'It was business: you would not understand. Perhaps she thought he was a real painter, not a cheap little Jewish forger.'

Iris felt her scalp prickle at the ugly insult. 'What were you going to do?' she whispered.

Anna Massi's head tilted towards her, that predatory bird again. 'I was waiting,' she said. 'I thought, I will know, when the time comes; I was powerful, listening to the two of them, and they didn't know I was there. Do you believe in fate?'

Iris stared at her, unable to speak. *She is mad.*

'Oh, I do,' Anna Massi didn't need an answer. 'When I heard him tell her, that stupid, senile old goat, heard him telling her all our secrets, of course then I had to act. She wasn't important, she was nothing, but when it ended, her little fling with Paolo, her little Sicilian honeymoon, because he always ends it—then she might tell someone. I couldn't let that happen, not again.' She drew herself up. 'And then I knew what to do, to stop it.'

She gazed off through the window to the night sky, where sirens came and went in the darkness. Then she turned back to look into Iris's eyes and when she spoke she was full of triumph and exuberant, as though she'd never been listened to before.

'It was so easy! I simply accused him of touching her improperly.' She smiled beatifically, a wide joyful smile.

'Oh, the way he looked at me when I told him to get his hands off her, as if he really had touched her; full of panic, full of guilt!' Her laugh was almost merry. 'And then instead of defending himself, he ran away, so incriminating, and she after him. Oh, and when I said—it just came to me, also fate, don't you think?—don't you remember, your wife's dead, such a face! You silly old fool, you lecherous old goat, you might as well be dead yourself.' She spread her long fingers in a throw-away gesture. 'What had I to lose? Even if he didn't do what I wanted him to do and just disappear, just go and kill himself, who would believe a senile old man?'

'You told him his wife had died?' whispered Iris, trying to understand the casual cruelty of it, knowing that she must not cry.

Anna Massi shrugged. 'What good was he in the world? Everyone knew he was losing his mind, Paolo had told me, we might not be able to use him any more. And of course then I understood that the police would believe that if he was demented, he might do—anything. Might molest a girl; most men would, even him, given the opportunity, a little whore like that offering herself on a plate. No marriage is perfect, why should his be? Even if that old fool of a wife might have thought she was all in all to him.'

Claudio Gentileschi had loved his wife: that much Iris remembered. Anna Massi pursed her lips.

'It was when I took her *telefonino* and smashed it, that frightened him, and he ran away. Iris thought of the violence with which that phone had been destroyed. She was afraid herself; she would run away now, if she could. She looked towards the door.

Anna Massi didn't seem to see where Iris was looking; she drew a breath, a satisfied sigh. 'And then, to deal with Paolo's little whore was not difficult. She was afraid of me, you see, when I told her who I was. She was crying; she was guilty, and she knew it. And I know where to walk in that place, not to be seen. I told her I was taking her back to the gallery, and she came; only a small amount of force was necessary. I took her back the same way I came, back to the gallery, where she will be punished, as a child. And then...' She made a magician's gesture in the air, letting Iris's hands drop. 'She is gone. I make her disappear.' She stood, took a pace or two towards a massive stone fireplace.

'I return for Claudio Gentileschi later; Paolo has told me of the bar where he takes a drink after work every day, before he goes back to his wife. Maybe he will be there. And it was fate: he was there. I told him again why there was no point in going home. I could smell whisky on his breath.' She reached for something on the mantelpiece, and held it up. 'He even gave me his keys.'

Iris struggled with the information; she could not bear to stop and think about it because it wasn't Claudio she needed to know about. Her wrists were free and she knew she should run and she would, but first she had to know.

'Where did you put her?' she said, hearing herself close to begging, close to crying. 'What do you mean, you punished her, like a child? She was harmless, you didn't need to be jealous of Ronnie.'

And then the sob rose in her throat, when she saw what she had done. Too late.

'You think I would be jealous?' Anna Massi said with soft, whispering fury and seized her, forced her back down, her mouth so close to Iris that Iris could smell her breath, slightly sour, the chemical smell of madness, of medication, of something wrong deep down. 'He always comes back.'

Over Anna Massi's head a mirrored dreamcatcher swayed and tinkled, and beside her elbow the grey filament of smoke from an incense cone spiralled into the air, chokingly sweet. Iris thought she didn't want these to be the last things she saw and smelled; she squeezed her eyes shut.

'He always comes back?' She forced the words out. 'To this horrible place? Well, more fool him.' And as one of Anna Massi's hands moved to her throat she found she couldn't even cry out, any more, for the open spaces, for hills and trees, to be out of this great, dark, wet, suffocating doom-laden city, to be home with Ma.

The doorbell screeched again, a desperate, protracted, sound: too late, thought Iris, as the blood pulsed behind her eyelids.

❀ ❀ ❀

His new-found confidence evaporated, Jackson was about to turn and go—to the nearest police station, or where? He had no idea—only then the door opened in his face and a middle-aged man came out. The man gave him a curious look, but he didn't pull the door shut behind him, only let it swing slowly shut.

Jackson put out a hand to hold it, just in time. He was inside.

Chapter Twenty-eight

'SO WHAT DID you do with the body?'

As Sandro spoke, Paolo Massi sat at the desk, summoning up some ghastly imitation of composure. He didn't reply, but Sandro saw he was trying to rebuild his position.

Sandro held up the single caramel-coloured hair. 'She was here, and now she's gone.'

They stared at each other, then Massi spoke. 'That's not evidence,' he said, his voice oddly high-pitched. 'She was a student, she had been here to the gallery as had all the students, one hair is not evidence. I had nothing to do with her disappearance. You should find her, then you will have evidence.' He rattled off his defence, ending with something like the old sneer, then he clamped his mouth shut.

'I'll find her,' said Sandro, slowly. 'I'll find her all right.' He turned on his heel, walked along the row of artworks, staring blindly at them, a tinted ink sketch of the Santo Spirito, a muddy little oil he couldn't even make out. He concentrated on what he knew; they had kept her here.

He turned back to face his audience enclosed in the blood-red room, Giulietta and Luisa, watching him intently from the door to the street, Antonella Scarpa in the shadows, and at the centre of the picture Paolo Massi, downlit, and under interrogation.

'*Stay there*, she must have said, *Stay right where you are*, and you did what you were told. Sat obediently at your fine desk, as Gabi over the road will testify, until she came back.'

Nobody moved. Sandro continued, following his thread through the dark.

'You must have heard them, first, sitting there; you must have heard her dragging Veronica down from the Boboli, through that gate, inside. Your wife must have managed to manhandle her all the way down here after she saw Claudio off. Strong woman, is she? Not only cleverer than you, but stronger?' Sandro paused to consider the fine-boned features he'd seen in the photograph on Massi's desk; they could be made of steel, those pretty, highly strung women.

'Did she even let you see the girl? Or did she just lock her in there, in the dark? Did she tie her up? Or did you do it together? You must have helped her, mustn't you? Are you afraid of your wife?' Paolo Massi's twitching face as Sandro spoke told him that he was right.

'I suppose she might have been dead by then,' Sandro continued regardless. 'But I don't think so. There are scuff marks, and nothing else; killing tends to leave a trace of one kind or another.' He paused, to observe Paolo Massi's reaction; the man's eyes were wide and fixed, as if the idea of death had only just occurred to him.

Sandro went on. 'You kept her here—how long? Did you have a row, about what she'd done, about the right thing to do next?' He paused. 'Did your wife tell you what she'd over-heard? Did she say, with Veronica Hutton out of sight, so you didn't have to look at her, bound and gagged in that hole, did she say, *I'm going after the old man*? Or something like that. Because by then it was too late, she had to get him to shut up.'

'I don't know what she did,' said Massi, pale. 'She went out, she said she was—she was getting me something to eat. I can't be responsible—I didn't know where she went.'

Sandro looked at him with disgust. 'She left Veronica Hutton locked in that room, that—that cupboard, where she might have suffocated, and she went out in the car to find Claudio Gentileschi, to finish him off. How did she find him? I imagine you must have told her where to look. Did she mean to drive him to suicide, or just to discredit him? The result was the same, wasn't it?'

He paused to watch Massi's composure disintegrate. 'Was she crying, little Veronica Hutton? Did she beg you to let her out? Or was she already dead?'

Massi's lip trembled, 'No, no, she...' And he faltered, his eyes filling up, overflowing with self-pity.

Sandro took a step towards him, then no further. 'You were too frightened of your wife, weren't you? Did she say, too late to let her go now, think of everything she might say? No one would suspect us, pillars of the community; let the senile old man take the blame, alive or dead.'

Massi swallowed, and Sandro moved on; his end was in sight and he would not stop for anyone.

'She was seen leaving here by Gabi over the road, in the car; then she was seen talking to Claudio on the Lungarno Santa Rosa, a witness...' and he paused a moment, thinking of the boy, because Massi didn't need to know what kind of witness he was '...a witness saw them. Will identify her.' He barely drew breath. 'What would your father have thought, eh? Persuading an old man to kill himself, to save your shoddy little business, sucking up to foreigners, selling fakes, sleeping with girls young enough to be your daughter?'

Paolo Massi remained quiet, though behind him Sandro heard Antonella Scarpa make a small sound of self-disgust.

'Oh, I'm sorry, I forgot, it was all your wife's fault, wasn't it? She did everything.'

'She...' Paolo Massi choked on the words, self-pitying. 'She didn't like my father.'

'That figures,' said Sandro, knowing that the man had broken, now: it hadn't been so difficult after all. 'But let's get back to the point, shall we? I want to know what happened next, because I need to find Veronica Hutton, you see. I need to give her back, alive or dead, to the people who love her.' He felt Luisa's eyes on him but he didn't look away from Massi.

'So you decided between you that Claudio Gentileschi would be a very handy suspect when her body was found, eventually? Particularly if he was dead; nothing neater than a murderer who kills himself out of remorse. Was she dead, by then, little Ronnie, by Wednesday evening when you told Antonella not to come to the gallery because your wife was helping? Was she dead when you took her out of the back and bundled her into the car? Or didn't you dare? I bet your wife would dare.'

'No, she...' Massi had the slack-jawed look of an idiot now, but even an idiot knew when to shut up.

'People saw Claudio, or thought they saw him, molesting the girl, didn't they? And he was losing his marbles, wasn't he, it'd be easy enough to make it stick. And then she had a better idea, didn't she? Persuade him he'd be better off dead, what with the shame of it all.'

Luisa's voice broke in, clear and firm.

'She told Claudio his wife was dead,' she said. 'Fiamma DiTommaso overheard them.' Massi turned to look at Luisa as she added, 'She heard her say, *Don't you remember, your wife's dead?*'

Giulietta was nodding, at her side. Massi turned to look at them, shrunk small, cornered.

Sandro took over. 'It wouldn't have been hard, would it? Dirty old man, you'd be better off dead. What was there for him to live for? There'd always been just the two of them.'

And as the words were spoken Luisa turned her head just slightly, so as not to look at him, and the chill was there, across his heart too. He forced himself to say what he had to say next.

'And then she held out her hand for his keys.' Sandro pulled the set of keys Lucia Gentileschi had taken from the scroll-top desk out of his pocket. 'He had a spare set at home, did you know that? His wife found them, and gave them to me.

'Why did she ask for the keys, Paolo?' Sandro went on. 'What proposal did she make to you when she came back here from the Lungarno Santa Rosa, still in her white coat? Remove the evidence, the stock of fakes, worth a penny or two, and then what? Plant a bit of evidence, instead? Just to make sure, when they found the body, that the finger pointed right at Claudio? That must be why you left that Post-it note up in the studio, after you'd taken such care to clear the place out? Very helpful. And what other evidence did you plant?'

Sandro held up the Yale key. 'This is the front door key,' he said.

The next key. 'This is the key to the studio.'

Then, finally, the tiny key, the key to a letterbox, only the building where Claudio had his studio had been too cheap for letterboxes, the post lay on the floor in the hallway. He held it up between thumb and finger, dangling it in Massi's face.

'And this key? A padlock? Some kind of storage shed, some lock-up somewhere? Outhouse, doghouse, *cantina*?'

Giulietta was on her feet, hand in the air as though she was in school. Sandro held up a hand to tell her, wait. 'I know,' she whispered. 'The dog, the boy told me Claudio had a dog, he was worried about the dog. Only there is no dog; Claudio never had a dog.' Sandro nodded, still intent, fixed on Paolo Massi.

But the answer came from Antonella Scarpa.

'He kept some stuff in a shed,' she said quietly, and they all turned; she was looking at Massi. 'Inflammables, thinners, that kind of thing. I can take you there.'

❀ ❀ ❀

Iris was on the edge of unconsciousness when the next sound came; she was at the point of reaching out for it with longing, to ease the bursting in her head. But the sound was so loud she jerked in response, just as Anna Massi's attention slackened, just fractionally. She managed to free one of her hands from the woman's grip, her elbow came up and she crashed it, painfully, into the bridge of Anna Massi's nose.

Falling back, Anna Massi shrieked, a horrible noise. With the blessed release of pressure from her windpipe Iris was on her feet and bellowing; she wasn't even aware of whether the sounds she was making were words.

'Iris?' The voice was muffled and panicky, but she recognized it; it guided her through the dark towards the door.

Oh, God, she thought, oh, thank you. Jackson. She blundered across footstools and coffee tables, and it wasn't until she got to the door that she realized Anna Massi wasn't behind her. She fumbled with chains and bolts, every moment waiting for the woman to lay hold of her again, but there was nothing. The door opened and there he was; she thought she'd never been so glad to see anyone her whole life.

The first thing he did was reach past her and turn on the light.

Chapter Twenty-nine

AS HE STEPPED out of the car, it came to Sandro that somehow he had always known he would end up back here. He had sat in his car gazing up at the Boboli, imagining it as somewhere evil had been done, yet it seemed to him now that it must have been this place that had occupied that space in his thoughts, all along. It had been this dirty, neglected stretch of river that ended in marshland; where the homeless foraged for food in rubbish and weeds, where the city stored its detritus in a shambles of crumbling shacks.

The place where Claudio Gentileschi had last seen the sky and breathed the city's polluted, lovely air, one bright November day before the rains began. The Lungarno Santa Rosa.

Giulietta and Luisa agreed to stay in the car with Massi; on the far side of him in the back seat Giulietta was intent on punching numbers into her mobile. On the near side Luisa gave him a thumbs up through the window as Sandro locked them in, grateful for a car so ancient such a procedure was possible. Sandro failed to return the gesture, so reluctant was he, suddenly, to take another step towards the inevitable. He straightened, Antonella Scarpa stiffly obedient at his side, and forced himself on.

'You know exactly where it is?' He'd asked the question as they'd crawled through the traffic to traverse the kilometre or so from the Via Romana to the Lungarno Santa Rosa. They might have walked, but Sandro wanted everyone together, he wanted his eye on them all.

'More or less,' said Scarpa. 'Behind the social club, whatever it's called.'

'The Circolo Rondinella.'

He'd had to blink away the vision of that place, the pergola under the rain and the Portakabin where someone had been watching him, it made him feel so sick with foreboding.

'I could call Tomi,' Giulietta had piped up. 'Comic-book Boy?'

'You have his number?' Sandro had taken his eyes off the traffic to look back at her, squeezed in the back seat. Next to her Massi's eyes were glazed with a look Sandro had seen in any number of guilty parties, absenting himself from the here and now, hoping it would all go away.

Blank denial; the trouble was, sometimes it worked. And then Sandro'd had to stifle the fear that, between them, Massi and his wife had been clever enough to eliminate the evidence, to shove it all on to Claudio. Which was really the fear of finding her; it was what all this was all about, wasn't it? He wasn't a police officer any more; he didn't have any of that apparatus that protected him from the dead, the feel and look and smell of the dead. No latex gloves, no evidence bags, no team of brothers, no jovial forensic technicians with their gallows humour, no fatherly, unshaven pathologist dragged from his bed to attend. Sandro was alone.

'Call the boy,' he'd said. 'Yeah.' But there'd been no answer.

Standing in the lee of the great wall of San Frediano, Scarpa beside him, Sandro realized that by some miracle the rain had stopped. The air was clear and cold, and without the soft sound of rain to muffle it, the roar of the river below them was like thunder.

'Here,' said Scarpa, and she stopped. Even she looked chastened now. They were in front of the steel gate of the Circolo Rondinella, the poster advertising ballroom dancing now no more than tattered pulp hanging from the wire.

Sandro pulled at the gate; it was locked. Silently Scarpa pointed to a gaping hole in the wire fence, then held it back as Sandro climbed through. Too old for this, he felt dread take hold, but before he could even complete the thought he felt something shift beneath his feet.

'Stay there,' he said sharply over his shoulder to Antonella Scarpa. 'Call a fire engine, call an ambulance, but don't move.' She nodded mutely.

'Where?' he asked. But she just pointed, helplessly, towards the ants' nest of broken palings and half-collapsed plasterboard behind the clubhouse of the Circolo Rondinella. 'Somewhere there,' she said.

And then, as he took a step, a sound cut through the roar of the water underneath Sandro, the tinny, high-pitched sound of a ringtone, incongruous and familiar, the theme tune of some ancient TV cartoon show Sandro couldn't place.

He moved towards the sound, around the side of the cabin and there it was, down a half-collapsed wooden walkway, the screen of a mobile phone blinking up at him in the dark as it rang. 'Tiger Man,' a tiny voice sang. Sandro reached for it and as he moved something came at him from the dark, took hold of his arm and held on for dear life.

Letting out an exclamation, Sandro struggled to free himself and saw beside him the painfully thin, upturned face of Tomi, Comic-book Boy, hair plastered all around it. He was holding a torch, its beam now directed at his own face, and he was making sounds.

'What?' said Sandro, holding the boy tight, looking him full in the face. 'What are you saying?'

'The dog,' said the boy distinctly, rearing and struggling to escape eye contact. 'The dog. Help him, Claudio's dog.'

'Where's the dog?' Sandro asked, and the boy shone the torch towards a battered door at a crazy angle near the far end of the disintegrating jetty, fastened shut by a brass padlock. And then below them something clattered and loosened, and the whole structure swayed. Bodily Sandro lifted the boy; he weighed next to nothing, all wire and bones; he hauled him back, across the terrace, pushed him out through the fence.

'Give me your torch,' he said, leaning through after him with his hand out.

'My phone,' said the boy, clinging to the fence, but Sandro was already gone.

It's all right, he told himself as he moved down the broken boards that had once formed a path, there are other sheds underneath, they'll go first.

He came to the phone and picked it up, put it in his pocket, but then when he straightened up his feet couldn't get a purchase on the splintered wood, greasy with days of rain, and he slipped. Sandro heard his own breath whistle out of him as he went down, but he was all right, he slid down three, four feet and then he was at the door.

Torch between his teeth, Sandro fumbled in his pocket for the keys, the blasted keys, while with his other hand holding on to some upright that might or might not represent something solid in this disintegrating rubbish heap. He was on his knees, rearing backwards to counteract the steep angle. The key went in.

She was at the back, more like a heap of clothes than a human being, like a sack of drowned animals, dead weight. Ankles, wrists protruding, bound with picture wire. Feeling a terrible pressure in his chest, Sandro reached for her, pulled her up; he thought she must weigh twice, three times, what the boy had. He slung her across his body; he couldn't manage a fireman's lift. He held her to him like a great child, and then he moved.

With each impossible step back up towards the far-off yellow gleam of the embankment's lighting, Sandro felt the whole structure under him being dismantled by the weight of the water and he knew that she was dead, that soon he would be too. Only he kept on, and underneath him the ground held, and then they were at the wire, and through the wire and on the pavement leaning against the low wall. And Sandro collapsed, the girl on top of him, and he held her against him as he sobbed.

There was no ambulance, there was no fire engine, but Antonella Scarpa was still there. 'No one answers,' she said, blankly, staring down at him—at them. 'Get Luisa,' he said, and he bowed his face over the girl's, his cheek, unshaven, against her cold, soaked one.

And it was Luisa, his Luisa. Afterwards it seemed to Sandro that when his wife took hold of the girl's wrist in hers, some mysterious exchange took place, from Luisa's warm beating heart to the girl's blue-veined arm, cold as marble. His Luisa brought her back to life.

She had to say it three times, before he stopped shaking his head and allowed himself to believe her. 'She's got a pulse,' said Luisa. And they sat there on the soaked stone of the Lungarno Santa Rosa, Sandro and Luisa holding the cold child between them, until finally the ambulance did arrive.

❀ ❀ ❀

'She can't have vanished into thin air,' said Jackson, and it turned out that he was mostly right.

In the bald, bright light of the central chandelier, the Massi's *salotto* was revealed in all its disarray, a wall of books thick with dust, a ragbag of crudely coloured throws torn off the sofa in their struggle, and all the hanging things jangling, but Anna Massi was not there.

Thumping at switches, Iris and Jackson blundered through the flat until every door in the place was thrown open and every space blinked back at them under overhead light, but they found only that Anna Massi was not in the small nun's cell, or in a neat, anonymous marital bedroom, or in the small, crowded bathroom.

It was only when they returned to the *salotto* and Iris realized that the long window had not been open before, and when the sounds of raised voices alerted them to the fact that something was happening in the street outside, that they came out to look for Anna Massi on the balcony. And failing to find her there, looked down into the street to realize that people had gathered not because something was happening but because something had happened, and they were gathered around that something.

Which was Anna Massi, who had not vanished into thin air in one sense, but in another, and was gone, beyond hope of return.

Chapter Thirty

IN THE END, Serena Hutton flew in from Dubai on the Wednesday. Iris had sat in Sandro Cellini's warm kitchen at close to two in the morning on Sunday, listening to him make the call, drinking camomile tea and thinking of Ronnie in her hospital bed. She had been airlifted across the city to Careggi by helicopter with Sandro and his wife, but Sandro had found the time to call Iris first to tell her. *She's alive, just. I have found your Veronica, and she is alive.*

Ronnie had lain pale and quiet next to a Roma girl with stomach pains and a drip and a half dozen members of her extended family hovering anxiously, batting away appeals from the nurses for some of them, at least, to go home. Ronnie had had only Iris.

Approaching the bed, Iris had been frightened; there were things she didn't want to think about. Massi, and his wife, stuffing cloth into Ronnie's mouth and bundling her into a dark place, quarrelling over what was to be done with her. Five days in the rain and the cold and the dark, with the smell of chemicals and paintstripper and the dirty river.

At first it had seemed that Ronnie was still unconscious; her eyes were closed, and her hands very straight at her sides with the palms turned upwards. Even like that, Iris felt herself unclench at the sight; it was still Ronnie. On her cheek, which was smudged and grubby, her eyelashes still curled, ridiculously long, and suddenly there was a new picture in Iris's head, Ronnie

315

at the mirror, leaning in to put on mascara. 'Ronnie?' she whispered. Nothing. She tried again. 'Ronnie?'

Ronnie's mouth moved; her tongue came out and she licked dry lips. Then she seemed to struggle and Iris felt herself panic, looked around for a nurse. She wanted to run. The spasm stopped, and Ronnie opened her eyes, tried to raise herself up, and failed. Iris put an arm around her shoulder and put the straw in her water glass to Ronnie's mouth until Ronnie put up a hand to say, that's enough, and Iris took the glass away, busying herself. Ronnie's gaze settled on Iris, and she let out a small sigh, and relaxed back against her piled pillows.

''Syou,' she said, eventually, and lifted her hand, gesturing; it took a minute for Iris to understand what she wanted. She took Ronnie's hand. 'Iris.'

'It's OK, Ronnie,' said Iris, not knowing what else to say.

'I shouldn'—shouldn't...' Her lip trembled and she controlled it. 'I was so stupid, Iris,' she said, searching Iris's face.

'Only a bit,' said Iris, holding her hand tighter. 'It wasn't your fault.'

Ronnie sighed, like a small, tired child, and let her eyes fall shut. Then suddenly they were open again, wide with alarm. 'God,' she said, struggling back up to prop herself on her elbows, tangling herself in the drip. 'Mum's not here, is she?'

Iris felt herself smile, hugely. 'Ronnie,' she said. 'It's all right.'

And by the time Serena Hutton did arrive, wrestling with a pile of designer luggage, red-haired with her sharp little face, complaining about the cold, the inefficiency of the airport, the uselessness of Italian hospitals, it mostly was all right. She walked in, and Iris walked out.

'It'll be OK,' Ronnie had said, when Iris had gone in to the hospital to warn her, and she'd sighed. 'I'm used to her, you know.' Weariness, Iris realized, was not something she'd heard in Ronnie's voice before, or acceptance, and almost never gratitude. She was different but, then, everything was. The world turned.

Jackson left the same day, a flight to Rome and then all the way across Europe, across the Atlantic, back to the New World. He had an errand to run first; Iris said she'd come as far as the house, for moral support. Lucia Gentileschi's house.

It had been Sandro Cellini's idea. He had summoned the two of them to his office, on the Tuesday.

The city had been in a strange mood; the skies had still been low and grey and the river still yellow but the waters had dropped, dramatically. All sorts of debris had been cast up on the mud-plastered embankments—shattered boards and bicycle wheels and dirty plastic bags—and traders had talked in hushed voices on their shop doorsteps about how bad it might have been. Sandbags were still stacked against the Uffizi's river façade.

'Both of us?' said Iris, on the phone.

'*Si*, Iris,' he'd said with weary patience. '*Tutte le due.*' He spoke to her in a mix of Italian and English now; it didn't seem quite real that they'd only known each other a week. She could hear tiredness in his voice; she knew there was something going on at home, with his wife. She wasn't well. 'I want you to come with him,' said Sandro. 'Because when he's with you, I think he is more of a man. Not so much a boy.'

It had taken her aback; Sandro had seen them together no more than twice, had spoken to Jackson alone once. But she was beginning to understand that he was an observant man.

'You have spoken to your mother yet, Iris?' he said, straight away when they arrived, fixing her in the eye. The three of them were standing in his small office, in San Frediano; Iris would have liked to be back in that kitchen of his but he'd said, quickly, no. Not home. Perhaps his wife was in bed.

'Not yet,' she said, with a hint of defiance. Would he understand, if she tried to explain how it was between her and Ma? That they had to be careful; there was just the two of them, and Iris had to be independent, for both of them. Perhaps he already understood; it wouldn't surprise her. She relented. 'I need to be sure of what I'm going to do next,' she said quickly to Sandro. 'That's all.'

He'd left it at that; beside her, Jackson had been listening, but he didn't say anything.

'Jackson,' said Sandro, with stern kindness. 'Now.'

Sandro had given Jackson a padded envelope containing six old sketchbooks, and the address of Claudio Gentileschi's widow, and told him to go and talk to her. 'He spoke to you,' Sandro had said roughly, clapping Jackson on the shoulder. 'You liked him. That will mean something to her.'

When he arrived with his bags in the Piazza d'Azeglio, ready to go, Jackson had stood square in front of her, folded his arms across his chest and said bluntly, 'Come with me. Please. You'd like the States.'

She'd shaken her head, smiling, because now she knew. What was going to happen next. 'I like it here,' she said.

It was a cold, bright morning, and Iris waited with Jackson's bags on the pavement in the Via dei Pilastri, in a thin slice of sun that fell on her between the eaves of two huge stone buildings, like a blessing. When he was gone she'd call Ma and tell her. Tell her she loved her, and that Antonella Scarpa had found her a place on another course and she was staying here.

❀ ❀ ❀

Under the great trees in the Piazza d'Azeglio, unknown to either of the two young people, Sandro watched Jackson and Iris emerge from the huge, ugly house of the Contessa Badigliani. He couldn't have said what he was doing here, only Luisa was at the shop and he couldn't seem to sit still at the moment. There was no way, she had said, that she wanted to mope around at home, no matter what the doctor said about taking it easy.

So he stood and watched as the two figures rounded the corner of the square, side by side but with no point of contact between their bodies, and disappeared down towards the Via dei Pilastri. Then he set off after them, unseen.

This is what private detectives do, he thought, mocking himself, but the sense of unreality with which he had embarked on his new career had gone. He had completed a job; was that it? He was too old and too disillusioned to expect anything like professional satisfaction, whatever Pietro had implied.

'We'd have you back in a shot, you know,' he had said on the phone only this morning; typical of Pietro to give him space, to leave things to settle.

'You wouldn't,' Sandro had said, smiling to himself. 'And I wouldn't go. I like things better this way.'

'Fair enough,' said Pietro, relieved. 'How's Luisa?'

Which had been a harder question to answer.

Maresciallo Falco had not given Sandro space. The carabiniere had phoned personally, Monday afternoon, and asked, politely, if Sandro would have the time to pay him a visit, to update him on the case. After the morning he'd had, not to mention the thirty-six hours without sleep, he should have said no, but blearily he'd kissed Luisa, who had been filling the washing machine and refusing to talk, said he'd be back in an hour, and walked down there, across the roaring Arno, to the Boboli. His senses had seemed sharpened by the lack of rest; he looked at everything he passed—the yellowing trees, the dirty pavements, the overflowing dumpsters—as if he was seeing them for the first—or last—time.

'You look rough,' had been the first thing Falco had said as Sandro entered his office. The carabiniere was sitting back in his chair with a sheepish look the cheerful insult attempted to disguise. He'd then gestured to the chair opposite him and Sandro had sat warily, not knowing what to expect. There was a degree of discomfiture on either side; Falco had underestimated Sandro, and knew as much, and in his turn Sandro found that he didn't relish this unfamiliar position on the moral high ground. If Falco ended up feeling humiliated, there'd be trouble.

But then the Maresciallo had begun to speak. Haltingly at first, but quite soon with something verging on enthusiasm, at least for a carabiniere, Falco had gone through the case with him, and it had slowly dawned on Sandro that the man actually admired him for what he'd done. He'd shifted in his chair; listening to praise had always made him uneasy, even in the force, but when Falco finished abruptly by standing, stiffly, with his hand out, Sandro had taken it.

Of course, Sandro had been there to hand over what he knew about Veronica Hutton's disappearance to the investigative body concerned, and he obliged. He told Falco about the Scuola Massi's forgery racket, but when it came to Claudio Gentileschi's part in it, Sandro hesitated. Was it their business, after all, Claudio's death being under the jurisdiction of the Polizia Statale, rather than the Carabiniere? He felt the tug of old loyalties, to his force, as well as to poor dead Claudio, unable to defend himself, unable to explain. Sandro's first duty was to protect his client, Lucia Gentileschi, but, then again, there were new alliances to consider. There was his new career.

Eventually he had taken a deep breath, and explained his position to Falco, who obliged him with a pair of palms face up: it was understood; it would go no further. Sandro could see that the quiet bargain struck left him in the weaker position once more, but curiously enough he was happier that way. And Lucia was safe. Antonella Scarpa wouldn't implicate Claudio; she'd said as much, although otherwise she was co-operating fully with both the Guardia della Finanza and Carabiniere investigations. He hoped she'd escape prison, although he imagined there wasn't much Antonella Scarpa couldn't handle in life.

It hadn't been perfect, he'd got it wrong time and again, yet when it mattered, he'd got it right. By the skin of his teeth, but sometimes that was all you needed, and the job was done. And although Sandro hoped that next time it might be just a matter of following someone's cheating husband, he knew that next time, he'd do better.

As Iris waited on the sunny pavement for the boy to come back out, her broad lovely face was tilted up, eyes closed, to catch the sun. Sandro realized with joy that he didn't have to worry about Iris March.

He watched the boy come out, saw them call a cab, saw her help him in with the bags and lean down to kiss him goodbye on the cheek, saw her wave at the departing taxi. Saw her pull her coat around herself, and walk off towards the river with her mobile pressed to her ear. And only then did Sandro walk across the road and ring at Lucia Gentileschi's door.

Chapter Thirty-one

IN THE SMALL, clean, featureless room, Sandro held Luisa's free hand as she lay on her side with the narrow plastic tube that was taped to what they called a port on her pale forearm. They were lucky, he told himself. This was what lucky was.

Of course, when the serious-faced surgeon had first spoken the words in the little consulting room, that other side of Sandro had thought only that this diagnosis was the deal. He had thought of the drained, white look on Luisa's face after they had loaded Veronica Hutton into the ambulance. A life for a life, he'd thought, before his rational side tore the thought to pieces in disgust. A life for a life.

The first lucky thing was, it had not spread. The exhaustive body scans and blood tests had definitively shown that it had not spread to any other location in the body. Not the lymph, not the lungs, nowhere else. And it was a—the surgeon had said what kind of cancer it was, it had a·name, but Sandro didn't want to name it. It was the opposite of aggressive, that was what mattered, and it was tiny.

'You were brave,' said the surgeon to Luisa. 'You examined the breast, that's brave to begin with, and when you found it, you came immediately.'

Of course, Sandro had thought impatiently as he gripped Luisa's hand, don't you know her?

There had been no need for a full mastectomy, but Luisa had demanded one. The chemotherapy was a precaution, but Luisa had insisted on it. Brave.

On the bed, she turned her head towards him, and smiled. Lucky.

7/24